T0323000

THE
STALKER

Also by Kate Rhodes

THE ISLES OF SCILLY MYSTERIES

Hell Bay
Ruin Beach
Burnt Island
Pulpit Rock
Devil's Table
The Brutal Tide
Hangman Island

ALICE QUENTIN SERIES

Crossbone's Yard
A Killing of Angels
The Winter Foundlings
River of Souls
Blood Symmetry
Fatal Harmony

THE
STALKER

KATE RHODES

SIMON &
SCHUSTER

London · New York · Sydney · Toronto · New Delhi

First published in Great Britain by Simon & Schuster UK Ltd, 2024

Copyright © Rhodes Pescod Ltd, 2024

1 3 5 7 9 10 8 6 4 2

Simon & Schuster UK Ltd
1st Floor
222 Gray's Inn Road
London WC1X 8HB

Simon & Schuster: Celebrating 100 Years of Publishing in 2024

Simon & Schuster Australia, Sydney
Simon & Schuster India, New Delhi

www.simonandschuster.co.uk
www.simonandschuster.com.au
www.simonandschuster.co.in

A CIP catalogue record for this book
is available from the British Library

Hardback ISBN: 978-1-3985-2930-4
Paperback ISBN: 978-1-3985-2933-5
eBook ISBN: 978-1-3985-2931-1
Audio ISBN: 978-1-3985-2932-8

Typeset in the UK by M Rules
Printed and Bound in the UK using 100% Renewable Electricity
at CPI Group (UK) Ltd

MIX
Paper | Supporting
responsible forestry
FSC® C171272

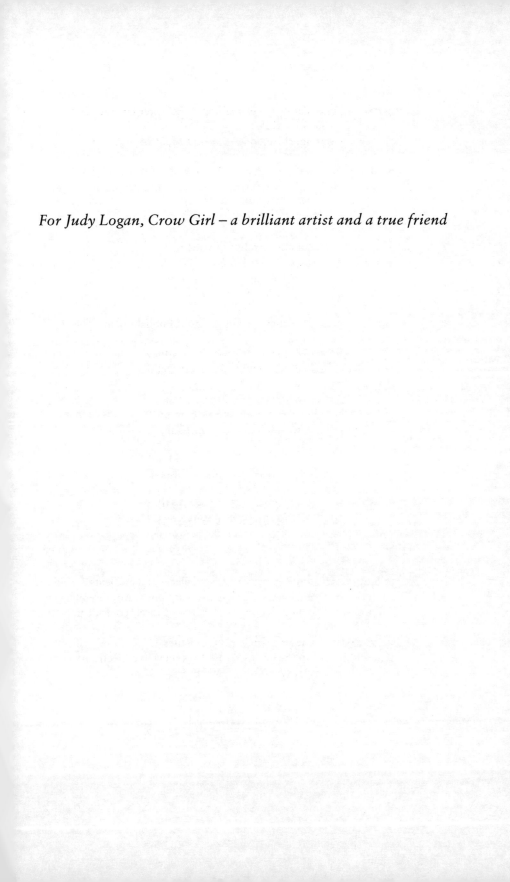

For Judy Logan, Crow Girl – a brilliant artist and a true friend

I see you everywhere,
in the stars, in the river,
to me you're everything that exists

Night and Day, Virginia Woolf, 1919

1

Bonfire Night, Friday 5 November

ME

Cambridge is a city that loves to celebrate, but I'm not in the mood tonight. The evening breeze feels icy. It's the coldest November on record, and I've been preoccupied all day, with you controlling my thoughts. All I want to do is lose myself in the crowd, as students spill out of pubs and cafés, looking for fun. They're winding towards King's College, to watch the lavish firework party it throws each year. I follow them through narrow Elizabethan streets, tangled together like string. I learned the art of invisibility years ago. It's no surprise when a group of girls push past, wearing headbands that glow in the dark, oblivious to my existence. Laughter and half-heard conversations jangle in my ears, until everything changes.

I see you walking directly ahead, with your back turned. I'd recognize that stance anywhere. You keep your head up, like a queen. Your arrogance is beautiful and ugly at the same time. My feelings towards you are getting harder to ignore. You move so purposefully, but I bet you're hating every minute. You get claustrophobic in crowds, and my pleasure drops away. Something inside me hurts. I'm divided between wanting to protect you and a stronger urge – to watch you fall apart.

Few people recognize the pain you carry. It doesn't show in your movements, or the fake confidence in your voice. You feel worthless sometimes. It comes from neglect, and being misunderstood, yet I feel little sympathy. You've cheated me out of something that should have been mine.

Fate has been generous for once. I close the gap, barging through the crowd until you're within touching distance. It's time to drop my mask and make you understand that only one of us can continue, or we'll be torn apart. You'd have to be stupid not to see the problem as I do, and you're not. You're the smartest woman I know. It shouldn't come down to a binary choice: my life, or yours, with just one of us left behind. But fairness tells me there's no other way. The sacrifice has to be yours, not mine.

I reach out to touch your shoulder, then someone jostles me from behind. My hand jerks too hard, shunting you off the pavement. You land badly, your head hitting the tarmac. Panic makes me lean closer. Your eyes are closed when I whisper my taunt in your ear, just three words, short and sweet. Then I escape into the sea of bodies.

When I glance back, people are taking care of you already, trying to bring you round. I don't know if you're dead or alive. Excitement fires my blood, giving me a sudden rush of energy, but whatever happens, I can't risk being caught. It's better to be safe than sorry.

I battle through a solid wall of people, heading in the opposite direction. It's exhausting, this life I've chosen, always swimming against the tide. They're moving faster now, craving the stink of gunpowder, and the sky is lit up by man-made comets. You can't die like this, before you've faced the truth. I'd rather kill myself than let that happen.

I wish someone had been honest with me as a child. No one ever explained that love can hurt, as well as heal. A heart can be intact or broken. I found out the hard way, with no one to comfort me. Sometimes you need patience: the person you love, or hate, has secrets that keep you apart. Every time we draw close, it renews the conversation between us, even when no words are spoken. But tonight was a mistake; I should have kept my distance.

I stop on the corner of Pembroke Street, pressing my back to the wall as people stream past. The display has started already. Fireworks sear the sky, writing gaudy letters on the clouds. The city looks more beautiful than ever, illuminated by artificial flares, but it no longer interests me. I've lost sight of you. Too many bodies block my view, surging forward, relentless as the sea. I catch one more glimpse of you, then retreat into the dark.

2

Saturday 6 November

YOU

There's silence as night-time closes in on me. My cheek rests against cold tarmac, smelling of petrol and decay. The sky is bright with colour when I come round. Someone tells me to lie still, the ambulance is coming. My body drifts out of control when I'm stretchered away, my vision blurred. Suddenly the pain feels like a grenade exploding inside my skull. The blackness helps this time, cradling me in its lap, soothing away confusion. A woman grasps my hand, her voice a slow whisper. She sounds like my mother, before she turned cruel; her voice tells me not to be afraid, but that's impossible. Fear has already crept into my life and taken hold of me.

I wake to the electronic bleep of my heartbeat, with the smell of bleach in my airways. The effort of thinking exhausts me. The woman that brought me here has vanished. A man I can't quite place is sitting a few feet away; fierce overhead light has turned his skin ashen. He's staring into my eyes like he can read the contents of my soul. His gaze is so intense it could burn through steel. I want to ask his name, but no words come, then sleep claims me again, the urge too powerful to fight.

The next time my eyes open, there's no one here. My vision's still hazy, but I can make out objects in this tiny hospital room. There's a mirror over the sink in the corner. My handbag lies on the bedside table, its strap broken. Someone has clipped a heart monitor to my finger, and the machine's regular bleep reminds me that I'm alive, like the pain when I turn my head on the pillow. It's a knife blow between my eyes, sharp enough to take my breath away. I keep trying to remember what happened. How much of my memory has gone this time? It was flawed already. Now it feels like a blank canvas.

A doctor appears at the end of my bed. He's too busy checking his clipboard to make eye contact. He's a decade younger than me, late twenties, with messy brown hair in need of a cut.

'Morning, Eloise.' His voice is deliberately upbeat. 'Feeling better today?'

Fine, I want to say, *now let me go home*, but no words emerge.

He asks for my full name and family details, giving me an easy start. My voice sounds like a lock being forced open, rusty and dry. I'm Dr Eloise Shaw, thirty-nine, married with one son. The day of the week is harder to recall, and the date. The doctor holds up four fingers and asks me to count them. He looks concerned when he peers into my eyes with a light pen, checking for damage.

'We'll do another MRI scan today. You've got a fracture in your cranial bone, here, from your fall.' He taps his forehead, just below his hairline. 'It will mend without surgery, if you take it easy. If you overdo it, there might be complications. Your husband knows about your accident. He should be here soon.'

My family feels like the distant past, too far off to recall, yet I need to convince the doctor that nothing's wrong, so I can go home. My son needs me.

'Discharge me, please, I'm fine now.' My voice still sounds unfamiliar.

'Trauma to this part of your skull can change your behaviour for a while, Eloise. It's near your amygdala. Do you know much about how the brain works?'

I force a smile. 'I hope so, I'm a psychologist.'

'So, you know about the symptoms frontal lobe inflammation can cause?'

My words are slow to arrive. 'Impulsivity, disinhibition, recklessness.'

'Exactly. People lose their sense of danger – it can make you paranoid too. We need you here, to monitor your injury. Do you have any questions?'

'A woman brought me in last night; there was a man too. Do you know who they were?'

He's flicking through his notes, already impatient to leave. 'Me, probably, and another doctor. You were semi-conscious. It's great your mind's clearer now.'

'I definitely saw them, they were older than you.'

'Your memory could be playing tricks, from your injury.'

I want to explain that it's already damaged, that parts of my childhood are lost for ever, but I need him to release me. The doctor's still talking when my thoughts come back into focus.

'This shouldn't affect your past memories long-term, but full recall takes time. It's lucky there was no haemorrhage last night. We need that second MRI scan to be sure.'

He doesn't need to spell out how the brain works; I understand how broken thought patterns can land you in jail. The anger I feel takes me by surprise. I've learned to suppress it over the years, but it feels closer to the surface. Why now, when the man's only trying to help me?

'I feel okay, apart from the brain fog.'

'People with concussion often say that. It causes problems if it's ignored.' He studies me again. 'Where do you work?'

'Cambridge University.' My voice still sounds flat and out of key. 'The psychology department. I run a treatment programme, to stop stalkers reoffending.'

'That sounds challenging.'

I'm running out of strength to reply. The truth is, psychology is the easiest part of my job. My social media has mushroomed recently, and now it's out of control. I do a weekly video, advising victims on how to cope with stalking. One of them went viral a few months ago, making me the go-to expert on the subject in the UK, even though I prefer anonymity. The round of interviews on daytime TV and news programmes has been punishing since my book, *Toxic Love*, was published this year. Everyone wants a guaranteed cure for a syndrome that terrifies us all. The idea of being pursued or threatened, sometimes by a complete stranger, is the stuff of nightmares. Avoiding the limelight was never an option.

When I look up again, the doctor is hovering by the door.

'It's great that you're calmer, Eloise. You talked about monsters chasing you in the dark last night.' He nods at the grey square of sky outside the window. 'Snow's coming, you're better off in bed.'

'Can I call my husband?'

'He should be on his way. Rest till he gets here, please. You'll be with us forty-eight hours at least. It could be weeks before you're safe to drive or spend time alone. Relax now and get some sleep.'

I can't switch off after the doctor leaves. The fear I've been denying keeps invading my thoughts, about the threat to my safety, even though my secure life at home keeps me protected. It began three months ago, after we got back from our cycling holiday in France. Letters containing just three words – 'me or you' – arrived at my office. Then came silent phone calls, first at work, then at home. I ignored the truth at first. I couldn't accept that the problem I've studied for years had come home to roost, but my husband and son saw me changing, and the slow erosion of my confidence. It's put us all under pressure. Jamie is permanently on edge, and Rafe watches me like a hawk, as though I've brought it on myself. I reported it to the police, of course. But they just issued a case number and told me to take more care over my personal safety. They can't act on psychological threats, only physical ones, because they're so short-staffed.

Last night changes everything. I remember that cold punch between my shoulder blades. Knowledge is what I need most of all, to help me fight back, yet I can't prove a thing, and never saw my attacker's face. Isolation presses in on me, increasing my fear. No one can fix this, except me. But who was it that sent me sprawling to the ground? Did they watch me being stretchered to the ambulance too?

I worry about the effect it's having on Jamie as my mind drifts. My son is a typical seventeen-year-old with a passion for music and a rebellious streak. We've always been a close family until he vanished for a whole week recently, not even answering his phone. Rafe and I called his friends and visited all his usual haunts, with no luck. I was too stressed to think straight, until he finally reappeared, tired and monosyllabic, unwilling to apologize for putting us through hell. Even now, he won't explain where he stayed all those nights.

Jamie's changed since my brother and sister came back into my life two years ago. It's like he can't forgive me for concealing the existence of his aunt and uncle, but I dealt with our enforced separation by trying to forget them. Since my siblings reappeared, my son has questioned me constantly, as though understanding our family history could anchor him deeper in the present, like a tree with long roots. It's out of character. He never showed any interest in my childhood until Leo and Carla arrived, but he's unlikely to stop until he gets the answers he wants. Jamie's strong-willed, like me.

I'm dozing, only half awake when a nurse arrives, holding a box with an Interflora label. She leaves it in the corner, then steals away. Time passes, maybe an hour or so, before the feel of a cool hand on my arm jolts me awake. My eyes open and the panic subsides. Lisa Shelby has been my closest friend and ally at the university since she arrived five years ago. We work in different departments, but instinct told me immediately that we'd become close when we met at a welcome event for new staff. I suddenly remember that I was on my way to meet her last night, to watch the fireworks, then go for a drink.

It's a surprise that she's my first visitor. I thought Rafe would be here by now. It's his comfort I'm craving, but Lisa is a good substitute. We're around the same age, but she always looks more glamorous, an art historian with a passion for bright, eccentric clothes. She's wearing a jade-green blouse that suits her olive skin, curly brown hair swept back from her face.

'Thank God you're all right, Elly. I panicked when you didn't show up last night, until Rafe phoned me. He said you'd fallen in the street, the poor guy sounded anxious.' Her gaze settles on my bandaged forehead. 'How's the bump?'

'On the mend, don't worry.'

She looks amused. 'I'd be screaming and wailing in your shoes, milking the drama. I bet you haven't even shed a tear.'

I smile, ignoring the pain. 'I'm okay, that's what counts.'

'Did you slip on some ice?'

'I just tripped on a kerb, it was nothing.'

I know it was a deliberate attack but announcing it would only make me feel more vulnerable, despite my trust in Lisa. No one has heard about my stalker, except Rafe and Jamie. That needs to change. I should follow the advice I give to victims of stalking more closely, yet it feels like the wrong time to go public. It would make my situation much too real and give my stalker the satisfaction of being centre stage, on social media. Exposure carries the risk of even greater vulnerability, and right now I'm still too exhausted to make sense of it all.

'I got you some stuff.' Lisa pulls items from her bag: a chocolate bar, a carton of pomegranate juice and a glossy interior design magazine. 'I thought you'd enjoy seeing how millionaires decorate their houses in Malibu. I checked out the pictures while you were asleep. It's pure kitsch, leopard-skin wallpaper and white leather sofas everywhere.'

'It's sweet of you to come, Lisa. You didn't need to bring anything.'

'You'd do the same for me.' Her face turns solemn. 'You're quiet, sweetheart. Are you okay?'

'Tired, that's all. It hurts to open my eyes.'

'Want me to bugger off and come back tomorrow?'

'No. Stay for a bit, please.'

She squeezes my hand. 'Don't scare me again, Elly. Only you listen to me bang on about my tragic love life. Feel free to doze, if it gets boring.'

Lisa describes her date for this evening. She's been single a long time and has decided it's time to get back in the saddle. Tonight's guy is someone she met online. She's got high hopes, but he'll need to tick a lot of boxes. Lisa wants someone sane, solvent and ready for kids, before her biological clock stops ticking. She's funny, as always. Her monologue is full of anecdotes about boyfriends that come and go in rapid succession, thanks to her short attention span. None of them meets the invisible standard that's lodged in her mind.

'He just has to be interesting and kind, with decent bedroom skills. Then I'll know he's a keeper.' She suppresses a laugh. 'Is this making your headache worse?'

I smile back at her. 'You'll find someone. Don't rush it, that's all.'

'Good advice, but sadly I've only got one gear.' She glances at her watch. 'I'd better go and beautify myself. It takes forever these days.'

Lisa leaves the room, fizzing with energy. I know from going on a spa break with her recently that she struggles to slow down. I loved the whole experience – taking life easy, swimming, having saunas and eating gorgeous food – while she never fully relaxed. We're chalk and cheese, but it still touches me that she rushed here the moment she knew I was ill.

I only remember the flowers the nurse delivered after she's gone. Lisa dumped them on my bed, then forgot to open them, so I reach for the box. It's lighter than I expected, like it contains only air. I bet it's from Rafe, or my sister, Carla, who prides herself on marking every occasion with an appropriate gift.

It takes effort to pull myself upright. I'm curious to see who sent the flowers, but when I prise the box open, something's wrong. The blooms inside are shrouded in tissue paper and are releasing a sour, musty smell. When I pull back the wrapping, I see the flowers have been sprayed black, a dozen roses carefully dried, the petals still intact. Leaves crumble under my hand to a dry powder. The note reads 'me or you', in a child's shaky handwriting, matching the others I've received.

The gift is so ugly and funereal that nausea chokes me, forcing me to breathe deeper, to steady myself. It feels like the successful life I've created is disintegrating. I want to hide under the covers and dream myself safe, but my heart's beating too hard for rest.

My stalker has proved that my life would be easy to snuff out, like the flowers. When my eyes blink shut I remember their voice, whispering 'me or you', then the night's cold silence, smothering me in the dark.

3

ME

I've been twitchy all morning. You've been the focus of my life for years while I've learned how you tick, but my feelings change like the breeze. Some days I want you dead, others alive. I want to see you suffer, like me, yet it triggers my guilt. I prefer to help people, normally, and enjoy their company, but you're different. The power you carry isn't showy or overplayed, just a fact of life. You're not even aware of it, which makes it harder to ignore.

The price of watching you is loneliness, even though my days are often spent among people. I feel isolated in the middle of a crowd, or with friends, because I'm so preoccupied. I'm growing tired of sending gifts, and that breathless pause when you pick up the phone, fearful and curious at the same time. It's not the conversation I've dreamed about, even though I loved making you afraid at the start. The endgame must be honest. I will tell you the truth about my feelings, but anger is difficult to describe. We're taught to suppress it from the day we're born.

You're the wound I can't heal. I should be able to recover, given my skills and experience, yet it remains there, always. Pain dominates my life. I control your destiny, but you've overpowered my thoughts. Even now, when I should be out enjoying myself, I'm thinking of ways to hurt you even more deeply than putting you in hospital. You're a psychologist, after all. The best way to destroy your life is to twist your thoughts out of shape, breaking your beliefs one by one, until your mind no longer functions.

I want to send you reeling into the dark alone. But that will take careful planning, with so much at stake. You have to understand that no one can outrun their past.

4

YOU

It's midday when a nurse appears to check on me. She's middle-aged, with a kind face, her movements slow and deliberate when she hands me a glass of water. I watch her flick through the chart at the end of my bed.

'How's the walking, Eloise? Let's see you in action, shall we?'

I seem to have aged decades overnight. My body feels weighty, like it's dragging a heavy burden, when I cross the room to the en suite loo at my fastest pace. I need to do well, to increase my chance of going home soon.

My reflection in the wall mirror feels like glimpsing a stranger on a train. My head's wrapped in a bandage, covering most of my short blonde hair. My Danish mother gave me sharp cheekbones, blue eyes set too deep in their sockets, and nothing else. I spent so little time in her company, I never found out if she was strong or weak. Her treatment taught me resilience, even though my memory of those days is patchy. The crisis that happened in my childhood is missing, and my mind is unwilling to return to so much betrayal, even though the facts speak for themselves. I can't recall the few weeks between my father being rushed to intensive care and my mother banishing me permanently from our London home. I don't dwell on it, normally, but my stamina has taken a battering since last night.

The nurse perches on the side of my bed. She explains that patients with skull fractures often experience severe headaches for weeks. I should hit the button beside my bed if the pain suddenly worsens, my vision changes or I feel nauseous. She takes my wrist to check my pulse.

'Your husband's a sweetheart, isn't he? Handsome too. He was here last night for ages. I can always tell the devoted ones. They sit there, holding your hand, not moving a muscle.'

The news is reassuring. Rafe and I have been married eighteen years. It's a long time since we gazed at each other with unblinking devotion, even though there's no one I trust more. It shows how confused I was, to mistake him for a stranger, but it's good to know I was his first priority.

'There was a woman here too. Do you know her name?'

'We don't keep a register, I'm afraid. I thought he was alone with you the whole time.'

My mind empties when an orderly trundles me down to the X-ray suite for a scan. I'm dreading it because confined spaces make me panic, but there's no escaping when the MRI machine closes around my head and shoulders, like I've been shoved headlong into a white plastic coffin. The air smells sterile, my skin freezing as the mechanism clunks and whirs. The fear in my chest makes me want to claw my way out, but I force myself to lie still and focus on certainties. I've seen plenty of brain images before now, but never my own. Colleagues of mine are working with neurosurgeons, to pinpoint where individual emotions lie in the brain's dense network of neurons and capillaries. It still strikes me as miraculous that dreams come alive inside such a drab grey organ, with the texture of clay.

I'm half-asleep as the orderly wheels me back to my room, still drifting when my husband and son finally arrive. The band of pain around my skull loosens as Jamie marches into the room. He's already six feet tall, the same height as his dad, with sleek brown hair falling to his shoulders. Jamie looks grown up from a distance, but his movements are twitchy, like he fears his own strength. He's dressed in a hooded top and jeans, deliberately anonymous. I sense his anger when he kisses my cheek. It's trapped in his clothes, along with the smells of tobacco and cannabis. I remember his bravery as a kid, hurling himself into the swimming pool from the top board, but there's a note of anxiety in his voice today.

'He put you here, didn't he? Your stalker tracked you down. We have to stop him, Mum.'

I hesitate for a moment too long. 'It's okay, I tripped, that's all.'

'You're just saying that to shut me up. It'll be one of those freaks from prison, or some psycho online. They'll have seen those films you keep posting.'

His dark eyes search my face for the truth. I've had the same thought myself, but each of the stalkers from my programme is tracked closely once they leave prison, by the National Anti-Stalking Centre and the probation service. It helps us to judge their progress over time. Stalkers occasionally shift from obsessing over their victim to pursuing their therapist, but transference is rare. It would be wrong to stop posting advice. I know that many victims of stalkers are desperate and trapped inside their homes. Helping them is the most important thing I've ever done in my work.

I want to reassure Jamie that it's unlikely to be a convicted stalker pursuing me, but he's paying the worst price for my situation. The late-night phone calls and anonymous letters have put him on edge. I'm almost certain he ran away to escape the stress, even though he's too macho to admit it. There are still nights when I hear him go downstairs at two or three in the morning, the sound of his guitar rising from the living room, like he's playing himself a lullaby. He sets off for sixth form college pale with tiredness. And when he gets home, he questions me about my past, as if understanding it could unlock the present. I get the feeling that anything I say will make things worse, and my headache sharpens. He's the only person in this world that I love unconditionally, yet the barrier between us seems to widen every day.

Rafe stands by the door with his arms folded, watching the conversation, like an umpire at a boxing match. He qualified as an architect the year we got married, after I graduated. He was eight years older than me, confident and far more certain about what he wanted from life. I was driven too, but for different reasons. Falling pregnant with Jamie was the best thing that happened to me. It delayed my plan to become a psychologist for five years, until he was settled at school, yet our lives seemed perfect. I never expected to find a man I could trust or create a family of my own with. Those goals seemed too distant, a vanishing point forever out of reach.

I can tell something's wrong from Rafe's body language. His salt-and-pepper hair is shaved close to his skull, making him look austere. The reality is different. He's one of the gentlest men I know. I can read all his expressions and nuances after so many years together. His face is gaunt today, his skin pale. That could be from the shock of seeing me lying here, helpless. The last time I needed hospital care was to give birth to our son. I'd like to comfort them both, but my head's pounding from the effort of speaking coherently while my thoughts are so muddled.

'Get your mum some coffee, can you?' Rafe asks, handing Jamie a banknote. 'There's a café downstairs.'

Rafe sits down at last, on the chair he used last night, once Jamie leaves.

'Sorry I didn't come sooner. Jamie stayed out all night and never answered my calls, he's been driving me round the bend.'

'But one of the nurses saw you here yesterday.'

He shakes his head. 'It felt wrong to leave, that's the thing. Jamie's volatile right now. I didn't want him coming back to an empty house.'

The news makes my stomach churn. Rafe has worried more about Jamie since he came back, even though he may only have been proving he's an adult, free to do as he likes. But who was the man holding my hand last night, if not Rafe? A stranger watched me sleep while I was too weak to move, and a woman hovered in the background, complicit. I still can't picture their faces. The man's gaze studied me with the force of a laser. That's all I remember. Panic's building inside my chest, but Rafe looks so uptight, I can't add fuel to the fire.

'You did the right thing, staying at home,' I say, keeping my voice level.

'Jamie bit my head off when I challenged him about skipping lessons. He needs you to straighten him out.' Rafe smiles at last, like he's been thrown a lifeline. 'I do too. How long will you be here?'

'Two more nights, probably. They're monitoring me for concussion, which is a pain in the arse.'

'Be patient, El. It's a skull fracture. You need to recover.'

'I know the risks, don't worry.'

'Want me to call your brother and sister?'

'I'll tell them once I'm out.'

He looks surprised. 'They should know today, surely? Or can't you face any more visitors?'

'Lisa was here earlier. I just want peace and quiet for now.'

Rafe shifts his gaze to the winter sky outside the window. The truth is, Carla tires me and Leo's condition keeps him at home.

I'm still adjusting to my biological family drifting back together, after a string of unexpected emails. It fell apart when I was young, but both my siblings have moved to Cambridge now, and my sister has transferred our mother to a nursing home nearby. I'd come to terms with never seeing any of them again, but the thrill I got the first time we reunited felt overwhelming. I can tolerate Carla's habit of ringing me every day, and Leo's mood swings, for the simple joy of having the two of them back in my life.

I study Rafe again, noticing how sombre he looks. He's dressed in a black turtleneck sweater and well-cut grey trousers, his rain-coat abandoned on the chair, a rime of stubble on his jaw. It's like he's playing the part of a successful architect for the world to admire. He's changed from the charismatic livewire I placed on a pedestal in my twenties, always ready to travel to far-flung countries at the drop of a hat. This man seems to need a more sophisticated type of love.

'Jamie's right,' he says, quietly. 'The police should know what happened to you.'

'I got caught in a crowd, leaving work. Someone shoved me off the pavement. I didn't see their face, so I can't prove a thing.'

'What else do you remember?'

I hesitate for a moment. 'Someone said "me or you", before I blacked out.'

'That's what his bloody notes say, isn't it?' Rafe's voice is suddenly hot with anger. 'I'm calling the police.'

Suddenly I'm tired of going round in circles, and none of it making a difference. 'Fine, put it on record, but don't expect a result. Tell them dead flowers were delivered here too: a box full, with the same message.'

'Are you serious?'

I point at the package dumped in the corner. Rafe prefers more unusual bouquets, full of thistles and sea poppies, but he's empty-handed today, apart from my overnight bag, containing a fresh set of clothes. I can see how rattled he is when he peers inside the box. It forces me to stay calm again, for his sake.

'Jesus, that's a sick thing to do,' he mutters.

'The police won't care about a stupid prank. Remember what happened after we reported it last time? No one rang back.'

'It's their job to keep the community safe, El. I'll speak to them when I get home. Call me when you get the all-clear,' Rafe says. 'I'll pick you up, okay?'

'I can get a taxi home, if you're working.'

'Let me look after you, for once.' His voice is softer than before when he leans over to kiss my cheek. 'Jamie's okay, trust me on that. If they want you here for observation, don't argue. You should rest until you're fully well.'

'I can do that at home. The university's given us a reading week, for the first time ever, so I'm not teaching. We're meant to do admin and research.'

My energy is plummeting. I can hardly keep my eyes open while Rafe keeps insisting that I'll need more than a week off to recover properly. Minutes pass before he finally falls silent, then sits by me, his hand gentle on my shoulder. I'm not strong enough yet for lectures on personal safety, even though he's just being protective. It still feels like a pneumatic drill is pounding my skull, so I close my eyes, and when I open them again there's a takeaway coffee cup on the bedside table.

Rafe and Jamie must have left ages ago. The drink is stone cold, and the room is empty. Loneliness washes over me, until sleep steals in once more.

5

Hospitals are easy to enter unseen, if you wait until 10 p.m., when the shifts change. Staff are so busy handing over duties that they don't notice me hanging around. I can't risk being spotted, because I've been here too many times already. It's lucky that the security signs on every corridor are meaning- less. I just have to pick the right fire escape, then cut through rooms that patients never get to see. I pass the laundry, where huge tumble dryers spin in unison, churning out towels and bed linen, day and night. Then I pause outside the boiler room to catch my breath, keeping my head down to avoid a CCTV camera.

I hurry up the back stairs, emerging on the right ward. It's riskier now. I know it's unwise to visit the same place often and expect to stay invisible. The NHS have done me a favour when I reach your ward. The hospital is so understaffed there isn't a single nurse in sight. I'm free to loiter outside your room and peer through the glass panel.

You look restless in sleep. Much more delicate than in the films you post online, lecturing all those sad victims on staying safe, even though your perfect life is fraying at the seams. You don't know it yet, but it's already slipping away. I can't risk going inside again, in case you wake up and see my face.

When I look at the thick white bandage concealing your hair, it wounds me to my core. I never intended to hurt you so badly at this stage, yet I can't deny the relief it brought. You've ruled my thoughts for so long, it felt good to reduce you to nothing for a few short hours. Now you know how I feel every day. It makes us equals; you can never look down on me again.

I linger, knowing I'm in danger, as a doctor strides down the corridor. He's bound to ask what I'm doing here, so I offer him my best smile. It's a perfect defence. No one ever sees a happy person as a threat. The medic returns my smile then hurries on, focused on his duties ahead.

When I peer back inside the room your eyes are opening at last, so I mutter goodbye under my breath, then turn away. I retrace my steps, fast, like I'm late for an important meeting. My sadness has lifted. It was worth taking another risk to see you lying in that bed again, pale and broken, like an abandoned rag doll.

6

YOU

It's 2 a.m. when I wake again. The room is dark, and the clock ticking on the wall sounds thunderous now the hospital's quiet. Something about this place makes me desperate to leave, even though I'm lucky to have my own room. Leaving home as a child left me afraid of the dark. I missed my brother and sister so much, I cried out for them sometimes, in my dreams. I thought that phobia had gone, but my hands fumble for the bedside light. It's a relief when every corner of the room is illuminated. No monsters are hiding there, or under my bed. The past has loosened its grip for now, but its effect remains, like the pain throbbing behind my eyes.

Someone has left a local newspaper by my bed, which cheers me up. Rafe prefers print, while I always browse online. He scours the *Cambridge Gazette* each week for news about local building plans. He's always been ambitious, setting out to create a successful architecture practice. There are six partners now, all working on different projects, and it's still expanding. He's taken on a personal assistant, and an intern too, in the past year.

My phone is charging on the bedside table. No personal messages have arrived, but thousands of people have reacted to the film I posted recently on social media. I advised victims of severe stalking on ways to build a strong security network around them, like a forcefield, and how to maintain it every day. Most of the replies are positive, with people sharing their own ways of handling the threat. A few haters have left toxic messages too. I ignore them, until one catches my eye. It's written in strident capitals, like someone's shouting in my face.

FUCKING MANHATER. GET A
LIFE, YOU STUPID BITCH.

I receive dozens of similar messages every day and blocking them doesn't work. Anonymous trolls just set up new temporary accounts, to vent their rage at anyone they see as a do-gooder trying to help the vulnerable. Most are missing the point. Stalking behaviour isn't a gender battle: one in ten stalkers is female, capable of making their victims' lives hell through threats, blackmail and online abuse. I've learned to live with online aggression by believing that it's not a serious threat. Sticking my head above the parapet makes me a target for a few angry followers, but violent stalkers are normally people from your intimate circle.

My mind flicks through the facts about stalking, to identify why I've been singled out. I've done this countless times already, trying to control the fear by rationalizing it. The most common trigger is rejection after a breakup. It can tip a healthy mind into psychosis if the trauma's deep enough. Predatory stalkers are the most dangerous, often planning a sexual attack, which terrifies me most of all. My stalker's acting like I've stolen something valuable from them that can't be replaced, yet no one in my family or friendship group seems a likely contender for such a bitter campaign.

When I check my voice messages again, one has just arrived from my sister Carla, sounding irritable. She's asking me to call back soon, because we haven't spoken for several days, which throws her into a panic. I know she wants us to become close, but trust is a process that can't be rushed. Fortunately, my brother Leo is less demanding. There's a reminder from work about prison visits over the next month, but I don't reply. I can't think about counselling stalkers while I'm recovering from my own injuries.

I skim through the paper, comforted by the trivia it contains, plus local campaigns for cleaner air and a congestion charge. There's even a story about stray sheep from Lammas Field bringing rush-hour traffic to a halt by wandering onto a main road and refusing to budge. One of Cambridge's biggest appeals is that it's a thriving city which still feels like a market town, moving at a sedate pace.

A picture on page five stops me in my tracks. It shows a man in his mid-thirties gazing back at me. His clean-shaven face appears bland and trustworthy; he could be any pleasant acquaintance or neighbour. I know from dozens of meetings with him in Greenhill Prison that the reality is darker. Joe Sinclair was released recently after serving time for stalking his ex-girlfriend, Georgia Reed. He love-bombed her at first, sending gifts and messages, lulling her into a false sense of security. Then his coercive and controlling behaviour increased. By the end of their relationship, he only allowed her to leave home to shop for food or go to work. He wrestled her into submission through mind games alone, never resorting to physical violence. I spent months counselling him on my treatment programme, until his thinking seemed to evolve. It often takes dozens of therapeutic conversations before a stalker's viewpoint shifts back to normality, and they accept responsibility for terrifying their victim. Sinclair was judged fit for release by a panel of experts, including me. Our decision was confirmed by the parole board.

Reading the story makes my eyes hurt, like they're full of sand, until shock takes over. Sinclair broke into his ex's flat in Huntingdon, holding her captive until morning. He left her with such severe injuries that she was hospitalized, just twenty-four hours before me. Pity turns to anger in my head. I screw the paper up, then hurl it at the wall. The gesture releases something that's been trapped inside me for too long. I've spent years denying my feelings, acting like nothing can hurt me. It's a relief to let out some tension. I hate being the victim of someone else's obsession and hate the way it impacts on other victims too.

I keep picturing Georgia Reed, lying in hospital, with far worse injuries than mine. Sinclair seemed like a cast-iron success story, describing his plans to put his life back on track so convincingly. It sounded like his impulses were fully under control. It seems too much of a coincidence that Georgia was attacked so soon before my stalker put me here. It makes me wonder if he drove twenty miles the next day and came hunting for me too, shoving me to the ground, but the facts don't add up. I started counselling him months before my own stalking began. Sinclair can't have made the silent phone calls I've been getting from his prison cell. He couldn't have sent me the letters or unwanted gifts either.

It will be my duty to assess him again, now he's back in jail, to discover what went wrong in the period leading up to the attack. Review meetings often provide clues about preventive measures we should take next time. It's vital research, to see how the pro-gramme failed, but I hate the idea of sitting opposite him after he's committed such a monstrous crime. It's a new feeling for me; I've rarely struggled with professional distance, until now.

I turn out the light and panic smothers me again. I can't get

Georgia Reed's suffering out of my head; I've got too many black marks on my conscience to cope with any more. I focus on the glass panel in the doorway, where a dim light shines. The quiet feels like a lead weight on my chest.

Anyone could walk back into my room while I'm helpless. I try to calm myself, using the techniques I taught patients for years to help control anxiety. Slowing my breathing eases my racing thoughts. The sense of danger makes me determined to face the problem at last. I'll fight to defend myself, whatever it takes.

Heels click on the lino outside, accompanied by the sound of a trolley being pushed past my door, its wheels grinding in slow revolutions. Hospital staff keep busy all night long, the corridor rarely empty. *You're safe*, I tell myself, even though it's a lie. No amount of professional knowledge can shield me here. The man that sat by my bed could be waiting in the corridor, and there's no one to protect me. I battle to stay awake, but am soon conquered by sleep again.

7

YOU

It's almost ten when I wake up, feeling stronger. A nurse has left a breakfast tray by my bedside, and the curtains are open. The winter sky is pallid blue, with jet trails from planes flying to Stansted slowly dispersing. It hits me again that another woman is lying in intensive care, following the release of an offender from my treatment programme. The coincidence of us being assaulted on consecutive nights still feels unnatural, but I won't find out the exact details until I leave.

My gaze lands on the dead flowers by the bin. *You reap what you sow.* My mother's words creep into my head, uninvited. I think she quoted that parable before sending me away to live with my aunt and uncle, but I can't be certain, my memory hazy. Even now, her actions don't make sense. I love Jamie more than anything, my maternal instinct at the core of everything I do, yet she banished me at the age of ten, and never made contact again. Maybe I did something she couldn't accept, overstepping an invisible boundary. Now it's happened again. I've put myself in danger, trying to fix a problem that ruins people's lives, and it's too late to complain about repercussions.

When I fumble for my phone, my social media is still jammed

with questions from followers seeking ways to de-escalate their stalking and reclaim their lives. Answering them all would be like trying to climb Everest alone, never reaching the summit. But I can't ignore a message from a young woman whose profile picture makes her look like a rabbit caught in headlights, her eyes stretched open a little too wide.

> A bloke at work has been hassling me for weeks.
> He hangs round my desk, leaves me poems
> and stupid gifts. I'm worried that something I've
> done has given him the wrong idea. Everyone
> knows I'm not interested, but he won't listen. He's
> been at the firm for years, so I'm worried that
> complaining could threaten my job security. The
> other day he followed me home. How do I stop
> this? Help me, please. I can't take much more.

Her situation is a classic example. It follows the rule of four: fixated, obsessive, unwanted and repeated behaviour from her stalker. I share contact details for the National Stalking Helpline, and Paladin, the Stalking Advocacy service, then remind her that she's the innocent party. She needs to be brave and confide in her boss and colleagues, so everyone knows the truth. It's isolation that puts victims in danger, and shame that they may have brought it on themselves. I scan more messages and see familiar scenarios, from male or female ex-partners who refuse to let go, to obsessives who focus on total strangers.

I've been a reluctant guru since my boss asked me to post some talks online, to raise the profile of my research. Stalking is such a common problem worldwide that each video brings thousands more followers. Victims clamour for advice, like I could cast a magic spell to make their problem vanish. They confide intimate details about stalkers who have made their lives miserable for years. It seems ironic, now that my own defences have been stripped away. I'm failing to follow my own advice, about making sure everyone around you knows the truth. I've always hated being the centre of attention. If I tell all my colleagues, friends and family that I'm being stalked, the problem could take over my life.

I push myself upright, then swing my legs out of bed, my feet hitting cold lino. It's best to keep my head up and walk, even when the destination's uncertain. My pain reduces to a dull throbbing behind my eyes when I enter the bathroom. I stand by the mirror, then unwind my bandage to assess the damage. There's a cut high on my forehead, held together by butterfly tape, almost hidden under my hairline. Flakes of dried blood land in the sink when I brush my teeth. The pain comes back suddenly, rocking me on my feet, but I'm determined to take a shower, unsupervised. I keep my hand flat against the tiled wall as water courses down my body, hot and comforting.

The muscle weakness has returned when I finally climb back into bed. My mind's blank as I stare out of the window again. This is the calm after the storm, but I can't help remembering Georgia Reed. I need to understand the connection between our attacks, if one exists, but my brain won't co-operate. My thoughts are still jumbled as I watch swallows winging south over the city in a skein. It looks like a wreath of smoke, forever changing shape.

When I check my phone again, my daydream ends. There's a voice message I haven't listened to before, sent on Friday by Jamie's college tutor. The man sounds grave when he explains that Jamie has missed so many lessons, he's jeopardizing his course. He must submit last term's assignments soon, or he'll be excluded. The tutor asks me to ring him back on Monday. I try to call Rafe, then Jamie, about it, but neither of them pick up.

I can't just lie here while Jamie drifts deeper into trouble. He could be with Billy, his closest friend for years, but I don't have his mobile number. When I call his parents' house next, I get only his mother's chilly voice message. Jennifer Rawle and her husband Mike are acquaintances rather than friends, their life-styles too different from ours for an easy fit. Jennifer and Mike are tech entrepreneurs, running a huge training business, often travelling to exotic countries. They live in an immaculate house just outside Cambridge, but their son seems lost. Billy is taking a gap year before going to art school and seems to spend his days driving around in his dad's BMW, visiting friends. I've always liked him, but he's directionless right now, and Jamie could be following his lead.

I'm on autopilot when I get out of bed, determined to see Jamie. My skin feels tender when I put on the clothes Rafe brought me from home – black trousers and a grey merino wool jumper, from an expensive shop in town. He bought them for my birthday, but I'd have preferred something vibrant. My thoughts jitter back to the past, when I used to wear every colour of the rainbow: turquoise, orange, aquamarine. It's years since I chose such bold colours, but I bought a crimson dress recently, which hangs at the back of my wardrobe, unworn. Rafe dislikes anything too vivid, so I abandoned it for him, my life turning monochrome. It seems a small price to pay for a rock-solid marriage. Suddenly I want his arms around me, more than anything I can imagine. It's another good reason to go home immediately.

The nurse on the desk at the end of the ward looks furious when I discharge myself. She keeps her voice low when she ex-plains that a doctor must sign my form when I'm well enough to go home. I've got concussion. She repeats the doctor's warning: there's a chance I'll have a seizure, or a haemorrhage. I hear her concern, but it doesn't frighten me. I understand the risk yet can't stop myself from taking it.

'We need to monitor you here,' she insists, refusing to listen when I explain that my son's welfare matters more. She places her hand on my arm when I turn away, like she plans to restrain me, then thinks better of it. Her voice follows me down the corridor, telling someone on the phone that a patient with a head injury has discharged herself without authorization.

I make it to the corner, then lean against the wall. My sight's still blurred, a row of gurneys seeming to hover in mid-air. I wait for the lift, then hurry out of the front entrance, into the freezing air. It's lucky that a taxi is waiting by the rank because I still feel weak. I give the driver my home address on the outskirts of town. We've lived there ever since Jamie was born, in one of the first houses Rafe ever designed. His Audi is in the driveway, so he must be at home, but Jamie's ancient Ford Fiesta is missing. If he's not here, where the hell is he?

I see my home now with fresh eyes. It's a jagged glass citadel sprouting up from the ground, perfect for a family with nothing to hide. The place has been featured in several architecture magazines for its clever use of materials. I loved watching it evolve while I was pregnant with Jamie, feeling him stir when steel joists slotted into place. Rafe created a space that's sheltered us for years, great for entertaining, with a square garden at the back full of fruit trees we planted together. The project put us in debt for a long time, yet we've never regretted it. It was the perfect place to raise a child. Jamie had an idyllic childhood here, in a house that's always filled with light, but now it feels like he's losing his way. I let myself in, calling Rafe's name, but there's no answer.

I stop in the kitchen to gather my strength, still wrapped in my coat. Rafe designed every detail for usability and warmth as well as space, using oak and polished concrete. It was fitted eighteen years ago, in the days when we had a huge mortgage, but it's still my favourite room. I'd like to rest for a minute, but Jamie's in trouble, so I stumble to my feet again immediately. Rafe will be outside in his garden studio, where he often works at the weekend if there's a deadline. He spends countless Sundays hunched over his drawing board or doing admin for clients.

When I open the French doors, the buddleia and lilac trees that attract butterflies each summer are just leafless sticks. I brace myself for Rafe's anger about me leaving hospital early, but his studio is empty, which is rare. I sink onto his chair, trying to blink my headache away. I must lie down soon, before I keel over. He's rushed out in a hurry, leaving drawings scattered across his table, the screensaver on his computer showing a Paris skyline. I felt sure he'd be here, so we could plan how to support Jamie.

I'm about to return inside when something catches my eye. A silk scarf hangs from a hook on the wall, a beautiful strip of vermillion. When I gather it in my hands it releases a scent that's vaguely familiar, and something shifts inside my chest. Rafe has never given me reason to fear other women, always dependable as a husband and a dad, but what if the rules are changing? I banish the thought fast because it's ridiculous. We love each other, we always have. The paranoia must be from my injury. Rafe will have brought a colleague here, to work on a project. That happens all the time. I stumble outside, closing the door behind me.

Jamie's still not answering his phone when I try his number again. I keep a tight hold of the handrail as I go upstairs, my head swimming. Our bedroom's a mess. The duvet is piled on the floor and Rafe's clothes lie abandoned on a chair, the light shining in our en suite. I don't care about any of the clutter. I just need to recover, then find Jamie.

I pause by the bathroom door, where something glitters next to the sink. It's a bracelet, made from twisted gold wires, that only a woman with slim wrists could wear. It feels weightless on the palm of my hand, very different from my own plain silver jewellery. Why would a woman leave something this expensive in our bathroom? There must be a safe explanation.

I'm still puzzling over it when the door slams and Rafe pounds upstairs, calling my name.

'What's happened, El? The hospital said you discharged yourself.'

'I got a message from Jamie's college. He's close to being chucked out, so I came home, looking for him.'

'You should have let me deal with it.'

The anger on his face only fades when he sees the bracelet in my hand. I'm willing to accept whatever he says, but he's silent. The colour is draining from his face.

Knowledge settles in my gut, making me nauseous. 'I found this by the sink, just now. Who does it belong to?'

'One of Jamie's friends, probably. They often use our bathroom.' He won't meet my eye.

'No teenager could afford something this expensive. But you already know that, don't you?'

Rafe's communication skills are second to none. He's famed for his ability to persuade any client to spend huge sums of money on building their dream home, but he doesn't answer my question. The picture's starting to make sense, and panic stifles me.

'You brought someone here. Is that it?'

He takes ages to reply. 'Once, that's all. It was a mistake.'

'Sex is a choice, not a mistake.'

'Listen to me. It was nothing, I promise.'

'You screwed her in our bed. Is that nothing too?'

My thoughts scatter. I remember learning the Greek myth of Ariadne at school. She laid a trail of golden thread so the man she loved could find his way home through a labyrinth. This story is uglier. A stranger has littered things around my house, expensive and obvious. How many more clues has she dropped that she plans to replace me?

'Your car's in the drive. Did you walk her home?'

'No, I went out alone, just now, to clear my head.'

'I need the truth, for fuck's sake. Show me that much respect, at least.'

He drops his gaze. 'We can get over this. It was just once, like I said.'

'Liar. She's been here before, laying a trail.' Tears keep threatening to spill over. 'You wanted me to ring for a ride home, so you could cover your tracks.'

'Let's focus on what matters. You should be in hospital.'

'Shut up, Rafe. Just tell me what happened.'

'Nothing serious. I've been loyal to you, all these years.'

'Just sex then, like scratching an itch?' I spit the words at him. 'Does Jamie know you've got a mistress?'

'Of course not. He's been at Billy's the last few nights, anyway. This is about you and me, no one else. Can't you see?'

'If you're blaming me, that's bollocks.'

'It's both of us,' he snaps. 'I've built my practice single-handed, while you chased your career. You prefer those stalkers' company to mine. I was lonely, all right?'

'That's a pathetic excuse.'

My body aches when I wrench the bracelet apart, gold strands peppering the floor. I grab my holdall and stuff clothes inside with my tablet and phone charger. Instinct makes me chuck my passport in there as well, too furious to speak. Escape is the only thing on my mind. I need to get out fast, before this place collapses around my ears.

'You can't just leave me over one mistake.' Rafe watches me in the bathroom, where I chuck my makeup bag into the holdall, his hands twitching at his sides. 'Is that all our marriage is worth?'

'Ask yourself that. You broke it, not me.'

When he stands in the doorway, blocking my exit, there's disappointment in his eyes. Anger almost blinds me. It's the look he gives Jamie when he skips college, like I've failed some vital test.

'Let me go, Rafe.'

'Listen to me, please.'

I barge past him, then stumble back downstairs. My strength's returned, adrenaline-fuelled, heart pounding in my throat. Rafe touches my shoulder, but I shrug his hand away and grab my keys from the hall table. He's pacing behind me when I leave, talking too loudly, giving lame excuses. I need him to shut up, more than anything. Rafe keeps saying that our marriage can recover, even though he's lobbed a grenade at our beautiful glass house. Did he do it just for the fun of watching it shatter?

'You can't drive in this state. We can sort this out . . .'

Rafe looks different from the man I loved until today. He's standing by my car, blocking my escape route again when, without any warning, instinct takes over. I want him to suffer, like me. I can't stop myself when I draw back, then punch him hard in the face. There's a burst of relief in my chest when he reels backwards. Shock washes over me, as if someone else has lashed out, but I feel no regret. One more denial would make me do it again. Rafe stares at me, while blood leaks from his nose. I must be sicker than I feel. Physical violence horrifies me normally, but now it seems justified. It must have been lurking inside me all this time.

I swing round suddenly, aware of someone's gaze crawling across the back of my neck. But there's only Rafe standing on the driveway, blotting his damaged nose with tissue. I bet the neighbours are peeking from their upstairs windows, loving this Sunday-morning drama in a genteel street where nothing bad ever happens. But that doesn't matter. Rafe's the one that cares about public opinion, not me.

My mind feels numb when I get into my car and drive away, leaving behind the possessions I've collected so carefully over the years, barricading them around me, believing I was safe.

8

ME

I watch you leave, shocked to my core. My feelings are too jumbled to accept what just happened. Your violence is too crude to fit my image of your quiet strength, yet it excites me too. It will make our last battle a genuine challenge. You're clever enough to cause lasting damage with words, but you've revealed a primitive side that I never knew existed.

I'm discovering what love means from watching you break down. When it turns sour the pieces are too jagged to handle. It damages everyone close by, yet I don't care. The person you've lied to most often is yourself, pretending to be innocent and that your past is over. My ability to pull the wool over people's eyes has never equalled yours, even though we're driven by the same purpose.

Are you really prepared to abandon the world you've created? It looks perfect to me. The certainties you take for granted are fragile, yet you've marched on, regardless. You've made it your life's work to leave people like me in the shadows. Any happiness I feel, any praise I get, you always have to do better.

Your rage stays with me. I knew it was there, but now it's exposed to the light. Violence begets violence. You've kick-started a process that fate will decide, the result beyond our control.

9

Instinct takes me in a direction I normally avoid. I haven't seen my mother since I was a child, but she now lives on the outskirts of Cambridge. My sister visits her every week. It's a specialist care home for Alzheimer's sufferers, but I've never been inside. I'd love to have the kind of mother that phones often and enjoys every visit. Mine was never like that. She locked me out of her life so completely thirty years ago that it feels stupid to seek her out now, even though I'd welcome some maternal kindness.

I pull up in the car park and stare at the building. It's a rambling Victorian mansion, with traces of its old grandeur still on display. The portico has stone columns either side and banks of windows gazing down at the road. My mother must be sitting behind one of them, guarding her secrets. I'd love to run inside and find her, even now. The reason my childhood home fell apart remains out of reach, and why she's refused to see me ever since, but I don't need answers today, just reassurance that life will get back to normal. There's an empty space in my gut where my beliefs used to live. It feels like the first strong wind could blow me away. I glance at the building one more time, before twisting my key in the ignition. I've always hated self-pity. Revisiting my past won't change anything, and there's no comfort waiting for me behind that grand facade.

When my phone rings I keep driving, unwilling to hear Rafe's excuses. The pain is still too raw. I need time alone, but there are few options. I pull over, resting my forehead against the steering wheel, weighing up choices. My brother and sister would expect me to explain if I turned up at either of their homes. I could stay with friends from work, like Lisa, or Clive Wadsworth, my old PhD supervisor. Clive and his wife have treated me like a daughter since I joined the psychology department. He's retiring this week, but I know they'd never turn me away. I can hear the doctor telling me it could be weeks before it's safe to drive, yet the risk doesn't scare me. I feel safer inside my car than at home, cocooned by metal and glass, even though my head's still pulsing.

My best choice is to return to the cottage my aunt left me. It lies in the fenland countryside, unoccupied since she died three years ago. I still make occasional visits to absorb the peace and quiet. I used to take Jamie there as a child, but now it's a retreat for me alone. It's the place where I learned to feel safe, and it still feels precious. I'd hate to sell it. My mind flicks back to the day my aunt and uncle took me in when I was ten. Pete was my father's older brother, and I barely knew him and his wife Lucy. The couple were old enough to be my grandparents, Pete already hunched with arthritis, yet that soon stopped mattering. I was meant to stay there for just one summer, then return home to London, until they explained that the arrangement was permanent. They'd never had children, so I filled a gap in their lives. They understood my need for safety instinctively. It's easier to remember their quiet, slow-growing devotion than Rafe's betrayal.

I pass through Girton on the way. The village has changed since I was a kid. It used to be a pretty cluster of houses a mile from Cambridge, but now it's connected by an ugly sprawl of new builds. Blocks of flats stand too near the road, with slit-thin windows like narrowed eyes, watching the traffic pass.

The cottage I inherited lies four miles outside the city's limits. I take the road bridge over the M11, then drive deeper into the Fens, before turning down a single-track lane. It feels like time is slipping into reverse. The property is a nineteenth-century farm worker's cottage, with red brick walls, a low porch and tiles slipping from its roof. A row of identical properties once surrounded it, until the others fell into disrepair and were pulled down. The council would love to flatten mine too, to make way for yet another out-of-town development, full of boxy houses built from a single template. I keep on fighting their compulsory purchase orders out of loyalty to Pete and Lucy. It's worth very little in this state, but it was their pride and joy.

The air feels cold when I get inside because I haven't visited for a few months. It took me years to realize how lucky I was to be allowed to stay. If they'd turned me away, I would have ended up in the care system, deprived of love and encouragement. This place is the opposite of the glass palace Rafe built, but the walls still emanate kindness, the rooms packed with memories and worn-out furniture. I shut my eyes to remember how welcoming it felt the day I arrived, and Lucy's gentle smile. She used to hurry back from work early, to greet me when I got home from school. My mind feels calmer when I lock the door, then gaze outside.

The Fens look stark in the morning's harsh light. I've got a 180-degree view of the sky and the fields flatlining into the distance. I stood by this window often as a child, staring up at the sky's vastness. It put things back in perspective, numbing the pain of separation from my brother and sister. Maybe it can heal me this time too, but the wound's still raw.

I fiddle with the switch on the boiler, willing it to start. When it finally grinds into life, it feels like Pete's ghost has returned to help me. He was a handyman, able to fix anything, no matter how broken.

I pull out my phone and call Jamie again. This time he answers, thank God, but he already sounds defensive. I'd like to know if he's sensed his dad's betrayal, but it's the wrong time to ask.

'Your tutor called me, Jamie. You're close to being thrown off your course. Why haven't you done your written work?'

He gives a loud sigh. 'The course is shit, and the assignments are useless.'

'But you want a certificate at the end, don't you?'

'Let me decide. Stop nagging me, okay?'

'It's my job to nag. Where are you, anyway?'

'At Billy's.'

The news worries me. Billy is too ethereal these days, drifting in a cannabis haze. His camera is always slung over his shoulder, as if archiving every situation could keep him safe. Maybe all teenagers have to get lost before they can find themselves again.

'When do you come home, Mum?' The anger in his voice dies away.

'I'm out already, at Lucy and Pete's, tidying up. I just need a few days' quiet.'

'Dad said you'd take weeks to recover.'

'I'm fine, honestly.'

'You don't *sound* fine. Go home, please. We'll take care of you.'

'This isn't about me. Go to college from now on, Jamie. I'm not letting you fail that course. I'll be here if you need anything.'

I ring off fast, unable to worry about him while my head's pounding. I go upstairs to the bedroom that felt like a gift once I realized that it was mine alone. It was a pink-walled shrine to Barbie back then, and elements of my childhood linger. The curtains are still covered in silver unicorns and fairy-tale images, like Rapunzel letting down her hair. It's so cold my breath forms clouds when I crawl under the blanket, still wearing my coat.

Darkness has fallen when I wake up. My head feels like an eggshell that could crack open any minute, and there's a void where my feelings should be. I've treated patients with concussion after-effects in the past, when I worked for the NHS, but never experienced it myself until now. It's like someone else's brain has been transplanted into my skull. The idea of Rafe having sex with a stranger hurts too much to remember, so I let practical needs take over, and pick up my phone. Lisa called an hour ago, the ringtone failing to wake me.

She answers my return call fast. 'Where are you, Elly? The hospital told me you'd checked out early, you fool.'

'Are you busy?'

'Hell, no. Last night's date was hopeless. He banged on about his ex-wife non-stop, so I legged it.'

'You'll find the right one soon, don't worry.'

She laughs. 'I love your optimism.'

'Can you do me a favour, Lisa?'

'Fire away.'

'I'm staying outside town, a ten-minute drive away. Can you pick up some food and bring it here?'

There's silence while I give her the postcode, hoping her satnav finds the cottage. The boiler's making a racket when I go downstairs. The temperature only feels a couple of degrees higher, the system working overtime to heat rooms that have stood empty too long, but at least the pipes haven't frozen.

I walk around, surveying for damage. There's mildew on the hall ceiling and the air smells damp, yet it still seems like a refuge. I felt protected here, until I left for York University to study psychology. The same sense of security returned every time I came home to visit. Instinct tells me I'm still safe here now, but I pull the curtains shut in every room anyway, unwilling to face the infinite blackness outside.

Lisa soon arrives, carrying a bag from a Korean takeaway in town. Food is a much bigger deal for Lisa than for me: she grew up with an Italian mother and developed a passion for it. I can tell she's dying to ask what's wrong, but is biding her time. She unloads cartons of dumplings, rice cakes, vegetables and crispy beef, then watches me eat. It's the first time I've felt hungry since leaving hospital. I can feel my strength reviving with each mouthful, even though my thoughts lag behind my actions, my movements clumsy. Red wine splashes on the table as I seize my glass.

'Should you be having alcohol with a head injury?' she asks.

'Probably not, but I'll risk it.'

Lisa studies me again. 'You seem different, Elly. It's normally me throwing caution to the wind.'

'Maybe that's been my biggest problem all along.'

'Finally, you agree.' She laughs with her head back, the sound infectious. 'This place is amazing, it's like a shrine to the seventies. Is it yours?'

Lisa gazes around in wonder as I explain. It looked dated to me even as a child. Pete and Lucy didn't believe in replacing anything until it was worn beyond repair. My friend seems transfixed by the black-and-white lino, Formica work surfaces, orange tiles and woodchip wallpaper.

'They spent all their spare cash on me. I was lucky to get a second chance.' I want to shut the subject down, to avoid having to lie about my past. 'Thanks for coming, Lisa. There's no one else I could face.'

'You're still feeling rough, I can tell. You can talk to me, you know.'

'It's too complicated.'

'Come on, Elly, you've heard me rant plenty of times. Let me be the listener, for once.'

Words stick in my throat, but she's not asking for my full life history. I only need to describe the present. I tell her about Jamie running away without explanation, and her eyes widen when I announce that Rafe was unfaithful during my stay in hospital; some nameless woman slept in my bed while I lay there, unconscious.

She looks appalled. 'You seemed great together. I thought he was better than that.'

'Me too. Rafe says it's my fault, for focusing too hard on my work.'

'I bet he's done the same,' she says, frowning. 'Who's the woman, anyway?'

'He won't say, but I'll find out. He's no good at secrets. I bet it's his assistant, Mia. She's in her twenties, blonde and textbook gorgeous.'

'So, it's a midlife crisis?' Lisa hesitates. 'I've only met Rafe a few times, but your marriage looked rock solid to me, and Jamie's a great kid. I envied you, to be honest.'

'He's broken my trust. I'll never get it back.'

'Think before you walk away, that's all I'm saying. You've loved him all these years, and I'm living proof that a good man is hard to find. A flawed one might be better than nothing.' Sadness narrows her smile. 'But there's something else, isn't there? You've been quiet for weeks.'

Words gush from my mouth unchecked. 'I've got a stalker. It's been going on since August: silent phone calls and scary messages.'

Lisa looks shocked. 'That's nuts, when you're the big expert. You should have told me straight away.'

'Maybe I've been in denial.' Knowledge gives its own protection, but she's got a point. I always advise victims of stalking that visibility can keep you safe. The trouble is, I learned to hold my troubles inside as a child. It's a hard lesson to forget.

'Is it an ex?'

'They won't reveal their identity, which raises the danger level. Anonymous stalkers will do anything to keep their secret hidden, including hurting their victims. It's often someone from your intimate circle.'

'A student, maybe, or a colleague?'

'No one gets near my personal life until I'm sure they're no threat.'

Lisa's eyes widen. 'What about that creepy American guy on your research team?'

'Dan Fender? He's been vetted by the university, like all our research students.'

'That doesn't mean a thing. I tried chatting to him at a party once, but gave up. His focus was on you, a hundred per cent.'

'He probably wanted to discuss professional stuff. Dan's very committed to the programme.'

'It was about you, not work. I'm a good judge, so keep an eye on him. He gives me a bad feeling.'

'I can't see him hurting anyone.' Dan has worked alongside me for two years, without a hint of discomfort. He seems like a gentle giant to me. He's shy, but gets on well with the whole team, when stalkers are normally lonely, isolated figures.

'You've got a million followers online. Could it be some stranger who's seen you there, or on TV?'

'Possibly – there are plenty of warped mindsets out there. Some hate me just for telling women how to keep safe, even though I support male victims too.'

'Stay at mine for a bit, Elly, please.' Lisa's face is full of worry. 'The flat's warm and quiet, and there's an intercom. No one gets inside without an invite.'

I'm touched, but decline, patting her hand in gratitude. 'Thanks, but I need to fix things here. I'll call a security company tomorrow to get better locks fitted and install CCTV.'

'It's too exposed, even if you turn it into a fortress. Can't you see? There's literally nowhere to run. You'd be safer at home, even if Rafe's been an idiot.'

Lisa's advice makes sense. It's wrong to be pig-headed, but this place has always been my ideal shelter. It's small and self-contained, easy to barricade. There are plenty of reasons why I can't be at home. Jamie shouldn't have to witness Rafe and me arguing, when he's struggling to recover his confidence. I've got a low threshold for cruelty and emotional abuse, so going back right now isn't an option. I can't return to a house full of lies.

'You haven't mentioned the personal impact of all this,' Lisa says. 'You seem so calm, like nothing's hurt you, even Rafe letting you down. Maybe you should let some of it out.'

'I hate his guts right now, for destroying our life together.' A fresh wave of anger bubbles in my chest. 'It'll hurt Jamie too, which is unforgivable.' There's pressure behind my eyes, from unreleased tears.

'Rafe would be mad to let you go.'

'Maybe not. I punched him in the face, hard, before I left.'

She blinks at me. 'Seriously? I can't imagine you hurting anyone.'

'I don't feel great about it. It was a shock reaction, but it was still wrong.'

Lisa's shoulders are set, her tone decisive. 'He deserved it, and the cow that targeted him. She must know he's married.'

My phone rings before I can reply. It's Rafe, so I mute it, only willing to pick up for Jamie. The truth is, I don't care who lured Rafe into bed. He should have said no. It still amazes me that I lashed out. Normally, my temper stays firmly in check. The memory of my voice resonates inside my head, flat and emotion-less, like a vital element of my personality is missing.

Lisa urges me to go back to the hospital, to make sure I'm okay, but I resist. I do my best to reassure her, and when she offers to stay over, I refuse. Pete and Lucy's kindness seeped into the bricks and mortar for fifty years. This place has always kept me safe, but Lisa is still objecting when we finally part.

It's 10 p.m. and my head's pounding, but I stand on the thres-hold, watching her car disappear down the rutted lane. It's a clear night, the northern hemisphere overhead glittering with stars. Tomorrow there will be frost on the ground, and my situation feels like the land – raw and exposed, my securities all stripped away. There's nothing protecting me from the cold.

When I go back indoors, climbing the stairs feels exhausting. My mind is too tired to make sense of anything, and I've left my phone on mute in the kitchen. I need a good night's sleep, to piece my fractured thoughts together. I brush my teeth, then switch off the bathroom lights. The absolute silence here at night overwhelms me, just like it did as a child. All I can hear now is the wind moaning in the chimney, but when I peer out of my bedroom window, another car has arrived. It's Rafe's electric Audi that never makes a sound.

He approaches the house, bathed in light from the car's head-lights, then I hear him rap on the door. Anger floods my system again. He's had a key to this place for years, but at least he's show-ing some respect by waiting for me to answer. Rafe used to talk about demolishing this place and building us a state-of-the-art new home, surrounded by open fenland and amazing sunsets, but I wasn't interested. There's no way anyone's erasing my memories.

I stand on the landing, battling my impulses. I can't open the door because I don't trust myself to speak calmly without hurting him again. Two sides of me seem to be at war. The rational part knows that my injury is winning. It's pulling me in two directions at once: calm and crazed, kind and cruel. I shut my eyes to block out the panic, then enter my bedroom.

Rafe is welcome to brave the cold outside all night if he wants. It's his choice. The pain in my head eases when I lie down, but sleep keeps its distance. My thoughts shift to Joe Sinclair, back in prison after my therapy programme failed, his obsession even more violent. The decision to release him nags at me. It was made by a whole team of professionals, yet I still feel culpable. If Georgia Reed dies, it will be partly my fault. Starlight floods through the thin curtains, or is it the beam from Rafe's headlights? Shadows chase across the ceiling like phantoms. I can't forget that nightmares could be lurking in the dark, just like when I was a child.

10

Monday 8 November

YOU

Sleep must have arrived suddenly, leaving me comfortable at last, tension easing from my muscles, until I startle awake. A noise comes from the floor below. Someone's inside the cottage. My eyes jerk open fast, and pain sears my temple like a firebrand when I strain to hear it again. I get up to peer out of the window. All I can see is the moonlit fen, with fields stretching to infinity. Rafe has tired of sentry duty, deserting me while I slept, just when I need him most.

The sound starts again once I get back into bed. It's like finger-tips drumming on the kitchen table. They're quick and impatient, saying *me or you, you or me*. The taunt makes me shiver, but I get up anyway. If someone's managed to break in, I can't let them find me cowering in bed. There's no need to hit the light switch as moonlight spills across the landing. I try not to make a sound going downstairs, but the ancient treads creak with each step. The kitchen door is closed. There's a yellow line underneath it, even though I switched the light off hours ago.

I'm frozen to the spot, too afraid to move, until instinct takes over. I grab a broom from the hallway then rush inside. The space is empty, and my head spins, my heart racing. Where's the noise coming from? Was someone tapping on the window, or did I imagine the whole thing? My head injury could be confusing me. I switch off the light and study the darkness outside. There's no one there, only a stunted apple tree, its branches pale with moonlight, tamarisk bushes shivering in the breeze.

I only locate the sound after checking every corner. A tap is dripping, slow and relentless, water on steel. It was magnified by the night-time silence, and I must look like a madwoman, clutching a broom at shoulder height like it's a shotgun. I place a rag under the tap to muffle the noise, then release a shaky laugh. No one broke into my safe haven, I just forgot to turn off the light, and the tap needs a new washer. I should go back to bed, but I'm too wired to rest, even though it's only 3 a.m. My stalker is probably fast sleep, without a single concern.

My aunt used to limp around this kitchen, making camomile tea and telling me to switch off my brain, for once in my life. I can picture Lucy with my eyes shut. A thin woman with a thatch of pure white hair, who worked as a laundress and loved growing vegetables in her garden. She knew how to listen without judgement. But when my eyes open again, her ghost has vanished. There's no one to protect me.

I don't even know if I have enough strength to fight an intruder. I did a self-defence course years ago, but that didn't help me on Bonfire Night. I never realized until now that obsession is infectious. My stalker is fixated on me, but the feeling's mutual. My mind's not my own. It never will be until the exchange between us ends. The advice I give to my followers online, to try and resist spiralling into panic, is hard to follow. Anxiety is churning in my gut, impossible to deny.

*

It's still early when I wake up on the sofa in the living room, even though I don't remember lying down, or using my coat as a blanket. The pain behind my eyes feels less severe. It's as though the tight band of metal around my skull has loosened slightly, and the solitude is comforting. The fields outside are rimed with frost, acres of rough soil bleached white by the cold. The only building in sight is the condemned farmhouse that's stood empty for years, dominating the next field. The air is so still I can hear motorway traffic droning several miles away, even with the windows closed, like a whispered conversation in a quiet café. This place feels like a remnant, left over from a bygone time.

When I switch my phone back on there's a message from Jamie, saying he'll come over tonight. I'll have time to devote to him this week, undistracted by work during research week. Most undergraduates have gone home, giving me time to sort this place out. A trickle of pale brown water emerges from the shower when I stand under it. I try not to study myself too closely in the bathroom mirror. My skin's too pale, like I've been living underground, the swelling under my hairline still pink and tender.

I make a list of things to fix. The fridge is empty apart from last night's leftovers, so I eat cold pork balls, dumplings and congealed plum sauce for breakfast. Jamie will expect better. I'll have to go to the supermarket and stock up on supplies. The kitchen looks even more neglected in the morning's raw light. I turn on the radio and dance music from twenty years ago pumps out as I mop the floor, then wash the dishes I left in the sink last night. The room still looks shabby, but at least it's clean.

It's easier to focus on practicalities than on my life falling apart, so I make half a dozen phone calls, summoning help. It's amazing how quickly people respond when offered a cash incentive. A locksmith promises to drive here immediately to work on my windows and doors, and a security firm can fit two CCTV cameras on an emergency contract tonight. It's going to cost a fortune, and I'm never impulsive with money, but right now it feels liberating. This place matters to me; I need to feel safe here.

Something shuts down inside my head as I cross the kitchen, before I can protect myself. I'm fully conscious when my body hits the cold lino, too shocked to be afraid. I shake uncontrollably and my jaw locks so tight my face spasms; my limbs convulse too, like a fish writhing on a hook. A new memory surfaces, of my brother running towards me, screaming, and my sister covering her face with her hands. It floods back, then vanishes again in a blink. That's how they looked before I was sent away. I want to know what terrified them, but the answer hovers out of reach.

The seizure seems to last for hours. Now I'm wrung out and dizzy, still on the floor. What the hell am I doing here, alone, with no company except ghosts? My body is sending out distress signals. It's crazy to stay here, fighting my demons alone, yet I feel frozen in place, unable to see any alternatives.

My legs shake when I get back onto my feet. I'm lucky not to have banged my head again, but my shoulder feels bruised when I return to the sofa, where I fall asleep instantly. The light has changed when I wake, and my vision's clearer. When I look outside, the locksmith's van has arrived, and an old man stands in the porch, wearing a toolbelt, his grey hair neatly combed. He looks so like my uncle Pete, I trust him immediately. He hums quietly to himself as he checks each door and window. It's only when a new mortice lock and deadbolt have been set into the front door that he speaks to me directly.

'Just moved in, have you, love?'

'I grew up here, but the place has stood empty a while.'

His voice has a low fenland burr. 'There's not much burglary out here, if that's your worry. I've lived nearby for years, without any trouble. There's richer pickings in town.'

'That's true, but I'd still like bolts fitted on the internal doors too, please.'

'All of them?'

'Just the bedrooms and bathroom.'

The man produces a box from his toolkit, letting me choose which type of bolt I prefer. I pick the sturdiest and he goes upstairs at the slowest pace imaginable. Another hour passes and it's midday before he completes his work. He stands in the doorway, telling me he'll send an invoice soon.

'Anything else I can do for you today?'

'Nothing. Thank you for coming so quickly.'

'Take care of yourself, love.' His smile reappears. 'No one can get inside now, unless you want company.'

I lean against the wall after he's gone. There was pity in the old man's eyes and suddenly I'm crying, for the first time in years, in loud wrenching sobs, unable to stop myself. I've always hated self-pity, but feel lighter afterwards. The outburst gives me a reprieve from worry about my marriage, being stalked, and Georgia Reed, the young woman I failed to protect.

I'm too weak to drive, so I find a supermarket online that will deliver my food shopping today, soon after I place my order. The mundanity of clicking on apples, oranges and milk helps to steady me. Lucy used to cook all our meals from scratch, but I take the easy option: soup, ready meals and pizza. I remember how much Jamie loved chocolate-chip ice cream when he was small and order some, out of nostalgia.

Hours pass by unnoticed. My brain remains idle while I sit at the kitchen table, staring at paint flaking from the wall. I'm on autopilot when the delivery van arrives. It seems to take me forever to fill the fridge, leaving tins and packets of rice on the work surface. Loading them into the empty cupboards feels too strenuous. My phone is pulsing with messages, which I chose to ignore.

My next visitors are two young women from the security firm. They look about the same age as Jamie, but soon rig CCTV cameras and security lights over the front and back doors from wiring in the hall. One of them shows me which app to download on my phone, to check what my cameras are seeing round the clock, night or day. Neither of them seem curious about why I need full security in such a quiet setting. They say a cheery goodbye and jump back into their van as dusk settles over the fen. I walk outside to check that the motion sensors work, and lights flash on immediately, their beams dazzling. It should reassure me, yet I've felt numb since learning about Rafe's affair. Blankness feels easier than facing the pain of his betrayal.

I pick up my phone next time it rings, the noise pulling me out of my stupor. It's my boss, Professor Marina Westbrook, from the university's psychology department. It's rare for her to call anyone outside office hours. The woman is famously self-contained, preferring to breeze through the corridors without making any human contact, unless there's a professional problem to resolve. She's always offered me a chilly form of courtesy, but some claim she can be hostile. Instinct tells me not to share information about an offender from my anti-stalking programme turning violent. I won't mention my injury either, unless she asks a direct question.

'Feeling better, I hope, Eloise? Did the hospital release you already?'

There's a moment's silence before it sinks in. 'I'm at home, doing okay, thanks. How did you know I was hurt?'

'I called the ambulance and went with you to A&E. Don't you remember? I was on my way to dinner at Corpus when I saw you fall.'

'I had no idea.' My voice is flat with shock.

'You were out cold. I was afraid it might be serious.'

'I'm fine now, but thanks for your help.' It amazes me that my cool-eyed boss turned Florence Nightingale. I want to ask about the male stranger by my bedside, clutching my hand, but she's already onto the next subject.

'Thank heavens you're recovering.' Her words canter along at their usual brisk pace. 'Have you checked your work email today?'

'Not yet.'

'Good. I want you to take another day off to recover properly, but I've got news about your book.' She takes a breath, building the drama. 'You've won the Cambridge Prize, for *Toxic Love*. It's just been announced online. Congratulations, it's a huge achievement so early in your career.'

I can't summon a reply. The Cambridge Prize is given by the university each year for outstanding research by a member of the teaching staff. I knew that my book was in contention, among hundreds of others, but never expected to hit the jackpot. Marina seems certain that my colleagues will want to celebrate my success.

'I'll arrange a drinks party in your honour, tomorrow night at work, if you're well enough to attend?'

'Why not announce the prize at Clive's leaving do on Sunday?'

She sounds appalled. 'This is a career-defining moment, Eloise, not an afterthought. I'd like you to give an acceptance speech, if you feel up to it.'

'Okay, thanks. I'm still adjusting, that's all.'

'I hate to spoil the mood, but remember your annual report's overdue. I can only give you a few more days.'

'Sorry, it's ready. I'll email it from work tomorrow.'

'Fine, and congratulations again. Believe me, I know how hard it is to win. I've written eight books without getting close.

Most of your colleagues are in the same boat, so it's a boost for the whole department.'

She rings off fast, her tone an odd combination of delight and resentment. Marina appears to enjoy her role as head of department, but she'd have more respect if she'd won the prize herself. Surely she wouldn't have called if there were any sour grapes. She'd have sent an email instead. Trust her to remind me that my annual research review is overdue, even though she nursed me while I lay on the ground, unconscious. It's a requirement that every lecturer submits a detailed account of their teaching and research once a year. Mine is complete, but I want to check it once more before submitting it, when my head's clear.

The news about the prize still feels unreal, even though my work has received a lot of attention recently, thanks to some high-profile advocates. Several actors and politicians who've experienced stalking have lent us their support. It's helpful that some popular celebrities have taken up the baton, arguing for long-term government funding.

I should be overjoyed, but the irony of my situation is clearer than ever. I've won a prize, even though one of the offenders I treated just put his ex at death's door, and my own stalker's campaign is intensifying. My marriage has suffered as a result; it may even be beyond repair.

I focus on checking my voice messages. The first is from my old PhD supervisor, Clive Wadsworth, congratulating me. There's one from Lisa, too, sounding giddy with excitement after seeing my prize announced, like she's drunk too much champagne. The next is from Rafe. Apparently the hospital have mixed up our phone numbers. He's been getting messages intended for me. I should listen and follow their instructions. Some trust in him must still exist because I play back the voice note he's forwarded, from the doctor who treated me.

'Your scan shows a subdural haematoma. That means your brain's inflamed at the site of your injury. You need to take dexamethasone straight away, to avoid a haemorrhage. The tablets are waiting at the hospital pharmacy, but they won't work on their own. You need urgent medical attention. Call me back, please, when you get this message.'

The medic's speech is slow and insistent, like he's explaining something complex to a child. I've worked in psychology long enough to know that overworked doctors rarely phone patients unless it's serious. I should ring for a taxi back to the hospital, but numbness wins out. I'm drowsy with exhaustion, and Jamie will be here soon. I need to see him most of all.

I stand by the kitchen window, waiting for my son's rattletrap car and trying to imagine how Pete and Lucy would react to my prize. They greeted every success with the same quiet pride, followed by a trip to the village pub. But the outside world doesn't look celebratory tonight. There are no stars, the universe blotted out by cloud. The night sky is dirty with light pollution, forming an orange line on the horizon.

Better to be safe than sorry.

The phrase arrives in my head, without invitation. It's my father's voice I can hear, still sharing his favourite philosophy, even though he died thirty years ago. But safety feels out of reach, despite my best efforts. There's a flicker of light at the edge of the next field. It could be from a passing car, or someone skirting the hedgerow, getting closer all the time, holding a torch. It's important to be prepared. Pete taught me that you can't work without the right tools, yet I've got no weapons. Instinct keeps telling me to be ready for attack, even though the idea is ridiculous. Some victims of violent stalking campaigns carry knives, believing it will keep them safe, when the reverse is true. The best way to avoid harm is not to engage with my stalker at all and stay out of reach. My hands shake as I go from room to room, testing the new locks and bolts, trying to swallow my panic.

11

I finish checking the cottage by 8 p.m., and my sense of safety is returning. The place is fully secure now. I can barricade myself inside until help arrives, if my stalker appears. I'm about to make myself a hot drink when I hear a car pulling up outside. I'm expecting Jamie, but Rafe's car is back on the driveway, floodlit by my security lights. There's a grim look on his face when he trudges up the path, in full sight of my CCTV. I don't have the energy for another row, whatever he says. He taps on the door at first, but soon it's like hammer blows, increasing my headache.

'Open up, El, for God's sake.'

He's yelling through the letterbox, and I'm only a few metres away, standing in the hall. I could call his bluff and try to ride it out until he leaves, but Jamie will arrive soon. I don't want him to witness a full-scale row between us.

Rafe glowers at me when I finally slide back the bolt. The damage I've caused looks dramatic; he's got a black eye and his nose is bandaged. It makes us even: the pain he's given me is just as bad, even though it's invisible. Hurting him causes me little shame. There seems to be a vacuum in my head where emotions like pity used to exist.

'I collected your tablets from the hospital. They made me beg, but the doctor left a note on your file. The pharmacist knew you should be readmitted.' Anger resonates in his voice as he drops a paper bag on the table. 'I'm not leaving till you take the pills.'

He's done me a favour after all, and seems determined to help, against my wishes. Rafe marches into the kitchen, pours me a glass of water, then offers me tablets on the palm of his hand. I know he'll stand there forever, if need be, so I swallow them with a glug of water.

'Two, every four hours.' His voice is softer now I'm following his rules.

'I can read the instructions, thanks. Now you can leave.'

'Not yet. The doctor's message scared me. You're too fragile to be left alone right now.' Rafe deposits himself on a kitchen chair. 'And I came here to apologize.'

'Do you honestly think that'll fix it?'

'At least give me a chance, El. I deserve that, surely?' His tone is pleading, not angry. 'You broke my nose, for God's sake.'

'Sorry.' I regret lashing out, but pain triggered a violence in me that I never knew existed. 'Emotional damage hurts too. You did something unforgivable.'

'I can't lose you over this. I need you, so does Jamie.' The panic in his voice sounds real, but it doesn't fix anything.

'I never thought you'd betray me, then lie through your teeth. If you're screwing your assistant that's a pathetic cliché.'

Rafe leans forward, invading my space. 'You're not perfect, either. You work too hard, and there are no-go areas we never discuss, like your past. Jamie hates all that mystery.'

'And it bothers you too?'

'You shouldn't lock us out.' His voice rings with certainty. 'I'll make you a promise, El. I'll be open with you, if you do the same.

Help me understand why you're always so private. You should get it off your chest, once and for all.'

'My past isn't a bargaining chip, for God's sake. Some things should stay private, but your affair affects us all. You betrayed me, Rafe. Nothing can change that.'

'I regret it more than anything.' Confidence fades from his voice suddenly. 'I'll keep on apologizing forever if it helps. I've been an idiot, I know.'

'That's true, at least.'

'It's not safe for you here. Anything could happen.'

'I'm protected, by the cameras. My stalker's terrified of exposure.' I rise to my feet, trying to regain my equilibrium. 'Jamie's coming over soon, so you should leave, please. He's got enough to handle without hearing about your exciting new sex life.'

Rafe shakes his head. 'I haven't always prioritized him, but neither have you. We should put on a united front, to get him back on track. This isn't down to just me or you. Can't you see? His interests have to come first, for once.'

I almost spit out that I gave up five years to be a stay-at-home mum, but weaponizing my decision feels wrong. Nothing can harm that memory. It was my choice, and I loved every minute.

'Don't lecture me on responsibility. You broke my trust. It wasn't easy letting you get that close.'

Rafe pulls me into his arms, but my body stiffens. I've been guided by his emotional reactions for years, but now there's a wall between us. Memories define us, good and bad. The fear I experienced as a kid has shaped our marriage, still hidden too deep to access. I owe him an apology too, but my messed-up past didn't trigger his affair. If Rafe wants me to explain the blurred mess of my childhood, where do I begin? There's a gap that I can't fill. Only my mother knows the truth, and she won't see me. What am I meant to tell him and Jamie, exactly?

'Take those pills, and don't drive anywhere.' Rafe releases me at last, his body language weary. 'It's good you've installed those lights and cameras, but if someone really wants to hurt you, they'll smash a window or kick in the door.'

'Glass houses are vulnerable too. I'm safer here.'

Our conversation has levelled me, and exhaustion is affecting my balance. I need him to go, right now, before I fall again. The security lights blaze when he steps outside, and I feel more confused than ever, stranded between past and present. Part of me wants to call after him and beg him to stay.

12

ME

I'm forced to withdraw gracefully. What choice do I have? It frustrates me that you've blundered ahead, trying to keep yourself safe. Those cameras and lights force me to remain distant, watching through my binoculars. I must follow your rules for now, but you can't stop me returning, no matter how much kit you buy. It's a desperate attempt on your part, and ugly too. Those lights irradiate the landscape, like distress flares, cancelling out the stars.

My gaze scans the night for landmarks. The Fens resemble the ocean in darkness; the lights of distant houses are ships going nowhere, on a flat sea. The peace is illusory, of course. You must have sensed the drama I'm planning, or you wouldn't have spent a fortune on gadgets and locks.

The black outline of an abandoned farmhouse is the nearest building. It rises from the ground half a mile away, condemned and waiting to be demolished. It must be fifty years since a family lived there, when lives moved slower and labourers tended the land instead of machines. I make a mental note to check the place out another time. It could serve me well in future.

I had dreams years ago about our lives combining in some rural idyll, undoing the damage of the past, until I learned how much you've stolen from me. I could never live out here either. Soon it will cease to exist. The empty fields will be obliterated by a city that's expanding at a breathless pace.

I wait until your cottage falls dark again, only one downstairs window glowing behind closed curtains. You're afraid, which is satisfying, but the feeling's mutual. We've caused each other so much hurt. You terrify me too, for different reasons.

It's a reminder not to let you fight back. I need to break down your defences, one by one, until you have nowhere left to turn.

13

YOU

It's midnight when Jamie finally arrives, while I'm slumped on the sofa. His old Ford rattles down the lane like a drum roll, jerking me awake. I'm grabbing my dressing gown when I hear him twist the door handle. My aunt used to leave the door unlocked, certain that no one would bother her in this blank landscape, but now the door is bolted, and he doesn't have a key to the new lock.

It's obvious Jamie's been smoking dope when he walks inside. I can smell it on his clothes and in his hair when he reaches down for a hug. It terrifies me that he's driven here high, but I'm in no position to preach. My son's face is turning from boyish to handsome, right in front of my eyes.

'Have you been with Billy all evening?'

Jamie nods. 'I almost brought him here; his mum's being a nightmare.'

I'm still blinking myself awake, struggling to keep up. 'I thought you got on well with Jennifer.'

'Not anymore. She keeps hassling him to work for the family business. She's been on his back ever since he got his place on that photography course.'

'And his dad?'

'He's always off on business trips,' Jamie says, heading for the kitchen. 'Is there any food? I'm starving.'

'The fridge is full, help yourself.'

He's always hungry after smoking too much weed. I want to remind him of the statistics linking cannabis to poor long-term mental health, but the relationship between us feels too fragile to nag him again. That doesn't stop me worrying, of course. Twenty-five per cent of all teenage referrals to acute psychiatric wards are triggered by dope. I check his appearance for signs of damage. He's watching me too, with the same wary expression, like I'm a bomb set to explode.

I sit at the kitchen table while be builds a sandwich from his three favourite ingredients: ham, salami and cheese. It bothers me that I can't seem to meet his emotional needs, but at least I can provide the basics. He swallows a colossal bite, then finally speaks.

'How come you left hospital early?'

'To see you, partly, and make sure you go to college. Plus, I'm fine. It was only a bump on the head.'

'I was there, remember? You looked like a ghost in that hospital bed. And I know what's really happening. You and Dad are splitting up, aren't you?' Fear resonates in his voice.

'Nothing's decided. We both love you, whatever happens.'

'You keep hiding stuff, and Dad's the same. We hardly talk these days.' He waves the subject away with a swipe of his hand. 'This place is so different from home. What was it like for you, growing up here? You're half of me, Mum, but you never talk about that time. It's like you're hiding something.'

'There are no secrets here.' I glance around the kitchen. 'The cottage was calm, after London. Pete and Lucy knew I needed stability. They were kind, from day one.'

He's still frowning. 'You said they were your parents, not your aunt and uncle. I loved them too. I even called them Grandma and Grandad. Why lie to me like that?'

'You were too young to understand, and names don't matter. It's about who loves us most. They were your grandparents, a hundred per cent.' The muscles in my chest tighten. He's skirting close to the part of me I try to ignore. The last thing he needs is an ugly story about rejection while he navigates his way to adulthood. 'Want to see some photos? It might help you understand.'

'Go on then.' Tension slowly eases from his face.

I reach for my favourite photo album on the kitchen shelf. I showed it to him years ago, but he'll have forgotten. Jamie pores over each image. He lingers over one of me, aged nine. My blonde hair was long, my smile uncertain, legs bony in a pink summer dress that failed to reach my knees. My son keeps his gaze on the picture. His eyes are wide as he hunts for clues.

'How come you never talk about your life before here?'

'Some of my memories are out of reach.'

He looks startled. 'How do you mean?'

'There are psychological names for it – selective amnesia, or buried memory syndrome. I can't remember the period between my father's death and being sent to live here. Those few weeks are a blank.'

'What happens if you try to remember?'

'Nothing. Bits drift back sometimes, but they soon vanish again.' It's the first time I've been honest with him. He's asking grown-up questions, so he'll have to accept adult answers.

'I can't believe you never told me you had a brother and sister till last year.'

'Mum kept us apart. Lots of families split up, Jamie, it's not rare.'

'But ours felt solid until now. We were this safe little unit of three, but that's changed. I had a right to know my aunt and uncle, and you kept them from me. I've been round to Carla's flat recently; she says I can go there any time. I've phoned Leo too.'

'That's good. He'd welcome seeing more of you.'

I keep my voice steady, but the news feels like another betrayal. How dare Carla not tell me that Jamie paid her a visit? I can't guess what she's told him about our family before it fell apart. I know my anger's irrational – my son has a right to contact her and Leo, they're his relatives too – yet the feeling refuses to lift.

When the phone rings, the sound is so jarring I jump out of my skin. The landline hasn't been used in years. I didn't even know it was still connected. Who would call me on it but my stalker, proving they're one step ahead?

'It's him, isn't it?' Jamie hisses. 'That bastard knows you're here.'

I'm sure he's right. I often get calls at home at the same time, but this place is meant to be my sanctuary. It feels like the worst violation yet. When Jamie reaches for the receiver, I have to press my hand down on it so he can't pick up.

'Stalkers want a reaction from us. It's what they crave most of all.'

'He's a fucking coward, Mum. Give me the phone.'

'That would make it worse.'

Jamie looks furious, but I have to protect us both. Stalkers sometimes target people their victims love, so there's a chance he's in danger too. When he rushes upstairs, boots pounding on each tread, my sense of loneliness magnifies. My stalker has found me, in the place where I felt safest, and their campaign is driving a wedge between me and my son. I let the phone ring until the sound dies. Few people know the number out here, mostly old friends from the surrounding cottages that no longer exist. I can't think of anyone who'd call me on it, except Rafe, and a thought takes shape at last.

What if Rafe is doing all this? I could never have imagined him setting out to hurt me, but the rules have changed now he's slept with someone else. My thoughts are spiralling. Maybe he resents all the attention I'm getting at work. I'm closer to Jamie, too, because our minds are similar, always analysing, never fully at rest. He told the truth about me being emotionally absent at times, which must be hurtful. But why would Rafe set out to destroy me, and harm Jamie too? It's out of character for him to do anything without weighing up all the consequences. Maybe he wants to install his new woman in the house he built for us? The idea horrifies me, my hands clammy with sweat, but loyalties can change in a heartbeat. My mother taught me that as a child. One minute she was taking care of me, then she sent me away. The idea that Rafe could be my tormentor is ridiculous, but it's here now. I can't get it out of my mind.

14

YOU

My head feels tender but clear when I wake up. It takes time to remember that I'm in the cottage, my eyes blinking at the unicorn curtains shifting in the draught. Mornings were my favourite time here as a girl, waking up certain I was safe, with no one to criticize or punish me. Trust developed over time. It came because Pete and Lucy let it grow naturally, at my pace, not theirs. Loving Rafe was a shock to my system. It left me nowhere to hide. I can't escape the feeling that the emotions between us have turned toxic, his ability to hate as powerful as his need for love.

Jamie is waking up too. I let him choose where to sleep last night, and he picked my aunt and uncle's old bedroom. I can hear him through the wall, yawning as daylight arrives. He's still drifting when I place a mug of tea beside him, then perch on his bed.

'Breakfast, sweetheart? Then you're going to college.'

He rolls over, blocking me out. 'Maybe I'll stay in bed.'

I try to keep my tone light. 'Sleeping all day's never a good plan.'

'The lectures are so boring. I should have gone straight out and got a job last year.'

'But you're seeing your tutor today, and you can finish those assignments.'

He sits up slowly, rubbing his face. 'Maybe I won't. I hate it there.'

'Because of your classmates? I thought you liked them.'

'They're okay, but the stuff they teach is out of date. Technology can do it all in a blink.'

I can't argue with the truth. We both know AI is removing jobs faster than anyone predicted. 'Don't throw two years of your life away, that's all I'm saying. I can come and see your tutor with you, if that helps.'

'Let me deal with it.' His face looks shadowy, and older than his years. But he doesn't pull back when I touch his shoulder.

'It gets easier, you know.'

'What does?'

'Life in general. It's only hard right now because you're dealing with everything for the first time.'

'No more psychology, please.'

'It might help.'

'Okay, if you must, but no long words.'

His pained expression makes me smile. 'Erikson calls it human development stage five, identity versus confusion. It happens to us all between the ages of twelve and eighteen. We struggle to work out who we are, and what we want, at that point in our lives.'

'So, by nineteen I'll be sorted?'

'Of course you will.'

He gives a theatrical sigh. 'You win, Mum. I'll go to college, work in a coal mine or anything you want, to stop you analysing me.'

'Deal.'

Jamie takes ages to get ready. I can hear his steps, slow and heavy, until he finally appears downstairs in last night's clothes. I can still smell dope on the fabric. I'd love to tackle the subject now, but I'm afraid he'll vanish again. Rafe and I were both terrified we'd end up searching for him for years, a missing person, forever out of reach. When he finally returned, the relief was overwhelming. It felt like a tsunami, knocking me off my feet.

When I look out of the window, the landscape looks too clean for danger, the ploughed fields frosted white, the sky pale with cloud. I've never minded silence, at mealtimes or at work. The gaps between words expose other types of communication. Jamie's quiet as he butters his toast, but his anxiety shows itself anyway, his legs tapping out a rhythm as he eats.

'Dad texted just now. He wants you to go home.'

The idea that Rafe is my stalker returns, my mouth suddenly dry. 'I need to figure out what to do with this place first.'

'Have you taken your pills?'

'Earlier. Don't worry, I won't forget. What time's your first lesson?'

'Not till ten.' Jamie gazes outside at the empty fields. 'You could throw great parties here, with no one to complain about noise. It feels like we're the last two people alive.'

'Not to me.' My memories of this place are still strong, ghosts keeping me company.

He studies me again. 'You seem worried, Mum, since you got hurt. I'll stay here every night till you come home.'

'I'll be okay, you know.'

'You're hard to understand at the best of times.' He frowns at me. 'Carla's way easier. She likes having me around, last time she even baked me a cake.'

His words sting. 'I love you being here too. But it's a long way from college.'

'I can drive there.' He nods at his ancient Ford on the driveway, his pride and joy, freshly painted a brilliant orange. 'Do you like the respray?'

'It's eye-catching, for sure.'

'A mate had some leftover paint.'

'Listen to me, Jamie. You'd be more comfortable at home, with your dad.'

He seizes my hand. 'You don't get it, do you? Your stalker knows you're here. I want to protect you.'

I make an effort to sound calm. 'No, Jamie. You'll be a target too if you try. It's important you keep out of it.'

We're standing toe to toe, but he's not listening.

'Promise me you'll tell the police everything today. Go there and hassle them for protection. I'm not leaving till you agree.' He sounds like Rafe, the power between us shifting again. 'Yes or no?'

'Remember, it's my job to protect you, not the other way round. But I'll do it. Okay?'

Jamie gives a victory smile, then hurries outside before I can change my mind. His car engine spits out exhaust fumes as it kicks into life. I should have extracted a promise from him too, to spend the day at college, not with his older mates getting stoned. I don't know whether to be glad or afraid that he's so determined to keep me company, but it's my responsibility to keep him safe. I can't let him get hurt if my stalker launches another attack.

I feel a stab of pain behind my eyes, sharp enough to make me wince. It soon lifts, but it's a reminder to slow down. There's no need to race into town. I can spend a few quiet hours here first. I use the time to check each room for signs of neglect. If I'm going to stay here long-term, the place needs an overhaul, and I'll have to keep fighting the council's demolition order. When I check the unread mail stacked on the counter, there are two more letters threatening compulsory purchase. I can't let this place be razed to the ground, but that battle must wait until I feel stronger. There are letters from the water board too, energy suppliers, and leaflets from self-employed gardeners, which go straight in the recycling bin.

It pulls me up short to find a letter in a manila envelope at the bottom of the pile. The stamp carries a Cambridge postmark, dated a week ago. The writing is my stalker's unmistakable spidery scrawl.

'Me or you,' I whisper.

There's no need to open it to know the message it contains. They've found me here. But how, exactly, unless someone watched me every day, like Rafe? It's months since I last drove here. Have they been following me so closely they realize it's where I grew up, and that I can't bear to sell it? They must have guessed that circumstances would bring me here eventually. The idea makes me feel dirty, as though a stranger's eyes have crawled all over my skin, like a bee seeking nectar, leaving a sticky trail.

I check the feed from the CCTV cameras to see if my stalker has been invading my territory. But when I fast forward through last night's footage, nothing appears, except a brilliant winter moon. I remember Rafe's words, saying that all the security measures in the world can't protect me from someone determined to do harm. Sooner or later, they'll catch me alone. It sounded like blackmail, to force me to go home, but now it seems like an empty threat. The security here feels watertight. I'll take more steps, if necessary, to regain my old sense of ease. I hate turning Lucy and Pete's home into a fortress, but there's no other choice.

My legs still feel shaky when I lower myself onto a kitchen chair, despite counselling myself to stay calm. It's easy to keep tabs on people these days. Anyone can track your phone via GPS, with the right software, and I may be being cyber-stalked too, by any number of followers. I study the fragile writing on the envelope again. It's possible that the gap in my memory is causing all this. Maybe I did something unforgivable as a child and it's engraved on someone's memory. They could be old by now, with trembling hands, and plenty of time to follow me. Would I even notice an elderly man or woman in the driver's seat of the car behind me?

I think about the rare cases of stalkers hiding their identity before launching a vicious attack, recalling how I told Lisa that it's ten times more likely to be someone from your intimate circle, sexually motivated, leading to violence or rape. I remember a case when a stalker pursued his sister-in-law relentlessly with letters, anonymous emails and gifts. He hid his identity so well she had no idea, until he attacked her in her car, then drove to a wood and set it on fire, with her locked inside.

But this feels different. My stalker has had plenty of chances to get me alone, yet chose to attack me in a crowd, with the greatest likelihood of getting caught. They want to destroy my mind, as well as my body. But I can't imagine any of the people close to me concealing that kind of hatred. The message is unchanging, as though it's a given that only one of us can win. The tone feels like a direct challenge, but it's a one-sided dialogue, never allowing me to reply. That could be what they're building towards: a big showdown, two bare-knuckle fighters entering the ring.

My phone is pulsing with messages. I should have done my weekly broadcast yesterday, supporting victims of stalking by reminding them of safety protocols: record all your stalker's actions, never react, and keep friends, family and the police informed. I'm not following my own advice because keeping secrets is in my DNA. It was safer to keep my fears quiet growing up, until the habit became engrained. At least Rafe and Jamie know the truth, and I've kept a written record of everything my stalker has done in a notebook at home, even though the police have shown no interest in protecting me.

I scroll through hundreds of requests for support. It feels overwhelming now we're all in the same boat. No matter how quickly I bail out water, I'm still sinking. I glance at isolated phrases: thousands of texts, public shaming, sex videos, bullying. The process never changes, and it's the same in every country across the world. If a highly motivated stalker can't possess you, they dismantle your life instead. And there are so many ways to do it. It only takes a moment to upload a film of your ex, naked in bed, but the results can blow their life apart. Many of the stories resonate with me. One man describes his ex-wife's endless pursuit, even though he's got a new partner and a baby. She still believes that one day he'll walk back into her life, if she can only make him listen.

When I look outside again, sleet is splashing onto the roof of my car. I've got a wide view of the surrounding countryside as I move from room to room, but the confidence I learned here has drained away. There's no one watching the place at close range now, but they could come back any minute. Rafe's words about windows being easy to break return to me. If my stalker wants to hurt me badly enough, they won't care how many cameras point in their direction. I take a deep breath and try to shrug the thought away.

I confront myself in the mirror upstairs. I need to look presentable for the drinks party tonight in my honour, but the clothes I threw into my holdall on Sunday are a random assortment. I pick a midnight-blue silk shirt, slim black trousers and high-heeled boots. I make an effort with my face too, brushing my short fringe over my swollen forehead, then applying foundation and concealer to camouflage the bruising, plus a dash of lipstick. It lifts my mood, but instinct makes me choose trainers, too. I place the spike-heeled boots in my bag to wear later. I have to be ready to run from danger, no matter how weak I'm feeling. The band of pain around my forehead tightens then releases again. The boundary between sensible and risky behaviour has blurred. I should be following the doctor's advice to rest, but that feels impossible. It's best to keep busy and surround myself with people, holding my stalker at arm's length.

I've got an itinerary to follow when I get into my car. I shouldn't drive, but I start the ignition anyway, even though my internal voice is warning me against it. I need to collect more clothes and possessions. The cottage looks bare; I must try and make it homely, for Jamie's sake. I'd rather not have to face Rafe again, but it's a price I'm willing to pay. The ten-minute drive home passes without incident, apart from a flurry of snow landing on my windscreen, dissolving as the wipers clear it away.

Rafe's Audi isn't on the drive, thank God. I can grab what I need, without another tough conversation, until I spot a familiar red Mazda parked close by. My sister, Carla, is in the driving seat, staring at my house. We got back in contact two years ago, yet it still feels strange. I'd learned to accept that I had no relatives, until her email arrived in my inbox at work, out of the blue. Her expression's furious when she beckons me over, always bossy, despite being my youngest sibling. The sleet is thicker now, landing on my face as I open the passenger door and slide into the seat.

Carla is thirty-six, but looks twenty-five, dressed in the blue scrubs she wears to work as a freelance physio. There's no makeup on her pretty, heart-shaped face, her blonde hair scraped into a ponytail.

'Rafe called me,' she snaps. 'He said you've got a head injury. Why the hell are you driving?'

'He's overreacting, Carla. I didn't want to worry you or Leo.'

'We'd have come straight to the hospital.'

'Thanks, but I'm fine now.'

Carla doesn't seem convinced. 'Your speech sounds slurred, Elly. What on earth happened?'

'I had a fall. It's left me tired, that's all.'

'How can I help if you won't even tell me you're in trouble?'

'I was going to explain next time we met.'

'You're coming to mine tomorrow afternoon, remember? Or maybe you've got more important things that I don't know about?'

I feel a sudden flash of anger. 'You've hidden stuff from me too. Why didn't you say Jamie's been visiting you?'

'I assumed you knew, and it's not a crime, is it? God knows, we needed relatives' support as kids. That's no reason to lock me out.' Carla's expression softens at last, her eyes glossy with tears. 'Rafe's message scared the shit out of me, Elly. He said you've been acting weird. I've been ringing your doorbell. I was terrified you were in there, unconscious. I was about to call emergency services.'

'I'm sorry, okay?'

Now's the moment to explain that Rafe and I are living apart, but I still don't trust her completely, after such a long separation. I smile instead, dispersing the tension.

Carla heaves in a breath. 'I'd better go – a client's waiting for me. See you tomorrow. Call me later if you feel rough.'

I don't remember making the arrangement to meet, but nod anyway, to avoid any more conflict. Then I step back into the sleet and watch her leave. My sister's car looks happier than its owner. Last year's Glastonbury sticker is still clinging to the rear window, plus a faded NHS rainbow and a heart-shaped sign announcing that cats make great boyfriends, because they never let you down. It might do Carla good to take an active role in Jamie's life, and help him too. But trust is the one thing missing between us, and I can't magic it out of thin air.

I'm reluctant to enter the house again, knowing that Rafe's

mistress followed the same path to our weathered steel door. The idea hurts, so I bat it away. If he'd taken her to a hotel the effect on our marriage would be the same, but my home already feels different. The atmosphere seems airless when I stand in the hallway, like there's no oxygen left to breathe. I slump on a chair in the living room, then fall asleep instantly. It's 3 p.m. when I wake up, and it's stopped sleeting outside. My brain seems to grab extra sleep, trying to mend itself, whenever it can.

I fill two suitcases with clothes and items with personal value. I pick a sculpture of a figure reaching for the sky with arms outstretched, carved from teak. I bought it in Mexico after watching a woman carving it by the side of the road. That was my first big journey with Rafe, at a time when our life together seemed perfect. I pack photo albums, two small paintings and a handmade blanket from a recent holiday in Shetland. Its abstract blue woollen pattern reminds me of the sea.

My car is piled to the roof with bags and boxes by the time I finish, and it's almost 5 p.m. I need to leave before Rafe gets home. I pour myself some water in the kitchen, then swallow two more tablets. The pain is back, even though I've been working slowly. I wash the glass, dry it, then place it back in the cupboard. It seems important to leave no trace of myself behind, except gaps on the shelves and walls. The spiteful part of me wants Rafe to grieve long and hard for the space I leave behind.

I spot something under an eye-level cabinet as I turn away. It's a small silver bump. When I touch it, something drops into the palm of my hand, no bigger than my thumbnail. It's a plastic chip, like an earpiece, the same grey as the units. Shock leaves me unsteady on my feet.

I'm almost certain it's a bugging device, allowing someone to overhear every one of our conversations. My hands shake when I check online and my suspicions are confirmed by the photos I see. Did my stalker listen to my last row with Rafe? And how the hell did they get inside? The only people with keys are me, Rafe and Jamie. I remember suddenly that my sister has one too, even though she'd forgotten it today. She used it to water our plants while we were away. But surely she'd never hurt me? Carla always wants to look after people, not cause them pain.

I've been too lax about security at work in the past. It's possible someone walked into my office months ago, before this threat existed. Few of my colleagues bother to lock their doors. We often leave our offices open for hours, while we're teaching or in the library. Someone from my department could easily have taken my keys from the pocket of my coat as it hung behind the door, then made copies at a locksmith's in town, returning the originals immediately. The idea of my stalker traipsing around our home is even worse than being shoved to the ground. Now nothing is sacred.

'You sick bastard.'

I hiss out the words, aware that someone is listening, even though it's wrong to give them a reaction. Stalkers view any response, positive or negative, as permission to escalate their campaign. They want to be the only thing in your mind. It's part of the psychological process of creating terror. Fury burns in my throat when I spot some crockery, stacked by the sink. I grab a cup and hurl it at the wall, then watch it shatter. Next a dinner plate, and glass tumbler. I want to break everything I see, but make myself stop as the pain behind my eyes intensifies. My actions leave me shocked, my hands still shaky. I've never vented my feelings like this. It's as though some foreign influence that I don't trust is controlling my thoughts.

I have to understand what's happening to me. Once stalkers accept that their victim won't return their feelings, they set out to wound and abuse. Any form of power satisfies them. I fight my temptation to drop the bug into a glass of water, placing it in my pocket instead. I feel hollow when I find a dustpan and brush to clear up the mess I created, suddenly desperate to leave.

I pause by the open door of my office. It used to be a refuge. I wrote three books here while Rafe and I juggled childcare. It gave me so much pleasure to look up from my computer in summer and see them outside, kicking a football around. When I glance through the window now, the garden's barren, the water in the birdbath frozen solid. I can't stay any longer. I pick up a shoebox full of letters from my stalker, closing the lid to avoid seeing the handwriting. Then I grab the notebook I've used to record every act of intimidation and hurry down the hallway.

It feels good to slam the door hard enough to make it shudder on its hinges, the noise like a crash of cymbals. The rational side of me knows I'm not myself. My head injury's making me behave out of character. My anger is focused on my stalker's invasion of my life, but something primitive is at work too, something I can't control. Protests collect inside my mouth, waiting to be spat out, like bullets from a machine gun.

15

I head for the police station at 5.30 p.m., to honour my promise to Jamie. Commuters are flooding in the opposite direction, leaving the city in a slow crawl up Huntingdon Road while I wait at the traffic lights. I glance at the 1930s semis lining the roadside, and the college playing fields covered in ice. Cambridge never used to be so congested, but new villages are cropping up on every brownfield site, leaving the main routes gridlocked. We're running short of water too, and the air quality is compromised. My chest feels tighter with every mile, but that could be down to anxiety. My situation's changing too fast, swinging from one extreme to another like a pendulum.

Rafe supported me for so long. He believed in me, and his architecture practice prospered too, allowing him to rent a swanky office in town and employ Mia, his beautiful assistant. I blink my eyes shut, hands clenching the wheel. Rafe still hasn't given the mystery woman a name. It seems ironic that I've never been unfaithful, and believed he was too principled to cheat. Maybe he's right after all. What's the point in dwelling on something that broke us apart? It would be better to focus on curing the damage, but that's easier said than done. How can a marriage heal from an invisible wound?

It takes me twenty minutes to cross the city centre to Parker's Piece. The common becomes a fairground every holiday, the rides designed to catch children's imaginations. It must be half term. Teenagers are milling around on the grass, even though it's freezing. They stand in the floodlights, waiting to ride the waltzers. Tinny music echoes through my car windows, the carousel's vivid colours shine in the cold, the Ferris wheel spins.

The city's police headquarters stands on the edge of the common, beside the fire station. It's a square 1970s block, built from grey concrete. I park in a visitor's bay and remove my notebook from the box I collected. I need to keep on logging everything my stalker does, but I'm keen to pass on the letters as proof. My dealings with the police haven't helped me so far, but I'm hoping to be surprised. If the worst happens, it's important to leave an evidence trail behind. My expertise is no comfort. I know all the statistics about stalking as a predictor for violence: many campaigns escalate, with more than fifty per cent resulting in a physical assault. Over one million people reported being stalked in the UK last year, and the police are so understaffed and badly trained they often fail to handle cases properly. I try to rally my optimism, but the waiting room is no place for positivity. It's crowded with people sitting on hard plastic chairs, with a baby screaming loud enough to leave a ringing noise in my ears.

The officer behind the desk looks prematurely old, like he's seen too much tragedy. He only cheers up when he reports that I'll have a long wait to speak to an officer. I try to explain my situation, but he's already shooing me away, dealing with the next person in line. I must wait until the number on my ticket's called.

Places like this used to fascinate me as a student, where every type of anxiety behaviour is on display. The young girl opposite is agitated, experiencing facial tics every few seconds: Tourette's syndrome, exacerbated by stress. The old man next to her has forgotten his way home. That'll be Alzheimer's or secondary dementia. I don't know whether it's a blessing or a curse that my job has taught me to observe body language and human behaviour obsessively, including my own. Hyper-vigilance can be tiring, but it's useful in my line of work. It helps me spot warning signs before a client turns violent. But my old sense of certainty about diagnosing violence early has left me since Georgia Reed was attacked. It feels like my safety instinct is damaged. I used to depend on it, but now it's a compass spinning out of control.

I keep my head down, unwilling to enter random conversations, rarely meeting anyone's eye, with pain squeezing my temples like a vice. Forty minutes later I'm still waiting. The atmosphere in the waiting room is getting tenser all the time. A young couple are having a screaming match over custody of their baby, while the child dozes in her pram.

Ten more minutes pass before I look around again. This time I notice a man sitting in the corner, and his gaze locks onto mine, putting me on edge. He's middle-aged, in a brown leather jacket that gapes open, exposing his paunch, with grey hair hanging in greasy curls. He seems unembarrassed about staring at me. I've never seen my stalker, as far as I'm aware, but this is the ideal location to hide in plain sight. No one else is paying me any attention, all focused on reporting crimes they've witnessed. I want to escape the building fast, but the man's behaviour is erratic. When I glance at him again his gaze is fixed on the wall opposite, and my panic dwindles.

An administrator emerges after an hour, passing me a familiar form to complete. I helped design this prompt list for Scotland Yard. It's intended to assess the risk level victims face, so every report follows the same protocol. Am I in immediate danger? Have I been attacked recently, or in the past? Does my stalker loiter by my house or car? Has there been material damage, including vandalism to my property or possessions?

I write on the back of the form once it's complete, explaining that my stalker is hiding their identity, which makes the threat level worse. They put me in hospital for two days, without ever showing their face. I also report that one of the stalkers I've counselled in prison, Joe Sinclair, launched a brutal attack on his victim twenty miles away, the night before I ended up in hospital.

When I check my statement again, my story sounds like the ramblings of a crazed conspiracy theorist. Who will believe that a stranger sat by my hospital bed, holding my hand, and broke into my home unnoticed to place listening devices there? Any hard-pressed detective will question my sanity. When I look up, leather-jacket man is watching me again, making me queasy. He offers a nicotine-yellow smile, but I'm already on my feet. I've faced too much unwanted attention to welcome a middle-aged admirer leering at me in public, whether he's my stalker or not.

I dump the letters on the duty officer's desk. He peers at the box with a frown, like it might be booby-trapped, then explains that I must stay in my seat. If I leave without seeing an officer, my evidence may not get seen for days. I feel sure that my stalkers' notes will be archived, or binned, whether I stay or leave. I hate cynicism as a rule, but sometimes it's built into the system. I've dealt with enough well-intentioned welfare officers, police and social workers to know the pressures they face. The system's creaking at the seams, and the only crimes that get investigated fully involve physical violence of the worst kind. The one person who looks disappointed to see me exit the building is my fan in his leather jacket, but at least he doesn't follow me outside.

It's a relief to return to the evening's cold air. I stand with my back to the car door, catching my breath, my head pulsing again, irritated by the waste of time. The fairground ahead of me is a blur of colour. Thrill-seekers are caught on a ride that jerks in a half-circle, leaving them suspended upside down until gravity flips them upright again. I remember going on it with Jamie when he was nine or ten, his eyes wide with excitement. He used to be so fearless, and I still see sparks of his old courage behind the cool mask most teenagers like to wear.

I leave my car in the Lion Yard car park in the centre of town. I could have chosen the one for staff at the university, but the access path is dark at night. It's the ideal place for my stalker to hide. It feels safer to pick somewhere with CCTV cameras on every floor.

My presentation is just twenty minutes away when I reach the department. It's an imposing building, tall and austere. Its walls form a three-storey square, enclosing a cobbled quadrangle. Most of the building is given over to research and teaching, with only a few flats for postgraduate accommodation. The limestone has been greyed by exhaust fumes from the traffic on Regent's Street, or the despair patients felt a hundred years ago, when psychology was in its infancy. The building houses the old laboratory, with an exhibition of photos and instruments from the earliest days of experimental treatments. Surgeons believed back then that madness could be cut from a patient's brain. There's even a glass case full of scalpels, hand drills and knives, including the steel chisel used to perform the first lobotomy in the UK. Just thinking about those savage treatments makes the air feel colder.

I pause by the department's entrance, where the porter's lodge stands beside the ironwork gates. I normally stop to collect my post from Reg Bellamy, who runs the building and spends long hours policing it, but I need to scan the speech I scribbled this morning. I handle stress by overpreparing, like all good perfectionists, but this time my strategy has failed. I feel nauseous and light-headed as I hurry across the quadrangle, hemmed in by the high walls and unlit windows. It's a relief to use my pass card and enter the department. The atmosphere inside disturbed me when I began my PhD, but its echoing corridors, which undergraduates claim to be haunted, are familiar territory now.

Someone has reached my office on the third floor before me, an envelope shoved under my door. It seems ironic that I've only started locking my office door recently, while few of my colleagues bother, but my stalker has walked straight to the heart of my professional world, unchecked. My name and title are written in delicate black ink: Dr Eloise Shaw. I've been crossing my fingers that no more would come, but this is a change of style. The messages have arrived by post until now, proving that the sender can invade my privacy any time they like. But how did they get inside, unless they have a pass card, or managed to borrow one? Whoever is stalking me is a bold risk-taker, and the fear nagging at me is growing stronger all the time.

The card inside holds the same three words, in a child's shaky handwriting. But this time the message is emphatic, written in jagged block capitals, a new sign of escalation. My stalker must be feeling powerful after putting me in hospital. Their aggression has shifted up a gear. It feels like they're yelling in my face, making my heart rate increase:

ME OR YOU

The words linger on my retinas, even when I look away. My stalker is announcing their latest victory. I still can't pinpoint why I've been chosen, despite analysing their behaviour for weeks. The university's high walls protected me well until my attack. I still can't figure out whether it's someone I trust or a random stranger. Most of my colleagues still have no idea what happened to me three days ago, except Marina and Lisa. My visit to the police station has convinced me that nothing will happen if I call emergency services about three words scribbled on a postcard. They're too short-staffed to care, and a squad car pulling up right now would make me visible for all the wrong reasons.

I suddenly remember my boss's warning to submit my research report in time for the departmental audit, so I start my computer. I need to meet every requirement at work because I'm waiting to hear if my application to become a reader has been approved. It's one level below a professorship, and it would guarantee funding for my research project for years to come. I could reduce my teaching load and concentrate on my anti-stalking work, but high-level academic jobs at Cambridge are like hen's teeth. There's no certainty I'll get it, however much external funding my research attracts.

Marina will have to deal with a few missed commas in my report – I can't face checking the densely typed pages again. But when I open the folder, the report's not there. Maybe I filed it somewhere else by mistake? There's no trace of it on the computer, or backed up online, and I'm starting to feel nauseous. It took me days to produce, containing case studies and an overview of my recent work with stalkers and the students I supervise.

I must have saved it to my desktop on the day of my attack, yet it seems to have vanished. I check my backup files and other folders where it could be stored, but there's no trace. It's like the report never existed. I was stupid not to upload it to the university's system, where data is fully protected. It dawns on me that someone might have stolen it. But why the hell would they hack into my computer – to destroy the one document I can't afford to lose?

My stalker has broken into my home, and now here too. The idea sickens me. It feels like they've crawled inside my head. The weight of it settles on the back of my neck, a burden I never predicted. I can't deny this is a big escalation from phone calls and letters. If my stalker really tampered with my computer, they must have nerves of steel. I should be honest with all my colleagues, including Marina, as damage limitation, and to keep myself safe. The problem is, old habits die hard. Guarding my privacy has served me well until now. I'm not yet ready to ring the alarm bell and announce that I've fallen victim to the very syndrome I'm trying to cure.

My legs feel weak when I peer at the quadrangle below, my thoughts overtaken by half-formed memories. I yank the window open to give myself some fresh air, allowing the winter chill to touch my face. I know how my father died because I was told about it. Apparently I was in the house when he got hurt. I should be able to look the facts in the eye, but they always evade me. I stare down at the flagstones below and try to remember his last act. The sound of someone screaming enters my mind, then falls silent. My mind seems to be full of someone else's doubts.

I pass my hand over my eyes, trying to clear my confusion. Colleagues are crossing the quadrangle in gaggles now, wearing black academic gowns, their outlines picked out by lamplight. No one bothers to look up. They resemble a flock of crows, chattering in the dark. My stalker could be among them or may have sneaked up the back stairs before I arrived. It must be thrilling, to remain anonymous for so long, unlike most stalkers, who prefer to stand outside victims' homes, fully visible, tracking their movements at close range. Visitors are meant to sign in at the porters' lodge by the front gate, but the system's flawed. Deliveroo drivers and tourists often march inside, unchecked, and the CCTV is basic. There are just two cameras, both over the main entrances. The back gate is sometimes left wedged open. Once you're inside the building, you can do as you please.

I'm still feeling shaky when Reg Bellamy appears in the doorway. The porter looks like he's worked here for a hundred years, a stocky figure in an old-fashioned black suit, the jacket always buttoned, even in high summer. He's around fifty, and this is his second career, after decades as a railway guard. Reg sees it as his duty to support all the academic staff, as well as students. He seems amused when I ask if many strangers have visited the department today. Apparently, there are far too many to count. The lobby outside the meeting room is packed, with invitees waiting for the drinks party in my honour.

Reg seems in a hurry when he hands over a box. It's just like the one I received in hospital, marked with an Interflora label, full of dead flowers. I thank him and he scurries away. My stalker's latest gift remains sealed when nausea returns suddenly. I make it to the women's loo just in time to spew the contents of my guts into the toilet bowl.

'It stops here.' I hiss out the words. 'You can't hurt me again.'

It's rubbish, of course. The only things defending me from my stalker are my professional knowledge and my certainty that they'll try to hurt me again. They'll already be hunting for another opportunity, and next time I might not be so lucky. Whatever happens, I have to keep going, for Jamie's sake and mine.

The woman in the mirror looks shell-shocked when I wash my hands, with grey strands in her short blonde hair. My Danish mother stares back at me. It disturbs me that I'm the spitting image, almost the same age as she was when she sent me away. I've tried dyeing my hair and wearing different clothes, but the resemblance between us is undeniable. The wound under my hairline from where my head hit the pavement is fading, yet my mind's chaotic. I can't even tell if I look like a victim or a survivor.

I rinse my mouth with water, then apply fresh lipstick. My lips look like a vampire's snarl, but it's too late to rummage in my bag for a paler shade before heading back out. My colleague, Clive Wadsworth, is in his office. He calls to me when I pass his door.

Clive is a bluff Yorkshireman of sixty, with an exceptional mind and a passion for football. I wouldn't be here without him. He picked my application over hundreds of others, agreeing to supervise my PhD, ten years ago. Clive and his wife have treated me kindly ever since. Thanks to his guidance I work independently now, with my own research team. Clive's waistline has expanded a little since he took me on, thanks to his love of curry and beer, but he's ageing well. His face is craggy but handsome, like a character actor, not yet old enough to play King Lear.

'Are you okay, Elly?' His voice is a smoker's low grumble. 'You're as white as a sheet.'

'Thanks for telling me, just before my event.'

'Stage fright, is it? Don't worry, you'll be great.' Clive taps me on the shoulder. 'Help me find my glasses, will you?'

'It starts in five minutes. Can we get moving, Clive?'

'I need them for my speech about your prize. My memory's rubbish these days.'

'I'm glad you're doing it. I thought Marina would take charge.'

'She prefers invisibility. You got me instead, an old man with a dying career.' He rummages through a chaos of paperwork, his voice full of self-mockery and a hint of genuine sadness.

'Rubbish, they've made you an emeritus professor.'

'It's a title, not a job, Elly. They're showing me the door.'

'Don't be silly. You'll have to come in for coffee with me, as usual.'

We've spent hours together in the fellows' canteen. I don't like the idea of him going any more than he does.

'Where the fuck are they? Marina hates lateness, and she's vicious, at the best of times.'

It's hard to imagine our head of department venting her temper in public. I expect her usual icy remoteness when I confess that my research report is lost. Professor Westbrook never announces her plans, making it impossible to track her movements unless you're summoned for a meeting. She passes through the building like a ghost most days.

Clive grabs a crumpled sheet of paper at last, and I spot his glasses on a stack of psychology journals.

'They're here. Now let's go, please.'

'You're the main event, remember? They can't leave until you've had your say, then it's wine and snacks. Hilary and I will take you out to dinner for a proper celebration after. The rest can bugger off to their colleges, leaving us in peace. Okay?'

'Dinner sounds great, thanks, but I'd rather skip the first bit.' Tension echoes in my voice.

'Stop winning bloody prizes, then. All you have to do is smile sweetly and say thanks. You know the drill.'

Clive's lighthearted tone barely conceals a brisk reminder to stop being churlish. Plenty of staff in the department would love to win an award of any kind, in a place dedicated to celebrating only the elite.

The quad's empty when we reach the bottom of the stairs, with orange light pulsing through the meeting room's windows. We enter via the back entrance to avoid the crowded lobby. The space inside looks pristine. Tables stand in neat rows, covered with wine bottles and trays of canapés. The architecture is high Victorian with ornate plasterwork on the ceiling. I found the formality daunting at first, but it suits me better now. I'll never be a Cambridge insider, but at least I understand how the system works. The place smells like it always does – of dust, history and overcooked food.

I stand by the stage while academics troop inside. Fellows, readers and professors from departments littered across the city have marched through the cold to hear my prize announced. I should be grateful, but I feel like a fraud. I can't tell if the pain behind my eyes is from nerves or my head injury.

'Let's do this,' Clive whispers.

My anxiety lingers when we walk on stage, even though no one can attack me in such a public setting, surrounded by allies. Clive is in his element, with his wife Hilary beaming from the front row. He's a lumbering figure in a scruffy suit, but his charisma is undeniable any time he faces a crowd. He makes complex information sound easy, holding audiences in the palm of his hand.

'Raise your glasses, please, everyone. It's my great pleasure to announce that Dr Eloise Shaw has won this year's Cambridge Prize for her book, *Toxic Love*. It describes her groundbreaking anti-stalking programme, currently being trialled in UK prisons, making her the UK's chief forensic expert in the field. Excellent news, of course, but it presents me with a thorny dilemma. How does an egotist like me claim some reflected glory?' He pauses for a moment while the crowd laughs. 'By telling you that I honed her razor-sharp mind, of course. I supervised her PhD, which was a true privilege. She's one of life's great problem solvers, dynamic enough to fix a broken system. We're all proud of you, Elly.'

Applause erupts before I can reply. My boss is hiding in the middle of the crowd, her face neutral, unlike my colleagues'. Several are on their feet, grinning as they clap. I'd like to savour the moment, but I'm unsteady on my feet. My stalker could be out there in the audience. I won't give them the pleasure of seeing me rattled, but the pain in my head feels emotional as well as physical. I'd rather be in a darkened room than addressing a crowd, unsure if my words even make sense.

Gripping the podium tightly, I begin my speech.

'People often ask me why I picked stalking as my research area when it's such a tough syndrome to fix. But for me that's its biggest draw. Obsession destroys our self-control, replacing it with a yearning to control someone else, and there's been a huge rise in stalking in the UK, with over eighty thousand police cases last year. Many more go unreported. That will only improve if society's mindset shifts away from punishment towards creating an effective cure.

'My treatment programme evolved through working with the UK's most dangerous stalkers in prisons. Those conversations have taught me that stalking exists as a delusional illness long before it becomes a crime. Offenders need an intensive nine-month therapy programme to bring their obsession under control.'

I feel more comfortable taking questions and comments from the audience at the end. A colleague states that she's glad psychological interventions are starting to take place long before harm's done. If we can remove the stigma from seeking help before stalking begins, we can end victims' suffering by solving the problem before it's begun.

I escape from the podium, relieved. A few high-level bureaucrats shake my hand, then Noah Jagiello approaches me. He joined the department after a stint at Harvard last year, already an expert on childhood trauma and PTSD. I noticed him the first day he arrived because he's an imposing figure – tall, with an athletic build and relaxed manner, his black hair cropped short. If he feels self-conscious about the deep scar that bisects his left cheek, he gives no sign of it. I don't know him well enough to ask how he picked up the injury. His appearance is smart, apart from his three-day beard. Noah's office is next to mine so we run into each other all the time, and I hear the jazz he plays at low volume whenever he's at work. It never bothers me. In fact, there's something uplifting about the melodies he chooses.

I've worked with plenty of attractive men before without

getting into trouble, but Noah is hard to ignore. Attraction is subliminal, anyway. We show it in our movements and reactions, through dozens of involuntary signs. I've noticed him, and the feeling appears to be mutual. If he's aware of my stress tonight, he's too polite to say.

Noah stands two feet away, silent, like he's waiting for an answer that's overdue, or doing some behavioural research. The truth could be far simpler. He's flirting with me, for reasons unknown. I'm in no position to encourage personal interest while my life's in a mess, and neither is he. A wedding ring glitters on his left hand, yellow gold, almost a centimetre wide.

'Those numbers are terrifying,' he says. 'If one in five women in the UK experiences stalking, and one in ten men, at some point in their lives, how come treating offenders has been so badly neglected?'

I'm glad to return to familiar topics. 'Maybe the problem seems too overwhelming. Stalkers are often unwilling to accept therapy or medication.'

'How did you get the police onside?'

'That's a work in progress. They still see stalking as a public nuisance, and they don't trust therapy.'

'Because it's expensive?'

'Not compared to time in prison, but it's viewed as a soft option for offenders.'

'I know you want empathy for them, but the victims suffer more, don't they?' Noah's tone is gentle.

'Obsession can ruin a stalker's life too.'

He studies me again. 'Is it a personal thing? Have you ever experienced stalking yourself?'

'Direct, aren't you?'

'I was born curious, that's all. Don't feel obliged to answer.'

I still feel cornered. 'My work puts me in the line of fire, I accepted that at the start. The stalking mindset can lead to a new fixation, straight after the first.'

'Yet you go on doing it, that's what interests me.'

'Tonight's meant to be fun, Noah. No more psychoanalysis, please.'

'Sorry, I've been in the library all day, overthinking,' he says, laughing. 'Got any plans for reading week?'

'There's stuff to do at home. I moved recently and the house is a mess.'

'I need a new place too. My flat's tiny, that's why I spend so much time here.' Noah turns to me again. 'I've been meaning to ask you for a favour, Eloise. Could I observe you at work for a few days, on your prison visits?'

I return his gaze. 'You're interested in my programme?'

'It would help my research. I'm writing about the link between childhood trauma and delusional illnesses, like stalking. If you let me tag along, I'd need some anonymized case histories too, for my next book.'

'That sounds worthwhile. Hardly anyone's looking closely at the role of childhood neglect as a trigger for stalking.'

He smiles again. 'We'll be ahead of the curve then. Maybe we could co-author the chapter?'

'God no, I've been writing all year. But you're welcome to observe my work, if it helps. I'll send you some dates when you could shadow me.'

I survive the rest of the event on small talk and a single glass of wine. I still feel weak, as if the first strong wind could blow me away. It's a relief to be among people, and the distractions they provide. I should pace myself for the meal with Clive because my head's still throbbing. I'm about to retreat when a stranger strides over just as the event is closing. So many people have offered me congratulations already, I prepare a grateful smile. The man's skin is florid, his grey hair in need of a comb. I assume he's another dignitary, but his frown looks like it's been set in concrete.

'Does the name Georgia Reed ring any bells, Dr Shaw?' His voice is almost too low to hear, but his words trigger the guilt I've been carrying. He rushes on without waiting for my answer. 'It should do. You almost got her killed.'

'I read about what happened. I'm so—'

'I'm her dad, Alan Reed. Her stalker was released early, thanks to you saying he was cured. That sick bastard broke into her flat and tried to kill her three days ago. Georgia's injuries are so bad she's unrecognizable.'

I can't think of a reply. Nothing I say can relieve his family's suffering.

'That monster's back in jail, but she's in intensive care. Sinclair must be overjoyed,' Reed hisses. 'I'll destroy you for that, do you hear? I'll get you disqualified.'

'I'm sorry if—'

'Her blood's on your hands.' His voice rises to a shout. 'I bet you think you're some kind of feminist, but you set those psychos free to hurt innocent girls like Georgia. She could die because of you.'

He flings the contents of his wine glass at my face. I dodge, but the liquid hits my shoulder, leaving a dark red stain. Noah grabs the man's arm immediately, and another tutor helps to restrain him. The room falls silent, everyone gripped by his furious yelling as he's marched away.

The pain in my head feels sharper than ever. My programme should protect lives, not put them at risk. I've been so self-absorbed since my own attack, I'd almost forgotten Joe Sinclair's victim, and her family's trauma. When I look up again, Marina Westbrook is studying me like I'm a specimen smeared across a slide. Her expression is too cold for sympathy, and I can tell she has no intention of rescuing me this time. You could hear a pin drop. Disturbances like this rarely happen inside ivory towers like Cambridge.

I can't stay here with dozens of people observing my panic, so I stumble through the crowd, then exit the meeting room fast, too upset to care who might be waiting for me in the shadows.

16

YOU

I'm breathless when I reach my office, which forces me to stand still and recover before I rummage in my cupboard. My gym clothes are in there, for the rare occasions when I do an exercise class. I dump my ruined blouse in the bin, then pull on a clean T-shirt, desperate to feel normal. My thoughts refuse to settle. I wanted to apologize, even though every stalking prevention programme has casualties. My system beats any other, but statistics are no defence now Georgia Reed is in intensive care.

I'll have to assess Joe Sinclair again soon, as part of the treatment programme. My work is focused on learning why a minority reoffend, but I'm only human. Right now, I just want him to pay for his crime, so he suffers worse than Georgia. The violence I've ignored for so long makes a comeback, an acid taste burning in my throat. I try to suppress it because it can't be trusted. It could get me into even more trouble. The evening's events replay in my mind; my boss stared at me like I was a stranger, when any normal person would have rushed to help. Her behaviour's contradictory. She rode with me in the ambulance and arranged a party to celebrate my success, yet spent the whole evening looking aggrieved.

Marina's attitude is the least of my worries. Today's visit to the police station made me certain that official help will be thin on the ground. It's possible that my stalker is in the same position as Georgia Reed's dad. That would explain why I'm being targeted, if they're getting even for all that suffering, even though parole-board decisions are never made alone. There may be others who'd love to see me disqualified as a psychologist. Anger destroys logic. If Jamie was lying in intensive care, I'd be hunting for a scapegoat too.

I'm by the window when someone barges through the door without knocking. It's Lisa, riding to my rescue again. My friend looks glamorous as always, her dark hair a shoulder-length mass of curls. She's dressed in a scarlet top, with matching earrings and lipstick. She's so out of breath she must have run straight here from the meeting room. She's the one person at work who knows my situation, and I'm certain she's kept her mouth shut.

'What did that nutter say to you?' She puts her arm around my shoulders.

I shake my head. 'His daughter's in intensive care because an offender from my programme beat her up.'

'That's not your fault, he'll realize that in time. The stalker's to blame, no one else.' Lisa's ability to see the world in black and white is one of many traits I admire. Her eyes are calm, like she's never experienced any doubt. 'Forget it for now. Let's go out and celebrate.'

'It's spoiled the mood, Lisa. I need to get home anyway.'

'Stay at mine, for God's sake. The Cambridge Prize is massive. We should be in the Ivy, downing cocktails.'

'One would finish me.'

'Prosecco then.'

'Sorry, I need time to process this.'

Lisa parks herself on my desk. 'I'm worried about you, Elly.

Things have been so hard, since your accident and at home. Let's have coffee at mine if you just want to talk.'

I want to explain about finding the bugging device in our kitchen, but someone could have broken into my office as well. It's possible our conversation is being monitored here too, yet words pour out of my mouth, like a radio with no off button. The icy look on my boss's face lingers in my mind.

'Did you know Marina Westbrook took me to the hospital? She's the one I heard comforting me. It doesn't make sense.' I blurt out the words without thinking.

Lisa looks puzzled. 'Maybe she's got a heart after all. People change in an emergency, don't they? It's human instinct to help someone that's hurt.'

'Marina looked so hostile tonight, but she was the first to congratulate me on the prize.'

'Sour grapes, maybe. I'll bet she wanted it herself.'

'I'll have to face her soon and make a confession. I've lost my research report.'

Lisa frowns in reply. 'It must be backed up somewhere, surely?'

I shake my head. 'I don't even have a version history. It's like someone's hacked into my files.'

'Could it be Marina? She must have a master key for the whole department.'

'Why would she? The auditors need it.'

'Professional jealousy's rife here. I see it every day.'

'It's possible, I suppose, but hard to believe.' I drop my face into my hands, my head aching. 'It's all such a mess. Rafe would normally support me at an event like that, and now we're living apart.'

I used to be sure that I could identify any trigger that would make a relationship collapse, but there must be reasons I don't understand. Rafe could be listening right now, the bugs at home just a decoy.

'The stalking's put us all under pressure. He's asked me to go back, but how can I? He could even be behind all this, for some mad reason.'

'Is it often the boyfriend, or husband?'

'Anonymous stalkers normally come from your immediate circle. It can be a family member, terrified of exposure. Love and hate are such strong emotions, sometimes the barrier between them breaks down.'

'It sounds frightening.' Sadness resonates in Lisa's voice. 'You must be in bits, you poor soul.'

Her sympathy makes me well up. 'I don't want it to affect Jamie. He's busy being a teenage rebel, figuring out what to do with his life.'

'Maybe a clean break's better than him seeing conflict between you and Rafe. Is there anyone else involved, on your side?'

'No one. I'm still reeling, to be honest.'

'It's an ideal excuse for a fling with Dr Handsome, next door.'

'Noah?' She forces a laugh out of me at last. 'I'm in no state for that right now. When I went home today, I felt like smashing everything in the building.'

'Maybe some rebound sex would help. He made a beeline for you after your speech.'

'Only because he wants to observe my work.'

'That old chestnut.' She smirks at me. 'It's just a sneaky way to get close.'

'I'm not on the market, Lisa, but thanks for listening. Can you find Clive and Hilary Wadsworth and apologize for me? Tell them I'm going home. They wanted to take me out for dinner.'

'Those two are sweethearts. I'll go in your place. Text me dates tomorrow, to meet up. And remember my private view on Saturday.'

Lisa blows me a kiss then rushes away, and suddenly I'm exhausted. I'd forgotten about the exhibition she's been preparing for months, borrowing paintings from galleries all over the world. She's always so lighthearted, but she takes her work seriously. Worry has made me forget that everyone else has a life too.

It's 10 p.m. when I finally get the chance to search my office for listening devices, running my hands along bookshelves and under my desk, even checking inside the light fitting. There's nothing suspicious, but the flower box Reg delivered is still dumped in the corner. I don't want to open it, but it's part of the conversation between me and my stalker. Dust flies in my face when I pull off the lid. There are no flowers this time, just ash that smells of woodsmoke. The sight leaves me breathless. Ashes to ashes, dust to dust. *Me or you.* For the first time I'm afraid that my stalker doesn't just want to taunt me; they want me dead and buried. My hands shake as I replace the lid. It's caught me off guard, still weakened by my injury. I hate the fear nagging at my core, but it can't be denied.

I'm still holding the box when footsteps pass down the corridor outside. I hear Noah push open his office door without unlocking it first. I envy his sense of safety. He seems to be the only colleague in the building after the party ended so abruptly. Jazz music soon pulses through the wall, but now the footsteps have returned. I feel sure someone's loitering outside my door, making me relieved that Noah is only a shout away. The building always feels ghostly when it's deserted, echoing with remembered pain. Logic tells me to keep safe, but a louder voice in my head is insisting this mess has to end.

I throw open the door, but see only dark air. When I flick the light switch, nothing happens. My eyes gradually adjust to the dark, and I notice the white line under Noah's door. Saxophone music is still drifting on the air. Instinct tells me that he wouldn't make judgements, but I can't tell him about my situation, or any other colleagues, while I feel this vulnerable. I hit the light switch again, relieved when it finally works. Panic is driving me to make bad choices. My professional head knows I should have hunkered inside my office and called security if there was an intruder. But fear only amplifies once it's announced, like yelling into an echo chamber.

17

ME

I follow you, of course, to see what happens next. It's my only option until you realize it's time for us to have a real conversation, instead of threats and gestures. I'll be able to relax once every pretence is stripped away.

I remember why Cambridge is my favourite city at night. The college buildings are elegant and pale, turning their backs on the lanes that bind this city's ancient heart. The crowds are thinning now. Students are drifting back to their colleges, on bikes and on foot, oblivious to danger.

You walk fast, which never works. I've been following on your heels all this time. You might as well slow down and accept that fate has caught up with you. You halt under a streetlight, rummaging for your car keys, a muscle ticking in your cheek. I melt back into the shadows. It's always a privilege to watch you, unobserved. Artifice drops away, revealing your true nature. I can tell you're furious, which fascinates me. Your injury has brought your anger boiling to the surface, just like mine, but for a different reason.

We're so similar, you and I. We'll both fight hard when the time comes. I'll need to recruit a helper too, who'll do exactly as I say.

I've got someone in mind, already primed to follow my instructions. I'd prefer to complete the task alone, but it's too ambitious.
I hate the idea of placing my trust in someone else to reach my
goal, but it's unavoidable.

I want everything from now on to happen in sequence. It would
be easy to hurt you again while you're so distracted, but it's too
soon. When I look up, you're entering the car park by Lion Yard,
and the reason is obvious. You believe you're safe there, which is
laughable. Security cameras are easy to dodge.

I let you vanish upstairs, happy to have seen you vulnerable.
I could wait here until your sleek new car drives away, but it's
best to quit while I'm ahead. I walk away with my hands buried
in my pockets, whistling to myself, my collar turned up against
the breeze.

18

YOU

Pressure settles on the back of my neck. I felt it when I fled the building, the certainty that someone's watching me again. It's like the sixth sense I developed as a child to protect myself from harm, but it could just be growing paranoia.

I check my car door's locked and the dashcam fires up, which reassures me. Anyone that comes close will be instantly identifiable. Overhead light flickers down on empty cars as I read my texts. One is from Carla, asking if I'm okay. You'd think that her duties as a physio would exhaust her desire to nurture, but she checks on me constantly since we got back in touch. I fire off a quick message telling her not to worry. My brother Leo prefers his own company, which is easier to handle.

I drive west through the city, passing a gaggle of students, drunk on their bikes, freewheeling down Huntingdon Road. I slow down to let them pass and my fear eases. Night driving demands all my concentration, my racing thoughts steadying at last. I drive past the turn-off to my old home without hesitation, then head into open fenland. Miles tick by while the night sky opens before me, full of stars, like a skein of fairy lights suspended from a high ceiling. Exhaustion closes around me as I park by the cottage. The security lights cast an ugly blue glare that burns my retinas. It's just one of many changes that I've had to make since the stalking began. I can't let it strip away everything I own.

My first action once I get indoors is to check for listening devices. It feels like I've entered a parallel universe where my every movement and conversation are on public display. I won't allow it in a place that was my childhood sanctuary. I work my way through every room, running my hands under furniture, checking inside wardrobes and drawers. It takes me over an hour, even though the cottage is small. I'm satisfied that no intruder has broken in, yet I'm still on edge. This is my only safe haven since my home and my office have been accessed.

I need to face some ugly truths, now Georgia Reed's father has hunted me down. What did I miss in Joe Sinclair's behaviour during our conversations? He sounded increasingly contrite and passed our psychometric tests with flying colours. It convinced me, his psychiatrist, the prison wardens and a social worker that he was fit for release. I fire off an email requesting a review meeting at Greenhill Prison this week, to help me work out why and how the programme failed.

When I tap Georgia's name into my phone, her story is even sadder than I realized. There are half a dozen photos on news websites, taken before her assault. She's a pretty twenty-six-year-old veterinary nurse, with red hair and a confident gaze. It's only when she's pictured alongside Joe Sinclair that her smile turns brittle.

Georgia Reed lives in a busy block of flats, twenty miles away, surrounded by neighbours, yet he still managed to put her in hospital. I can imagine the terror she experienced during Sinclair's attack. The only reason she's alive is because a neighbour heard her screaming. My work gives me access to encrypted police files for all the stalkers I treat, including crime scene pictures, but I can't face visual details tonight. Culpability has soaked into my mind like an ink stain, too deep to remove.

I shove my phone back into my pocket. Obsession and madness can look just like sanity when someone's a skilled liar, but I should have spotted the signs in Sinclair. Maybe I was too preoccupied to notice telltale clues.

My heart rate increases when my landline rings at the same time as last night. My stalker could have found the number by hacking into my computer, and deleted my report at the same time. I should let it ring, or unplug it, but instinct makes me pick up. There's only a hiss of white noise. Someone is listening to me breathe, but I won't give them the satisfaction of speech, and they withdraw first. There's a click before the phone line dies. I punch in 1471, then scribble down the number. The late-night calls come from public phone boxes in Cambridge, or service stations, never a private number. It's a clever trick, guaranteeing that they're the last thing on my mind when I lie down to sleep.

It hits me again that Rafe knows exactly where I am, as well as all my passwords, and he's smart enough to cover every trace. But how could our relationship turn vicious without me realizing? Maybe I never really knew him. I'm starting to question my own judgement. I've always believed that I'm a good judge of character, but that certainty is slipping away.

I walk around the house, checking the locks on every window and door. The fields look pale under tonight's fierce moonlight, and I reassure myself that there's nowhere for an assailant to hide in such a flat landscape. The cameras would see anyone approaching from every direction, even while I sleep, yet my safety feels gossamer-thin. My stalker might be ready to throw caution to the wind, because stalking campaigns intensify in the majority of cases. It's a struggle to put my fear aside, the muscles in my shoulders pulsing with tension.

When I reach my childhood bedroom, I look outside one last time before pulling the curtains. Frost is forming on the glass, with no cloud cover overhead. A light is flickering in an abandoned farmhouse on the horizon. It glints for a moment, then dies. Why would anyone enter a place that's been empty for decades on a freezing night? It could be my stalker, keeping me in their sights, but I push the thought away, reminding myself that this place is fully secure. My room's freezing temperature reminds me of my first winter here. I've adopted Pete and Lucy's spartan outlook since coming back. They used to say that heating was a luxury. Why turn on a radiator when you can wear a thicker jumper?

I swallow a few deep breaths to calm myself. Jamie said he'd stay here every night until I'm fully recovered, but I'm relieved that he's changed his mind. My situation can't put him in danger too. He's so young and hot-headed, he could easily stray into the line of fire. I climb into bed still wearing my T-shirt, pants and socks, then put out the light, hoping to sleep soundly for the first time since my assault. But my body fights to stay awake, my thoughts in freefall.

Joe Sinclair enters my head again, uninvited. He had no record of physical violence, despite the mental torment he inflicted on Georgia Reed, before going to jail the first time. Was he planning the attack while he sat opposite me in the interview room at Greenhill Prison, pretending to recover? The majority of our meetings were witnessed by my PhD student, Dan Fender. I'll have to find out if he spotted any sign that Sinclair's contrition was fake. My eyes blink at the dark. I'd like to release some of the anger welling inside me, but my tear ducts have run dry.

19

Wednesday 10 November

YOU

My phone buzzes on my bedside table when I wake from a night full of ghosts. It's a message from Rafe, asking me to go home immediately to talk about Jamie. His voice sounds resentful. We started out with meandering conversations that never seemed long enough, yet now our communication is so terse it barely makes sense. I could refuse to go, but that would be childish. It's better to hear his message straight from the horse's mouth. The nausea that's dogged me since my attack lingers, but I force down some dry toast anyway, hoping it will steady me.

I peer out at my car, calculating how long it would take me to cross that gap with someone chasing me. Four seconds, maybe five? Part of me feels numb, while the rest fights to stay alive. I force myself to move slowly in case I'm being watched from a distance, unwilling to show my anxiety. It takes me ten minutes to unload the items I took from home yesterday, piling them in the hallway. It seems weird that my only possessions with any sentimental value take up so little space, after years with Rafe. Maybe it's best to jettison anything unnecessary and walk on, lighter than before.

My old home looks different when I park outside again this morning, its glass walls reflecting dull sunlight. My home life was exposed to the public eye for years, but that never bothered me. I feel less confident now I know that my stalker found his way inside, to leave listening devices while we were out. If they're bold enough to risk that, none of us are safe.

I see Rafe in the kitchen with his phone pressed to his ear. My nerve endings are jangling already. He used to be my best friend and confidante, as well as my partner. The loss feels so huge it could swallow me whole. A new thought arrives, out of the blue. Maybe the woman he's sleeping with is so in love with him she wants to destroy me and dismantle our marriage too? Could it be a personal vendetta? The idea seems crazy. Our lives together used to be so safe and predictable; Jamie must be confused by the mess we've created. Our son still has no idea why I left, unless Rafe told him last night.

When I walk inside I see the houseplants I nurtured are already wilting, but the living room's tidier than before, without my books lying around. It's quieter too. Jamie's presence is usually hard to ignore, with his music drifting down from upstairs.

Rafe appears while I hover in the doorway. His face is normally animated, his zest for life spilling over into everything he does, but now he's solemn. Why didn't I notice him retreating as our jobs took first place? His arms hang open at his sides, like it would only take a small gesture to walk back into his embrace. Instead, we keep three metres of clear air between us. He's wiry, and thinner than before, as he approaches fifty. People used to say we looked more like twins than a married couple. It was true for years, but not now. We're both medium height but he's projecting his image as a successful architect through his smart, monochrome clothes. He's shaved this morning, like he wants to impress a new client, but his features tell a different story. His nose still looks swollen.

The dark shadow under his right eye is another giveaway that my fist connected with his face, hard enough to shatter bone. I can still hardly believe I caused that damage. Rafe looks more like a victim than an aggressor, but appearances are deceiving.

'You shouldn't be driving,' he says. 'Why won't you listen?'

'I'm feeling better.'

'Come home, for God's safe. We can fix things between us, I promise.'

'That's not my biggest priority.' I look him in the eye. 'This place is bugged, Rafe. We need to do a search.'

His laughter sounds off-key. 'Are you joking?'

'I found a listening device in the kitchen yesterday, stuck under a cabinet. I took it to the police, but they've done nothing so far.'

'Who could get in here? This place is fully secure.'

'Someone's managed it. They could be recording us right now. I bet there are microphones in each room.'

'That sounds like paranoia. How do you even know it was a bug?'

'I checked online. Who else has a key?'

'Just you, me and Jamie.' His rapid eye movements give him away.

'You lie so well these days.'

Rafe's skin flushes. 'It could be your fault. How about your sister or brother? Do either of them have a key?'

'Of course, Carla watered our plants while we were away. Do you seriously think she'd do something that nuts?'

He shrugs. 'I barely know her, remember? The whole idea's mad, El. I leave my keys on my desk at work sometimes, and I bet you do too, but why would a colleague terrorize you? If you really think this place is bugged, you'll have to prove it.'

'Fine, let's do a search.'

Rafe looks sceptical, but sets to work anyway. I'm determined to prove my point, so I check under coffee tables and chairs, and over every doorframe. Twenty minutes pass before I hear Rafe swearing to himself in the kitchen. He's staring down at a plastic chip in his hand, just like the one I found.

'There could be more, in every room.'

'Jesus, this is madness.' He turns to face me. 'Shut the door, El. There are no more in here, I've looked everywhere.'

My discomfort remains, even when he drops the device on the floor and grinds it apart with his heel.

'Is it you doing all this, Rafe?'

His eyes snap wide open at my bombshell. 'I can't believe you just said that.'

'Maybe you feel overlooked. Stalking often happens when a relationship's breaking down.'

'Why would I post letters and arrange phone calls to my own house?' His angry tone gives way to tiredness. 'You should go back to hospital, El. You've lost your mind.'

'Or you're gaslighting me.'

'You can't be serious.' He sounds stunned.

'Who else has been here recently?'

'Jamie, his mates and an electrician, sorting out some lights.'

'And your mistress.'

'She never had a key.'

'No?' My anger's rising with each word. 'She could have done it while you slept, and it must be someone I know, or you'd tell me her name.'

'I told you, it's irrelevant.'

'Not to me. Where's Jamie, anyway?'

'I haven't clapped eyes on him since last night, that's why I called you.'

The sadness in his voice makes the situation feel worse. I used to love his refusal to sulk. He'd always clear the air first after a row, with no brooding or recriminations, forcing me to do the same. I can't let rage overtake me again. I owe him that much, at least.

'I expected him at the cottage last night. Has something upset him?'

Rafe folds his arms across his chest. 'Like his mum doing a runner, you mean, out of the blue?'

'I thought you wanted a conversation, not a row.'

'We need a strategy to help Jamie. He's skipping college to hang out with his druggie mates. He'll chuck his future away if we don't act. Let's sit down and talk properly, for God's sake.'

I can hear his distress, and our shared history makes me want to comfort him, more than anything. Still loving him makes it worse. That fact is so raw, there's no safe place to hide. Rafe keeps his back turned while he makes coffee, then sits down beside me. It's a psychological trick I taught him myself. Sit adjacent to your client, not opposite, for tough conversations. It's less confrontational than talking head on.

'Jamie seems lost right now, behind all that fake confidence,' Rafe says. 'I think he's planning some aimless gap year, like Billy Rawle.'

'What happened to being a musician?'

'He says he'll keep writing songs, but only as a hobby, thank God. One more drum roll and I'd have flogged his kit on eBay.'

We laugh in unison, the barrier between us cracking at last. Rafe leans closer, his hand on mine.

'Don't leave us, El. I couldn't stand it.' He sounded like that in the old days, kind and contrite, if he ever upset me. 'This whole shitshow's my fault.'

'Help me to understand what went wrong.'

'The truth would do us more damage.'

'Tell me anyway, I can't heal without it.'

He grits his teeth, like I'd have to wrench his jaw open to prise out the words.

'Is she a client, or a colleague? You can't hide it forever.'

'That's one hell of a double standard.' His face flushes. 'Your whole past is out of bounds. It's the stuff between us we should fix.'

I spot some old photos in the hallway, through the open door. Relics from another life. One was taken the year we met, when I was at university and Rafe was completing his architecture training. The eight-year gap between us never seemed to matter. Our smiles are incandescent. The next one shows the three of us when Jamie was small. He looks shy and elfin as he peers at the camera from his dad's shoulders.

Rafe's voice jerks me back to the present.

'You've kept me at arm's length all these years. I found that sexy at first, but Jamie hates deception. You lied to him about Lucy and Pete being his grandparents, and about getting back in contact with siblings he never knew existed. No wonder we're all keeping secrets – it was you that showed us how.' His tone is harsh when he spits out the words. 'Did you even know that one of Jamie's college mates has been arrested for drug dealing?'

'Billy, you mean?' I look back at him, stunned.

'Another pal, but he's in the same gang. They're all using cheap dope, and I bet they've tried cocaine too. I don't even know where Jamie stayed last night.'

'Are you sure he's safe?'

'God knows. I got a text this morning saying he's not coming home tonight, either.'

'I worry about him driving, if he's high.'

'It beats doing it with a head injury.'

'You're not listening to me, Rafe.' My frustration's building, along with the pulsing in my temples.

'Jamie's immature, not stupid. Passing his test straight after he turned seventeen proves it.' He raises his palms to the air, like he's testing for rain. 'He'll contact you soon enough, don't worry. The umbilical cord between you's still intact, isn't it?'

'What do you mean?'

'He matters to you more than anything. You stopped asking me if I was okay years ago.'

'Is that it? You're jealous of your own son?' I can't hide my scorn.

Rafe's voice is flat with anger. 'How do you think he'd react, if he knew your mother blamed you for your dad's suicide? You think that's why she threw you out, don't you?'

I stand opposite him, open-mouthed. I trusted him enough to confess my worst fears, leaving myself vulnerable. Now he's using them to wound me, and he doesn't even look ashamed.

'Don't attack me with that. I was just speculating.' His words trigger a noise I've heard before, a man's voice screaming in pain. I try to force my mind back through the years, but the sound fades. 'I told Jamie the truth. I can't remember anything, from the day Dad got hurt to my being sent away.'

'You're great at burying things, El. Nothing's ever your fault, is it?'

The old Rafe was gentler than this. Now it feels like he's dredging through our shared past, looking for weapons. There's a glint of fury in his eyes.

'I can't explain something I don't remember. You're the one hiding what you did, just a few days ago.'

'You prioritize your brother and sister over us. I don't trust them. They shunned you for years. *We* deserve your loyalty, not them.' He appears more upset than angry now, blinking back tears. 'It hasn't stopped, has it? Those phone calls and threats. You still look haunted, and letters keep arriving here too.'

'Why didn't you say?'

'I couldn't put you under more pressure. You need medical care, and staying at the cottage is a bad decision. It's too vulnerable.'

'I'm no safer here, with someone listening to every word. You need to search every room, and get the locks changed too.'

'Will you come back, if I do?'

'Only if you agree to marriage counselling.' The words emerge before I can stop them. I'm suddenly exhausted, close to defeat.

'That never works.' His jaw sets in a hard line. 'So, we're stuck, aren't we?'

Rafe picks up a manila folder from the work surface, then hands it to me. Surely he can't have seen a lawyer already about a divorce? The picture only makes sense when I realize it's the letters he mentioned: five sealed envelopes, with my name and address written in the same childish script as the rest. The stamps all carry Cambridge postmarks. My stalker's been busy, sending me new messages almost every day.

'I felt like burning them, but they're yours,' Rafe mutters. 'Can you clear your office too, please? Jamie shouldn't have to worry about it every day. It looks like an episode of *CSI* in there.'

I rise to my feet fast to avoid escalating the row, then head next door. Rafe has placed a cardboard box on my desk, already full of items from the drawers. It contains notes I made about the timing of each contact, looking for patterns or details to expose my stalker's identity. All I see now is a jumble of scribbled comments. I'm still packing documents away when Rafe reappears. He doesn't speak before beginning to help me, like the old days, when we did everything together.

'I don't want you facing that monster alone.' His voice sounds broken.

'They watch this place, and now they're listening too.'

'I'll put an end to that.'

'I can't come back, Jamie needs stability.'

'Don't use our son to justify leaving me.' Rafe's voice carries an edge of desperation. 'I was wild too, at his age, but he's a young adult now, and he's smart. Jamie knows relationships go through rough patches.'

I'm too weary to argue. 'Just tell him to call me, please.'

'I already did.'

Rafe helps me carry boxes out to my car. Instinct tells me to throw them all away, but I need an evidence trail. I'm about to get into the driver's seat when he pulls me into an embrace.

'I know you're scared, El, and I've been an idiot, but I'd never harm you intentionally. Remember that, okay?'

I rest my head on his shoulder for a second, then step back, fast. It feels like the fracture between my past and present could swallow me whole, the ground collapsing under my feet.

I twist the key in the ignition, then glimpse Rafe in my rear-view mirror, wearing an odd smile. It looks as though he's glad to see me driving away, but when I glance over my shoulder again, his expression is sombre. That grin could have been just a trick of the light, or maybe I imagined it, my mind failing me again. It feels like everything I care about is breaking down. I gasp in a few deep breaths, then flee from our glass palace, even though it's tempting to stay.

20

My first action after I leave is to ring Jamie. His new voicemail message is a raucous clash of cymbals, like he's trying to scare callers away. I leave a message anyway, telling him I'd love to see him tonight, then make one more call, to my brother Leo. He likes to keep his distance, especially since he grew ill, but his advice is sound. The trust between us came back faster than with Carla because he's not trying too hard. There's no reply, as usual. If I want his company, I'll need to go there in person and push the doorbell until he's forced to answer.

I put the thought aside and head for work, even though the pain in my head is still there. My mind still feels chaotic, but at least my anger is back under control. Rafe's cheating hurts too much to consider. It's better to stay busy and focus on my work until I'm strong enough to look the problem in the eye.

I park my car in the small car park on Downing Street that's reserved for psychology staff and official visitors. I've avoided using it at night since the stalking began because it's poorly lit, with a narrow path threading between the blank sides of neighbouring buildings. The ginnel opens directly onto the back of the quadrangle, which is deserted now the students are away. Light still shines down from the window of my office. Maybe I was too shaken to remember to turn it off last night? The air's frigid this morning, burning my cheeks with cold. Noah Jagiello's light is on too, so I won't be alone in the building.

Habit makes me look around before I enter, checking that no one's followed me here. The odd atmosphere of the place has disturbed me more since my injury, as though ghosts are waiting to fly at me from the walls. I swipe my card through the reader, but nothing happens. The entry door remains locked after three attempts, making me curse under my breath. It's never happened before, and now I'll have to seek help. The porter's lodge on the far side of the quad is only a minute's walk away. It's the place where all practical problems get fixed, so I head straight there. The sign on the door reads 'Mr Reginald Bellamy, Senior Porter'. The university is stuck in an era where hierarchies still matter. Everyone's name, rank and job description are on permanent display.

The lodge is small and airless. Reg is still dressed in his tidy black suit, his sparse grey hair waxed into place. He stands behind the counter he polishes to a gleam, where dozens of keys hang from hooks on the wall, proving that he can access every room in the building. There's a shelf crammed with books that students abandon when they finish their studies. It holds novels and poetry, as well as old psychology textbooks. Two chairs and a coffee table fill the remaining space. Students and fellows often sit here, like I did at the start, to hear Reg's stories. The man is always courteous and dignified, his expression unshockable.

'Morning, Dr Shaw.' He raises a hand in a half-salute. 'I hear there was an intruder at your drinks party. I hope it didn't spoil things for you?'

'No, Reg. I'm fine, honestly.'

His gaze searches my face. 'I'd have sent him packing, but I was off duty by then.'

'It was dealt with, don't worry. But can you help me with my pass card? It's stopped working.'

'That's odd. Can I see?'

He checks my card on his reader, re-enters the code, then passes it back. 'It looks like someone cancelled it, but there's no name on the system. I'll try and find out, but there's only one guy on the IT helpdesk till the students come back.'

'Do you know much about IT security here, Reg? I've lost some documents from my computer too.'

'They just spent a fortune on encryption. But any system can be hacked these days, can't it? Maybe Professor Westbrook can help.'

He collects my mail from one of the pigeonholes behind his desk, then stands perfectly still with the letters clutched in his hands. 'I hope you'll call me if there are any more problems.'

'Of course, Reg. You always fix things for me.'

My comment must have struck the right note because he hands over my mail immediately and wishes me a pleasant day. I glance down at the letters, but for once there's nothing suspicious, just circulars from American universities, advertising journals or calling for conference papers. I don't know why, but the conversation leaves me unsettled. Reg's behaviour is always old-school, but I've never seen him look tense until now, as if he's let me down.

The porter soon leaves my mind when I return to the psychology building. The lobby is empty, the overhead light flickering and the long corridors extending into the distance. The building's dark history hangs in the air. Some of the very first electro-convulsive shock treatments for depression were carried out here, in the laboratory on the ground floor. Patients were so desperate for a cure that they accepted the pain and confusion that followed. It's still used occasionally even now, in a milder form, with few side effects.

Noah's jazz is still pulsing through the walls when I let myself into my office, as though he's been there all night. The room looks exactly as I left it, the longest wall covered by books and the old mahogany desk criss-crossed with scratches. But something's changed. The air smells floral, like it's been spritzed with an aerosol. I spot an envelope on my desk, bearing my name. Panic rises in my throat. How did they get inside when the door was locked? There was no sign of damage.

It turns out to be a card from Marina Westbrook, congratulating me again on my prize and asking me to meet her early tomorrow morning. I'll have to give her the bad news about my missing report then, but my discomfort about her accessing my workspace with her master key lingers. My boss positioned the card where I was bound to see it, then forgot to turn off the light, leaving the fragrance of her perfume behind. I've spent so little time in her company that I've never noticed it before. The card is subtler than her scent: a monochrome image of a seaside town in winter, with a beach that stretches for miles. I shut my eyes to imagine myself there. The nearest coastline is two hours' drive away. I'd love to stand on that beach now, the sea's slow drumbeat steadying my nerves. It bothers me that Marina invaded my space, but this is her empire, after all.

I'm still standing there when someone raps on the door. It swings open before I can respond. My mouth is suddenly dry, until I see it's Dan Fender. He's the PhD student Lisa suspects, and a member of my team. Dan came here from Ohio University three years ago, and we've spent a lot of time together on prison visits. Most psychologists hunch over their computers all day, turning their skin pasty, but Dan could be an American football player, brimming with health. He's tall, with hulking shoulders and a thatch of white-blond hair. His physique makes him appear to be a natural leader, yet he never seems fully at ease.

Dan has done some excellent interviews under my supervision, his quiet manner perfect for extracting secrets. He's keen to develop treatment options for female de Clérambault's sufferers too, one of the toughest delusional illnesses to cure. It mainly affects women, leaving them obsessed with the idea that their target, often a complete stranger, adores them from a distance.

'Sorry to barge in – I didn't think you'd be around in reading week. I was going to leave this.' He passes me a wad of paper, then hovers in the doorway.

'Is it part of your thesis, Dan?'

'Primary research, but the introduction's weak. Would you mind taking a look?'

'Of course not. I'll email you a time for feedback.'

He shuffles awkwardly on his feet. 'Congrats on your prize, by the way. I could only stay for your speech last night, I'm afraid.'

'Prior engagement?'

His face reddens. 'My girlfriend's over on a flying visit till tomorrow. I thought a roomful of shrinks and professors might be too much. She's on vacation, after all.'

'It would terrify most people,' I say, smiling. 'Let's meet soon to discuss your work.'

'I'm free pretty much any morning, Dr Shaw.'

'Please don't use my title. We're colleagues, remember?'

'Old habits die hard. Back home we have to call every teacher "ma'am", or "sir", from nursery through grad school.' His flush deepens.

I'm suddenly keen to share something that's been troubling me; to confide in someone with specialist knowledge. 'Have you heard about Joe Sinclair attacking his victim, Georgia Reed?'

He nods rapidly. 'I saw the news, about her still being in intensive care.'

'Did you spot anything in Sinclair's behaviour to suggest he was planning to hurt her?'

'No way.' Dan sounds adamant. 'I thought his obsession was under control. Sinclair was compliant about taking anti-psychotic meds and agreed to more therapy after his release. No one could have predicted it.'

'Maybe he went through our programme in good faith. If there's even a shred of obsession left behind, it multiplies.'

'Like cancer cells, you mean?'

I nod in reply. 'We'll have to adapt the programme. We can't just accept that some cases are incurable.'

'Can I observe his review meeting?'

'It'll be this week, I'll let you know when it's set up.' I smile at him, pushing away my dread at seeing Sinclair again. 'Did you find a better place to stay? You mentioned your bedsit was cold.'

'Professor Westbrook found me postgrad accommodation in the block opposite. They say it's haunted, but who cares, if the heating works?'

'I'm glad you're comfortable.'

A moment passes before he speaks again. 'I told Stacey about our work together, and realized I should have thanked you for your support. Homesickness hit me pretty hard in my first year, and culture shock too. I considered flying home to finish my PhD.'

His admission takes me by surprise; I hadn't realized he was struggling. 'It's good that you stayed, you're doing well here.'

'Thanks, Eloise, that means a lot.'

Dan mumbles goodbye then vanishes into the corridor. I never knew he had a girlfriend back in the States, but it's good news, and makes Lisa's theory seem less likely. I've seen him in the department common room over too many weekends, when he should have been taking a break, but it must be hard to switch off while he lives so close to work. His quiet, matter-of-fact demeanour makes him seem an unlikely aggressor, even though that's often the case with stalkers. I don't want to suspect him, but I'll have to keep watch.

The first page of Dan's research describes a specific case study. It's about a fifty-eight-year-old woman so gripped by de Clérambault's syndrome that she believes Prince William is in love with her, prompting her to send him hundreds of letters. She thinks he replies in coded messages via her TV. Delusions like hers can seem funny when you're not dealing with it yourself, but the reality wastes lives, with the sufferer unable to work or communicate, until they're consumed by loneliness. I put his chapter aside, unable to concentrate.

When I turn on my computer to hunt for my missing report again, Georgia Reed's name is the first thing I spot in my emails. The National Centre for Anti-Stalking Research has confirmed the assessment meeting I requested with Joe Sinclair at Greenhill Prison. Staff there have been working alongside the police since the attack happened. I scan the update, which states that Georgia is still alive, in ICU. It strikes me that although Sinclair was her ex-partner, his approach was the same as my stalker. A steady flow of messages, darkening over time, evolving into death threats. Mine feels like the dripping tap that woke me in the night. Fear can build a cell around you, brick by brick, leaving you trapped inside.

My next duty won't be easy. But I have to follow the protocol I designed, in which every member of the therapy team must assess the impact of a stalker's campaign after a repeat offence, from physical evidence. Often, it's just a raft of unsolicited emails and texts, but sometimes there's a police crime scene photo too. This time, I'm facing it alone.

I open the only photo provided by the police, taken in Georgia Reed's flat in Huntingdon, twenty miles away. An officer must have taken it before she was carried to the ambulance. Her hair is soaked with blood, and so is the carpet she's lying on, red liquid still trailing from her nose. There's a gash on her throat too, from a ligature. Her eyes are too puffy to open, facial bruises turning purple. My hands fumble as I close the image down fast. If she survives, she'll need plastic surgery to reset those broken cheek-bones. I force myself to read every piece of evidence relating to Joe Sinclair's attack, noting that he showed no contrition at all when he was finally rearrested.

Georgia's suffering leaves its imprint on my mind. Maybe her father's right and I'm to blame for failing to extract the root of her stalker's obsession. I bet she pleaded for help, yet the police did nothing, and my own situation is no different. I'm alone, with only my knowledge to protect me, if I can quell the panic.

21

ME

It takes me fifteen minutes to return to your cottage. It's the ideal time to come, while you're at work. The location is perfect, too. I can see immediately when your car is missing because the property's so exposed, without a single fence. I'm no fan of rural isolation myself. I prefer people around me, and cafés from which to watch the world go by. There's nothing here except open fields and fallow black soil. It's rich with sediments from epochs ago, when the whole county lay submerged. Now it's overworked farmland, stretching for 400,000 hectares, lying below sea level. It's a struggle to prevent this region from drowning. These fields require a vast network of canals, ditches and dams to keep them alive. It'll be the first place to vanish when sea levels rise.

I shut my eyes and imagine your house being hit by a tidal surge, washing your refuge away. It lessens my pain to imagine it being scoured from the earth's surface, leaving nothing behind. You took everything from me. Soon you'll learn exactly how it feels to wake up lost, with nowhere safe to hide.

I collect my camera from the back seat, then walk closer, taking care to hide my face in case your CCTV's range extends this far. I've taken plenty of photos of you in the past year, and enjoy the camera's solid weight in my hand, a tool that never fails me. Your property is surrounded by traces of rural life that no longer exist. Foundations of cottages like yours, with bricks and broken tiles scattered among the weeds. There would have been a community of farm workers here once, rising at dawn to spend long days in the fields. You must enjoy the company of ghosts.

Your CCTV forces me to keep my distance for now. I could short-circuit it, but that would take effort and time. That burglar alarm must have cost thousands. I study the place through my zoom lens, then snap a few shots to identify the make and model of each device. It will help me to disable them from a distance.

The cold makes me long to wait inside. I'd love to be sitting at the kitchen table when you get home, ready for our chat, but the wind is too bitter to remain outside for long. There's nothing protecting me from the north wind's icy breath. It amazes me that you grew up here, with no shelter from the elements except a draughty, ramshackle cottage, protected only by sparse laurel hedges.

I circle the place again, taking care to remain distant. My zoom lens gives me all the access I need, right down to the serial numbers on the alarm. If your cameras see me at all, I'll be no more than a blur. I can see floral wallpaper through the magnifying lens, and an ugly fireplace in the lounge. I doubt the place has changed at all since you were a girl. I could stand here for another hour, photographing every corner of your refuge, but it's too risky.

The car feels warm when I get back inside and drive north, to avoid crossing paths with you coming back from town. I imagine you'll be alone now your marriage is breaking down, licking your wounds. Your existence looks miserable already, and there's worse to come. Soon you'll have no job, no family, no place to lay your head.

I thread my way through fenland villages, where thatched cottages lie beside cheap modern in-fills and boarded-up pubs.

This area has no charming hills or chocolate-box prettiness. The land's so flat it looks like it's been steamrollered, yet it suits your personality: beauty and ugliness lying side by side.

I'm still unpicking the riddle of your life. I've enjoyed the challenge until now, but I need to step out of the shadows again soon, to explain why you're always in my mind. I could never leave you alone, now our lives are interconnected. I drive faster, keen to protect my secrets. I need to be in the right place, at the right time, for the next part of our conversation.

22

Carla rings me when she gets in from work. My sister's voice sounds tired when she reminds me that we're due to meet this afternoon at her place. It slipped my mind, despite her messages. Our relationship's still too fragile for me to cancel, even though the tablets Rafe gave me don't bring much relief. The pain behind my eyes is throbbing as I listen to my sister talk.

'I'll be there soon,' I tell her.

'Don't bring cake.'

Carla rings off immediately. She always takes charge, despite being younger than me, and the years of absence separating us.

It's getting dark when I return to the car. My hand fists around the rape alarm in my pocket when a man approaches from the opposite direction. He passes me on the narrow pathway without a glance, his footsteps thudding into the distance while I catch my breath. Hyper-vigilance is one of my biggest challenges. Everyone seems like a potential stalker, stopping me from greeting the world with confidence. The habit's become so engrained it's already second nature.

The afternoon traffic is thinning when I head for Carla's place in south Cambridge. I've never liked this suburb much.

It feels centreless, and the only shops are huge supermarkets on the ring road. She lives in a maisonette she bought last year, with a private garden, in a neat Victorian semi. The mat by her front door is decorated with flowers, the word 'Welcome' picked out in scarlet. The reality is different. She takes ages to answer the doorbell and her expression is flustered. Carla's blonde hair is pulled back, her face bearing no sign of makeup. The only adornments on display are a small gold nose ring and a row of studs in each ear. She's wearing an apron over her jeans and T-shirt, with flour dusting the fabric. I notice a tattoo on her arm for the first time. The number nine peeps out, almost hidden by her sleeve.

'Sorry I'm late,' I say. 'What are you baking?'

'Scones. Is that okay?'

'Any cake works for me.'

She smiles for the first time, then hurries back downstairs. Her home seems to showcase her personality, full of photos and artwork, so I linger in the hallway, searching for glimpses of her past that I never witnessed. A photo by the door shows her beaming, dressed in her brand-new NHS uniform. Carla's done well since then, moving to different hospitals in the UK before going freelance and saving enough cash to buy this place. Her walls are painted a cheery yellow, a string of vivid landscape paintings bringing them to life.

When I peer into her living room, it's spotless, as usual, with a vase of daffodils on her coffee table. They must have been flown in from abroad because spring is still months away here. I see a deep indentation on one of her sofa cushions. Maybe she slumps there alone most nights by the telly, or reads a novel from her packed bookshelf. I'm curious about her personal life, but conversations between us are still a tightrope act. The only companion I see is her cat, Alfie, fast asleep, his body draped across a stool.

Carla calls me from the floor below, startling him awake. The cat leaps away in a haze of black-and-white panic. By the time I get downstairs to the basement kitchen, the air smells of burnt sugar and Alfie is on the window ledge, mewing for his freedom.

'What did you do to him?' Carla asks.

'Nothing, he just woke up suddenly.'

My sister looks uncertain. It makes me wonder what lies our mother spun about my behaviour after sending me away. She runs her hand down the cat's spine. 'The poor thing's terrified.'

'I didn't come here to scare your cat, Carla.'

Her face softens again. 'It doesn't take much. I got him from a rescue centre in a dreadful state. People should be jailed for treating animals like that. His fur was all filthy and matted. He hid behind my wardrobe for days; I had to coax him out with bits of chicken.'

'He seems fine now.'

'Don't ask me how much the vet bills cost.'

'That's one reason I don't have pets.'

'He's a sweetie. You're the one missing out.' She takes a tray of scones out of her oven, inspects them, then slams them back inside. 'Five more minutes.'

'Great, I'm in no hurry.'

'Take a seat, then. Make yourself at home.'

I do as I'm told because Carla is kind but brittle, easy to upset by the smallest gesture. I notice a camera case lying on her table, which surprises me. It's an expensive Pentax, just like the one Rafe uses on-site, to document every stage of a build.

'Are you into photography these days, Carla? That's a posh camera.'

'It's for work.' She swings round to face me. 'Patients like to see their bodies getting stronger over time. I've got one guy with advanced curvature of the spine. The photos show how much it's improved through the exercises we do.'

'That must be satisfying.' I hesitate for a moment. 'I meant to ask, how come you didn't use your key at my house yesterday? You've still got it, haven't you?'

'Why? Do you want it returned?' Carla has her back turned again, hands in the sink.

'Of course not. I'm just asking.'

'I keep yours and Leo's together, here, in my key box.'

Rafe criticized her, saying she could be behind all the notes and strange gifts, but why would someone who's spent her life relieving people's pain suddenly turn cruel? My stalker is hell bent on making me and my family suffer. I can't imagine my sister doing anything so terrible, but logic tells me it must be someone who's watching me at close range.

She's busy washing up her mixing bowl and wooden spoons, humming under her breath, giving me time to look around. Her kitchen window provides little light because it's below pavement level. A potted fern is struggling to survive on her windowsill. There's a prettier view from the back, where French doors open onto a sunken garden.

We sat there every few weeks last summer, joined sometimes by Leo, trying to fill in the gaps. Our conversations still feel jerky and incomplete. I always tread cautiously because Carla's so touchy. God knows how she deals with her clients' pain every day, yet there's plenty of evidence that she does a good job. A pinboard on the kitchen wall is covered with thank-you cards.

'Want me to make tea, Carla?'

'Go ahead. You know where everything is.'

I open a cupboard, then freeze. The past leaps out at me like an attack dog. It's the bone china coffee set our mother used for special occasions, before our family collapsed, stacked in piles. The cups are so fine they're almost see-through. I can hear her voice even now, telling me not to touch. I may have seen them here before, but my aching head makes me forgetful. Carla must have a different relationship with our shared history if she enjoys seeing Mum's favourite possessions every day.

'Not that cupboard, Elly. Mugs live in here.'

Carla shuts the door, then opens the next, her movements quick and defensive. It's like she doesn't want me to touch Mum's treasures. If she's noticed me stumble, she doesn't comment. I focus on the task in hand, putting teabags in the pot while the kettle boils. By the time I've located the milk jug, Carla's scones are heaped on a platter in the middle of her table.

'Dive in,' she says. 'I'm bloody starving.'

'Didn't you get a lunch break?'

'God, no, today's been full-on.'

My sister's in a hurry when she spreads two scones with butter and jam. I take my time selecting one, while she bolts hers down. Food seems to calm her. There's more colour in her cheeks as she sips her tea, revealing how beautiful she is when she's relaxed, but her expression's guarded.

'I called your landline last night,' she says. 'Rafe said you've been staying at your cottage since the accident. I felt like a right idiot, not knowing. Sisters should tell each other important stuff first, shouldn't they?'

'Is that why you're angry?'

'Upset, more than anything. We're meant to be getting closer, aren't we? You never said a word about your marriage being in trouble.'

I can feel my shoulders tensing. 'It was still too raw.'

'Sorry, El, it must be awful for you.' Her eyes are stretched wide, like she's forgotten how to blink. 'Jamie's struggling too right now, isn't he?'

'How do you mean?'

'He made me promise not to tell you something, but it feels wrong to keep it quiet.'

I swallow my anger, but the taste is bitter. How dare she take my place, exchanging confidences with my son after such a long absence?

'Jamie stayed here one night, that week when he left home,' Carla says.

I shake my head in disbelief. 'You knew I was going crazy with worry, but didn't say anything?'

'He needed shelter. What was I meant to do?'

'Call me, if it happens again. Don't get involved without telling me first.'

'I couldn't say no. Remember how bad things got for us after Dad died?'

'How could I forget?'

Carla misses the irony. 'None of us will,' she says. 'I still don't understand why you've left Rafe.'

'He screwed another woman in our bed, if you must know. He didn't even have the decency to use a hotel. She left a scarf and a bracelet behind, as calling cards for me to find.'

'Jesus, what a bitch,' she says, her gaze holding mine.

'Rafe probably gave them to her. He showered me with gifts at the start.' I choke out a laugh. 'I never imagined letting anyone get that close. Trust's still an issue for me.'

'Because of what happened to us?'

'Maybe you feel the same.'

Her eyes blink rapidly. 'You have to know something, El. I was bullied at school after you left. I used to dream you'd come back to save me. It wasn't my choice to make you leave. I missed you every day.'

'Why didn't you come looking for me years ago?'

We've circled round the subject plenty of times, but never

addressed it head on until today. I can feel my heart kicking against my ribcage. We're getting close to the past, and the gaps I always avoid.

'Mum made us promise never to contact you. She said you had an evil spirit, she saw it in your eyes when you were born. You'd hurt us, like you hurt Dad. She told us that the whole time we were growing up.'

Words explode out of me. 'I was ten, Carla. I behaved badly sometimes, out of anxiety, because of all the crap going on at home.'

'I see that now, of course. No one's born evil, anyway.' She bites her bottom lip. 'It was worse for Leo. He kept begging her to bring you home, then she'd hit him, or lock him in his room. I envied you sometimes, for escaping. I bet he did too.'

'If it was that bad, why move her to a care home nearby?'

'I'm all she has, so I visit when I can. It's only me caring for her now.'

'That's her choice. I wrote to her loads of times as a kid, but never got a reply.'

'I still think you should go, before it's too late.'

'Why, exactly?' I don't mention all the times I've driven there but failed to go inside.

She holds my gaze. 'To say goodbye. She's been hanging on, since her stroke, in case you visit.'

'Mum told you that?'

'Not in so many words, but it's what she needs. It might help you too.'

'I doubt it.' The past keeps on threatening to derail us. 'What about you, anyway? You don't say much about boyfriends. Is there anyone special?'

'I've met a guy recently, but it's early days. I don't want to screw it up.' Carla frowns at me, then hurries on. 'My last boyfriend decided he didn't want kids with me, after four years together. The flat was empty when I got back from work one night. He'd taken all his stuff and some of mine too. The bastard legged it, leaving no forwarding address and months of unpaid rent.'

'That's a shitty way to ghost someone.'

'Blokes like me at first, then get bored.' She leans forward, her hand grasping mine. 'We should take care of each other from now on, Elly. I thought losing Dad in that awful way was the worst thing we'd ever face, but some people enjoy causing pain, don't they?'

'Let's not talk about it today.'

She bites her lip. 'Have you heard from Leo?'

'Not lately, he never picks up. You?'

'The odd text and that's it. I worry about him more now he's ill. It's crazy that he lives in Cambridge but only sees us once in a blue moon.'

'You can't take care of everyone, Carla.'

'It's in my nature – that's why I love my job. My clients keep me going.' She squeezes my hand. 'Will you promise me something? If anything bad happens again, something terrible that you can't fix, come here. Make me your first choice and stay as long as you need.'

'That's generous, Carla.'

'I don't want you to suffer again, or me. We could even buy a place together.'

'I've got the cottage, don't worry.'

'It could be our sanctuary, and Jamie's.' Her grip tightens around my wrist. 'Sometimes I hated you for escaping, but you suffered too. I can see it in your face. Promise you'll remember my offer.'

I know why she wants to protect me, but it's too late; the

damage is past, not present. I could mention our mother again, and the way she loved to divide and rule. We're still doing it, fighting over Jamie like a trophy that's out of reach. When I stay silent, our mother's presence hangs between us, like smoke neither of us wants to inhale.

23

It's 6 p.m. when I leave Carla's flat. I sit in the car with my hands braced on the steering wheel, processing new facts. I should be grateful that she sheltered Jamie in a crisis, yet it still feels like a betrayal. The news that my mother said I was evil hurts too. My head's pounding so hard I scrabble inside my bag for my tablets and gulp one down. I can't tell if it's my injury causing the pain, or the plain truth about the past.

Carla seems keen to discuss our family history, but I'm not ready for that yet. I can barely remember the time when all three of us attended the same primary school in London. Leo was two years below me, and Carla was the youngest. He was a sporty, boisterous kid, and she was always tidy, with neatly plaited hair. Her classroom was next to mine and I'd hear her voice through the wall, eager and loud, always keen to please.

The anxiety we faced at home affected me differently. We never knew what mood Mum would be in when we got home. The uncertainty left me unable to concentrate, gazing out of the window or disrupting lessons and running from the classroom when the teacher's back was turned. Our mother could be kind or cruel, for no reason. But I still hated being sent away. I'd always sheltered my siblings, as the oldest child, and the shock of separation left me with déjà vu. I'd imagine Carla in the playground at my new school, plaits flying as she ran. When I looked more closely, it was always another girl, but she haunted me for years, and so did Leo. My mindset's changed since my injury. I've tried to keep a lid on our past, but I'm losing strength. It feels like Pandora's box could soon fly open, releasing any number of vicious ghosts.

Sainsbury's car park is crowded when I stop at the edge of town. I feel safest in places like this, with security cameras monitoring every aisle and dozens of people grabbing items from the shelves. There's something reassuring about loading my trolley with everyday essentials. Soon my cart's full of fruit, teabags and stuff for the freezer. I drop a bumper-sized pack of loo roll in the trolley with a bottle of detergent, then dig out my purse. I'm relaxed, until someone taps me on the shoulder. It's a dark-haired man, about my age, standing much too close. I step back fast, like he's carrying a deadly disease.

He looks apologetic. 'Sorry to scare you, love. You dropped this just now.' He holds out one of my grey leather gloves. 'Are you all right?'

'You made me jump, that's all.'

'It's okay, no harm done.'

The man is walking back to his wife, who's pushing their child in a buggy. It's too late to thank him properly, like a normal human being. The woman must have seen my reaction, because she scowls at me, and I don't blame her, after his good deed. Adrenaline's still rushing through my veins and I'm sick of shadowboxing. I need to work harder at finding the truth. Living with this much rage trapped inside me isn't sustainable. My hands are still trembling when I drive back to the cottage.

It's dark by the time I turn down the lane, with no streetlights and the moon hidden by clouds. A car is parked outside my house, making me slow down. I need to get close enough to see the registration number, then do a U-turn. My heartrate only returns to normal when I recognize Jamie's Day-Glo orange Fiesta.

He steps out of his car when I pull up, reminding me that he needs a new set of keys. I want to hug him, but his eyes, the same mid-blue as mine, are wary. His hair is pulled back in a ponytail.

'Where've you been, Mum?' His tone's accusatory.

'Shopping. You didn't say when you'd arrive.'

'I meant to call you. Dad's been nagging me so much, I can't stay there.' His voice is quick and defensive.

'He's a bit worried about you, that's all. We both want to help.'

'He doesn't give a shit about either of us.'

'That's not true, Jamie.'

'Dad's got someone else.' His eyes screw shut, holding back tears. 'I've known for weeks. Sorry, Mum, I should have told you, shouldn't I?'

Something inside me shifts, like water being sucked down a plughole. 'How did you find out?'

He looks away. 'I was stuck in the middle. Dad went out most nights when you were in America on your book tour. He pretended it was work dinners and stuff, but when I confronted him he just made excuses.' Jamie's arms are wrapped tight around his chest, holding himself together by the skin of his teeth.

I trust my son's instincts. If he believes Rafe's affair has been going on for months, it's likely to be true. Ideas blur in my mind. Did Rafe's affair start when the stalking began, just after we got back from our holiday, or before? Maybe I was right, he could be behind all of it.

'I'm sorry, Jamie. None of it's your fault,' I say, reaching for his hand. 'Come inside, it's cold out here.'

He grabs his guitar from the boot of his car, then helps me carry groceries indoors. He's dressed head to toe in black, silent and watchful as we dump bags on the kitchen table. His voice is flat when he speaks again.

'I want to move in here, with you, for good.'

'You don't have to take sides. Divide your time between us, however you like.' He's swaying on his feet. 'When's the last time you ate?'

'I'm not hungry.'

'We should have something anyway. How about pizza and salad?'

'Whatever.' Jamie heads away, his biker boots leaving mud on the worn lino I cleaned this morning, but it's the wrong time to pick holes in his behaviour. He reappears just as I'm sliding pizzas loaded with toppings into the oven.

'It's freezing, Mum. Can I light the fire?'

'It'll be smoky, the chimney needs cleaning.'

'Let me try anyway.'

He vanishes again, while I throw a salad together. My head's still spinning from the news about Rafe's affair. I don't understand why he's pleading with me to go back if he's been seeing someone else for months. For all I know, they're together right now. I block the idea out and focus on the task in hand. Jamie's welfare matters more than all of it.

When I put my head round the living room door he's performed a miracle, crouched by the hearth, warming his hands by flames that are starting to leap. I don't need to announce that dinner's ready as the air drifting from the kitchen smells of oregano and burnt cheese. Jamie used to love mealtimes, but tonight he picks at his food, shifting lettuce leaves around with his fork. His face is changing all the time. He's morphing into an adult before my eyes, but the lost look in his eyes belongs to a distressed child.

'I'll listen, if you feel like talking.'

'Don't analyse me, Mum, please. I'm sick of it.'

'Just let off some steam. Tell me how you're feeling.'

'Dad's been a total prick. What else can I say?'

'He's still your father, no matter what.'

Jamie hesitates. 'I had a few beers last night, that's why I couldn't drive here. But I'm never going back there unless you do.'

His hand movements are twitchy, and it hurts that his angular bone structure is a direct copy of Rafe's. It feels like my heart's shrivelling inside my chest. I was so confident that my marriage was unbreakable. That the family we created would stay united, unlike my own.

Jamie's gaze searches my face. 'What time of year did you move here, as a kid?'

'Winter, in driving rain. I was already homesick.' My words slow to a halt.

'Your mum's still alive, isn't she? How come you never visit her?'

'That was her choice, not mine.'

'I'm lucky then, aren't I? You'd never send me away.'

I manage a smile. 'Don't bet on it. If you drop out of college I might just change the locks again.'

He rolls his eyes. 'What do those letters say? The ones that came this week.'

'That's a neat change of subject. I took them straight to the police, unopened.'

'Thank God. You've wasted hours studying every detail.'

'I need to understand it to end it, Jamie. Knowledge is power, as they say. One of the stalkers I worked with may have switched their obsession to me.' I don't want to scare him, but he needs honesty.

'Why work with them, if it's that dangerous?'

'Mental illnesses need cures, just like physical ones. I want to fix something that's broken.'

Jamie's voice rises. 'Even if it destroys our family? This guy's too smart to give himself away.'

'There's always some clue to chase. They want me to guess their identity, it's part of the game.' I try to keep calm. If he sees my fear, he'll absorb it too.

'Leave it to the police, Mum.'

'They'd need thousands more officers to protect every victim.'

'You can't just accept they're doing a crap job. We should complain.' His expression sours again. 'You must have some clue who's doing this. What about ex-boyfriends?'

'There was no one serious before your dad. I met him when I was twenty-one, then you arrived the next year, so they'd need a really long memory. It's someone who feels slighted – there's always a trigger to start an obsession.'

Jamie's gaze is solemn. 'It could even be Dad, couldn't it?'

'He'd never hurt either of us.' I do my best to sound convinced. The idea of Rafe hurting me still doesn't make sense.

'It can't be him making the phone calls, can it?' He pushes his plate away, still half full. 'Our landline rings most nights between ten and eleven, like the stalker's saying goodnight. He knows your number here and at home.'

'It could be a woman.'

'You think one of your girl students has a crush on you?' He lets out a laugh.

'Female stalkers can be vicious too,' I remind him.

'We can't just wait for them to act again, Mum. The pressure's getting to you. It's great you've installed CCTV, but it shows you're scared. You expect him to break in any time, don't you?'

'It's just a precaution. They're too clever to risk exposure.'

He shakes his head, clearly deflated. 'If we're staying here, can I keep that room upstairs, and change it a bit?'

'Show me what you mean.'

I follow him as he heads upstairs, canvas bag slung over his shoulder, guitar in hand. He's been playing it often recently, and carries it everywhere. I realize again that this place needs work when we enter the bedroom. The carpet's worn out, smudges of mould blossoming on the ceiling. I offered to renovate all the rooms, but Lucy refused, always reluctant to accept change after Pete died.

Jamie studies the rose-print wallpaper and battered furniture. 'It's shabby, but the view's amazing. I can paint the walls midnight blue. I want to take up the carpet and paint the floor the same colour.'

'You can, if you promise to finish college.'

'That's a big ask.' He hesitates, then gives a slow nod. 'I want a blackout blind too, not curtains.'

'We may not even be staying, Jamie.'

'I like it out here. All this land was seabed till a few centuries ago. I want my room to look like it's still under water.' He glances down at his phone. 'Can I have Billy over for a bit? He texted me just now.'

'Okay, but not for too long, please.'

Jamie pulls me close for a hug. It's tempting to cling on for some much-needed comfort, but we both withdraw at the same moment.

'You still look tired, Mum. Remember, no one can hurt you with me around, okay? I can't be here in the daytime, but I'll stay every night. He's got two of us to deal with now.' He studies me again, deciding whether to tell me something. 'If I have to finish my course, I'll need a gap year, like Billy, to recover. I'm thinking of doing computer design at uni, if I go.'

'Great, if you'll enjoy it.'

'I'd rather do music, but songwriting's not a career,' he says.

I try to imagine Pete and Lucy's old room converted into a den fit for a tech nerd, but my head's too foggy to look that far into the future.

Jamie seems happier after his declaration. He chats about his future when we sit by the fire downstairs. He dreams of travelling and writing songs for famous artists as a hobby, but he's a realist too. I'm relieved to hear that he wants a job that makes him a good living.

It's 9 p.m. and I'm washing up in the kitchen when Billy arrives in his dad's BMW. He's been more like a brother to Jamie than a friend since primary school. I remember him as a talkative, sweet-natured boy, but he's retreated into himself recently. The boys are inseparable, even though Billy's a year older and they're from different backgrounds. His parents are millionaires with a huge house in a village nearby, their wealth protecting him from the need to get a job, even though it would do him good. He seems to spend most of his time wandering around, taking pictures.

Billy has his camera slung over his shoulder, as usual. He carries it everywhere, like Jamie and his guitar. He used to talk about becoming a doctor one day, but now his biggest ambition is to become a music photographer, following pop stars all over the world. He dumps his leather jacket on a chair, then greets me politely. His smile soon fades, like he's guessed he's not fully welcome. Billy's tall and thin, with a gaze that's far too adult. Something about him sets my teeth on edge, and the fact that he's high, on substances I've never tried. His gaze flits from wall to wall, unable to settle on anything for long.

'Nice to see you, Eloise.' He drawls out the words. 'Jamie says you've run away from home.'

'Are you okay, Billy? You seem spaced out.'

'I might copy you. My parents have been rowing for months, the house is a warzone.'

'I'm sorry to hear that.' I've only been to Billy's place a handful of times. It's immaculate, and his parents always look glossy with health and perfectly in tune, like they've just done a long workout at the gym.

'Dad's always away, and my mother's a nightmare. You never know when she'll strike next. If it goes to court, he won't stand a chance.'

'Don't bother Mum with it, Billy,' Jamie hisses. 'She's got enough on her plate.'

My son looks embarrassed when he leads Billy upstairs, still wearing his vacuous smile. That's the beauty of drugs. They dis-inhibit you, and they're easy to buy if you've got the cash. Anger rises in my chest again, my head throbbing. This time it's aimed at dealers that flog skunk to teenagers when they're vulnerable, just as their adult minds are developing.

Music echoes through the ceiling from the boombox Jamie brought from home, the base pulsing in my ears. It's the retro American rock he's been playing for months, but the melody's distorted, setting my teeth on edge. I block it out to focus on my own mess. The first step will be understanding exactly how my stalking began. I've been obsessing over it, but it has to be someone from my immediate circle, to get so close. My talk with Jamie makes me want to call Rafe immediately to find out the truth about his affair and whether it could be linked in some way, but there's no point. He'd lie to me again, for reasons I still don't understand.

I stand in the small room off the kitchen that my uncle used as his office until he died. The space still carries Pete's atmosphere, even though it's virtually empty. I can picture him at his desk, typing out invoices for the odd jobs he completed. He spent most of his life driving between fenland villages in his van full of tools, fixing leaking taps, plastering walls and trimming hedges. I realize now that he deserved even more respect. He was a jack of all trades, able to fix almost anything.

I unpack one of my boxes onto his desk. It contains the notebook in which I logged every contact my stalker made, from the very first letter. I was stronger back then, and less daunted, but it helps to see how much groundwork I covered, instead of sitting around with the word 'victim' on my forehead. I tried to act, even though the police have shown no interest.

My first task was to track every stalker I've worked with through the probation service, but the majority have moved on, establishing new relationships and getting jobs. They're unlikely to focus on someone from the past as they rebuild their lives, but I still need to keep watch. There's also an outside chance that my stalker is one of the critical voices online, telling me to stop offering advice. I scan my social media accounts, but something's changed. An anonymous sender has posted a picture of Joe Sinclair. It looks like a police mugshot. He's gazing directly at the camera, his expression intense, eyes almost black. There's a caption in block capitals underneath:

MEET JOE SINCLAIR, CONVICTED STALKER.
DR ELOISE SHAW FOUGHT TO GET HIM
RELEASED EARLY AND HE ATTACKED HIS
VICTIM DAYS LATER. SHE'S STILL IN ICU. DON'T
BELIEVE A SINGLE WORD THAT BITCH SAYS.

Whoever sent the message has no followers, and their online name is 'Righteous'. But their lack of accountability doesn't matter. The message is out there now; it will be hard to fight. The comment already has a thousand likes and the court of public opinion always believes there's no smoke without fire.

I'm still shaken by it, scrolling through messages and checking for more attacks on my reputation, when the landline rings, just like last night. A door slams on the floor above, and Jamie thunders downstairs. I hear him grab the phone in the kitchen before I can stop him. His voice is a raw shout.

'Leave her alone, you scumbag, or I'll fucking kill you.'

His eyes glitter with outrage and suddenly I'm terrified he'll put himself in danger. He only calms down when his friend appears in the doorway. Billy is still wearing his odd Cheshire Cat grin when he grabs his jacket and camera, then slips out of the door.

Jamie is pale with tiredness. He doesn't say a word before heading up to bed, but his outburst has left me uneasy. I check each door and window, performing safety rituals. Then I study the camera feed outside. Each CCTV camera is filming acres of empty darkness. There's no immediate threat tonight, so why am I still tense? My stomach is clenched like a fist when I finally go upstairs.

24

Thursday 11 November

YOU

I sleep better knowing Jamie's here, despite the ugly messages appearing online, but he's gone when I wake up. His guitar is propped against his bedroom wall. The only other thing he's left behind is a note on the kitchen table, telling me he'll be back tonight. He's left the room so tidy I doubt he ate anything before going to college. I've got an hour to fill before meeting my boss, so I return to the study, unpacking the remaining boxes onto the desk. Soon it's littered with envelopes. Some are sealed, but others have been torn open. Most contain just the familiar words, 'Me or you', but a few are more lyrical. I'm not a big reader of literature, but they seem like quotes from poems. The first one appears to be a promise, as well as a threat:

I will not let you go into the unknown alone.

I search on my phone and find out that it's by Bram Stoker, the author of *Dracula*, which seems fitting. My stalker is depleting my energy, as though my lifeblood is draining away. I've never read the book, apart from skimming a few pages in Jamie's copy at our old house. He loved anything to do with vampires during his Goth phase, but his taste in reading has evolved since then. The line reminds me of the past. My stalker may be trying to capture their own feelings, but sometimes they hit the jackpot and trigger my buried memories too. I used to believe that Rafe and I could beat any challenge, confident we'd remain in lockstep. My stalker appears to feel the same about me. It would make a fascinating study if I was reading about it in a psychology journal, instead of living it every day.

When I go back through my records, I see the first message arrived in August. I remember opening it, still tanned and happy after our holiday. Letters started to arrive daily, all stamped in Cambridge. Fear took longer to materialize, slowly eroding my sense of safety. The records give me something to build on, at least. I make sure to pull down my office blind when I finish constructing a timeline. My stalker can't approach the house without getting caught on camera, but I cover the windows anyway, in case they have a reckless moment. I'd hate them to see their letters piled here, like precious keepsakes.

I prepare to go out carefully because my boss is always immaculate. I pick a skirt and smart blouse, then dab on foundation to bring colour to my cheeks, followed by mascara and lip gloss. I study myself again in the bathroom mirror. I can't tell if I look whole or broken, only that my hair needs a trim. The makeup helps, but when I drive into town my stomach feels like I'm stuck in a lift that's dropped fifty storeys in the blink of an eye.

It comforts me to follow the usual rituals when I get to the department, until my pass card fails to work again. Reg's smile lights up when I enter his domain. This time he looks apologetic when he resets my entry card, and promises to get the IT department to look into the problem once reading week ends. He passes me my mail without delay. It's only when my hand brushes his by accident that he startles, like he's touched a live wire. The look in his eye is hard to interpret, as though he needs to share vital information but can't find the words. I notice an odd smell in his lodge for the first time. The dry, dusty scent of loneliness that never goes away.

'Did you hear the forecast, Dr Shaw? Snow at the weekend, they say.' His voice falls quiet.

'Let's hope they're wrong.'

'My nephew's praying for a blizzard so he can build snowmen.'

Reg nods goodbye, indicating that I'm free to leave. College life is governed by protocols I took years to understand. Porters still wear bowler hats in some colleges, but Reg follows his own rules. He circulates the building constantly, checking lightbulbs and sockets, but seems to enjoy human company more. He once showed me a wad of postcards from overseas students after they graduated. They'd written back from their home countries, thanking him for his support. He handled the cards delicately, like they were precious relics, demonstrating that he's more sensitive than he appears.

Marina Westbrook is a tougher prospect. I've witnessed more than one postgrad student emerge weeping from her office after hearing that their research funding has been cut. It surprised me that she pulled strings to provide Dan Fender with university ac-commodation. Maybe there's a softer side to her, but I can't forget how hostile she looked when my prize was announced.

She's waiting for me in her office, effortlessly chic, as ever, in a blue dress that makes her look pencil-thin. Her grey hair is cut in a sleek, jaw-length bob. Marina's room takes minimalism to a new level. It contains just a desk, a state-of-the-art computer and two beautifully designed armchairs. The only sign of softness is her lemony perfume scenting the air. If she has a home life, it's not on display. There are no houseplants or pictures, just pristine white walls. It feels like I've been summoned to the headmistress for poor behaviour.

'Thanks for coming by, Eloise. Are you fully recovered now?'

'I'm much better, thanks. Would you mind sharing what happened the night I fell?'

Her grey stare meets mine. 'I was close by when someone barged into you, then vanished. I didn't see their face in the crowd. Calling an ambulance took priority.'

'Thanks for helping me.'

'Anyone would have done the same. I hope you're getting proper aftercare?'

'I'm fine, apart from my patchy memory of that evening.'

'Maybe that's for the best. I waited until the doctor assessed you, then left you to sleep.' Marina looks curious, like she's observing a new case study.

'I think a man visited my room that night. Did you see anyone?'

'You were alone when I left,' she says, firmly. 'Look, I hate to rush you, but there are some work issues to discuss, and I've got a meeting later. Can we move on?'

It crosses my mind that I should come clean and tell Marina about the stalking, and no longer feeling safe here, but she's already onto the next topic.

'I still need your annual report.'

I take a breath before answering. 'I'm afraid there's a problem, Marina. It's been deleted from my computer.'

Her eyebrows rise. 'Reports don't just vanish without a trace.'

'Mine has. It's not on the cloud either, and I've been locked out of the building a couple of times too. Someone keeps deleting my name from the system.'

'Are you suggesting the two things are linked? That sounds like a conspiracy theory.'

'I don't know what's happened, but I'll need time to rewrite my report, I'm afraid. There's no one on the IT helpdesk till the students come back.'

'Every department must submit its report on time, for the annual audit. HR will have to know you're the reason we're late. Call IT on Monday, please, and get it resolved.' She tuts under her breath. 'Let's shelve that for now. I can tell the spotlight makes you uncomfortable, Eloise, but the Cambridge Prize puts you in a different league. Many academics crave that prize, like I said, for their whole career.'

'I feel honoured, obviously.'

Her thin smile vanishes. 'Two of your colleagues were also in the running this year: Noah Jagiello and Clive Wadsworth.'

I stare back at her. 'Neither of them mentioned it.'

'Due to pride, I expect. No one likes missing out. It must be particularly galling for Clive. His work on memory dysfunction is respected worldwide, yet he's never won. I hope you're coming to his retirement do on Sunday, at Corpus?'

'Of course, I owe him my career.'

'That's not strictly true. I would have supervised you if he hadn't taken your application. Your research proposal was the best in your year.' Her voice still sounds cold, despite her praise. 'Clive will still be an emeritus professor, but his contact with students ends this week.'

I can hardly believe Marina's latest revelation about her initial support for my research, but it's Clive's situation that sticks in my mind. I remember him snapping at me before his speech. Maybe he was hiding his disappointment.

'Why did you choose Clive for the announcement speech if he came so close to winning?'

'He insisted, quite forcefully, which impressed me a great deal. I might not have been so generous in his shoes. It's just something to be aware of, Eloise. Professional sensitivities can be a minefield.'

'I'll keep it in mind.'

Marina leans back in her chair. 'The other issue is more serious. It concerns Alan Reed, the man who gatecrashed your celebration. He meant what he said, I'm afraid. It's not going away.'

'How do you mean?' Panic rises in my throat.

'He's suing you for professional negligence. His lawyer's phoned me several times already, asking for your licence to be revoked. I've explained that parole board decisions are collective, not personal, but they're not backing down.'

'I can't be sued for acting in good faith. My programme is successful in ninety per cent of cases. The outcomes are much worse without it. Sixty per cent of stalkers reoffend soon after release, often more aggressively than ever. The ones we treat return to normal lives in almost every case, setting their victims free.'

'This forces us to consider the ones that fail,' she says, frowning. 'The press love to criticize Oxbridge for being elitist and out of touch. If we take the high ground, it will be seen as arrogance.'

'I don't understand.' The shock of her message is making me dizzy.

'His lawyers want to see all your paperwork relating to Sinclair, and the programme itself. I assume that's still on your computer?'

'Yes, but the files are encrypted.'

'I've got police clearance to see them. If they get involved, we can—'

'The police? Are you serious?'

'We'll conduct an internal enquiry first.' She extends her hands, palm down, like she's smoothing a tablecloth. 'Be prepared, that's all. I've already reported Reed's assault on you to the local force.'

'He didn't attack me. It was just a glass of wine.'

'It was physical abuse, Eloise, and disturbing the peace.'

Marina's voice is firm. 'It could give us some leverage. I intend to pull out all the stops to prevent him from damaging the department's reputation.'

'But I've got work to do this week, at Greenhill Prison. Sinclair needs an assessment tomorrow.'

'You're still licensed to practise at this stage, but keep your professional duties to a minimum, please.' She gives a curt nod. 'HR were planning to offer you a readership, with my approval, but that could be harder now. They hate adverse publicity, and your report arriving late won't help. They'll see it as a lack of professionalism.'

'It was a computer failure, for God's sake.' My voice is rising now my job's at risk.

'Let's see what the IT team can do.' Her eyes glitter like wet chips of coal. 'Mr Reed will keep on calling for your dismissal while his daughter's so ill. Let's hope she recovers soon.'

'Her family must be terrified.'

'Empathy is a fine emotion, but not when your back's against the wall.' Her lips twist, like she's suppressing a smile. 'Send me that information today, please. We can't keep the lawyers waiting.'

I'm still reeling from the unexpected sea-change: I was a prize-winner when I walked in here, but now my whole career's in jeopardy, according to Marina.

'Post your weekly video soon,' she adds. 'Your social media profile is valuable to the university, and you can announce your prize. It will remind the decision-makers that your work attracts positive attention, as well as criticism.'

I keep my silence. The truth is, I don't feel equipped to offer anyone guidance right now. It seems fraudulent, pretending to have all the answers, especially now the haters know about Joe Sinclair's actions.

'One more thing. Keep the enquiry into your professional conduct quiet, please, until we have an outcome.' Marina passes me her card, effectively dismissing me. 'I realize this must be stressful. Contact me outside office hours, on my home number, if you need to talk.'

When I glance at her address, it seems fitting. She lives on one of the most elegant roads in Cambridge. Maid's Causeway is full of huge, austere Georgian houses. If she lives there alone, those empty rooms must echo with loneliness. The properties are separated from the road by front gardens, where every hedge is clipped to perfection, as though a single stray leaf would be a punishable crime.

'We'll fix this between us, Eloise.'

There's something odd about Marina's reaction, as though she'd sacrifice me in a blink if her own career was under threat. She appears to have forgotten me already. Her gaze is focused on her computer screen when I let myself out.

I return to my office with my head pounding. The house of cards sheltering me feels more fragile than ever, discomfort hitting me when I sit in front of my computer to deliver an impromptu video to get Marina off my back. My image gazes back at me from the screen, poised and fully made up, with no cracks visible. I remind myself that it doesn't matter if people are turning against me; I acted in good faith, based on my professional knowledge. If just one victim feels less alone after seeing my film, it's worth doing.

It's surprising how easy it is to click into professional mode when I press the record button. I always make the films sitting in the same chair by the window, yet it feels uncomfortable today. I'll be giving out guidance that contradicts my own behaviour, but I have no choice. I've told the police about my situation, yet they've been no help at all, and my work situation is suddenly too precarious to risk telling the senior managers. Even my husband can no longer be trusted to offer me protection. I swallow a deep breath, then begin the film by introducing myself and sharing the stalking helpline numbers for the UK, as I do every week. I lean closer to the screen when I tell my audience not to feel ashamed, like I'm in a café, chatting to a friend.

'No one sets out to get stalked, and self-blame only makes things worse. You didn't create this problem, your stalker did. The best way to stay safe is to force them out into the open, by letting people know what you're experiencing. That way you're enlisting help from every family member, friend and colleague, so the stalker is isolated, not you.'

I talk about a case I worked on, years ago, taking care to conceal the victim's identity. She managed to prosecute her stalker successfully by keeping evidence of every threat over several years. I choose not to announce my prize, ignoring Marina's suggestion. It feels inappropriate while my job hangs in the balance. I offer a professional smile instead, then say goodbye.

'Remember to call the helpline for support if you need it. You're not alone.'

I've never felt more fraudulent when I upload the film, then watch the counter click upwards. Within a minute, five thousand people have viewed it worldwide, with the number rising every second. People just like me are searching for a solution, members of a club we never asked to join. It's only when I check across all my social media accounts that I realize Alan Reed's accusations are making others question my expertise already. A few haters have been posting defamatory messages, too crude to be taken seriously. I can't guess whether it's stalkers or their victims who are turning their backs on me.

When I check my emails, my interview with Joe Sinclair has been confirmed; it's at 9 a.m. tomorrow morning, at Greenhill

Prison. I forward the message to Dan Fender, then gaze down at the cobbles below. It feels like my life's fragmenting: my marriage, my reputation and my future. This is the same panic I felt as a child, after losing my family. The biggest thing preventing me from launching myself through the window is Jamie. I shut my eyes and listen for familiar sounds to anchor me. Noah's music is silent for once. All I can hear is the heater in the corner rattling as it spits out hot air.

There's no one I trust enough to call, except Lisa. She sounds glad to hear from me, inviting me to the art gallery at Downing College in an hour's time, then to lunch afterwards. *Focus*, I tell myself. *Get the job done.* I turn on my computer screen and bring up the encrypted files containing every document relating to Joe Sinclair. It starts with an initial assessment, carried out jointly with a forensic psychiatrist. We both judged him a suitable candidate for the recovery programme, and so did his prison governor. There are dozens of reports from every meeting on his treatment plan, most of them witnessed by Dan Fender, plus Sinclair's psychometric test results. I never guessed that he would outwit the system and ruin the Reed family's lives, leaving my career hanging in the balance.

My stress lifts a fraction when I forward the case file to Marina. If the police find any flaw in my work, I'll be vulnerable, but all the correct protocols were followed. Every mental health professional knows that record keeping is our best defence when dealing with volatile patients. All I can do now is wait for news and remember that I've done nothing wrong. I hate this sense of powerlessness after experiencing it so often in the past.

My office suddenly feels stifling, my skin clammy. My headache's still there, the pressure in my temples refusing to lift. I need fresh air before I see Lisa, so I reach for my coat. The yellow light in the porter's lodge looks welcoming when I pass by, but I don't stop. Kindness when I'm this brittle could tip me over the edge. I'm determined not to cry in front of colleagues, which is a skill I've honed over the years. Holding back tears is a requirement as a psychologist. We often hear heartbreaking life stories, but personal reactions aren't an option. I have to remain dispassionate, no matter how much trauma a patient describes.

I hurry along Downing Street, passing the anthropology museum, which Jamie loved as a kid. The ancient pottery fascinated him, making him dream of becoming an archaeologist until music took over. Thinking about him helps me breathe more easily. He's gone through so many phases, from his passion for dinosaurs, to skateboarding, always coming home with bumps and bruises. I can't let him live with me until the stalking ends, whatever he says. I'm not prepared to put him at risk too, so I'll have to find another solution.

I stop walking for a moment to scan the environment. The street stands at the edge of the town's historic section, with Lion Yard Shopping Centre on one side, a square-edged sprawl of concrete boxes four storeys high. My meeting with Marina has left me too distracted to look over my shoulder until now. I watch the street, searching for anyone suspicious, but people are keeping their distance. An elderly couple overtake me, their Jack Russell on a short lead. Passers-by are going about their business, perfectly innocent. I spot a figure in the distance wearing a shapeless winter coat, a cap pulled low over their face, moving slower than the rest. But it's a false alarm. He soon disappears into the shopping centre. I don't even know if my stalker is male or female, familiar or a complete stranger. All my professional certainties seem to have ebbed away. I glance up and down the street one more time, then head for a quiet section of the river, hoping for some peace of mind.

25

ME

It's lucky you're too preoccupied to notice me hiding in a gap between buildings when you look back. I'm taking a risk today, following you down a street with few pedestrians. It's the main route for drivers hunting for a parking space in town. I can tell you're upset. Your movements are jerky, yet you keep your head high, like nothing could go wrong. You need love, yet can't trust it, worried the emotion could suck you down into a whirlpool beyond your control, just like when you were a child.

I watch you balance on the pavement's edge at the junction on Trumpington Lane as a bus hurtles past. Vehicles thunder by, inches from your face. It looks like you're preparing to throw yourself under the next lorry, making me freeze on the spot. How would I cope if you took your own life?

It's not how our story should end. You must see that because you wait for the road to clear, then hurry down Mill Lane towards the river. It's a spot that fills with tourists in summer, eager to hire a punt from Scudamore's and follow the Cam to Grantchester, through wide green meadows. The boatyard's shut today and there are ice fragments floating on the river's surface. There's only a scattering of people, taking photos of scenery that has changed little in the past three hundred years. Shepherds used to drive their flocks across Lammas Field to drink from the river, but no sane person would risk swallowing the water today. You could catch Weil's disease from the effluent it holds.

You come to a halt, looking down at the ink-black river, and this is where we part company. After a moment's reflection, you keep walking, and I turn away, fast. I want to be exactly where you expect to find me, whenever you come looking.

26

Water always soothes me. I often walk here after work, in summer. There's something reassuring about the river's slow tide, as though it understands that a long journey lies ahead, winding through forty miles of empty fen to King's Lynn and the open sea. I sit on a park bench and watch a young woman teaching her toddler to feed the ducks. I did the same with Jamie when he was small and I was happier than ever before. Those days were exhausting but unforgettable.

I try to imagine myself back in that safe time, but when my eyes reopen, winter air chills my face and the puddles at my feet are icy. Someone told me once that Virginia Woolf died by suicide, filling her pockets with stones, then walking into the river Ouse. She took her life just as winter ended. My own death would have to be fast if I ever made that choice. My father lingered in agony for weeks, according to my brother and sister, yet the idea refuses to go. The water looks tempting, despite the cold. My security is vanishing. It would be logical to end the process now, before the pain comes back.

'Get a grip, you idiot,' I whisper to myself.

I'm back on my feet, leaving the river behind, telling myself

I'm tired, not broken. It's time to shed this burden. I take the ten-minute walk to Downing College, on Regent Street, at the heart of town. Lisa works here, in the art history department, but she's rarely in her office. Running the Heong Gallery is her passion, and far more than a professional duty. It's a single-storey modern building just inside the college gates. I've been here often for private views, when guests spill out into the college grounds, enjoying the party atmosphere she creates so effortlessly.

The gallery door hangs open despite the cold, the place a hive of activity. The theme of Lisa's new exhibition is 'Winter Solstice', and I catch sight of a landscape painting full of snow-clad fields propped against the wall. Research students stand in clusters, debating whether pieces are hung correctly, reflecting the light that spills through the gallery's glass ceiling.

Lisa hasn't seen me. She's supervising students as they unload a cargo box full of packing materials. She's wearing Levi's, baseball boots and a bright yellow jumper. From this distance she could be in her twenties, like them. Her face is animated, curls pinned into a ragged bun. I wait until the picture is safely removed and I can see the canvas, shining with cold radiance. The picture depicts a *fin de siècle* mansion house, backed by miles of slate-grey sea.

I'm still admiring it when a young man swings round suddenly, almost bumping into me. His gaze lingers on my face for a beat too long and panic strikes me again. Sometimes that's all it takes. Age gaps are no obstacle to stalkers. Fixation is about power and control, not beauty. I've met offenders in their twenties obsessed by victims who are decades older. I escape outside to catch my breath.

Lisa soon appears at my side. 'There you are. Why did you rush off just now?'

'You're too busy. Let's have lunch another day.'

'No way, I want to see you. Give me two minutes to grab my coat.'

I wait outside, unwilling to get spooked again. Lisa takes longer than she promised. I watch how she interacts with her researchers through the window, handing out instructions. Her charm looks effortless from where I'm standing. My friend is still beaming when she finally reappears.

'It's mad in there, Elly. We've been flat-out. The French pictures finally arrived, just now. I was terrified we'd have nothing to show at the private view.'

Lisa chatters away as we walk, asking how I'm recovering. Her ability to talk fluently on any topic is one of the things I love about her. She flits between subjects at lightning speed until we arrive at the Italian café across the street, which is her favourite haunt. The waiter greets her like an old friend, then leads us to a booth at the back.

'Wine or beer?' she asks.

'Water for me. I should work after this.'

'God, you're a killjoy. Why are we even friends? You need to loosen up before Saturday. Wear something fabulous and bring Dr Handsome. I might even try him out myself.' She leans closer, inspecting my face. 'Spill the beans, then. Something's upset you today, I can tell.'

I ignore Marina Westbrook's instruction and share my news. It seems unbelievable that my boss looked after me in the ambulance. I felt so grateful, but now I'm facing a lawsuit, she won't back me, in case it damages her own reputation. Lisa looks outraged. She's always good at keeping secrets, making me certain the details won't be shared with anyone.

'Marina should be supporting you. I'd contact the union, in your shoes. I bet you've done nothing wrong. You always get a second opinion before releasing a prisoner, don't you?'

I nod rapidly. 'An expert panel agreed it, and a consultant psychiatrist.'

'So, it's not your fault. You're safe. Take her to court for harassing you.' Lisa's words reassure me. I'm still overshadowed by the past, too quick to believe I'm in the wrong.

'It's how Marina operates with everyone.'

'Don't let her bully you. The management are all the same. Those bastards keep giving me two-year contracts, then telling me to be grateful.'

'You're bound to get tenure soon. You're brilliant at your job.'

'I wish they agreed. I love my work more than anything, except my friends, of course.'

'They're stupid not to value you properly.'

'I'm more worried about you right now, Elly. What happened to that girl's not your fault. I'm amazed the university are taking her dad's threats seriously.'

The truth is, Marina's speech got to me. I'd hate to give up the programme I designed and see my hard-won reputation crumbling. My system offers better protection for victims than any other, but I can't let anyone else suffer like Georgia Reed. Her case proves that it's not perfect, and there's a risk it could fail someone else if I don't improve it.

'How are you doing at home?' Lisa asks.

'Jamie's guessed about Rafe's affair – he thinks it's been going on for months.'

She looks shocked. 'Is Rafe still keeping quiet?'

'He lies, that's the trouble. And he keeps on laying the blame on me. He thinks I should tell him and Jamie more about my past, like that could fix everything.'

'How exactly?'

'Rafe thinks it's overshadowing the present.'

Lisa chews her lip. 'I hate to say it, but he could be right. You know all about me being raised by a single mum, and my wild-child youth, but yours is a mystery.'

'Only because I don't remember the crucial bit, when it all went wrong.'

The restaurant is full by now, all the tables occupied. People are chatting in pairs or small groups, relaxed as they eat, but my discomfort's building. Lisa is trying hard to dispel my tension, but it won't go until I've learned the truth about my stalker's identity.

'What is it that makes people forget tough memories?' she asks.

'Past trauma. We're programmed to avoid reliving it.'

'So it gets sealed inside, like a volcano, waiting to blow?'

'It feels like that sometimes.'

'That sounds awful, Elly. You haven't said much about how you're doing, except at work.'

'I can't let my stalker spoil every conversation.'

'That guy on your team, Dan Fender, still bothers me. Can't you get a background check on him? It's creepy, the way he watches you all the time.'

I fiddle with my cutlery. 'I've known him for two years. He'd have acted by now, if it was a problem.'

'What if he's the slow, brooding kind? You're way braver than me. I've never recovered from seeing *It* at thirteen, I still have night-mares about clowns with pointy teeth.' She gives a mock shudder.

'Most stalkers are nothing like the movies. The violent mes-sages they send are just to make them feel stronger.'

'But he's already hurt you, Elly. He put you in hospital.' Her eyes glitter with concern. 'What drives it, normally?'

'Don't ask. A lecture on stalking would ruin your appetite.'

'Nothing gets between me and food. Come on, give me the basics.'

I look down at my hands. 'It normally starts after a breakup, then turns into an obsession that can last years. Resentful stalkers have grievances to settle. They believe you've slighted them in some way. Then there are predatory stalkers, who plan a sexual attack. They want to control and humiliate you.'

'What category does your stalker fall into?'

'Resentful, I think. Most of the notes say "me or you", like I've cheated them out of something precious, even though I don't remember hurting anyone.'

'No one you've crossed at work?'

I hesitate before replying. 'Noah Jagiello and Clive Wadsworth were both considered for the Cambridge Prize this year. But my stalking's gone on for months, and the prize was only announced recently.'

'Have either of them behaved oddly?'

'I don't think so, but that's not proof.'

'What if the stalker's predatory?'

'Then I'm in much deeper shit.'

'Don't take any risks, please.' She sounds alarmed. 'Stay at mine. It's better to be safe than sorry. My spare room's cramped, but you've coped with it before.'

I touch her shoulder. 'That's a lovely offer, but it would be playing into their hands. They want to back me into a corner. Stalkers are narcissists with grandiose ideas. They believe their victims should be grateful for their attention. When you're not, it makes them furious.'

Lisa pauses for a moment. 'Could it be someone from your past?'

'My last fling was twenty years ago, before I met Rafe.'

Our conversation falls silent when the waiter delivers two plates heaped with lasagne, and a salad to share. Lisa helps herself before speaking again.

'You know I'll always listen and try to help. I flap a bit, but I do okay in a crisis.'

'I'm lucky to have you.' Words stick in my throat, but I need to release my feelings before they drown me. 'Rafe's turned into someone else, that's what hurts. He's always been so honest. Now he's lying to me and accusing me of keeping secrets.'

'You've just confided in me properly, for the first time. That's progress, isn't it?' Her smile's gentle. 'But I've never met anyone who avoids their past like you.'

'I've spent too much time and energy trying to remember.'

'In therapy, you mean?'

'Years of it, in my twenties.'

'I saw a shrink too, before uni.' She looks embarrassed. 'I was out of control, partying too hard, until I burnt out.'

'Was there a trigger for it?'

She shrugs. 'I never got much guidance as a kid. Mum had different priorities, but I'm still not sure why I lost the plot for a few months.'

'I'm sorry, Lisa.' I'd like to comfort her, but she makes light of it.

'It was funny, really. She had to coax me out of my room for CBT like a frightened rabbit.'

'Did it help?'

'It got me back on my feet, ready to face the world, and keeping a diary was useful too. But that's enough about my murky past.' Her smile revives. 'Did I tell you, I've met a new guy? He's ticking a lot of boxes.'

Lisa tells me about her new admirer, and I hope this relationship doesn't follow the usual pattern. They desert her, or she ends up converting them into friends. The rest of our lunch passes in a blur. I'm so grateful to park my worries for a while that I abandon the idea of sharing any more secrets. The biggest one stays locked inside. I'm terrified that Jamie could get caught in the crossfire if my stalker hunts me down again.

'Promise you'll come to the private view, Elly. You deserve some fun.' She drops money on the table for her lunch. 'I'd better check how many precious artworks my lot have broken in my absence.'

Lisa hurries away, leaving a tang of jasmine and excitement on the air. Even her scent is carefree, and my thoughts feel lighter when I head back to my office, just one block away.

My stalker seems to be taking a day off. The corridor is empty when I go upstairs. It's impossible to tell how many colleagues are hiding in their offices, catching up on work, diligent and solitary. Academic work attracts obsessives – it's almost a prerequisite. You have to make hard choices to get this far, with your name and title bolted to the door. Your research area has to be your greatest passion, too.

I see a slip of paper on my office floor, stuffed under the door. The contents are innocent for once. It's from Clive Wadsworth, inviting me for a late lunch tomorrow, which puts a smile on my face. He and Hilary have been entertaining me at their place for years. I took Jamie there often when he was small. He loved exploring their rambling garden, and they spoiled him, like absent-minded grandparents. I leave Clive a quick voicemail, accepting the invite.

I pick up my notes for tomorrow's meeting at the research centre. When I look up from my desk, something catches my attention. One of the windows in the accommodation block opposite is brightly lit, revealing a figure hunched over his desk. It's Dan Fender; I recognize his messy hair and powerful build. He looks immersed in his work, and the sight of him unnerves me after my chat with Lisa. He must be able to see me too, any time he chooses to glance across the quadrangle, but his manner is so gentle I don't believe he'd harm anyone. I hate the way being stalked makes me doubt even the people I trust, including a member of my own research team.

When I step out into the corridor, I almost bump into Noah Jagiello. It's my second near collision with a man in the past few hours. He steps back, giving me room to breathe, yet I still feel unsafe, my paranoia mounting. Noah spends so much time in his office, it's the ideal position to monitor my movements. I notice for the first time that his lips twist slightly, his smile lopsided because of the scar at the centre of his cheek. Oddly enough, that flaw only adds to his appeal.

'You're in a hurry, Eloise.'

I still feel unsteady, but try to mask it. 'I only dropped by to collect notes for a prison visit tomorrow.'

'I've been hoping you'd email me some dates to shadow you, for my research. I'd love to find out more about your work.'

'Sorry, I forgot to check my calendar.' My next statement emerges before I can edit it. 'How about tomorrow morning? I start at nine, at Greenhill Prison.'

He looks surprised but pleased. 'Shall I meet you there, in the car park?'

'By eight forty-five. Expert witnesses can watch sessions via video, but can't be physically present in the therapy room.'

'Understood. I'll be on my best behaviour.'

'Bring ID, but not your phone. Security's tight there. If I email ahead, they'll put you on the safe list.'

'I appreciate it.' He pauses for a moment. 'I'm having dinner at King's tomorrow night. Why not come with me? Let it be my thank-you present.'

'There's no need.'

'Come anyway, you might even enjoy it.' He stands there, smiling. 'Remember, the offer's there.'

Noah enters his room, leaving me flustered. His door clicks shut as I walk down the corridor, followed moments later by a few bars of jazz. It's best to be honest about my motives. Noah has boosted my ego at a low moment. I'd almost forgotten how to flirt, but the skill must have been lying dormant, a relic from drunken teenage parties. I can't guess why he appears so comfortable inviting me for dinner, despite the wedding ring on his hand, but that's his story to tell. Noah has no reason to stalk me, or anyone. The man's laid-back confidence never falters.

I'm on my way out when I catch sight of Marina Westbrook returning to her office. It still surprises me that I can't recall her helping me the night I got hurt, and she had no fresh information to share. I'm almost certain that a man sat by my bedside while a shadowy woman loitered by the door, yet it's impossible to prove. Marina walks with her shoulders back, like nothing could break her stride. She raises her hand briefly when she spots me, then disappears back inside her lair.

27

YOU

I decide to pay my brother a visit on my way home. Leo moved from London to Cambridge two years ago, soon after the three of us reconnected. He's the middle child, often spiky and hard to please these days, with good reason. He was diagnosed with multiple sclerosis before he left London. He now lives in a bungalow off Huntingdon Road. I can't tell if he misses his glamorous life in Notting Hill, and he's unlikely to say. He came to Cambridge to take part in a clinical drug trial at Addenbrooke's Hospital, to combat his condition. He spends most of his time alone, protecting his independence. It's best to turn up unannounced instead of calling first, so he can't refuse. I try to recall the foods he liked as a boy, then stop at the Co-op on my way to pick up crumpets and blackcurrant jam.

Leo's wheelchair-adapted car is sitting in his drive, so I park on the street. There's no point in ringing his doorbell. He either takes ages to arrive or doesn't answer at all. I use the side entrance to his garden and catch sight of him immediately. He's in his conservatory, which he's converted into a workspace, too absorbed to spot me. Classical music whispers through his closed doors, low and mournful. He always plays it when he works. It sounds like a Mahler symphony, but my guesses are often wrong. Leo is the only classical music buff out of us three, and a voracious reader, like Carla. There are dozens of shelves in his house, packed with history books and novels.

He only looks up when I tap on his door. He's still the best-looking sibling, with great bone structure and blue eyes a shade darker than mine. There's no trace of a smile when he beckons me inside, out of the cold.

'Wait a minute, can you, Elly? I can't spoil this.'

I watch the fine movements of his hands. He's staring down at minute shards of pottery through a magnifying glass. The pieces are no bigger than my thumbnail. I'd like to ask where he gets his patience, but one tremor could cause irreparable damage as he lowers a fragment into place. It's his perfectionism that won him his role as chief ceramics conservator at the British Museum. He tried to resign when his MS started, but his boss insisted he continue as a freelancer. Leo gets consignments of broken pottery sent to him every few weeks, packed inside foam-lined cases, each piece swathed in bubble wrap.

My brother is so absorbed that I park myself on a stool to watch. Some of his brushes hold just three or four horsehairs, to apply minute dots of paint. The place smells of resin and chalk, the acrid stink of white spirits lingering in the air. He's designed the room perfectly to suit his needs. His table stands at wheelchair height, with shelving low on the wall so he can reach tools easily. I can see jars of cobalt-blue pigment, a dozen bottles of glue and rolls of surgical tape. He says it's the best material to bind pottery together because it leaves no fibres behind. It allows him to perform life-saving operations on every pot he rebuilds.

Leo takes less care with his own appearance these days, even though he used to be a dandy. Work consumes most of his energy.

I'm certain his hair hasn't been combed for days, and he's in need of a shave.

'Christ, that was tricky. I was trying not to breathe,' he says, finally pushing his wheelchair back from the table.

'What are you fixing?'

'Porcelain, from a Chinese nobleman's grave. It's Han dynasty, two hundred BCE, glazed with copper oxide.'

'It must be daunting, handling something that old.'

'Not really. It can't get any more broken than it is now.' He finally meets my eye. 'Why are you here?'

'What a delightful welcome. I brought crumpets, but maybe I'll take them home.'

'Ocado do just fine, delivering my food.'

'It's not about you, Leo. I need brotherly advice. Plus, for unknown reasons, you calm me down.'

Tension slips from his face. 'Sorry. I'm a rude bastard, aren't I? It's bloody Carla, bothering me every five minutes on the phone. Give me those crumpets, I'll try and come back human.'

I stifle my urge to rush to his messy kitchen and fill a tray, aware that the chore will waste his energy. Leo does everything now at a measured pace. He's nothing like the kid I remember before I was sent away, full of madcap energy, always racing outside to play football with his mates.

He trundles away in his motorized wheelchair. Leo can still walk, but it's becoming a challenge. I see him through his kitchen window, movements faltering as he prepares our drinks. His condition seems to be worsening fast, despite many hospital visits. I read an article recently about the link between autoimmune diseases like MS and childhood trauma. I can't help wondering if his condition was triggered by witnessing all that conflict. Leo greets every situation with gruff stoicism or blue jokes, but it must be horrifying, at thirty-eight, to be losing his mobility. So many other things have been sacrificed, too. He used to live with his TV producer boyfriend back in London, their evenings full of glamorous parties.

Leo looks triumphant when he returns with the tray on his lap, the battery on his wheelchair releasing a steady hum. He sets it on his table with the same slow precision as his work, then takes his time stirring the tea. He passes me a plate at last, always comfortable with silence.

'How did you know I hate all jam except blackcurrant?' he asks.

'You did as a boy.'

'And you hung onto that until now?'

'Why not? I remember loads of things, like you learning to ride a bike faster than me, and how badly that pissed me off. Your school reports always said you were clever but wayward, like me.'

'We've got rebel genes – Carla was the girly swot.' He produces a grin. 'No wonder we kicked off at school. You were a screamer, I seem to remember. The teachers used to put you in the corridor to cool off.'

I still recall that childhood rage; it's never felt closer to the surface. 'It's weird that I remember trivial details, but the important stuff's gone.'

He holds my gaze. 'I remember pretty much everything. Sometimes I wish I didn't. I could tell you about Dad getting hurt, but you don't want to hear, do you?'

'It's better to let my own memories surface without forcing them, but I may take you up on it one day.' I know he's trying to help, but Leo could only give me his version of events. It might add to my confusion.

'You only mention the past when you're upset, El. Are you okay?'

I hesitate before adding to his burdens. 'I've got two problems taking over my life right now.'

'Start with the biggest one.'

'My marriage is over.'

Leo barely reacts, so maybe Carla's already broken the news. 'Are you sure?'

'Definitely. Rafe's been screwing someone else.'

'That doesn't have to be a deal-breaker.' His voice softens. 'It can be a cry for help. You could stick around and find out why.'

'He won't even tell me her name. Could you accept that?'

'It's lies that hurt me, not the sex, or the guy's name. Simon was unfaithful loads of times, but I knew he loved me.'

'Betrayal still hurts, surely? We all want to come first in someone's life.'

Leo lets my words resonate. 'You must be in shock. Rafe seemed perfect for you. I thought you'd stick together for good.'

'Everyone says that, but it still collapsed.'

My brother nods. 'What's the second thing?'

I take a breath. 'Someone's been stalking me for months. I've never seen their face, but they attacked me in the street. It put me in hospital with concussion for two days last week. I can't tell what's safe or dangerous anymore.'

'Christ, that's a lot.' He stares back at me. 'The hunter, hunted. Is that it?'

'It's consumed my life since it started. Whoever's doing it knows where I live, where I work, and they ring me every night, just before I go to bed. They're listening to my conversations, maybe this one too.'

'That sounds paranoid, Elly.'

'Except it's real. I'm being bugged – I found listening devices at home. Then a few days ago they sent me a bouquet of dead flowers, and a box full of ashes.'

He releases a long whistle. 'Have you told Carla?'

'Not about the stalker. She heard about my injury and went nuts. You know how she loves melodrama.'

'That's for sure. She called me in floods the other day, about some spat with a colleague over absolutely nothing.'

'She wants to help, which is sweet, but it won't work. If a stalker really plans to hurt me, they'll find a way.'

Leo frowns. 'You can't just throw in the towel.'

'Nothing stops it, and it's exhausting. My expertise is no protection.'

'You need adrenaline to fight it, like in the old days. You protected me and Carla whenever Mum hit us. You even slapped her back a few times, which took serious guts.'

His words grind to a halt suddenly, a mournful look on his face. I don't know if he's grieving for our lost childhood, his mobility or the life his condition has stolen.

'Enough about me. How are you doing, Leo?'

'This thing cramps my style.' He taps the arm of his wheelchair. 'The drug regime's got shitty side effects, but I don't care, if it helps end this bastard MS. Gene editing could save the next generation of carriers from developing it.'

'You're doing the trial, even though it won't benefit you personally?'

'Surprising, isn't it? I never saw myself as an altruist, but it's not at all romantic. The pills give me the shakes, and blurred vision. Sometimes I feel like screaming my head off, to be honest.'

I keep quiet. It's so rare for him to vent, it's best not to interrupt.

'My sex life's crap too. God knows why Simon still visits me every week. We used to rip each other's clothes off with our teeth; now we go out for coffee, or to the cinema, like retirees. I keep telling him to bugger off, but he won't listen. The idiot's even thinking of moving up here.'

'I hope he does. You're great together.'

'It wouldn't work, El. Where's the fun for him? We can no

longer shag each other senseless. I don't want him cooking every meal and hauling me into the bath.'

'You're still gorgeous, Leo. And he must love you, or he wouldn't offer.'

'What kind of future would that be? This bloody condition is killing me and I've never been remotely brave.' He peers at me over the rim of his mug. 'Do you ever wonder if we've inherited the suicide gene?'

I hold his gaze for a moment. 'What are you saying?'

'Answer the question, El.'

'I worry more that it's skipped a generation and landed on Jamie.'

'That boy's too sorted for self-harm. He's phoned me a few times lately, asking to come round. I wanted to check with you first.'

'You're his long-lost uncle, and you'll do him good. Maybe he wants some pearls of wisdom.'

'He won't get any here.' Leo narrows his eyes. 'I asked you if you'd ever been tempted to self-harm, like Dad.'

'Only when I'm super stressed.'

'If a parent commits suicide, it's more likely the kids will, isn't it?'

I try to deflect. 'No one talks like that anymore. It makes it sound like they've committed a crime. It's better to say "died by suicide".'

Leo's reply is terse, but accepting. 'Okay, I get your point.' He waits expectantly for my answer.

I can't hide the truth. 'Children of people who have died by suicide are three times more likely to end their own lives, but it's not a given. We can have genetic markers for depression, yet still avoid it. No one's born with suicide as their destiny.'

'But we're already experts on the subject. If my hands stop

working, like my legs, I won't be able to mend pots anymore. What's the point of me then?'

'I like having my brother alive.'

'You managed okay without me for years.'

'Not by choice. If you're actively suicidal, tell me right now, Leo.'

'Don't have me sectioned just yet.' His smile flickers back into life. 'I'm too cowardly to chuck myself off a motorway bridge. If my body packs up completely, Carla can trundle me around in my wheelchair. She'd be overjoyed.'

I find myself picturing it, then feel guilty. 'That may not happen.'

'Come on, you know how MS works. I bet you've googled the shit out of it. Sooner or later the symptoms win. I'll be Stephen fucking Hawking.'

'But less clever, with no chance of a Nobel Prize.'

He barks out a laugh. 'God, you're the opposite of Carla. I love every atom in her body, but she's too bloody earnest to crack a joke.'

'Mine was in bad taste, sorry.'

'It's jolted me out of my mood, thank God. Self-pity's so boring.' He takes a bite of crumpet.

'You know Hawking had MND, don't you? People living with MS often stay well for decades.'

'Stop it, optimism annoys me.' Leo tuts at me. 'What will you do about the stalker?'

'Identify them. It's my best option – the police only respond to immediate threats. I'm already researching all the offenders I've worked with, to rule them out.'

'How about colleagues? Some of mine are real nutjobs.'

I run through the list in my mind, as I've done before. 'None of them fit the profile. It'll be some lonely obsessive, nursing a fantasy.'

'Shrinks go crazy too, remember. Sigmund Freud was a sex-freak, with a thing for his daughter, wasn't he?'

'That's over-simplifying.'

'I wish I could find the bastard for you, El. These days I'm only good for fixing china, feeding birds in my garden and staying in love far too long.'

'Simon appears to feel the same.'

Leo looks appalled. 'He's so fucking decent. I'd have run for the hills by now.'

'You might react the same, in his shoes.'

'Don't be wise today, please. I need facile jokes and distraction.'

'Come outside then, let's catch our death of cold. Show me these birds you claim to adore.'

Leo turns serious. 'I need a favour first. An old friend's getting married next month. Can you help me buy a suit? I've got a fitting in town on Saturday.'

'Text me the time, but be warned, I always give my honest opinion.'

'That's what I need. Why wear a suit if it looks crap? I used to love buying clothes, before my legs packed up.' His eyes glisten. 'Let's focus on the birds. I've got cheese in the fridge, it's their favourite.'

'Want me to get it?'

'Stay there, it won't take me long.'

I sit in his workroom, trying to inhale Leo's essence, to understand him better. His patience must be hard-won because there was no sign of it as a kid. I'd never guessed he'd become selfless, either. It takes bravery to become a human guinea pig so others can escape a condition that's deprived you of the things you love. When I look around, every object relates to his work, apart from the sound system, which has fallen silent. I can see him in his kitchen, preparing food for the birds he pampers.

That's when it hits me. The sensation of being watched, like a feather trailing across my cheek. Leo's workspace is mostly glass, exposing me to prying eyes. Suddenly I'm back on the night of my attack. My stalker had the perfect opportunity to kill me. It would have taken seconds to drive a knife between my ribs while I lay on the ground. They must be planning something even worse, to drag out the threat this long.

I rush into Leo's garden, looking for an intruder. The layout doesn't help me. It's protected by a fence on one side and thick bamboo on the other. I spin in a circle to find where they're hiding. They could be peering through a knothole in the wood. But when I scan the planks looking for gaps, there are none, and suddenly the feeling of danger lifts, leaving me breathless.

Instinct tells me the threat was real, but my professional head knows that panic reactions are often wrong. It's pure adrenaline, like deer in a forest startled into flight by the sound of a single twig breaking. But I'm certain my stalker is retreating already. It's the wrong time to follow them, with no one to help me. My brother gives good advice, but can't defend me in a crisis.

Leo looks happy when he emerges from his kitchen. A plate is balanced on his knees, covered in crumbs of cheese, and his expression's child-like, like he's been promised ice cream. He presses his index finger to his lips when I drop onto his garden bench.

'Quiet,' he whispers, positioning his chair next to me. 'And stop fidgeting.'

I watch him throw crumbs of cheese onto the path. Nothing happens for a minute; the only sound I hear is the breeze picking up, cold wind ruffling my hair. Leo seems oblivious to the chill, and his reward soon arrives. A robin lands first, then two house sparrows, competing for food. When I glance at Leo again, he's forgotten my presence. His gaze is so focused on the birds, it's as though nothing else exists.

28

ME

There's beauty in knowing you're afraid; it makes my situation easier to bear. I'd rather you came to me willingly, to learn the truth, but fear is a decent substitute. I want your pain to be emotional, not physical, for now. Seeing you run mad would be the best reward, and that will come from hurting the people you love. I watched you rush outside from an ideal vantage point. You looked everywhere to find me, spooked by my gaze, unable to pin me down. Thank God you searched in all the wrong places.

I'll have to be more careful in future because my face is so familiar to you. If I want to get close, I should cover my tracks, so I don't end up cowering in the shadows again.

Your car pulled away five minutes ago and now I'm on the street, my footsteps tracing yours. I remind myself that there are a thousand ways to get the job done. You can be close or distant. It doesn't matter, so long as I'm in control.

My heart is still pounding in my chest. The excitement comes from almost getting caught. That was my closest shave yet, but it won't stop me from doing it again, whatever the cost. I stare down at the pavement where you stood, thinking about the future. My life will end if I go to jail. I'd sooner die than let that happen. *Me or you*, over and done. The thought lingers until the freezing air burns my doubts away. My hands are numb with cold, so I hurry away to safety before anyone notices me loitering here.

29

YOU

I stop for petrol at a garage on the city's borderline, where it unravels into open fenland. The building looks like an Edward Hopper painting from a book Lisa gave me years ago, showing scenes from everyday American life, lit up in stark detail. My car is the only one on the forecourt, yet my sense of being watched lingers. It must be imaginary. No car followed me here, I checked my rear-view mirror a dozen times. The only person in sight is the elderly woman in the kiosk who accepts my payment without a word, then returns to her sudoku. I envy her lifestyle, even though the routine would soon drive me mad with boredom.

I sit in the driver's seat with my hands gripping the wheel, remembering Leo's attitude to his situation. It's an object lesson in facing an overwhelming problem with humour, even though he claims not to be brave. The prospect of losing his strength must terrify him, yet he keeps going anyway. Work sustains him, and so do simple pleasures. The tearaway I knew as a child has matured into a patient man, delighted by the wildlife in his garden, and generous enough to set his partner free. I can feel us getting closer, even though there are still huge voids where we should have shared memories. Carla wants to fill every gap instantly, while Leo seems content to let familiarity evolve with time. He pretends to hate impromptu visits, yet I saw his mood improve during our hour together.

I'm about to drive on when a text arrives from Billy Rawle's mother, Jennifer. It surprises me because we haven't spoken for months and have never been close, despite our sons' long friendship. She's driving to my cottage, asking me to confirm whether I'll be at home. I reply that I'm on my way there, then reserve judgement. Maybe she's making this impromptu visit because she's in trouble too, if Billy's speech about his miserable home life was accurate.

Jennifer Rawle is alone in her car when I arrive. It's a white Lexus, so new the paintwork sparkles. Her phone is pressed to her ear. She raises her hand when I stop by the door, smiles, then continues speaking, her face animated. I can't tell whether work or personal matters have produced that much excitement. She and her husband run a lucrative tech business that's spreading across the globe, so the pressure must be high. Her eyes are still glittering when she leaves the car. I'm struck by how perfect she looks in her smart winter coat, with dark hair rippling over her shoulders. Her gaze takes in the wide landscape before returning to me.

'Sorry to drop by at short notice, Elly. Have you got time for a chat?'

'Of course. Come in for a coffee.'

She follows me into the hallway, keeping her coat buttoned. I can tell she's making assessments, and not just about the temperature, which almost matches the winter chill outside. She's studying the faded wallpaper, damp patches on the ceiling and swirly carpet that went out of fashion decades ago. It looks like she's struggling to mask her distaste.

'This place is in a great spot, isn't it? The views are extraordinary. You can see for miles. Are you planning to do it up?'

'One day, maybe.'

Jennifer accepts my offer of a hot drink, but the small talk feels stilted, as though she's eager to focus on the matter at hand. I try to slow my racing thoughts. Maybe I'm being paranoid again. She's just the mother of Jamie's closest friend, an acquaintance, with no axe to grind. So far, she's kept her expression neutral, even though the shabbiness of this place seems to put her on edge.

'How've you been, Elly? We haven't spoken in ages. I thought it was time for a catch-up.'

'Fine, thanks. How about you?'

'The recession hurt our business, but it's bounced back, thank God. We've had to change how we operate, supply-wise.' Her gaze finally meets mine. 'I didn't come here to bore you with it. I was sorry to hear about you and Rafe splitting up.'

'Thanks, but nothing's decided between us yet. There was no need to drive here to show your sympathy.' I don't know her well enough to open up, and there's no genuine warmth in her smile. The anger that bubbles up feels inappropriate, and my headache's pulsing again, reminding me my injury's still not fully healed.

'It's time to be honest with each other, don't you think?' Jennifer says.

'How do you mean?'

'Our sons have been so close, ever since primary school.' She sucks in a breath. 'But the friendship isn't helping them right now.'

'What are you saying, exactly, Jennifer?'

'Billy needs direction. We're encouraging him to make better choices and focus on developing a proper work ethic. I want to separate them for a while. Mike agrees with me.'

I stare at her, open-mouthed. 'You think Jamie's a bad influence?'

'They bring out the worst in each other. Surely you can see that? Billy was planning to work in our firm, till Jamie persuaded him to go to art school.'

'Billy made his own decision. Photography's his passion, isn't it?'

Her voice gets louder. 'You're not listening to me. We want our son surrounded by stronger people, with more ambition.'

'Seriously? You came here to tell me my son's weak?' Fury makes my hands curl into fists. I want to launch myself at her physically, but manage to hold back.

'That's your word, not mine.'

'But you're blocking their friendship anyway?'

'Billy needs more time at home. We've given him a curfew.'

'It won't work, Jennifer. If you deny teenagers something, they only crave it more.'

'He's taking drugs, thanks to Jamie's influence.'

'Rubbish. Billy's a year older; he's much more likely to know where to buy them.'

The gloves are off now, her eyes dark and shiny, like onyx. 'I know the truth about your screwed-up family, your lost relatives coming out of the woodwork. No wonder Jamie's flunking his course.'

Her speech knocks me off balance. 'How do you know about my past?'

'I hear them talk.' She blinks rapidly. 'Just keep Jamie away from my son in future.'

'Tell him yourself. Good luck with that conversation.' I rise to my feet fast, then point at the door.

'I'll speak to Rafe. He's the rational one, I see that now.' She tosses back her hair. 'Have you looked online recently? There's a petition calling for you to resign. It's got thousands of signatures. That's another good reason to keep Billy with us.'

'Get out of here, right now.'

I control my impulse to kick her out forcibly, but only just. She wastes no time in driving away, leaving me fuming. She seemed to enjoy seeing my world implode, but our sons' friendship is off limits. I would have relied on Rafe to agree, back when we trusted each other, but now I can't guess second-guess his reaction.

When I close the door, I notice another envelope on the mat, and my chest tightens. It bears a Cambridge postmark. The sheet of paper inside contains just one line, written in familiar, child-like writing.

You may be proud, wise, and fine, but death will wipe you off the face of the earth.

I sway on my feet, my anger suddenly replaced by fear. Until now the messages have been about love or loss, not murder. When I tap the words into my phone, it's a quote from Chekhov, but the source is irrelevant. If a stalker makes a death threat, the risk level rises exponentially. I'll have to defend myself better, but how, when I can hardly breathe? I spend the next half hour inspecting locks and peering out of windows, aware that I'm not fully safe anywhere if my stalker is determined to throw caution to the wind and appear on my CCTV.

The floorboards creak under my feet as I pace between rooms. The noise continues when I come to a halt. What if I'm not alone here? I haven't had time to check if anyone's appeared on the cameras. There's a crawlspace under the house; the opening is secured with a padlock. You see them everywhere on the Fens, where houses are built on elevated platforms, as protection from flood damage. I didn't check it today. Anyone could have destroyed the padlock with bolt cutters, then crawled under, to loosen floorboards and get inside.

Now the sound seems to be coming from inside the walls, but I can't identify the source. My mind is playing tricks on me. Maybe someone broke in earlier and they're hiding in the attic. I force myself to swallow deep breaths to quell the panic. But my sense of danger is primal, and beyond my control. This place is the only one where I feel safe, and now even that's been taken. When I listen again, the sound has stopped. It feels like someone's toying with me, enjoying watching me fall apart.

I still feel unsettled when I switch on my computer, to check whether Jennifer was telling the truth about a petition against me. I hold my breath as I read the statement by Alan Reed, blaming me for his daughter's plight. It lays out his views in simple terms: without my intervention, Georgia would be safe and well. I should resign immediately, or have my licence revoked. Several thousand complete strangers have already signed it, and my stalker could be among them, delighted to see my reputation torn apart. It feels like the ground is shifting under my feet. My job is a huge part of my identity. If it's taken from me, there will be nothing left.

I pull the living room curtains shut fast. If someone's out there, watching, they're out of luck, for today at least. I'd rather avoid the endless blackness outside too. It's a reminder that most stalking attacks happen at night, like Joe Sinclair breaking into Georgia Reed's flat while she slept. I'm dreading having to confront him tomorrow, with my reputation in trouble, but it's the only way to learn what went wrong. I owe Georgia's family that much, at least.

30

YOU

I'm in my office at home at 9 p.m., and I've checked the CCTV for today. No one has approached the cottage except a postman, who drove his van down the rutted lane, smoked a cigarette, then trundled away again. My computer screen is lit up, showing views from the security cameras outside while I study old work diaries. I'm hunting for clues about who could be targeting me online. The task feels overwhelming. I've encountered so many people over the past year, including offenders on my programme, strangers at parties, friends and acquaintances, plus students I teach. It's tempting to procrastinate, but anonymous stalkers only get caught through rigorous analysis of every passing contact with strangers, and self-protection by the victim.

I'm scribbling down names when the computer screen flickers. My nerves are on a hair-trigger tonight, my heart rate doubling in seconds. I watch a car draw up outside, the image blurred by speed. My panic only subsides when I see Jamie's old Ford. I'm on the doorstep when he appears, reaching out for a hug. He's taller than me, with a solid build – a man now, not a boy.

'Don't run outside every time a car pulls up, Mum. It's not safe.'

'It's okay, I saw you on the camera feed.'

Jamie returns to his car for some possessions. His jaw's set hard when he props a baseball bat against the wall in the hallway, like a warrior abandoning his sword.

'Put that away, Jamie. I'm not having weapons here.'

'What happens if someone breaks in? We have to be prepared.'

His gaze locks onto mine, and I can tell he won't listen. There's no way he'd absorb my message or Jennifer Rawle's if I tell him now. It's a surprise when he offers to make us a meal. He's shown little interest in cooking until tonight, but my absence appears to be changing us all.

I go back to my computer while he crashes around in the kitchen. His boombox is blasting out Nashville music from fifty years ago. His musical taste is wider than mine, but tonight we're on the same wavelength, listening to Emmy Lou Harris and Joe Cocker – songs recorded before either of us was born.

Jamie's done his best with limited ingredients when he summons me at last. He's made cheese omelettes with herbs, garlic bread and salad. When I compliment him on it, he looks blasé, then says the internet's full of free recipes and no one uses cookery books anymore.

'Have you spoken to your dad since your row?'

He shakes his head. 'I can't forgive him for what he's done.'

'That's for me and him to sort out, remember? Don't let it upset you.'

Joni Mitchell's voice echoes from his stereo while we eat, impossibly high and pure. I introduced Jamie to her album *Blue* recently, and he's been playing it ever since. Her soaring voice returns me to a time when I felt invincible, after meeting Rafe, but it's clear Jamie won't discuss his father again tonight.

'What kind of meals did you eat here as a kid?' he asks. I still don't fully understand why the past draws him like a magnet.

'Simple things, mainly. Lucy made casseroles or soup with veg from the garden. The three of us sat at this table every dinnertime. Meals were quiet most nights.'

'No chatting?'

'Just catching up on stuff from the day. I needed a steady routine, and all they asked in return was that I try hard at school.'

'And did you?'

'I had to learn how to concentrate first. I'd been a tearaway.'

'You got the best results in the county, didn't you? Lucy showed me a newspaper cutting.' There's a hint of pride in Jamie's voice.

'I loved studying by then. It helped my self-esteem.'

'You must be strong, Mum. I'd have hated getting sent away from home, aged ten. Didn't anyone explain why?'

The curiosity in his gaze seems natural. I swallow, my throat suddenly dry. He deserves the facts at my disposal, yet most are still out of reach. 'I think my mother blamed me for Dad's death, but I can't be sure.'

His jaw drops. 'It can't have been your fault at that age, surely? Social Services should have prosecuted her.'

'You can't force someone to be a parent. It's better to be disowned.'

'Weren't you scared, leaving everything behind?'

'Losing Carla and Leo hurt most. I was the oldest, they needed me, but at least I got great surrogate parents.'

'Sorry to keep going back to it, I'm just trying to understand.' Jamie's hand settles on my shoulder, until his attention shifts elsewhere. 'Billy wants to come over again. Is that okay?'

I can't avoid telling him what happened earlier. 'Jennifer came round today. She's not happy about you two being so close, she wants to separate you for a while.'

Jamie's eyes widen. 'Are you serious?'

'I told her not to meddle, but she's determined.'

'She can't keep Billy locked up there.'

'Just give her time to cool down. Maybe you can meet tomorrow?'

I feel better when he hurries upstairs to make the call. We've passed two important milestones tonight. He cooked me his first ever meal and didn't sulk about not seeing his friend. I stand at the sink, washing up. This place is so full of ghosts, I can almost see Pete and Lucy relaxing at the table while I stack plates on the drying rack. I'd love to bring them back to life, just as they were when I arrived, for Jamie's sake. It must take a big imaginative leap for my son, who craves adventure, to understand why I loved the peace here.

I'm drying my hands when the lights suddenly flick out, making my pulse rate double. Jamie curses upstairs, then his footsteps blunder across the floor. The whole house is without power, but the fuse box is on the top landing. I have to find out who's doing this to us, and panic's not helping me. I grope my way along the wall to my office where my laptop screen is blank. The camera feed has stopped working. There's no way of knowing who's outside, watching us flounder in the dark.

'Stay in your room, Jamie,' I yell out, my voice shaky. 'Lock the door.'

I fumble in the drawer for a torch, but only find a box of matches, then Jamie rushes downstairs, ignoring my advice. He's using his mobile phone to light his way, no sign of fear on his face, only his determination to fight back.

'He's done this to us, and now the bastard's waiting outside,' he hisses.

'Could just be a blown fuse.'

'No, I heard someone, just now.' Light from his phone bounces off the walls as he grabs his baseball bat. I should have made him leave it in the car – a weapon will only make him more vulnerable.

'Don't go out there, Jamie, please. I'll ring the police. If we react, the stalking will escalate.'

'I'll catch him, Mum. That fucker can't terrorize us.' He shrugs my hand away when I try to restrain him.

Jamie's gone before I can stop him. Instinct makes me lock the door, then yank back the curtain, terrified. I hear him yelling curses, but the security lights aren't working. My stalker could be waiting to hurt him, danger on all sides. I have to stop myself from chasing outside too. How did they cut our electricity supply from a distance?

The darkness looks thick enough to slice. There's no moon tonight, only a smattering of stars. I can't see where Jamie's gone. But when I listen hard, footsteps are pounding over the frozen ground. Is it two sets, or one? They fall silent suddenly. I'm terrified Jamie's been hurt, until he bangs on the door, calling for me. When I unlock it, he barges inside and it slams shut behind him. His breath comes in shallow spurts.

'The bloke's a fucking coward. He ran away, then I dropped my phone and lost sight of him.'

The frustration in his voice bounces off the walls. I can feel his anger simmering in the dark air, making me afraid he'll rush outside again.

'I'll catch him next time. He's terrified to show his face.' Something drops to the ground, heavy and hard. He's thrown down his baseball bat. 'Where's the fuse box?'

'On the landing, above the bathroom door.'

I hear him stumble upstairs, then there's a fizzing sound and all the lights flick on again. Jamie didn't need to throw a switch; the external power supply has been restored automatically. I'm certain it wasn't an electrical fault because the wiring's sound. I had the circuitry tested a few months ago when I was considering putting the house up for sale.

Someone stopped our electricity supply from a distance, expecting me to rush outside in a panic. I feel like a goldfish trapped in a bowl, all my movements visible, day and night. But Jamie's my biggest worry. He's impetuous, like most teenage boys, putting himself at risk for my sake. He joins me in the office to check the camera feed. Whoever cast us into darkness knew exactly what they were doing. My cameras stopped filming until power was restored, hiding their identity.

'He's playing games, Mum. I bet he hates me protecting you.'

I have to seem calm, for his sake, even though my legs feel like jelly. 'It's manipulation, Jamie, that's how stalking works. It puts them in control. What makes you so certain it's a man, anyway?'

'A bloke's way more likely to taunt us than a woman. He's trying to prove he's in charge.' He gets to his feet. 'Come on, he's buggered off now. Let's check outside.'

Jamie grabs the baseball bat again when we step outside, triggering the security lights. I shield my eyes from the glare, expecting to see more dead flowers or ashes in a box. But it looks like they didn't bother with gifts this time, too afraid of getting caught.

'My car's damaged,' Jamie calls out.

A narrow groove runs down the side of his Fiesta and across the door. Paint has been gouged away by a key or screwdriver. I'm speechless with anger. Jamie worked hard to save money to buy his car. It's old, but it's his pride and joy. He's paid a high price for defending me.

'I'll get that fixed, I promise.'

'Don't bother, it would cost more than it's worth.' His face is tense when he catches my eye. 'They know how to interrupt our power supply. What if I'm not here when it happens again?' He shepherds me indoors. 'Go to Carla's, or Lisa's. Don't come back till it's safe. Protect yourself till this shit blows over.'

I hesitate before replying. 'The same goes for you. I'll look online and find us a hotel.'

'I can stay with mates. Promise to call me if you come back here for any reason.' He's about to go back upstairs when he swings round again. 'Give me a key, Mum. If you need anything from here, I'll fetch it for you.'

I dig in my bag for a spare key, then he hurries away. Soon I hear his guitar from his bedroom as he practises scales and chords to calm himself. I stand in the hallway with my fingers pressed to my lips. My stalker must hate Jamie acting as my bodyguard. They've shown it by sabotaging his car and proving they can throw us into darkness any time they like. It feels like they're mocking me, enjoying seeing me lose control.

I used to feel sure that Rafe and I could provide security for Jamie, far beyond him leaving home. I even had fantasies about playing with his kids in our garden, years from now, but the territory's shifting under my feet. Rafe could be behind all this if the closeness between me and Jamie made him feel left out. Who else could bug our house and know every detail about my movements at work? The idea that he's my stalker fills my mind, then fades again, leaving only the throbbing pain behind my eyes that never goes away.

I peer through a gap in the curtain for so long that my vision blurs, then there's a pinprick of light in the darkness. It looks like someone's in the deserted farmhouse, or they could be standing at the edge of the field again, sending out pulses of light from a torch. It's a coded message I don't understand. They're mocking me from a distance, and a sensation of pure anger fills my chest. How dare they encroach on my safest territory? All the cameras in the world can't buy me security, no matter how much comfort this cottage gave me in the past.

31

Friday 12 November

YOU

Jamie looks tired when he gets up this morning. There are grey circles under his eyes, and his gaze is watchful when he stands by the window, blocking the light. He asks if I'll ever go back home to Rafe. The truth is, retracing my steps feels impossible now the trust has gone, yet the pain of separation is still so raw, I hate revisiting it. I need the truth more than ever. Jamie still seems determined to act as my bodyguard, now I'm alone. His bravery touches me, but I can't let him risk himself again, like last night. He didn't hesitate to rush out into the dark to defend us both. I'm still concerned when he leaves, saying he'll spend tonight at Billy's – or another friend's house if Jennifer sends him away.

Last night's adventure slips from my mind. It only returns when I see the damage to his car clearly for the first time as I wave goodbye. The scratch is a long, continuous scar; his punishment for protecting me. Jamie doesn't look back when he drives away, over mud that's frozen into hard ridges. The sky is a solid wall of cloud extending for miles, pale grey and heavy with snow.

I choose warm clothes for my prison visit. A woollen knee-length dress, ankle boots and an electric-blue scarf to keep me warm in the car. Noah Jagiello enters my mind while I stand by the bathroom mirror, putting on silver hoop earrings and a dash of lipstick. He makes a good distraction from everything I can't fix. I'd love to be able to go home and tell Rafe we can start over, but that finishing line feels like a mirage. I can never return there until I know if he's the one that's hurting me.

The door to Jamie's room hangs open when I leave. His guitar is lying on a chair, inside its case, and his baseball bat is propped in the corner. I never recruited him to protect me, yet he's insisting on doing the job anyway, and stopping him appears to be beyond my control.

I complete one last task before putting on my coat, tapping Georgia Reed's name into my phone. A news site informs me that she's still in a coma, thanks to the severity of her injuries, which lowers my mood. The house offers its usual quiet reassurance as I leave, reminding me of Lucy waving goodbye each morning when I ran for the school bus. She was convinced I'd become a doctor or a lawyer one day. Her confidence and Pete's kindness rebuilt me as the years passed, and I can't let my job suffer. I'm unwilling to give up everything they helped me achieve.

Sleet is falling as I drive west along the A14, following the rush-hour traffic. Wet snowflakes plaster my windscreen, the landscape passing in a blur. The motorway chases past black stretches of water at Fen Stanton, where the wetlands are slick with ice. The landscape here only comes to life in summer, when flocks of swallows skim across acres of shallow water, chasing mayflies. The fen looks bleak today, concrete grey, while my windscreen wipers move at top speed.

There's no sign of Noah Jagiello outside Greenhill High Security Prison. It lies half an hour's drive from my cottage, surrounded by empty fields. The prison site is huge, encircled by wire security fences, alarms and spotlights. Opaque windows protect it from curious bystanders. The location is well chosen; if any inmate managed to escape, they'd have a long walk to the nearest village through countryside with few hiding places. HMP Greenhill houses prisoners with a history of violence or serious crime, serving long sentences. The entire prison is classified as high risk, so there's medical expertise on hand, day and night. There's never been a serious attack on a staff member, but there's a first time for everything.

Joe Sinclair is waiting to be tried, currently in the isolation wing for failing to follow orders. We'll have a guard in the inter-view room, just in case he lashes out, like he did with Georgia Reed. The risk level is nothing new after a decade working one-to-one with stalkers. I've even counselled offenders who have killed their victims, yet this time the violence feels much more personal. Georgia Reed was attacked the night before me, her injuries are horrific, and the fallout could cost me my job.

I step onto fresh snow when Noah arrives in a car that doesn't match his laid-back personality. It's a blue Lexus convertible, designed for speed, yet he's never struck me as a thrill seeker. I can't guess why he picked a vehicle designed for the Amalfi coast in summer instead of the freezing cold fens. His face is calm when he strolls towards me, relaxed because today's visit is just an interesting piece of research. It will never be that simple for me because I built the programme. All my therapy sessions are filmed and pored over by my research team, who are spread across several British universities. We're all working together to understand the healing process for one of the most destructive mental illnesses around. I try to put my doubts aside as Noah smiles down at me.

'Thanks for letting me tag along, Eloise. I appreciate it.'

'You may regret it. The offender I'm seeing today put his victim in ICU a few days ago.'

'Was it her dad that threw wine at you?'

I nod in reply. 'I can see why, but we followed all the protocols. We train offenders to seek help immediately, from their probation officer or therapist, if they're tempted to stalk again. They're battling a mental illness, so we try to remove the stigma around it, but Joe Sinclair slipped through the net.' We approach the gates faster as the cold bites. 'There are no quick epiphanies here. It can take months, or years, for a stalker to accept responsibility for their crime.'

'Kids are slow learners too,' Noah says. 'I'm not expecting miracles.'

Dan Fender is already inside the reception area, a lumbering figure shrugging off his coat and handing over his phone. Everyone who enters Greenhill goes through a body scan, limiting opportunities to carry anything inside except essential documents. The protocol's tightened since the drug problem here intensified. Security staff on the front desk check our IDs and place our belongings in lockers. The décor is reminiscent of a hospital, with bland, inoffensive paintings in the foyer and a sign identifying which services are sited in each building. When the doors click shut behind us automatically, the sound is jarring. It's a reminder that some Greenhill inmates are serving such long sentences, they will never leave.

Dan greets us politely, but his expression's cool. 'I didn't know you were interested in stalking, Dr Jagiello.'

'Noah, please. It's their childhood experience I want to understand. But don't worry, I'll keep out of your way.'

Dan seems withdrawn compared to his upbeat manner last time we met. Maybe it's because his girlfriend has flown home, but he barely speaks to either of us as we cross the prison site to the isolation block. There's nothing here except an exercise area fenced in with chicken wire and a few stunted shrubs. I'm aware for the first time that Dan seems over-focused on me, paying little attention to Noah. I store the idea away, then click into professional mode. It's a relief to be dealing with stalking objectively for the first time since my attack, and everyone will expect clear guidance from me, as programme manager. I can't let personal distractions trip me up.

I run through the safety protocol in my head once we enter the isolation block. One of the cells is being cleaned out, the door hanging open. It's a minute space, with a single bed frame bolted to the floor, barred windows, and little else. They've taken care that no light fitting or handle could be used to enable a suicide. The cleaner tells us the heating for the whole block is out of order today, which explains the chill. The air inside the building smells of stale air, coffee and panic. Joe Sinclair's status couldn't have fallen much lower. He was in a relaxed category C prison last year, but now he's locked in an isolation cell with his future in tatters.

Soon he'll be accompanied here by prison guards. One will remain inside the interview room, while the other waits in the corridor. Sinclair has been charged with attempted murder, while Georgia Reed remains in a coma. Some of my research team will watch the session via camera, with Noah observing too. Our goal will be to pinpoint which element of the treatment plan failed to identify future violence in Sinclair's behaviour.

The prison governor appears as the meeting is about to start. Sally Hammond has run Greenhill successfully for five years, fighting a pitched battle against the epidemic of drug abuse that has gripped every UK prison. She's about my age, and I sense that she's found her vocation, trying to make a difference after seeing growing numbers of stalkers jailed for terrorizing their victims. Sally looks more like a librarian than a top-level prison manager, wearing a cardigan over her blouse, her hair clipped into a tidy bun. I've always liked the way she remains silent unless she has something useful to say. She seizes a moment alone with me in the corridor before the review meeting starts.

'Are you okay, Eloise? This is a pity, after all the time you gave Sinclair.'

'I'm disappointed, obviously. Have you had any feedback from your guards since he reoffended?'

'He's agitated and refusing medication. He says someone co-erced him into attacking his ex.'

'We often see denial of responsibility at this stage.'

'I think some of it sounds plausible.' She scans my face again, studying my reaction. 'Remember, we'll assist immediately if you hit the panic button.'

I've worked in many prisons over the years but have only faced a couple of emergencies. Sally's manner is calm too. You can't beat years of working with male offenders as preparation for tackling life's challenges. We're both trained to de-escalate tension. I can only hope that the system works today, because I can't get Georgia Reed's battered face out of my mind.

Dan has his back turned when I enter the interview room, gazing up at the monitor on the wall. I've grown used to being ob-served. It's nothing like the panic I feel when my stalker watches me. My colleagues are there to protect me, as well as to analyse my work.

I stand beside Dan, waiting for Joe Sinclair to appear on the screen. We consider every element of the stalker's behaviour, including their demeanour before the session begins. Sinclair takes his time emerging from his cell. There's tension in the taut line of his shoulders as he's led down the corridor. His posture is hunched, his gaze fixed on the floor.

'Not thrilled to be here, is he?' Dan mutters.

'That's no surprise. He's facing trial for attempted murder. His sentence will increase if Georgia Reed dies.'

Dan faces me at last, his face blank. 'I sometimes wonder how I got here. I come from a long line of Baptist preachers. Maybe I should be delivering sermons instead of interviewing sadists.'

'Sit this one out, if you prefer. Another team member can take your place.'

'No thanks, I want to hear his explanation.'

I eye him carefully. 'I'm just checking you're emotionally prepared, Dan. We have to stay calm, or he'll mirror any tension back at us.'

He looks away. 'I've never let you down before, have I?'

'But it's fine to take a back seat, occasionally. We've all done it.'

'There's no need.'

Once I press the button on the wall, security staff will escort Sinclair inside. I'm suddenly aware of the room's austerity. It's blank, like Marina Westbrook's office, apart from a plastic table with four chairs, and a sealed window set so high in the wall there's no view, except distant clouds.

I keep my expression neutral when Sinclair arrives, handcuffed. He's wearing a grey prison sweatshirt and jogging trousers. His expensive Nike trainers are the only sign that he once earned a good wage as a tax inspector for HMRC, after finishing a finance degree. He's in his early thirties, average height, with neatly combed mid-brown hair. There's nothing unusual about him, except the violence he keeps hidden from view.

Sinclair's guard is careful as he handcuffs him to the chair. I'd rather not interview anyone under restraint, but there are strict rules for offenders who commit grievous bodily harm. This man appears to be struggling to contain his anger. The questions haven't even begun, but a muscle is ticking in his jaw, and his lips are pursed into a hard line.

'You know why you're here, Mr Sinclair. We need you to describe the events, please, from the date of your release, up to your attack on Georgia Reed.'

'What's in it for me? I'll do years here, whatever I say.'

'We need to review the circumstances, to stop crimes like yours happening again.'

'Your programme failed, that's all,' he snaps. 'I came to you with a problem, and you let me down. That advice you gave about self-acceptance was a joke. End of story.' His tone's accusatory, like a peevish child.

'You might feel better unburdening yourself.'

I let silence fill the room. Most people fill the void with words, if you allow enough time, and stalkers are narcissists at heart. They love the sound of their own voices, but only respond if it will benefit them personally. When I look at Sinclair again, he's bent forward in his seat. It doesn't take much expert knowledge to read shame in his body language, even if he's too macho to admit it. Sinclair gazes at Dan, not me, when he finally straightens up.

'Georgia brought it on herself. Some girls love winding men up, don't they?'

Dan keeps his voice level. 'Your ex didn't ask to be assaulted.'

'But she knew which buttons to press. You understand how it works, I can tell. We're on the same page.'

I study Sinclair again. 'Address your answers to me, please, not my assistant.'

He shuts his eyes, his voice falling to a mumble. 'I never meant to hurt her.'

'What went wrong?'

'Going back to my flat got to me. I wasted so many days phoning her. Sometimes she didn't even bother to pick up. That's an insult, right?'

'You committed the crime, remember. Your victim's innocent.'

'Use her name, for fuck's sake.' He spits out the words.

'No verbal abuse, please, or this discussion ends now.'

'Suits me.' He looks contrite for a split second. 'I got bad advice that night. I shouldn't have listened.'

'Explain what you mean, please.'

'I went to a pub, just for one beer, but ended up drowning my sorrows. I met someone and talked about Georgia for too long. It felt good letting off steam. I explained about her hurting me for stupid, selfish reasons. That conversation persuaded me to try, one last time, to make her see sense.'

'Who was this person?'

He shakes his head. 'Just some random stranger.'

'Female or male?'

'Why are you bothered?' His eyes glitter with anger. 'Women like you hate men like me, whatever I say. You think we're all evil to the bone.'

'I wouldn't work with stalkers if that was true. It's a mental illness we need to treat.'

'Maybe *you're* sick for trying, not me.'

'Focus on your crime, please. That's why we're here. Can you describe what you said to this stranger in more detail?'

'I spoke about Georgia abusing my trust, even though we were perfect together. We'd be married by now, if she hadn't humiliated me by ending it in front of all my mates. The talk made me realize I had to act.'

'How, exactly?'

'Asking her for another chance. I would never have gone to her place without all that encouragement.'

'You're taking no responsibility at all?'

'I worshipped that woman, body and soul,' he says, his eyes black and glinting, like wet tar. 'I bet you've never loved anyone in your life, you smug bitch.'

'This is your final warning about verbal abuse.'

His mouth shuts fast, like a trap.

'The prison says you're refusing your anti-psychotic medication. Is that correct?'

'It makes me feel dead inside. What's the point in living, then?'

'When did you stop taking the Largactil?'

'Three days after I got out.'

I study my notes again. 'You were suffering from delusions when you began the stalking, hearing voices telling you how to act. The advice you heard in the pub could have been inside your head, Joe. Was it a combination of alcohol and your old symptoms?'

'No way – it was a hundred per cent real.'

'Do you remember the pub's name?'

'The Carpenter's Arms.'

'How long were you there?'

'I can't remember, with you nagging at me.' His anger drops away suddenly, leaving him a vulnerable child. 'Georgia won't want me now, will she? She must hate my guts.'

He begins to cry. It's a dry, rending sound, like fabric being torn apart. Maybe he's only just worked out that she could die. Some perverse part of me wants to comfort him. The man's illness is so consuming, he's almost killed the woman he loves.

Sinclair is more compliant after his outburst, his voice flat with despair. He explains that his confidence dipped after his release. Going to probation meetings and therapy sessions seemed pointless, when no one would ever give him a job. He rejected all forms of support, which should have sounded alarm bells. He needed much closer monitoring.

I bring the meeting to an end after an hour. I've witnessed no deep contrition in Sinclair's behaviour, and there's little empathy for the pain he's caused, only sadness about the personal cost of his actions. He's refused to describe the stranger he claims spoke to him in the pub, building my belief that he was drinking alone until his delusions escalated. But there's a slim possibility that someone whispered toxic advice into his ear. The police will need to check CCTV footage from the pub he visited to see if he's telling the truth.

Sinclair has withdrawn into his shell, but he does something unexpected on his way out. He leans over to hiss a few words to Dan Fender, like they're sharing a secret. When the guard yanks him back, Sinclair looks triumphant. His eyes shine with victory as he's led away.

'What did he say?'

Dan frowns. 'That his ex got what she deserved.'

The review meeting with my team online takes longer than the session itself. They're tuning in from probation headquarters and universities across the UK, their faces appearing in a grid on the computer screen. Our main learning point is that Sinclair's stalking comes from deep-rooted mental illness, with a likely re-emergence of his psychosis. Failure to treat the underlying illness reignited his stalking behaviour. When we release more ex-offenders into the community, we need tighter monitoring systems and full compliance with their medical regimens.

Dan contributes little to our discussion, as if one ultra-violent act has destroyed his faith in the programme. His expression only brightens when Sally reminds us all that Sinclair is an anomaly. The system works in the vast majority of cases, but we need a holistic approach, with multi-agency backup from the probation service and the stalker's GP. Noah is watching me intently when I draw the meeting to a close. I'd rather not be scrutinized while I deal with the worst case in the programme's history, but it can't be helped. We have to accept that even stalkers who appear to fly through retraining can still pose a threat.

It's one o'clock by the time I leave. Dan remains behind to write up case notes. He'll continue shadowing another fully trained therapist today, as more stalkers in Greenhill attend their weekly discussions on our programme. My time in Joe Sinclair's company makes me long for a hot shower, to remove the stain. I hated the way he vacillated between pride in attacking his victim and sorrow about losing her. I've instructed Dan to get the police to investigate the conversation in the pub. If it was genuine and the individual is found, the nameless stranger should be prosecuted for incitement to violence. It might help me professionally too. If I can prove that someone urged Sinclair to attack Georgia, the Reed family might have a new target for some of their anger.

Noah stays silent as our possessions are returned. The world outside has turned even whiter during the morning, with snow muffling every sound. The bushes lining the car park appear dusted in icing sugar, the snow at our feet powdery as we stand by my car.

'Greenhill's not for the faint-hearted, is it?' he says. 'How could anyone beat an obsession in there?'

'Plenty do, believe me. The programme helps them replace their fixations with self-belief.'

'Sinclair only had sporadic parenting, according to your file. He was ferried between relatives and seen as a problem to offload. You'd need resilience to override that in adult life. It's classic terrain for adult PTSD.'

'That doesn't make him innocent.'

'No, but guilt and responsibility are different things, aren't they?'

I squirm a little, the conversation cutting close to the bone. 'Negligent parenting sometimes makes kids strong. It can motivate them to live better lives.'

'That's true, but rare. They're more likely to experience rampant anxiety.' His half-smile remains in place. 'Staying objective must be tough with offenders like that, Eloise. I don't have your patience. I wanted to punch his lights out, for what it's worth.'

I choke out a laugh. 'That's a measured professional response.'

'I'm just being honest.' He stands his ground. 'Dinner tonight, then. I assume you're coming?'

'Not if you're going to grill me about work.'

'I won't mention it. See you at seven thirty, outside King's?'

Words slip from my mouth unchecked. 'Will it get you off my back?'

'We'll have to wait and see. I'll text you later.'

'You don't have my number.'

'I do, actually. Your art history pal handed it over, in the fellows' common room, yesterday.'

'Lisa? Are you serious?'

'She said you needed some fun.' His smile widens into a grin. 'See you tonight.'

I'm amazed Lisa gave out my number so casually. Maybe she's done it before, not understanding the risk. The snow returns as I drive away, following Noah's low-slung sports car down the A road. My thoughts feel jangled. I noticed him months ago, in the casual way you spot someone attractive on the Tube, then quickly look away. Noah seems harmless, but I was wrong about Sinclair. I could have refused to agree to his release. It feels like I'm losing my judgement about human nature.

Snow whirls in a vortex as I approach the lights, then reality dawns on me. My stalker has got the upper hand after last night's drama. I glance at my rear-view mirror. The same black estate car has followed me since leaving Greenhill. Panic rises in my throat again, making my mouth taste bitter. I indicate, then pull over on a side road, much too fast. My car reels across the ice. I pump the brakes until it ricochets off a lamppost, then spins full circle. My heart hammers in my throat. If a vehicle had been coming in the opposite direction, I'd be dead by now. The black car that was following me sails by, oblivious, leaving me on the hard shoulder to assess the damage.

32

YOU

I'm still shaken when I reach Clive Wadsworth's house on Searle Street, a bunch of hothouse roses from a petrol station on the back seat. I stop to check my damaged front bumper is still attached. It's hanging on by a whisker, like me. I can't tell if the pressure throbbing behind my eyes is from my injury or untapped stress. I should go to Lisa's flat or check into a hotel for some rest, but I need the company of old friends to steady me. Their home lies in a typical Cambridge neighbourhood, near the heart of town, with terraced Victorian properties set back from the pavement by narrow front gardens. The houses huddle together in the snow, like people waiting in a bus queue. The Wadsworths' eccentricity shows in the appearance of their property. The replacement sash windows look expensive, but the rest of the fascia is a mess. The guttering looks set to fall at any minute, and paint is flaking from the front door.

Hilary greets me in the porch. She's a pretty, round-faced woman with a smile that never falters and a distracted air, as if nothing captures her attention for long. Clive told me once that he married her because she's brighter than him and keeps him on his toes. She's in her fifties, with sleek brown hair cut short, wearing a silk shirt and jeans. Her appearance is always far smarter than Clive's. Hilary works as a translator for Cambridge University Press; she's fluent in three European languages. She gives me a hug, then draws me inside, where a small, excitable dog is chasing its tail in circles.

'This one's new, isn't he?' I hand over the flowers, then lean down to pet him.

'Clive insisted, but I have to walk him every day, of course. His name's Byron.'

'Female dogs had better watch out then. What breed is he?'

'A schnoodle – bright but naughty.' Hilary leans closer, speaking in a stage whisper. 'Be warned, Clive's dreading his retirement do. Please don't mention it unless he does.'

'I'll steer clear, don't worry.'

I follow her down the hallway. The wallpaper is faded William Morris, the quarry tiles worn from decades of footsteps. Clive is dressed in a butcher's apron when we enter the kitchen. He appears to have used a dozen pans to cook our meal, leaving them strewn across the worktop. He abandons his apron and pulls me into a hug, then frowns at his wife.

'There's no Worcester sauce, Hills. How can anyone be expected to make a decent fish pie?'

She looks amused. 'Parsley will do fine to flavour it.'

'Can you finish it, please? Nothing's gone to plan.'

'Take Eloise into the living room, then. I'll attempt a rescue.'

'If it's a disaster, call Deliveroo.'

Clive beckons me to come with him. The visit has followed our usual routine so far, the familiarity calming. The Wadsworths' marriage thrives on casual insults and teasing. I loved visiting them when I started my PhD, our friendship gradually evolving from professional to personal. Their living room still resembles a set for a Victorian period drama; books line every wall and a chaise longue faces the French windows, as if the couple take it in turns to lie there and read. The upright piano must be a hundred years old, and their sofas look antique too.

Clive throws himself down on one with his usual drama. 'Cooking traumatizes me, Elly. It triggers memories of lumpy mashed potato, homesickness and watery rice pudding at school. I keep telling Hilary we should eat ready meals and avoid the stress.'

'Cooking's not my forte, either.'

'Lucky for you that Rafe's great in the kitchen. He made us an excellent seafood linguine last time. We thought you'd bring him along.'

I hesitate for a moment. It's tempting to offload every detail of my messy personal life, yet something stops me. Clive has proved his loyalty many times over the years, but he's facing his own problems, so I keep my tone light. 'We're having some problems. I've moved out for now, to get some breathing space.'

His jokey manner vanishes. 'I'm so sorry to hear it. How are you coping?'

'Up and down, to be honest.'

'I couldn't exist without Hilary. But don't tell her that, obviously. It would give her the upper hand.' He shunts his glasses back onto the bridge of his nose. 'You can always stay here, with Jamie. Our place is full of empty rooms.'

The couple have spent plenty of time with Jamie over the years, encouraging him, like adopted grandparents.

'Don't worry, Clive. We're at my aunt's old cottage.'

'Past Girton, on the Fens?'

'How did you know?'

'You mentioned it last year. It sounds terribly remote out there. The Fens give me existential doubt. That huge, echoing landscape is like a blank page.'

'I love it, even in winter.'

'You must be a hardy soul. Freezing north wind, and nowhere to hide.' He gives a mock shiver.

'The sky's ever-changing from my back window, like the sea.'

Clive leans forward. 'Very poetic, but you're low, I can tell. I thought you'd be elated, after your prize.'

'Marina told me your book was considered too. Why didn't you say?'

'Prizes have never motivated me, and why give it to some old fool who's halfway out the door? I've been writing about the same thing for so long, I'm like a cracked record.'

'You'll keep working on buried memory, I hope? Your research is groundbreaking. It's part of every new psychologist's training these days.'

His smile fades. 'It fascinates me, even now, and I've still got to write up my latest study. Fear stops us looking over our shoulders. It takes real emotional maturity to confront your demons.'

Clive's words describe just how I feel. The present is full of hazards, and my past keeps bubbling under the surface, threatening to overwhelm me.

'What are the clinical outcomes like, from your latest research?'

'Worse than the last, I'm afraid. Living with concealed memories is damaging, in most cases. My interviews with army veterans show long-term symptoms like night terrors, addictions and increased risk of suicide. Therapy improves things, but it's still a major indicator for lifelong mental health problems.'

'They never recover on their own?'

'Occasionally new trauma can release a trapped memory. There are studies showing that fresh grief or shock can bring them to the surface. It can be an epiphany, if it doesn't break you in the process.' His eyes glint with interest. 'I'm more bothered about you right now, Elly. I insisted on giving that speech. Marina would have downplayed your success out of jealousy. She wouldn't recognize generosity if it bit her on the arse.'

I'd like to tell Clive about my conversation with our boss. The inquiry hanging over me feels like a burden, as do her veiled threats to my career, but he's still talking.

'Marina hates anyone doing well. Now you've won the prize she'll be gunning for you. Be ready for it.'

'Is she really that toxic?' Clive's ominous tone surprises me.

'She'll try to bring you down, and she doesn't play fair. The woman lies through her teeth. I bet she gives a poisonous little speech at my leaving do, about me never quite achieving my potential after a lifetime's hard work.'

'It's not like you to be so negative about anyone.'

'Marina snatched the top job from me years ago by running a relentless smear campaign. She's still planting rumours to this day.'

I lean in, curious. 'What did she say about you?'

'She told HR I'd been harassing her, which was nonsense, of course.' He shrugs. 'Maybe it worked out for the best in the long run. I've loved my job, without having to boss anyone else around.'

I want to ask more about their vendetta, but the hurt on his face puts the subject off limits. 'You'd have hated being in charge, anyway. Paperwork kills you.'

'Marina should still have paid for her cruelty.' Clive's shoulders are rigid with tension. It surprises me – he's normally so laid back – but maybe he's taking stock, now his career is ending.

The air only clears when Hilary appears in the doorway. 'Lunch is ready, if you can handle some burnt bits.'

The afternoon passes in a flurry of conversation about the

history books Hilary's been translating, and how the couple should celebrate their thirtieth wedding anniversary next summer. Hilary's smile brightens when she asks about Jamie.

'What's he up to these days? Is he still into music?'

'He's having a Joni Mitchell phase, but his rock star dream's over. He's threatening to study IT instead.'

'Stop him, for God's sake. Jamie's too sensitive for a robotic world. Noah Jagiello could tell him about that. He did something clever with computers, in California, before switching back to humanity.' Clive looks amused. 'Hilary has all the details. She's been smitten with him since the department dinner last year.'

'Noah's so charming, it was love at first sight. I hope it's mutual.' She pours herself more wine. 'I plan to leave you, and your silly dog, Clive.'

'Who'd feed me then?' He pats the back of her hand, then turns in my direction. 'Tell me how to survive my leaving do, Elly. I know it's traditional to ruin a Sunday afternoon with a glass of cheap bubbly and tedious chit-chat, but I'd rather skip it. Why deprive everyone of their leisure time to watch me sloping out the door?'

'So we can celebrate your work. You've had a brilliant career, and emeritus professors get full visiting rights, remember? This is just a new phase.'

He smiles at last. 'Bless you, Elly. You're always so comforting.'

Clive's anxiety echoes in his voice, but my own stress levels are falling. The Wadsworths' lifestyle feels like a step back to a gentler time, when intellectual pursuits and conversations mattered above all. When I glance at some photos on their shelf, I spot one I've never noticed before. It was taken when they were young, at a festival somewhere, surrounded by friends in a summer meadow. Hilary's pretty in a flowery dress, but Clive looks like a film star. He's got rugged good looks and appears confident enough to win any challenge. When I look at him now, thirty years later, the echo of his attractiveness remains, but his face is shadowed by sadness.

'They should have promoted you by now,' he says, as I finish my coffee. 'But don't get worn down chasing it. Ambition's no substitute for real life. Too many bright young things burn out along the way.'

'I'm not young anymore, don't worry.'

He looks puzzled. 'Rubbish, you're not even forty. And I bet you're going to the department now, while I take a siesta.'

'Not for long.' I want to go on checking everyone I've had meetings with during the past year, to help identify my stalker.

'I'm warning you, that way madness lies,' Clive says.

'Don't be bossy,' Hilary retorts, her manner teasing. 'Remember, you're not her supervisor anymore.'

'I'm nothing anymore, that's the trouble.'

'You're such a grump,' she says, patting his hand.

Hilary follows me down the hallway to say goodbye, leaving Clive on his favourite sofa with Byron draped across his lap.

She hugs me again. 'Come back soon, won't you? Clive loves seeing old friends. He's quite fragile at the moment.'

'How do you mean?'

'His depression's back, but the old bugger's in denial. The prospect of retiring has knocked him for six.'

'Let me know what I can do.'

'Just keep visiting us, Elly. Seeing younger friends always lifts him. I think he's terrified of losing contact with you all. Lisa Shelby popped round the other night, and he loved every minute. That girl's a hoot, isn't she?' She presses a finger to her lips. 'Don't mention the depression thing to anyone, will you? He'd think me disloyal.'

'Of course not. I'll catch up with you on Sunday.'

It's fully dark by the time I leave at 5 p.m. The snow has stopped falling, but the road is still slick with ice. Hilary is standing in the porch when I look back from my car. She must be freezing, yet she's waiting to wave me on my journey. The news about Clive's mental health is a surprise. He's been an ally ever since I joined the university, his mercurial spirit making him fun to be around.

I caught a glimpse of the negativity he must battle every day from his speech about Marina. Our boss strikes me as too cool for such a heated vendetta, yet there must be a grain of truth in it. I can't imagine her fabricating a story about Clive harassing her without a trigger of some kind, but the picture's confused. I still can't reconcile the way she helped me with her announcement that my career is at risk.

The streets are quiet when I drive away towards the town centre. Most people have retreated indoors, with curtains closed in houses by the roadside as I reach Jesus Green. Church spires are lit up in the distance, needle-sharp against the sky. The empty parkland is carpeted with snow, but I remember many summer days there with Rafe and Jamie, eating picnics by the river and watching punts sail by. Those memories seem out of reach, but they linger on my retinas, like I've gazed too long at the sun.

I leave my car on Regent Street instead of risking the department parking area after dark. The city is quieter than usual, with few students around to enjoy happy hour in the bars that line both sides of the streets. There's no sign of Reg Bellamy when I enter the quadrangle, even though his lodge is brightly lit. My pass card only works on my third attempt, as if the system resents having to allow me inside. I wait for the lights to stop flickering before climbing the stairs. The place is so empty, the only sound my heels clicking on lino. The building appears to be holding its breath, waiting for students to return. Its odd atmosphere hits me again.

No more messages have been shoved under my door when I enter my office, but even that feels like a trick, to give me a false sense of security. I switch on my computer to download more contact details to check. I focused on my stalker being an ex-offender at the start, but I must have missed someone obvious. Anonymous stalking is normally done by people close to the victim, aware of their every move but terrified of exposure. I still can't rule out my friends and family, yet the only one who's hurt me is Rafe.

When I check my phone half an hour later, Jamie has texted to say that he's spending the night at Billy Rawle's house, which makes me smile. Jennifer's intervention has failed, just as I predicted. He reminds me of my promise not to go back to the cottage tonight. I'm relieved that Jamie will be somewhere safe, after last night's ordeal.

The quadrangle is deserted when I glance out of the window, the building still in hibernation. The only lit window is directly opposite, where I spot Dan Fender in his bare living room. He probably got back from Greenhill an hour or two ago, after witnessing more stalkers describing their obsessions. When I look closer, he's hunched over his desk again, and his posture suddenly makes sense. His head's down, hands clasped tight in front of his chest. He's praying, not studying, lost in silent contemplation, and I can understand why. Listening to people's delusions for hours can warp your view of the world. Many are so convinced their fantasies are real that it takes a strong personality to avoid getting sucked into the whirlpool.

Dan's religious background sets us apart. I don't believe that anyone's born good or evil: life is more complex, with plenty of grey areas in between. We all carry the capacity to wound or to heal, driven by mixed emotions. If faith is central to his life, the stalkers we treat must seem like the worst sinners, determined to hurt victims they claim to love, yet maybe it gives him greater compassion too.

Lisa's warning has stayed with me, so I key Dan's name into my search engine. Nothing comes up apart from Facebook photos and his Cambridge credentials as a research assistant. I keep trying to find anything that might incriminate him, but all I discover is his last picture from high school. He looks clean-cut and likable, his smile genuine. The picture only changes when I finally tap in the name of his old university and find a news story that's six years old. My tension rises as I check the details and learn that a fellow student sued him for harassment. Her charges weren't upheld, but the case wasn't cut and dried. The judge ordered Dan's family to pay her legal fees. The following year, his father, a Baptist preacher, sued her for reputational damages, but lost his case.

It amazes me that no one in human resources did a thorough enough background check to realize Dan was accused of the very crime he's chosen to research. It should have ruled him out, on ethical grounds, yet his behaviour has given me no cause for concern until today.

Dan's window is dark now, the curtains closed, and my discomfort's growing. Maybe Lisa has been right all along. It makes sense that a stalker might choose to study the subject, hoping to beat their obsession, only to fall prey to it again. It feels like things are coming to a head. I'll have to put my own situation in the public eye at last, even if it leads to conflict at work. HR have to know the truth about Dan. I concentrate on downloading information about his trial in the US, passing it on, making it their responsibility. Even if they take no action, it will be on record, if he turns out to be the culprit.

It's almost time to meet Noah. The idea of being his dinner companion puts me on edge, even though we'll be surrounded by dozens more guests. I'm just putting on my academic gown when footsteps echo in the corridor, slow and regular. It sounds like someone's carrying a heavy weight, or they're built on a giant scale, like Dan Fender. The noise is magnified now everything else is silent, like the dripping tap at the cottage. Each footstep raises my stress level.

I scrabble with the bolt on my door, locking myself inside. The footsteps continue. It could be one of my colleagues, or Reg Bellamy doing final checks before locking up for the night. Suddenly a door slams, and my heart thumps in my chest. Someone's running downstairs, the noise like a fist battering on metal. The building's ghosts couldn't create that much racket. But when I look out of the window again, no one emerges into the quadrangle. They must be waiting downstairs, where the corridors are a labyrinth of offices and treatment rooms.

My stalker could be hiding by the exit to catch me as I leave. Suddenly a story pops into my head that made the news years ago. It took place one evening at another university, but the situation was like mine. A female lecturer and one of her male students were the only people left in college when he became psychotic. She locked herself in a broom cupboard, with no access to her phone, while he screamed abuse through the door. The woman waited hours, until the building fell silent, believing she was safe to come out. He was still there. The man strangled her, then ran away. It took the police days to track him down.

I keep my back to the door, shaky with adrenaline. I was stupid to take this risk in a deserted building. I can't put myself in danger again, so I pick up the phone and call the porter's mobile number. Reg Bellamy picks up after three rings, his tone courteous.

'Where are you right now, Reg?'

'Take a guess, Dr Shaw.' He gives a quiet laugh. 'The lodge is my second home.'

'I've heard noises outside my office and I think there's an intruder in the building. Would you mind checking for me?'

'No problem. Wait there, please. I'm on my way.'

I watch him round the corner below from my window, yellow light spilling onto the snow. Whoever came here is probably long gone, but I can't risk it. Reg looks solemn when he arrives a few minutes later. The place has been quiet all day, he says. Only a few postgraduate students are staying in the accommodation block opposite, although he wouldn't have seen any staff members entering by the back gates using pass cards. The only other members of staff he's spoken to this afternoon are Dan Fender and Professor Westbrook.

'Please call me straight away if anything odd happens again. It's my job to keep you all safe.' He looks at my door. 'Want me to fit a stronger bolt, just in case?'

'I'm probably overreacting.'

'I'll get it sorted tomorrow. All the doors on this floor need maintenance. They're the originals, so the hinges are weak. I've told the bursar, but getting money out of them's like squeezing blood from a stone. I'll see what I can do with yours.'

'Sorry to give you more work.'

'It's no problem. Things are quiet with the students away. It was like that in my day too, at the end of term.'

'That's a surprise. You never mentioned studying here yourself, Reg.'

'I only did two years in the engineering department, then had to leave to find work.'

'I'm sorry you didn't get to complete.'

'It's ancient history, but if I had my time over, I'd pick

psychology, like you. The human mind fascinates me, although I don't pretend to understand what motivates us to do good or evil.' He's gazing down at me with fierce concentration. 'Would you like me to escort you out of the building?'

The man's politeness never fails, but he puts me on edge, walking at my side a fraction too close. His words are more reassuring than his physical presence. He suggests that the noise may have been perfectly innocent, just a colleague collecting something from their office then rushing back downstairs. Most people cross the quadrangle and pass the lodge on their way out, but they could easily have used the back exit. I know my fear is spiralling if even a colleague like Reg makes me feel nervous. He may have the ideal job to keep tabs on me, but he's trusted by everyone.

I must still look spooked, because Reg offers to walk me to my car, until I explain that I'll be fine heading to King's on my own. When I glance back, he's standing by the entrance to his lodge, watching me leave. The story he told helps to explain why he's so invested in the university. He came here with hopes and dreams, like every other student. Now he's made it his life's work to safeguard everyone inside the building he sees as his own.

There are more people on Regent Street now, swaddled in winter coats, their breath freezing in clouds as they choose which bar to visit. My heart rate slows as I head for the market square. The pressure inside my skull has eased since earlier today, although pain still needles the crown of my head. I know the wisest thing would be to call Noah and apologize, then wait in Casualty for another scan. But the rational side of me keeps losing the argument.

Town seems quiet as I pass the Arts Cinema and Emmanuel

College lying in darkness. The market square is empty, with the striped awnings of stalls rolled up for the evening, the cobbles slick with ice.

My tension returns, suddenly, like before. Someone is watching me again. Maybe they followed me from work. The sensation brings me to a halt, my feet slipping on the icy pavement. I steady myself fast, my hand resting against the nearest building. The square appears empty, until I spot something flickering in the darkness and pain burns my temples again. If it's my stalker there's no one here to help me.

A figure is standing in an alleyway opposite, across the square, half-hidden by shadows. They're wrapped in a long coat, hood raised, already retreating. I need to see their face before they vanish.

'Coward,' I yell at the top of my voice.

My fear has been replaced by anger about everything I'm losing. If Dan Fender was haunting my corridor, he could easily have followed me here, but the figure's vanishing. I approach the alleyway at a steady pace. It's madness to risk it, but the feelings boiling in my chest are too hot to control. If I had a gun, I'd fire bullets into that dark opening, to end this stand-off at last.

I've only covered ten metres when footsteps pound into the distance. I feel elated now they're the one running scared. The tables might be turning in my favour at last. My good mood is short-lived. My actions contradict the advice I give to stalking victims every week about staying safe, never letting your aggressor get close.

My recklessness only hits me once I've calmed down. It feels like I'm standing on the edge of a precipice, with thoughts no longer my own. Is this how madness feels? I tried to be the best mother, wife and colleague, yet none of it's worked. It feels like

I'm losing myself. I don't even know if the figure I saw tonight was real or imaginary, just like I can't be certain if my hands are shaking from fear, or the bone-deep cold.

33

ME

Anger wells in my chest for the first time today. How dare you call me a coward, when you're the one that quakes when you open my letters? There's fear in your voice when I play back your private conversations at night. Your words are hesitant, even though you pretend to be calm. I could have exposed my identity just now, to enjoy the shock on your face, but there are steps to complete first. I need to hurt the people closest to you, with help from my ally. I've been keeping tabs on the people you love too, without triggering their suspicion.

You need to understand how it feels to lose everything, with no one left to trust. I experienced catastrophic loss when I was too young to understand the consequences, thanks to you. Why should your existence be happier than mine when you've caused me so much suffering?

I had to take back control. I'm amazed how straightforward it's been to damage your career, once the basics were achieved. It took effort to hack into your work email and the files you've downloaded, but I've always enjoyed playing around on computers. That allowed me to delete your report and deny you access to your workplace whenever I like.

I found out the release dates of the prisoners on your programme, too. Joe Sinclair was lonely and broken after his spell in jail. It only took two beers to win his confidence, and the pair of us must have looked so innocent. A murmured conversation between strangers in a bar. Sinclair was like an attack dog. All I had to do was bait him, then watch him leap. I regret what happened to the girl, of course, but that was a necessary evil. I had to prove you're fallible, like the rest of us. Georgia Reed's father is helping my cause. Soon your professional reputation will be destroyed, and Cambridge University will cut you adrift the minute your licence is revoked. Then you'll have nowhere left to turn.

I want you to guess my identity without any crude revelations. We're reaching a tipping point in our battle. I could still stop my campaign and pretend nothing has happened, leaving the calm surface of my life undisturbed, but soon there will be no turning back. It's fortunate that I've found someone naïve to help me with the final stage, prepared to do whatever I ask. The fight between us needs to end soon. I can't rest while you're alive. Sometimes I regret watching you so closely. I've grown to respect you in the process of tearing you apart. Maybe that was inevitable, but it makes my goal harder to achieve.

34

YOU

I have to calm myself before heading to King's College, inhaling deep breaths of icy air. Noah is waiting outside, tall and distinguished in his black gown, smiling like we're conspirators. I feel like a fraud in this setting, now my status is undermined, but Cambridge has always attracted dissemblers. It used to be a breeding ground for spies and is rumoured still to be a favourite spot for MI6 recruiters. Noah would make a good double agent. His manner is always relaxed and confident, as if nothing troubles him.

We join the line of fellows trooping towards the Great Hall in the uniform that makes us interchangeable. Our gowns allow us to march through any college or department, unchecked. Maybe that's what happened tonight? Reg Bellamy is so used to seeing teaching staff stroll by in their black cloaks, he may not have noticed my stalker in disguise.

'You look thoughtful,' Noah says.

'I'm just processing my day.'

'But work's off limits tonight, isn't it?'

'Definitely, I need to unwind. How come you were invited here?' King's is the top destination for fine dining in Cambridge, and invitations are highly prized.

'The Master's from Warsaw. Maybe he scoured the staff lists for Polish names and found mine.'

'Are you serious?'

'No, but it's a nice theory. Or he may know about my legendary conversation skills.'

'Or your ridiculous car?' It's easier to tease him than stray onto serious topics.

He laughs back at me. 'It was a whim, but I have no regrets.'

Noah's arm brushes mine as we wait to enter the hall. There's a crackle of attraction between us, but the timing's wrong. Rafe made a stupid decision; that doesn't mean I should do the same. The buzz of conversation falls silent as the heavy wooden doors swing open. The hall's grandeur is humbling, even though I've dined here plenty of times. Its vaulted ceiling towers fifty feet over our heads, the space full of echoes. It's big enough to accommodate three hundred guests, with lit candles flickering on ranks of tables covered in white damask cloths.

I glance up at the stained-glass windows and panelled walls, gradually calming myself. Portraits of ancient scholars gaze down at us, observing the crowd with no sign of judgement. My stalker may have got here first, but they can't harm me in such a packed environment, surely? A dozen waiters are already weaving between tables, serving drinks and hors d'oeuvres. We sit at a table laid for ten guests. Even the white linen and silver cutlery feel sedate, and I'm determined to stay in the moment. I'll finish the meal then walk straight to a hotel to honour my promise to Jamie.

Cambridge dinners always follow the same protocol. It's considered rude to speak only to one guest; shared meals are meant to encourage networking and break down barriers between academic disciplines. The woman next to me is a visiting astrophysicist from Tokyo. She's been invited here to give a guest lecture on the origins of the universe. It's a relief to listen to her talk about quantum physics and deep space. The concepts sound beautiful, even though most of them fly over my head. She tells me about a Dark Sky festival that takes place in the Arizona desert, where there's minimal light pollution. Thousands of stargazers spend the night outside every year, watching for shooting stars and meteor showers. Her manner is so calm it's hard to believe any external threats exist, in this universe or another.

Waiters bring more delicacies to our table. I don't have much appetite and the hors d'oeuvres look too perfect to eat. They're soon followed by fish and meat dishes. It's easy to see why fellows gain weight, eating regular five-course dinners. My attention only returns to Noah when the desserts are served. He's quiet but alert, his attention focused on me. Our chairs are squeezed so close together I can feel the heat from his body. It's time to leave, while this is still an innocent meeting between colleagues.

'I'll skip this course. Thanks for the invite, Noah, I've had a great evening.'

His voice drops, like he's sharing a secret. 'Have coffee with me before you go. You can see my nasty little flat.'

'It sounds so appealing.'

'Come anyway, I have a brand-new espresso machine.'

Noah's hand skims mine under the table, and it dawns on me that I don't have a marriage left to defend. Even so, the old me used to be cautious. I don't recognize this new recklessness, yet it's leading the way. It's too late to change my mind.

It's 10 p.m. when we emerge back into the market square. Noah's flat is close by, on Portugal Place. We exchange gossip about some university eccentrics, including one emeritus professor who's worn the same suit for so long it's falling apart at the seams. Hyper-intelligence seems to safeguard people from caring about public opinion, which must be a blessing. It used to hurt when people on social media criticized my appearance at the start, ignoring the information I share. I'm used to it now. A few still call me a hard-faced, ball-breaking bitch, determined to keep innocent men in jail. I used to believe that one of them could be my stalker, tracking my every word, but it feels much more personal now. They seem to know all my secrets.

I check our surroundings at Noah's turning, looking for anyone loitering between buildings. The streets are empty. People must still be drinking in the pubs along Bridge Street or keeping warm at home. I've got a nagging feeling that my stalker is close by, but there's nothing I can do about it, except book a taxi straight to a hotel after a quick coffee.

Portugal Place is easy to miss unless you're a Cambridge insider. The turning is only accessible on foot, lying between a Portuguese café and the Round Church, one of the city's oldest buildings. We cross snow-covered flagstones to reach Noah's flat. Georgian buildings wind towards Jesus Green and number four is the tallest, with light shining from its upstairs windows. The door clicks open after he presses numbers into a keypad.

The flat is on the ground floor. It looks studenty, with rugs on bare floorboards, IKEA furniture and rickety bookshelves. He leaves me alone and goes to make coffee. I can tell his friends play a crucial role in his life from the photos on his mantelpiece. The same gang appear on summer beaches, or on walking holidays, carrying backpacks. I'm still studying the pictures when Noah returns with mugs of coffee that smell bitter and rich.

'I hope you like Blue Mountain. I get it delivered from the importer.'

'It's wasted on me, sadly. I'm no connoisseur.'

'It's my biggest vice,' he says. 'I even grind my own beans. There's brandy somewhere too if you'd prefer a nightcap.'

'Just coffee's fine.'

His kitchen is small and tidy compared to the Wadsworths'. There are no candles burning on the table, so I can still pretend we're just two workmates being sociable. I spot a saxophone propped against the wall, covered in scratches, as if the silver metal has survived a long journey.

'Are you musical, Noah?'

'It's just a hobby. I can't play much here, but I might sound-proof a room in my new place.'

'Maybe it's a prop, like your car, to make you seem interesting?'

'Is that a dare?' Noah still seems happy to be teased. He picks up his saxophone, then breathes out a complex melody, minor notes lingering in the room.

'I stand corrected, that's beautiful. Only my son's got talent in my family. He plays the guitar and drums pretty well.'

'Like many teenage rebels.' Noah's still clutching the saxophone, like a lifeline. 'I wanted to invite you here sooner, Eloise, but I bottled out. A college dinner seemed like a good place to start.'

It's an odd speech from such a confident man. Until now he's seemed at ease in any social situation.

'I've eaten well today. Clive and his wife made me lunch earlier.'

'Those two are favourites of mine. Clive mentored me at the start. I loved his honesty about the toll academia can take on us all. He let slip that he's been depressed recently, but I imagine you know that already.'

'I've known him years, but never realized how tough it's been for him until his wife mentioned it today.'

'He was your supervisor, wasn't he? Maybe he still sees you as his protégé. The guy takes his work seriously, behind all that mock-cynicism.'

Noah explains that his own job in the department came as a

surprise. He was working at Harvard when Cambridge offered him a fellowship, out of the blue.

'I had to come back, sooner or later, to remind myself how to be British.'

'I hear you worked in IT for a while?'

He grimaces. 'A giant tech company in California needed shrinks to help their computers behave like humans. It bothered me after a while. Why create machines that can outwit us at every turn? I don't fancy life in a technocracy.'

'Me neither. Where did you grow up, Noah?'

He looks amused. 'Can't you tell, from my accent? My name's misleading – I've only been to Poland once.'

'There's some North America in there, but the rest's a mystery.'

'Take a guess, but it's high stakes. If you're wrong, our friendship's over.'

I consider for a minute. 'Liverpool?'

'Correct.'

A laugh escapes me. 'Thank God. I almost said Manchester.'

'My dad came over from Gdansk in the seventies. Mum's a true Scouser.' He studies me again. 'I bet you don't even remember us meeting for the first time, twenty years ago, do you?'

I can feel my backbone stiffening. 'What do you mean?'

'Don't look so worried. You were in the year below me at uni in York, always in the library, or hanging out with your mates in the bar.'

'You never mentioned it till now.'

'It's not important.' He's still staring, yet I don't pull back. 'I was already dating my wife, Suzanne. We lived together, in a flat on Wetherby Road.'

Tension eases from my body slowly. 'My house share was just round the corner. I must have seen you both loads of times, but I don't remember.'

'I was a mess back then. Suzanne had to fix my image from the ground up.' He shifts direction again. 'How are you feeling about your prize? Has it sunk in yet?'

'It feels awkward. I hear your book was considered too, and Clive's.'

He shrugs the comment away. 'I was just glad to reach the shortlist. You deserve it, for creating a programme to fix a social problem that won't go away.'

'It's not fail-safe, that's the problem, as you saw today.'

'Nothing in psychology's guaranteed, is it? I practised for months before accepting that some patients never get cured. We can only reduce their suffering by a fraction.'

'Where did you start out?'

'Serbia, working on juvenile trauma, with kids under ten. Most were orphans, so it was like psychological first aid.'

'That sounds like a baptism of fire.'

'The only thing I regret is almost losing an eye to flying mortar. They sewed me back together in a field hospital.'

He taps the scar on his cheek with his index finger, gently, like it still hurts, then describes his work for Médecins Sans Frontières in more detail. He spent years helping children from both sides of the battle cope with appalling losses. It reminds me of Leo claiming that there's nothing so broken it can't be rebuilt. But my brother was talking about ceramics, not flesh and blood.

Our conversation drifts between the past and present. I barely notice an hour passing until Noah reaches out to push a strand of hair back from my cheek. His gesture makes me freeze. I feel guilty, despite doing nothing wrong. I owe Rafe no loyalty at all. When Noah runs his fingertip along my jaw, I have to suppress a shiver.

'I forget to breathe sometimes, when you're around.' He looks embarrassed. 'Sorry, I shouldn't have told you.'

'It's okay to speak your mind.'

'You'd have guessed how I feel, sooner or later.'

'Where's your wife in all this?'

'Gone.' His eyes blink shut. 'I assumed you knew.'

When I shake my head, he begins to speak again, his words slow and quiet.

'It was Suzanne's idea for us to work abroad. She was the driving force in our marriage, until she died of breast cancer, two years ago. We wanted kids, but the treatment left her infertile.'

Noah appears to be scanning the table's wooden surface for flaws. I could tell him I'm sorry, but words seem pointless, so I touch his hand instead.

'Want to see a picture of her?'

'Please.'

A dark-haired woman in her thirties looks back at me from his phone. She's lying on a hospital bed with a cannula in her arm, beaming for the camera like she's the happiest person alive. She's beautiful, but skeletally thin. Noah's sports car makes more sense now; it was his reward for surviving the worst pain imaginable.

'I had to make sacrifices to win her at the start. Three trips to Oxfam with all my clothes in binbags,' he says, stifling a laugh. 'She was way stronger than me.'

'You must be resilient too. It takes guts, just to keep going.'

Something inside me is shifting position. I thought he could be my stalker, but his story seems to put him beyond suspicion. Still, my old doubt lingers. I could be exonerating him just because he's so attractive.

'Suzanne made me promise not to let years pass without fancying someone and acting on it.'

My laughter takes me by surprise. 'That's why I'm here?'

'Partly, yes.'

'I'm flattered, but I should go. The coffee was great, thanks.'

'Not yet, please. Something's bothering you too, isn't it?'

I take a deep breath before answering. 'I've got a stalker. It's been going on for months.'

The shock on his face looks real. 'That's a nasty irony, given your job, isn't it?'

I give him an outline, and find myself mentioning Rafe's affair too. It feels like I'm spinning. I can no longer tell right from wrong, and there's a well of fury in my gut because my world's fragmenting and I can't stop it.

'I can hardly believe it, Elly. You seemed like the most sorted person around when we met, keeping the world at bay. Forgive me for sounding like a shrink, but I assumed some kind of trauma, past or present, had made you that way.'

'That's perceptive. Childhood marks us all, doesn't it? I haven't seen my mother for years. She's dying now, in a care home.'

'My family's supported me better since losing Suzanne, but it could have gone either way. It's not too late to visit your mum.'

'I don't agree. You don't miss what you never had.'

'Or it makes you yearn for it even more. You know what they say about catharsis: the pain is easier to carry afterwards.'

Carla gave similar advice, yet he sounds more convincing. I can't tell if a last visit would fix anything, but the decision needs to be made soon.

'Stay here tonight, Eloise, don't be alone. I'll sleep on the sofa.'

'I need to go, for obvious reasons.'

'Why?'

'We'd end up in bed.'

'That sounds fine to me. I've wanted you for months, more than anything.'

I stumble to my feet. Fear only sets in when he stands by the door, blocking my escape route, yet I reach for him first, shocked by my own reaction. Noah's expression softens, then instinct takes over. I rise onto the balls of my feet to kiss him, his arms locking round my waist, pulling me close. His breath is warm against my neck, hands skimming my body.

It's the first time another man's touched me in years. My nerve endings feel electric. Everything's happening so fast, it seems like we're racing. My teeth graze the skin on his shoulder as he strips off his shirt. The only thing in my mind now is physical need. It burns my concerns away. Our hands fumble with buttons and zips, until every barrier's gone.

'Me and you, at last. Nothing in our way.'

He breathes the words into my ear as we land on his sofa. The echo of my stalker's threats is too loud, yet I don't care. Our limbs are entwined already. It's too late to stop. I'd forgotten how good it feels to explore a man's body for the first time: the new territory of his skin is breathtaking, exciting, raw. There's too much noise in my mind as I finally let go. It's the sound of my old world shattering, the wall I built around myself suddenly torn down. My legs are still tight around his waist when I feel him climax, the overhead light in his living room shining down on us.

When I look up, I see that his curtains aren't properly closed. There's an inch-wide gap in the fabric. My stalker could be staring inside right now, watching us. Noah spots it too. He stumbles to his feet, punch drunk, then pulls the curtains shut. It ensures our privacy, but his gesture may be too late. My reactions are still too visceral to care. Noah looks beautiful naked. He's tall and rangy, with ridged muscles on his arms from regular trips to the gym.

'You're safe here, with me,' he says. 'No one can hurt you.'

He leads me to his bedroom. There's a muted light by the bed illuminating dark green walls, and I'm too tired to argue.

Exhaustion soon takes over, the telltale pain behind my eyes needling me again. I fall asleep instantly, with his arm tight around my shoulders.

35

Saturday 13 November

YOU

A sound startles me alert. It's a car door slamming in a street nearby. The city is already waking up, but my brain is sluggish. I don't remember what happened last night until I see a framed wedding photo of Noah and his bride on the bedside table, taken before she got sick. The couple are standing outside a register office, their smiles incandescent, with friends crowding them on the steps. A haze of confetti lingers in the air like snowflakes, and I feel guilty for taking her place, even though she's gone. I don't know if the woman Rafe's been sleeping with ever feels the same, or if she's too blasé to care.

Noah is still asleep. The urge to escape is overwhelming, even though his face looks innocent. I can't just lie here until he opens his eyes and then talk about what happened. The sex was great, but I'm still too confused to understand what it means. I have to focus on the problem in hand. The stalking won't stop, and Jamie's life and mine can't go back to normal until I end it. I use Noah's bathroom, rinsing away doubt in the heat of his shower.

Last night doesn't have to be a problem between us, yet I feel like a teenager, embarrassed by our sudden intimacy.

The city is too loud when I escape onto Bridge Street before 8 a.m. It's humming with buses and taxis. People are heading to work or running early-morning errands when I set off for Bill's café. It used to be Jamie's favourite when he was small. He always ordered a huge stack of pancakes with fruit and maple syrup. I don't feel hungry, but it's one of the few places that opens early. I walk over melted snow that's frozen overnight, turning the pavements into an ice rink. It's impossible to be sure, but I'm almost certain no one's following me.

Bill's is a jumble of wooden tables and velvet-covered chairs, starting to look tatty. The place feels welcoming until I spot Dan Fender at a table nearby, peering at his laptop. My anxiety rises, knowing that he was accused of harassment back in the States. When he beckons me over it's too late to escape.

'You're working, Dan. I won't disturb you.'

He shuts his laptop with a hard, snapping sound. 'It's just a few emails. I'm surprised to see you, Eloise. You're normally in your office by now.'

There's a hint of anger in his voice. I know he could be my stalker, yet my gaze locks onto his, turning our conversation into a staring contest. My feelings have changed since learning the truth about him. Direct questions won't work, but I need to ask them anyway. If it was him in the square last night, following me, he must be terrified of exposure.

'How did it go at Greenhill yesterday afternoon, Dan?'

'Badly, to be honest. I kept seeing human cruelty all around me.'

'That's why professional boundaries matter.'

'You're the expert there, not me.' He spits out the words. 'I'm not cut out for forensic psychology, I realize that now.'

'I don't understand. You've always been so committed to our work.'

'You'll think I'm weak if I explain.'

'No, I'd never make judgements.'

He heaves in a breath. 'There's this gap between my old life and now, sitting here with you. Most days I hardly recognize myself.' He falls silent for a moment when the server brings his drink. 'My faith was a big part of my existence back in Ohio, especially after I had a crisis at university with my first girlfriend.'

'How do you mean?'

'She rejected me, but I couldn't handle it. It seems like madness now.' He screws his eyes shut. 'I used to drive to her apartment, then follow her down the street, begging her to come back. She tried letting me down gently, but that made it worse. I had the darkest thoughts imaginable.'

'Like what, exactly?'

'I considered throwing acid in her face to see her suffer, like me. That was the turning point. I knew it was crazy even to consider it.'

'Did you get therapy?'

'There was no need. God came back into my life, that was the turning point.'

'Your faith stopped you stalking her again?'

'And my family's support.' A tear spills down his cheek. 'Prayer doesn't work for me anymore, and Stacey's visit made it worse. She was mad at me for skipping church. She thinks God's the only one who can protect us from evil.'

'Are you afraid it could happen again?'

He looks upset. 'No way, I'd spot the signs. But my life feels hollow. There's this emptiness running through my core.'

The picture makes sense at last. Dan's crisis isn't about me. I knew there was nothing to fear – from him, at least. The band of pain around my skull loosens again.

'How can I help you?'

'I'll have to do it myself. There's just silence now, when I pray. It's this void nothing can fill.'

'Was it like that after your relationship ended?'

'The pain was all focused on my ex. Stalking was a sickness I conquered, with help from my church. It made me feel invincible for a while. I wanted to show others that recovery is possible, but our work forces me to remember the worst part of myself.'

'But that's in the past now, Dan. Maybe you just need a break.'

'I've made my decision. I'll finish my studies this term, then go home early and find another job, without so much pressure.' Dan stumbles to his feet abruptly, then hurries away. He leaves the door gaping until a waiter closes it, shutting out the cold.

The conversation leaves me shaken, as I swap seats to keep an eye on the street. It's another habit that's developed since my stalking began. I can no longer sit with my back to a door in a public place. I only spot a scrap of paper Dan's left behind when a waiter delivers my cappuccino. His handwriting is bold and easy to read, unlike my stalker's thin scrawl, reassuring me again that he's not involved. I study the words closely:

Our Father, who art in heaven, hallowed be thy name.

He's written the Lord's Prayer in full, the poetic version you hear in churches. He appears desperate to regain his faith, and I don't blame him. We all have crutches – people, or drugs – we rely on in a crisis. Dan's experiencing a dark night of the soul, and there's no point in regretting losing him from my team. I might not even have a job myself in few months' time.

It's snowing again as I finish my coffee, but the decision I've been seeking has finally crystallized. I've avoided entering my mother's care home on Histon Road until now. Maybe I should be grateful that I'm less fearful since my injury. I need to hear her explanation for sending me away, even if it hurts. I can't imagine any crime Jamie could commit that would make me reject him for ever, yet she was so eager to let me go.

The drive takes ages, my car slowed by traffic through the town centre. My thoughts jitter between the past and present. Thirty years have passed since my mother banished me from our home in Chiswick to the cottage in the middle of nowhere. I can't remember what happened that day, apart from crying in the car and arriving at the cottage in a state of shock. Pete and Lucy told me the arrangement was only temporary, at first, but weeks turned into years. It took me a long time to settle, even though they were loving. None of my other relatives came to visit, which didn't make sense. Did she throw down an ultimatum to them too: me or her?

I pull up in the car park outside the care home. The big Victorian building still looks grand, but there's no glamour today. An old man is being led outside, leaning on his Zimmer frame, to a waiting taxi. I'm certain he'll be going to a hospital appointment, not returning home. These places all share an unspoken rule: once you arrive, there's no going back.

The reception area is empty, so I follow the sound of voices. Residents are still eating breakfast, taking slow spoonfuls of cereal, like one meal could last them all day. The place feels claustrophobic, the air smelling of fried bacon, burnt toast and despair. I'm searching for my mother, but as she appeared thirty years ago, a tall blonde with a movie star's face that could switch from soft to hard in moments. Everything's changed since then. She's locked inside an institution with few comforts, and I've got no idea how she looks. She was exactly the age I am now the last time we were together.

'Are you looking for someone?' A young man in a blue carer's uniform appears at my side.

'Ingrid Kielsen.'

'Great, she loves having visitors. Are you family?'

'I'm her oldest daughter. We haven't spoken for a long time.'

'She'll be delighted. Come this way. Ingrid always sits in the garden room.'

He leads me down a corridor lined with closed doors which reminds me of Greenhill Prison. The air smells of bleach and boiled cabbage; kitchenhands must be preparing lunch already. We enter a large conservatory. It's chilly, and full of old rattan furniture, but it's brighter than the other rooms, at least. Cold light floods down through the glass roof. There's no sign of my mother, just a cluster of residents in a group, drinking tea.

'There's Ingrid,' the carer says, pointing ahead. 'Don't worry if she's snappy at first. The Alzheimer's can make her bad-tempered; she has good days and bad.'

My mother is alone, huddled by the window, looking out at the bedraggled garden. The plants are reduced to bare sticks, the lawn covered in snow. She had so much power over my life that it's a shock to see her white-haired and vulnerable. She appears frail, yet my heart's beating too fast, my mouth as dry as sand.

She remains focused on the garden, giving me time to observe her, at last. Her eyes have shrunk deep into their sockets and her skin is translucent, the veins at her temple dark blue, like a river's tributaries. Minutes pass before she turns in my direction.

'I hate this place,' she whispers. Her Danish accent is stronger than I remembered. 'Let me go home, please. There's nothing for me here.'

'I'm sorry you feel that way. Do you remember me?'

She gives me a sidelong glance. 'I've never seen you before.'

'You have, Ingrid. We're different people now, that's all.'

I can see traces of her old elegance. Her dark green dress is buttoned to the throat, a pearl necklace half-hidden under her collar.

'My children were such sweet babies. A boy and a girl. Do you want to see?' She scrabbles in her bag, but her hands emerge empty. 'Gone. They steal everything here, even pictures of my children.'

'You had three, didn't you? Eloise, Leo and Carla.'

'Just two.' Her voice is firm. 'A boy and a girl.'

'You must remember your first child, surely? You named me Eloise, after your mother.'

She glances at me, then gazes outside. 'It's a disgrace to leave a garden in that state. They should plant evergreens. It's a wilderness each winter.'

'Can I ask you a few questions? Then I'll leave you in peace.'

She gives a shallow laugh. 'Peace doesn't exist, only wars, my whole lifetime.'

'I can't remember what happened, after Dad got hurt. You could help me piece it together.'

'Leo and Carla. My sweet babies.' She repeats the words, like a mantra, drowning out my voice.

'They brought Dad home from hospital, Pete and Lucy told me that. You cared for him until he died a few weeks later, didn't you?'

'My husband fell. Broken, all broken. Nothing I could do.' Her hands tremble as she makes a shooing motion, sending me away, but I remain seated, still looking for the truth.

'Did you blame me for his death?'

'Go now, or I'll scream.' She turns her head away. 'I can't look at you.'

'Why not?'

'Your fault, not mine. That awful light in your eyes. Always fighting me,' she hisses. 'Devil child.'

'Dad loved me. What happened to make him so desperate?'

'You, not me. Lies from you, always lies.'

Her claw-like hands lash out suddenly, one of her nails scratching my cheek. My own flashes of temper since my fall must come from her, not Dad. I'm surprised by her strength. She looks shadowy, but it's deceiving. The force of her will is powerful, as is her ability to protect herself. She's shutting down now, eyes closed to block me out. A thin wail comes from her mouth, rising to a roar. It has the desired effect. The carer I met earlier hurries over, and her shrieking falls quiet.

'This happens sometimes, don't worry. Ingrid yelled at your brother last week too. She panics if her routine changes. That's why your sister Carla visits so often, to calm her down.'

'She's here a lot?'

'Almost every day.' He nods rapidly. 'Why not pop back one afternoon? Your mum's calmer after her medication.'

Carla implied that moving Mum so close was a duty that weighed on her, yet she spends so much time here. Why did she lie? The question lingers in my head. My mother is still moaning when the carer helps her out of her chair. She glowers at me, before being led away, leaving me shaken.

I've gained no fresh information from my visit, except that Ingrid is refusing to acknowledge my existence and still blames me for my father's death. The scratch on my cheek is nothing compared to the pain I've lived with since my attack. It only hurts because it's the one thing she's given me in thirty years. It feels even more urgent to know why she banished me, but I might be looking in the wrong place. When I head back to the exit, my mother's screaming again, in the distance. The sound cuts through the years like a laser. I heard the same cry as a child, but can't remember when, or why.

36

YOU

The air feels even colder when I get outside, my hands shaky. I should never have pressed my mother for information. She's a typical bully, still, even now her mind is failing. I'll only get the truth if she feels in control. The anger surging in my throat tastes sour as fragments of the past resurface. She called me evil as a child; that word lodged in my head, and traces of self-doubt remain. I'll need to go back another day, to try again, even if it hurts. I want to know why Carla has never mentioned her daily visits, and what she gains from seeing Mum so regularly. She keeps begging me to trust her, but this new information is testing the fragile bridge between us.

My brother has sent me a text reminding me to meet him in town, and I can't let him down – it's so rare for Leo to request help. I set off immediately, but it takes me ages to drive through the packed streets, then queue for a parking space at Lion Yard.

I reach the old-fashioned men's outfitters on King's Parade on time. There's no sign of Leo, just shelves full of cravats, college scarves and silk handkerchiefs. The place smells of wool and overheated air. Shops like this never seem to change. They sell the uniform rich British men have chosen for generations, plus dozens of expensive accessories. I'm safe here, at least. My stalker would be easy to spot among the Irish linen, Harris tweed and glossy leather belts lying on the counter in neat coils.

My brother's wheelchair rattles through the door, almost crashing into a display stand. Leo looks worse than last time we met, like he hasn't slept for days. He's too cross for a proper hello.

'Let's get this nightmare over with, then we can eat,' he hisses.

Two assistants descend on Leo with tape measures at the ready. He levers himself out of his chair with effort, then stands there swaying, like a strong wind could blow him over. I realize now why he's asked me along. He needs moral support to face the indignity of being helped in and out of his wheelchair repeatedly by strangers, but after an hour of false starts, he emerges from the changing room. He looks like any other handsome thirty-eight-year-old man, in a stylish blue wedding suit.

'What do you think, Elly?'

'I love it, the cut's perfect.'

'Thank God. I can't do this again; you'll have to bury me in it.'

He gives me a quicksilver grin and appears boyish again. I remember his ability to talk himself out of any tight corner as a kid, but the magic's faded. It saddens me that his condition can't be charmed into submission.

We emerge from the shop loaded with bags full of wedding regalia: tie, waistcoat and shoes. Leo could have managed the trip alone, but maybe he just wanted encouragement. I'm realizing that he would never admit to feeling lonely. He prefers to issue terse requests for practical help instead.

Leo suggests lunch at his favourite restaurant, an old-fashioned Chinese café nearby. Hong Kong Fusion lies on St John's Street. It's normally packed with students enjoying bowls of cheap noodles, but it's quiet when we pick a window table. My anxiety falls by a few notches, now I can keep watch on the world outside.

I'd like to blurt out the truth: I slept with a colleague last night, then went to see Mum at last. I have to understand the past's long shadow, for Jamie's sake and mine, but Leo seems preoccupied. He remains silent when the waitress delivers plates of dumplings, pak choi, chilli-fried beef and a pot of jasmine tea.

When he finally speaks, his gaze lingers on my face. 'You seem rattled, El. I can see why – I never imagined you leaving Rafe.'

'This isn't about him. I visited Mum and it didn't go well.'

He looks surprised. 'How do you mean?'

'She refused to accept me as her daughter, then lashed out. She almost screamed the house down.'

'That's her favourite trick if she feels cornered. I was honest with her last time and got the same reaction.'

'What did you say?'

'That she was a cruel, vindictive bitch.'

I put down my fork. 'What did she do to you back then, Leo?'

'Apart from filling my head with lies about you? She locked me in my room for days, without food, or toys to keep me occupied. You got the same treatment, before she banished you. Can you remember any of that?'

'It's blurred, but I remember you yelling to be let out.'

'That's when I started breaking things, for fun. I took my radio apart then rebuilt it loads of times, to stop myself going mad. I was her scapegoat after you went, not Carla.'

'I'm sorry she hurt you.' He's never admitted what happened then, until now. 'Did it help, telling Mum how you feel?'

'Not yet, but I'm ever hopeful.' He manages to grin.

'Carla goes there most days. One of the carers told me.'

Leo looks startled, then nods in acceptance. 'She's a masochist, that's why. Carla adored Mum as a kid, which kept her safe because she never argued. I think she knew the best way to survive was total submission. She did whatever Mum wanted in a blink, and maybe she still does.'

The strange, unequal bond between mother and daughter concerns me, but I can't explain why. Leo smooths the tablecloth with his palm, like he's trying to wipe the subject away.

'How's it going with Rafe?' he asks.

'Badly. He still hasn't told me the truth.'

'Relationships are a bloody minefield, aren't they? Simon's coming to see me tonight and I'm dreading it.' Leo gulps down some water. 'What's in it for him, except hospital trips and erectile dysfunction? He's so bloody persistent, I'll have to be cruel to end it once and for all. It feels like kicking a puppy.'

'Why not just admit that you love him and hate being a burden?'

'I'd rather pretend to have a toyboy. It sounds much more glamorous.'

'There's no shame in being honest. Let Simon make his own decision.'

'You said that before, El, and it's still wrong. I could be in this chair for fucking years. He should be having fun, exploring the world.'

I glance outside while Leo justifies abandoning the man he loves. That's when I spot Hilary Wadsworth across the street, inspecting her phone. Her dog is gazing up at her, but there's no sign of Clive. Cambridge is so small, you bump into people all the time, but Hilary looks different today. Her permanent smile is missing for once.

'Honesty's overrated,' Leo says. 'Let's get Carla's opinion. If she agrees, maybe I'll follow your advice and tell him how I feel.'

'She may not be home.'

'Of course she will. If she's not fixing someone's lumbago, she's in her dungeon, playing with her vicious cat or baking cakes. The poor girl's got no sex life whatsoever.'

I can't help laughing. 'I'll text, to let her know we're coming.'

When I glance at the clock on the wall, it's 3 p.m. I've got hours to kill before Lisa's private view, but my discomfort returns. It feels like someone's watching me again. When I look outside, Hilary is still there. Why would she wait so long, on a freezing cold day, with her dog tugging at its lead? Her gaze meets mine at last. It looks like she's about to rush over and say hello but changes her mind at the last minute.

Leo claims my attention again, and when I look back Hilary has vanished. I check the street once more as I do up my coat, looking for anyone behaving oddly, but it must have been a false alarm. The only immediate threat is dusk falling fast over the icy road.

37

ME

You're too self-absorbed to notice me, as usual, locked inside your selfish concerns. I've found the perfect vantage point to watch you up close, but you look straight through me.

I see you leave the café. It's one of my favourites too, but you've spoiled it for me now. I can't wipe out the image of you last night, head thrown back, animalistic, wild. Sex matters to you more than I realized. I'm forcing you to become someone else now your perfect life has fallen apart, but I never believed you'd sleep with a virtual stranger so casually.

We're both outside now, on the same street, with little separating us except the dark air. I used to draw comfort from being close to you, even when you ignored my existence. We breathe the same oxygen, see the same stars above us, feel the same pain. But none of that matters anymore.

Last night you walked towards me, hands outstretched, and I lacked the courage to face you with my pretences stripped away. Cold air seared my lungs as I ran from you. Now it's too late to turn back time.

I want you to disappear, leaving me free to walk on, unburdened. Nothing else will cure me, and the deadline is approaching.

It's hard to believe that my helper will do as I say, yet I have to trust them. I can't win this endgame alone. I need to see you lose everything, like I did, before letting you go.

38

I'm still on edge when we reach the car park. There's no one close by, except Leo, navigating his wheelchair over the bumpy concrete. His life needs planning down to the last detail, with no more spontaneous trips. I see how tough it's become when he manoeuvres his chair into his car. He doesn't complain, but frustration shows on his face at the slowness of it all.

When I walk up to the next floor, all the drivers seem to be following the same impulse to go somewhere warm. I give Jamie a quick call before setting off. He sounds upset to hear that Leo and I are going to see Carla.

'Why didn't you invite me, Mum? They're my relatives too.'

'It was a last-minute thing. Come now, we'll be at Carla's flat.'

'I can't. I'm with Billy, at the cottage. His mum's still being a nightmare.'

The news makes my hands tighten on the wheel. 'You promised me you wouldn't go back there until it's safe.'

'I know, but we can deal with him, Mum. I've got a feeling he'll come back tonight.'

'Promise not to sleep there, even if Billy wants to stay.'

'The line's bad. I'll ring you later, okay?'

He hangs up immediately, leaving me powerless. He's not a child anymore, and appears determined to fight my cause, even though his actions could make the stalking escalate. He never listens when I explain that passive resistance is the best option when your pursuer is longing for a reaction. Anxiety quickens my breathing, but I can't just stay here with my hands clenched so tightly my knuckles are turning white.

I follow Leo's tail lights as we crawl through the weekend traffic. There's no sign of Carla at her flat, but she pulls up a few minutes later. I'm more concerned about Leo. He hauls himself out of the car, leaving his wheelchair behind. I watch him cover the icy pavement at a snail's pace, leaning on his stick. It's the first time I've seen him walk any distance for weeks. His face is ashen when the three of us meet in the porch, as if the short journey has sapped his strength.

Carla is dressed in a black trench coat, far smarter than normal. Blonde hair cascades to her shoulders in a smooth ripple, and her makeup's perfect too, blue eyes glittering. I can tell she's uncomfortable, even though she loved dressing up as a kid. One of my strongest memories is of us trying on Mum's clothes, Carla's face smeared with mascara stolen from her makeup box. I'm certain we got into trouble for it, but can't remember our punishment.

'Hello, gorgeous,' Leo says. 'Let us in, before we freeze to death.'

Our sister's smile looks strained when she unlocks the door. Maybe seeing Leo and me together makes her jealous because she's never shared him until now. Her cat picks up on the atmosphere, bolting down the hallway to shelter under a table. Leo walks ahead of me down the stairs. I see him slip but manage to grab his arm. He regains his footing, thank God. I can see he's shaken. He avoided falling this time, but for how long? Carla's basement flat will soon be out of bounds.

Leo's mouth purses shut when Carla focuses on him. He stays silent while she promises to get a handrail fitted, then hovers close by, fussing over him. She's wearing a grey cashmere dress that I've never seen before. It's elegant and figure hugging, unlike her normal jeans and T-shirt, which leaves me confused. Her clothes are just like the ones Rafe chooses for me, understated and timeless.

'Tell us where you've been, in that sexy grown-up dress,' Leo says.

'Nowhere important.' She puts the kettle on, keeping her back turned.

'Let me guess then. Having wild hotel sex with your rich lover?' Leo continues.

'Or seeing Mum?' I ask in a neutral voice. 'I visited the home earlier. They said you go there all the time.'

Carla swings round to stare at us both. 'You two always ganged up on me. What's wrong with showing her some human kindness, when her life's so miserable? I'm the only one that gives a shit. She's our mum, for fuck's sake. She deserves our respect.'

'Respect has to be earned, Carla,' I reply.

Her movements are quick and brittle as she places our drinks on the table. I can tell there's no point in questioning her motives for all those trips to the nursing home. She only relaxes when Leo mentions his dilemma about Simon. We're old enough for lasting relationships, yet we're struggling. I was leading the way until this week, with my stable marriage, but now we're all in the same position.

Leo makes light of things when he describes his situation. He talks about his happiness when the relationship began. His MS has put it under strain, but Simon won't let him go. Carla's advice echoes mine. He should be honest about his feelings so he doesn't have any regrets.

Leo rolls his eyes. 'The poor bastard deserves someone healthy. I'll check into a care home like Mum's when my legs pack up.'

'Over my dead body,' Carla snaps. 'I'd never let that happen.'

I catch sight of us three in the wall mirror. We've got matching colouring and bone structure, but I'm the quietest, still finding my way. They spent their teenage years together, learning each other's gestures and nuances.

I'm grateful that Leo doesn't mention my stalker because Carla would never let it go. She obsesses about things that scare her. If she knew the truth, she'd try and take over. Leo appears to be tiring, the prospect of Simon's visit tonight weighing on him.

'What about you, Elly?' Carla asks. 'Sorry I snapped earlier. Things are difficult for me right now, that's all. How did it go with Mum?' She's watching me closely, her eyes shiny with tears, always the sensitive one.

'She called me a devil child, but it's just projection.'

'What does that mean, exactly?' Leo asks.

'It's when we project our self-doubts onto others, instead of accepting them ourselves. I couldn't even ask questions. She's too ill or confused to listen. The weeks around Dad's death are still a blur without her side of the story. I can't move on till I know what happened.' I rub my hand across my forehead. The pain's come back suddenly, emotional this time, not physical.

'I told you to let us help.' Leo's gaze holds mine. 'If we both describe what happened to us, maybe it'll come back.'

Carla nods. 'I didn't see much; you made me stay indoors. But I can share my angle on it too.'

'Go on then, I need to understand.' My body tenses.

'It was high summer, about noon,' Leo begins. 'The sun was scorching and I was kicking my football against the garden wall. The atmosphere felt weird. You and Carla were inside, and Mum was off somewhere, sulking.' He drags in a long breath. 'It was just us three and Dad at home. He was in his study, in the attic. I was pissed off because he wouldn't let me play with my mates on the street. I'd heard him and Mum rowing earlier on, but didn't know why.'

'You can stop if it hurts too much,' Carla whispers.

'Of course it fucking hurts.' He keeps his gaze on me. 'I saw Dad climb onto the window ledge. He looked up at the sky, then jumped. I couldn't stop it, so I shut my eyes. He landed on the path. There was no sound at first, then the screaming started. It sounded like an animal dying in the worst pain imaginable. His legs were shattered, and his back. You called the ambulance, Elly. But I was glued to the spot. I didn't even have the guts to run over and comfort him.'

'You mustn't blame yourself. It was his decision, not yours. I can't remember any of it.'

'Lucky you.' Carla keeps her eyes closed. 'I heard him yelling from indoors. I'd love to forget that sound.'

'He was paralysed from the neck down,' Leo says. 'He could only make that terrible moaning noise. The hospital said there was nothing they could do except try to manage his pain, but Mum wanted him home. She put a hospital bed, oxygen tanks and a ventilator in the living room. He needed full-time care. A nurse came on the days when she had to go out.'

'Mum sent me to stay with a schoolfriend,' Carla adds. 'Only you two were there with her when Dad died.'

'What happened that day?' I ask.

'The doctor said he'd choked on his tongue. Remember, he'd already tried to kill himself. It's the outcome he wanted. Mum told us these crazy stories to explain it. She said you made his life a misery, there was this evil seed inside you, which is bollocks, of course. Dad loved us all. I was too young to argue, but her version never made sense.'

Carla watches me react. 'It must be awful, hearing all this, Elly.'

'Either I did something bad, or she projected her anger onto me. It takes a lot for a mother to abandon a child.'

'It wasn't your fault, El.' Leo reaches for my hand, even though he rarely initiates touch with anyone. 'She should never have separated us.'

'I thought about you both for years,' I reply. 'I still need her version, but it's out in the open between us, at least.'

Carla's face is solemn when she finally pulls back her sleeve. The tattoo I noticed before is a row of dark blue numbers circling her bicep. 'Mum wouldn't let us see you, or even make contact. It hurt so much, I got our three birth dates inked like a bracelet when I turned eighteen.'

The line of numbers comforts me. It proves that Carla's on my side, after all. Tangible evidence that we're connected, even though the way ahead is uncertain. I feel safe for the first time in days, but my phone rings, spoiling the moment. The screen tells me the caller is withholding their number. I cancel it fast, but the threat lingers, like a bad smell.

39

YOU

I need an excuse to leave. The conversation has moved on, but the past has sucked all the oxygen from the room. It's a relief when a text arrives from Lisa, inviting me round before her private view. I know from experience that she gets nervous about every exhibition she organizes, with plenty of sleepless nights.

I'm still learning about my brother and sister's relationship as I leave Carla's flat. They irritate each other, but their closeness shows. I say goodbye to Leo in the kitchen, but Carla hugs me by her front door. I've smelled her perfume before, but can't remember when or where. She whispers something as we embrace, telling me she's glad I went to see Mum and hopes I got closure. It's like she wants to stick a plaster over our past, to heal the damage in only a couple of days.

I rest in the driver's seat of my car. My vision flickers, like strobe lights on a dance floor, making me giddy. I can't tell whether it's from my injury or revisiting the past's ugliness. When I shut my eyes time flips into reverse, and I'm standing in the attic of our old house, watching Dad climb onto the window ledge. The image lasts longer than before, leaving me weak. I still don't understand why his longing for death made him leap out to greet it, in front of his kids. He planted the same impulse in me, and Leo too. I can only hope that Carla has dodged the bullet.

Tiredness hits me suddenly. It feels like I've been dragging a heavy weight uphill for months. I need to cast it aside, but I don't know how, until I remember that the films I post online link me directly to my stalker. Something clicks inside my head. It's time to face them; I can't live in fear any longer. My childhood fell apart, but my adult life must stay intact. It's time we faced each other at last.

I always try to look professional when I make the films in my office each week. I keep the information accessible, giving victims tips on ways to stay confident and safe. Thousands of followers worldwide will see that we're connected now, like siblings. This time I'm the one in a mess, in need of support. I'm in my car, alone at night, with no script to follow, and I'm breaking a cardinal rule. All communication is courting danger, but I've run out of options. It's time to throw down the gauntlet and accept the consequences.

I hold up my phone, imagining my stalker standing close by, invading my space. My words must bring them close enough to catch. I take a long breath, then start to record.

'It's just us, at last, face to face. You began stalking me three months ago. You've broken into my home and my workplace and vandalized my son's car. But there's a problem, isn't there? You're a coward at heart. You'll lose your job, your family and your friends when the truth comes out. It's time for us to meet, in person. I'm ready for you. It's me or you from tonight, like you always say. No one else counts.'

My hands shake when I upload the film. Followers all over the world will see me wide-eyed and breathless, but at least it's au-thentic. My expertise has failed me, and thousands more people are calling for my resignation when I check the petition again. I have to confront whoever's ruining my life before I fall apart.

I leave my car on Hills Road, then walk to Lisa's block on the Highsett Estate. It's snowing again, flakes settling on the pavement, every footstep treacherous. I've almost reached the estate when someone emerges from an alley suddenly, a burly figure blocking my path. I'm so used to seeing Reg Bellamy at work, it's a surprise to encounter him in private. He looks uncomfortable too, his smile strained.

'Sorry, Reg. I didn't see you there.'

'No harm done, Dr Shaw. Are you visiting your friend Lisa?'

'How did you know she lives here?'

Reg's speech is slow, and I can smell alcohol on his breath. 'I grew up here. We often bump into each other. My sister still lives in Highsett. I called on her just now, for a drink after work.'

'You did a late shift at the department?'

'Someone tried to break in last night, apparently. The managers asked me to check the premises are secure, then lock up. If they had any sense they'd employ a night security firm, not leave it unguarded.' His gaze lingers on my face. 'Lisa mentioned you've been having problems recently concerning your safety. Is that right?'

'She's exaggerating. I'm annoyed she mentioned it.'

'I think she just wants to protect you. Let me know if you have any trouble at work, please, or elsewhere. I'd like to help.'

'Thanks, I appreciate it.'

I'm about to walk away, but he touches my sleeve.

'You've always been so courteous. Most of the other academics look straight through me, without a word of thanks. To them, I'm a nobody.'

'I'm sorry, Reg, that sounds upsetting.'

He's standing too close, his hand still on my wrist. I can tell he'd like to elaborate, but I make my excuses and hurry away. I've never noticed his bitterness about being overlooked until now, the smell of loneliness trapped in his clothes.

Reg slips from my mind when I approach Lisa's block. She's evangelical about Highsett Estate, which operates as a co-operative, with communal gardens and shared planning decisions. I can only see a set of ugly red-brick boxes. Rafe told me once that the architecture is known as sixties brutalism, without cladding or balconies to soften the outlines. The buildings are harsh lines scattered among gardens shrouded by snow.

My friend's voice sounds upbeat through the intercom when she invites me to the top floor. She flings her arms around me in welcome. I'm still annoyed that she shared my personal details with Reg but try not to let it show. Lisa's flat is colourful, the hallway painted ochre, with a neon-bright print of Jimi Hendrix's face dominating the wall. Her living room is full of quirky furniture, including an old record player and drinks cabinet. It's in keeping with the building's era. Two huge sofas dominate the space, designed to accommodate a dozen friends.

Lisa's scarlet dress falls to her ankles, skimming every curve and revealing spike-heeled boots. Her hair is a mass of corkscrew curls. There's a manic energy in her eyes, which always happens when she's under the spotlight. Excitement makes her like a kid on a sugar rush.

'You look amazing, Lisa.'

'The boots have to go,' she says, grinning. 'I can't dance in them.'

Her private views are legendary, often turning into parties with gallons of booze. When I glance outside, the estate looks quiet by comparison, all the flat-dwellers sheltering from the cold.

'I just ran into Reg Bellamy.'

She glances at me. 'Funny old soul, isn't he? A bit intense since his divorce. The other day he gave me a real grilling about you.'

'How do you mean?'

'He noticed you were upset. The guy wouldn't let up without an explanation.'

'You told him about my stalker?'

'Not in so many words, but security should know you've been followed from work, in case it happens again. I dropped a hint, that's all.'

'You gave Noah my number too. Please don't share anything about me again without asking first.'

'Come on, I did you a favour. The guy's gorgeous, and you deserve some happiness after such a shitty time.' She wafts my complaint away with a hand gesture. 'I know why you're on edge. Noah's called you, I bet. Have you got a hot date lined up?'

I could admit to sleeping with him last night but shake my head instead. My desire for privacy leaves me silent. I'm not ready to analyse my motives yet, and she'd expect every detail. It feels awkward claiming to have had no contact with Noah, but it's the safest choice.

Lisa moves on, giving me a reprieve. She takes me upstairs to see her newly renovated roof terrace. I haven't been up here since summer, when we sat drinking chilled white wine and chatting for hours, before the stalking began. Lisa has decorated it with fairy lights and plants, now whitened by snow. When I look out over the estate, its design makes better sense. The communal gardens have paths winding between trees and buildings, ensuring regular contact between neighbours. It appears safe and enclosed, unlike my cottage. It's perfect for Lisa, who's always gregarious, but I'd soon feel claustrophobic.

'I hope we get a decent crowd at the gallery,' she says. 'What if the snow keeps them at home?'

Lisa loves throwing parties, yet always panics that they won't be a success. When I turn to face her, she looks numb, her confidence dropping away.

'What's wrong, sweetheart?'

'I invited someone special. He texted just now to say he can't make it. I probably won't ever see him again. How come the good ones always drop me?' A tear rolls down her cheek.

'You're beautiful, Lisa, inside and out. He'll come back if he's got any sense.'

'Sorry, I'm being daft.' I brush the tear from her cheek and her fingers close round mine. 'People talk about finding their soulmate, but it never happens for me. I've done things I regret, prepared to sacrifice anything for it. Sorry, Elly, I'm a hopeless friend.'

'Rubbish, you've supported me brilliantly for years.'

'But I'm preoccupied, never really present.' Her smile slowly revives. 'God, I hate self-pity. He's just a bloke, isn't he? There are plenty more. Come on, let's get ourselves ready.'

Lisa comes to a halt on the landing downstairs, staring at my sober clothes.

'It's a celebration, Elly, not a funeral. You can't wear black.'

'This is all I've got.'

'Lucky my wardrobe's full of party gear. Quick, we don't have long.'

Resistance is futile, and it's a good way to escape my worries. In her bedroom, Lisa throws an electric-blue dress at me, followed by turquoise boots.

'I'm not wearing those.'

'You need some fun, remember?' She stands in front of me, dabbing on blusher, then runs wax through my hair. 'I should hate your guts. It takes five minutes to make you beautiful, while my face takes hours.'

'I don't believe you.'

She points at the wall-length mirror. Lisa has made me androgynous, my spiked hair elfin, the dress clinging to me like cellophane. The effect is sexy and off-kilter, designed to confuse. When I spin round to face Lisa again, she looks beautiful and flamboyant, until a stupid idea enters my head. She's exactly the kind of woman who'd wear the bracelet and scarf Rafe's mistress left behind. I bat the idea away. Lisa has only met him a handful of times. My paranoia must be growing if no one seems safe or trustworthy anymore, even my closest friend. My faith in humanity has faded. If Rafe's capable of lying, anyone could do the same. Thank God Lisa hasn't noticed my low mood. How can I suspect her of stealing my husband, even for a second? It doesn't make sense.

Lisa slips away when we reach the Heong Gallery. Two dozen guests are waiting outside already, with more drifting through the gates as she unlocks the building. She flits around keeping everyone happy, never settling anywhere for long. It's easier to focus on the artworks than to disappear down a rabbit-hole of suspicion. The paintings are a love letter to winter at its most beautiful, from the last century. They make me nostalgic for a time before I was born, when the landscape glinted with cleanliness. I stare at paintings of snow-covered mountains and freezing grey oceans. I'm standing in front of a seascape that's swimming in pale light, as though even the air is turning to ice, when someone appears next to me.

It's Hilary Wadsworth, wearing an anxious smile. 'Thank goodness you're here, Elly.'

'I saw you in town earlier. Is something wrong?'

'I didn't want to spoil your lunch. Clive left home this morning, without a word, in our car.' Her voice is shaky. 'We were planning to come here together, and he needs to write a speech for his leaving do tomorrow. It's so out of character. He always tells me where he's going, and he's been so upset lately. He won't even answer my calls.'

I touch her shoulder. 'What can I do?'

'Help me find him. I've been scouring his favourite haunts, like the café where I saw you, and the French one next door. I waited ages, without any luck.'

'Want me to try his number?'

'Please, Elly. He's so fond of you, he might pick up.'

'Let's go outside. It's so loud in here, I can't hear myself think.'

When we leave the gallery, icy air bites my skin. I call Clive twice, but it rings out, and Hilary looks miserable. Words spill from her mouth too fast to interrupt.

'Marina Westbrook started it. She told the university to sack him, but they refused, thank God.'

'He never mentioned it.'

'She claimed he'd been harassing her. Marina made up this ridiculous story about him pursuing her at work, like a lovesick fool.'

'Stalking her, you mean?' The words stick in my throat.

'It was a misunderstanding.' Misery echoes in Hilary's voice. 'But people always say there's no smoke without fire, and Clive's behaviour's easy to misread.'

'How do you mean?'

'He's like an impressionable teenager looking for new friendships. I think it's because we couldn't have kids, so he's never had to grow up. Clive can smother people when he's just being kind.'

'That sounds painful for you too.'

'It's not deliberate.' She seems embarrassed to reveal her situation, already edging away. 'Call me if you see him, Elly, please. I'll wait for him at home.'

Hilary rushes off, leaving my thoughts jangled. I know how

upset Clive would have been by Marina's allegations. Stalkers are normally jilted lovers, lonely obsessives or dogged by psychosis that clouds their reason, while Clive's gregarious, with a wide circle of friends. Yet the idea that he could be my stalker returns. He's heard all my secrets, even my marital problems. It could have been him beside my hospital bed, and last night, across the square. If he saw me and Noah through that gap in the curtains, he'd be raging, out of control. Maybe that's why he's disappeared, leaving poor Hilary guessing. I've considered him as a suspect before, but the idea still seems far-fetched after so much kindness.

There are two missed calls from Jamie on my phone. I ring him back, but there's no answer. The people I care about seem to be drifting out of reach. It's too cold to stay outside, so I re-enter the gallery, but the pictures seem less dazzling. They fail to capture the stark brilliance of winter, and their artifice shows. When I inspect one more closely, it breaks down into a mess of tiny brush-strokes, random dots stippling the canvas. The wine in my glass tastes sour, so I abandon it. My thoughts slow to a standstill; my mind's overloaded with information, and the ache at the front of my skull is making me dizzy.

I'm alone in a corner when my sixth sense returns. My skin prickles across the back of my neck, like someone is observing me too closely, in my borrowed clothes. I rise onto the balls of my feet to scan the room. There are familiar faces everywhere – Lisa's colleagues, and some of my own. The place is packed solid, exactly as she'd hoped.

I'm about to slip away when I spot Noah at the far end of the gallery, watching me. Was it his gaze I felt, travelling across my skin? His eyes remain locked on mine as he crosses the room to stand before me. I feel a jolt of lust, but suppress it quickly.

'You look amazing. Why did you disappear on me this morning, Eloise?'

'Sorry, I had something urgent to do.'

'But no regrets?'

'None at all.'

He touches my arm. 'Come back again tonight, I'd love it.'

'Sorry, it's bad timing. I've got too much baggage, Noah.'

His face blanks, masking emotions I can't read until his smile revives. 'No need to apologize. I might sulk for a bit, but I'll survive.' He nods at one of the paintings. 'How do you like the exhibition?'

We'll have to discuss what happened between us another time, to clear the air, but not in a packed art gallery. We're still exchanging opinions about the paintings when my phone pulses in my pocket. I apologize before reading the text from Jamie, telling me to go to the cottage straight away. Panic hits me immediately, and I'm annoyed he's still there. We promised not to go back while the danger exists, but neither of us enjoys following rules.

I say goodnight to Noah with a flicker of guilt. He's still wounded from losing his wife, but I can't leave Jamie on his own. My stalker will have seen my challenge online by now, calling them out from the shadows. It's bound to trigger a reaction. I race towards the car park at 9.30 p.m. The air feels static as I run, too laden with cold for even the slightest breeze.

40

The cottage looks defiant when I pull up outside. Jamie's left the curtains open, and light blazes from the downstairs windows. He stands on the doorstep when I leave my car, like he's a guardsman, wary about letting me inside.

'You promised to stay away, Jamie.'

'I had a good reason to change my mind.'

He pulls me into a hug and my anger subsides. We're here now, and I need to understand. I leave my coat on the banister and see a flash of amusement on Jamie's face.

'Is that fancy dress, Mum? You look like a nineties rock chick.'

When I catch myself in the mirror, the spell has broken. My eye makeup is smudged, the bruise under my hairline still visible, the dress a little too tight. Jamie leads me into the living room. There's a fire blazing in the hearth. I drop into an armchair to let the cold thaw from my bones.

'I saw your film, that's why I came back,' Jamie says.

My message was intended for my stalker, not as a call to arms for my family, but Jamie's reactions are beyond my control.

'You always seemed relaxed in the cottage, like this place matters to you more than anything. It was your secret world.' He leans forward to grab my hand. 'I want us to feel safe here again. I'm proud of you for challenging him.'

'It was probably a stupid idea.'

'No, it puts you in the driving seat. He's not calling the shots anymore.' His gaze drops to the floor. 'I tried calling Dad earlier, but he didn't answer, like loads of other times. Don't you think that's weird?'

'He's not the stalker, if that's what you're asking.'

Jamie still seems uncertain. 'Dad's changed. He's more worried about money and how the world sees him than you or me.'

'That's pretty harsh.'

'Forget it for now. I've got a game plan.'

Jamie's eyes glitter with excitement, like my stalker's campaign against me is a glorious battle. I try to remind him that any action we take against them will only increase their motivation, dragging us into a cat and mouse game, but he's too busy to listen. He's rigged up our old camping generator. It means that we'll never lose power downstairs if the mains fails us. All we need to do is flick the backup switch.

'It's a clever idea, but it won't help if they're determined to get inside.'

'We'll catch him by being prepared, Mum, and he'll come back soon. He may not be brave, but he's persistent.'

I might be crazy to stay here, but it seems better to fight than to hide in a hotel bedroom, even though I'm ignoring my own advice. The thing that worries me most is the messianic glint in Jamie's eye. His excitement might come from too many drugs, or the delusion that ending a stalker's campaign will be easy. I'm less optimistic after spending ten years working with offenders who keep on pursuing their victims, despite spells in jail. Sometimes the punishments they receive only make them more determined to continue.

I go upstairs for some respite from Jamie's wild energy. My reflection in the window's black glass looks ridiculous, all dressed up with nowhere to go, so I wash my face, then change into jeans and a jumper. Lisa's clothes lie on a chair, items that I would never choose for myself.

Jamie suggests that we sleep on the sofas in the living room, taking it in turns to keep guard.

'We'd be safer in town.'

'No, we have to end it, before he hurts you again.'

He speaks with the absolute conviction of a zealot. I should argue my case, but tiredness is winning out. All I want to do is stretch out on the sofa where Pete and Lucy used to sit together, happily watching soap operas. They'd be horrified to know that their home is no longer a safe haven.

'Check your phone, Mum. It was bleeping just now.'

Suddenly the lights flicker, then fail. Jamie's face is set in a frown when they reignite, a fraction brighter than before. It feels like we're lab rats trapped in a cage, waiting for the next experiment.

'We should stay indoors,' he says. 'Let him make the next move.'

We sit in silence, but the lights remain constant. Maybe that flicker is like the late-night phone calls – a reminder that my life's under siege. But when I check my phone messages, the latest is from the care home. My breathing quickens. My mother's had another stroke, and she's fading fast. I should go there now, if I want to see her again. The news takes a moment to register. My first thought is to call Leo and Carla, but the home will have contacted them too.

'Grab your coat, Jamie. We have to leave, straight away, in my car.'

'We can't, I—'

I swing round to face him. 'Don't argue, it's important. We're going right now.'

He protests for a minute, then does as he's told. I watch him pull on the grey skiing gloves I gave him last year. It's tiring how the power balance between us keeps changing, but I don't want any more regrets about my past. My mother brought me into this world after all, like Carla said. I owe her gratitude for my existence, whatever happened between us.

Jamie stays quiet as my car races south, too fast, on icy roads. It matters to see her one last time, which doesn't make sense. Maybe it's just the basic human urge not to let her die alone, no matter how much hurt she caused. I give Jamie the option to remain in the car when we reach the home, but he refuses, point-blank.

The same care assistant I met last time explains in a whisper that Ingrid fell ill several hours ago. The other residents are asleep, and we must try not to wake them. The man's kind manner reassures me. I'm surprised that Carla's not here already, given how vigilant she's been towards Mum, but maybe she missed the call.

My mouth feels dry when we reach the first floor. One of the assistants is sitting at Mum's bedside, keeping watch. When we approach, she slips from the room. My mother looks even more fragile than before, twitching in her sleep. Her chest barely rises each time she inhales. I'd like to protect Jamie from this, but he seems determined to stay, even though she showed no interest in meeting her only grandchild. When I take her hand, the gesture feels uncomfortable.

'It's Eloise,' I say. 'I came to see you earlier, remember?'

Her eyes fly open suddenly. 'Me, not you,' she whispers. Her words are so like my stalker's, I do a double take.

'What do you mean, Mum?'

'No one else involved.'

'I don't understand.'

'He did it to hurt me.'

'Go on, please. I need to hear.'

The brief conversation seems to have given her peace. The twitching has stopped and her breathing sounds more even as she drifts out of reach.

We wait at her bedside for an hour, but nothing changes, until the care assistant advises us to come back in the morning. He's nursed enough stroke victims to know they can linger for days. She looks relaxed at least, and my anger towards her fades. Blame is pointless at someone's deathbed. I think she was trying to offer me the truth, and that's better than nothing. The past seems to hover just out of reach. I wish I could smash the pane of glass protecting me from it, to see the whole picture.

Jamie looks upset when we return to the car, after seeing his estranged grandmother so ill. What he needs now is stability, so I explain what will happen in a quiet voice, leaving no room for protest. We're going back to Rafe's house. I'm done fighting, for tonight at least. There's nothing we can do about my stalker at two in the morning.

Rafe's car is missing from the driveway, which hurts, even though I spent last night with another man. Jamie goes straight to bed, while I settle in the spare room. It's far more comfortable than the cottage. The radiator is still warm, the bed linen pristine, yet my head is too full of ugly truths to fall asleep easily.

I'm drifting when I hear a door open and close, then footsteps on the stairs. Panic kicks in immediately. My stalker could have found their way into this house because Rafe still hasn't changed the locks. I put the deadbolt on, so whoever is down there must have come in the back way.

The house remains in darkness. Instinct makes me want to yell for Jamie, to keep him safe, but it was a false alarm. Rafe stands on the landing by the window, a ray of moonlight accenting him like a statue. He looks older than before, burdened by information he's sick of carrying. I want to know where he's been, but I'll never beg for answers again. If our marriage is going to survive, he'll have to explain his mistakes, and so will I.

Rafe's still motionless, like he's trying to decide which bedroom to enter. It's the expression on his face that chills me. He wore the same ambiguous smile when I drove away. He looks tired, but more relaxed than I've seen him for weeks. It's 3 a.m. Maybe he's been with her, planning their future, just like we did at the start?

Violence rises in me again. It's bubbling away, waiting to do more damage, after years of denial. I hear the door shut across the landing when Rafe finally enters the room we used to share. The clicking sound is hard-edged and final, reminding me of Greenhill Prison.

41

YOU

I wake mid-morning, still muzzy from my first decent sleep since being attacked. It's a surprise to be back in my marital home, with light filtering through the curtains. Our spare room is so minimal it could be a hotel. The walls are stark white, like an operating theatre, but it used to feel welcoming. The paintings and souvenirs I placed here after family holidays are now missing. Objects I cherished for their happy memories have vanished. Rafe must have seized his opportunity to shove them into cupboards the moment I left. The air feels warm when I get up, but it's deceiving. The atmosphere's as cold as Marina's office.

I put on yesterday's clothes, then step onto the landing. Jamie's still asleep when I peer into his room. He'll stay huddled under his duvet for hours, thanks to his teenage ability to dream all day. Rafe is padding around in the kitchen barefoot when I go downstairs. He doesn't hear me. His back's turned while he fiddles with the coffee machine. The tune he's humming is upbeat, an old pop song that I can't name. My husband sounds happy, given that our marriage is falling apart.

When Rafe swings round suddenly, the mugs in his hands slosh liquid onto the floor. 'I was just bringing you coffee, El.'

'We can drink it here.' I don't understand why he's pretending nothing's wrong, but I can't face another row, so I shift to a new topic. 'Did Jennifer Rawle contact you?'

'No. Why do you ask?'

'She wants to separate Jamie and Billy. Our son's a bad influence, apparently.'

'It won't work, they're like Siamese twins.' Rafe places the mugs on the island. It still hurts to look at him, but we need to agree a plan, for Jamie's sake, as well as ours.

'Jennifer said she'd come straight here. She thinks you're the rational one.'

'I haven't seen her in weeks.'

I study him, side-on. 'You seem happier, Rafe. Maybe your life's easier now.'

'That's not true.' He goes on before I can reply. 'I'm just glad you came back, even though you slept in the spare room. I've thought about your marriage counselling idea too. I'm willing, if it helps us fix things.'

'I only came here to keep Jamie safe.'

'Bollocks. You could have gone anywhere, El. We both need you home, can't you see?'

I avoid answering. 'You got back so late, I thought you'd stay out all night.'

'It's over. But you can't let it go, can you?'

I still want to know her name, but that's something to tackle in counselling sessions, if we ever get there. The headache I keep on ignoring is growing stronger, alongside my impulse to destroy any obstacle in my way.

'Speak your mind, El. Tell me what you're thinking.'

'My mother's dying. I'm going to the care home now. Everything else can wait.'

Rafe listens intently when I explain about Mum's stroke, and that Jamie still believes my stalker will target the cottage and wants to catch him out, even though the messages have turned violent. He can't go back there because I used my film last night to throw out a challenge. It's only a matter of time before whoever it is confronts me, face to face. We can't let Jamie be at risk.

The discussion feels strange, now I've slept with someone else. Part of me wants to blurt out the truth, but that could finish our marriage, and the idea of losing Rafe for good still terrifies me, despite his lies.

'I won't let Jamie out of my sight,' he promises.

We're talking politely, like strangers, but there are more pressing concerns. I hurry back upstairs to grab some clothes for Clive's leaving party tonight. I hope he's gone home to Hilary by now. He's given me so much help over the years that I can't let him down, even though celebrating will feel strange, with so much in the balance.

I drive straight to Leo's with my bag on the back seat, to see if he wants to visit the home one last time. The ache behind my eyes feels stronger, despite the medication, but ignoring it has become second nature. Leo's car is in the driveway, and habit makes me hurry down the side passage instead of ringing his doorbell. I catch sight of him in his workshop. He's on his feet for once, with his stick and walking frame propped against the wall. Leo's expression is intense, his phone pressed to his ear. The thing that strikes me first is the fluency of his movements. I've grown used to his faltering walk and the way he struggles up flights of stairs. Today he's pacing around his studio. He lost the ability to do that months ago, or so I thought.

Leo freezes when he spots me, clearly uncomfortable, until he beckons me inside. I can hear Carla's voice on his phone, high and tinny, telling him to get moving. It's his last chance to see Mum alive. He hangs up without saying goodbye.

'I can't do it, even for Carla,' he says. 'The old bitch can go straight to hell, as far as I'm concerned.'

'It's your decision, but you're moving well today, just like the old days. How come?'

A tear leaks from the corner of his eye. 'New medication. I have good spells and bad on the walking front. I was on cloud nine till Carla's phone call, but she's ruined it. I woke up feeling ten years younger.'

'Because of Simon?'

'I followed your advice.' Leo's smile reignites. 'He's rushed back to London to pack his stuff and move in here with me.'

'That's wonderful.'

'The fool even gave me a bloody engagement ring.' He holds out his hand to show me. 'I'll get married in that suit. You won't have to bury me in it just yet.'

'That's wonderful, Leo. You deserve to be happy.' His ring is an elegant strip of platinum, with symbols scratched on the surface, shaped like the pots he mends. 'How do you feel?'

'High as a kite, and terrified.' His smile vanishes. 'Have you been with Mum?'

'I went last night, with Jamie. She hasn't got long.'

Leo's voice hardens. 'I won't mourn her, not for a second. She broke me. A mother can do that to a son, you know? Punishment after punishment. I hated your guts sometimes, for abandoning us. She said you chose to leave us.'

'She told so many lies. It's good you're letting it out, at last.'

He blinks back tears. 'Carla needs support. You'd better go, El.

The daft cow's too soft to realize she doesn't owe Mum a thing. None of us do.'

Leo's unsteadiness has returned when I hug him goodbye. I'd like to stay longer and hear more about his good news, but it can wait. Carla's dealt with Mum single-handedly for years. I can't leave her by that bedside alone.

The atmosphere is quiet when I find Carla upstairs at the home, her gaze trained on our mother's face, clutching her hand. My sister's biting her lip, struggling not to cry. I dump my coat and sit down beside her. They say that we get the death we deserve, but it seems like random chance to me. Our mother looks serene as she slips from this world, oblivious to the hurt she's caused. I keep on remembering how strong she seemed when I questioned her on my first visit here, as if she still had plenty of time to brood over the past.

'Are you okay?' I whisper to Carla.

'Mum needs our help, nothing else matters.' She frowns at me. 'She said there's a box in her wardrobe. It sounded urgent.'

Our mother's closet is full of simple, elegant dresses when I look inside. It's like she was determined not to let old age ruin her style. I find the box hidden under a pile of shoes, its dark wood and inlaid mother of pearl instantly recognizable. She kept it on her dressing table when we were kids, full of lipsticks and mascara. The only thing it contains now is a yellowed envelope with her name on the front.

The sight of Dad's spiky black scrawl fills me with shock, then sadness. It must be his suicide note. I knew he wouldn't end his life without leaving a message. He may have been broken, but he was never cruel.

I read his words in silence:

I've been a fool, Ingrid. You plan to shame me in public, and I can't face that punishment, or your judgement. I know you want me dead, so I'm doing this for your sake. I let myself be dazzled by someone else, then so many lies followed it was too late to stop.

Now you can stop being so angry, and full of hate. Please take good care of our three precious ones.

My father's name is scrawled at the bottom, the word almost illegible. I screw my eyes shut, trying to picture him as he looked before sadness took over his life. He used to walk up the path after work, smiling, dressed in his smart suit and polished shoes. He had to travel constantly for his job, but was always far more present for us than Mum whenever he came home. He'd sling his briefcase down in the hall and demand hugs from all of us. I still remember the giddy weightlessness I felt when he swung me in the air. Whenever he went away Leo would cry himself to sleep until he returned, and sometimes I would too.

I place the letter back in the box for the other two to read. I can't predict whether it will bring them the same relief, but it's concrete proof that I didn't cause his death. Mum never hid her feelings. If she was furious about him having an affair she wouldn't have held back.

'Come here,' Carla mutters. 'Quick.'

Our mother is struggling to breathe. Each gasp seems hard won, a dry rattling sound in her throat.

'Want me to fetch someone?'

'There's no time.'

Mum drags in a long breath, then her face relaxes and her eyes turn vacant. I feel hollow when she dies, but Carla is already sobbing. All I can do is rub her back while tears run down her face.

My sister falls silent when two care assistants arrive. They were hovering in the corridor to give us privacy, but Carla's in no state to deal with the aftermath, while I feel oddly calm. I persuade her to go home and leave the rest to me. We'll need a death certificate, then undertakers must be booked and the funeral arranged.

I wait in the corridor until the doctor arrives with the home's resident nurse. The medic's face is grave when she introduces herself. She's around my age with greying hair cropped short. She asks how I'm coping before we enter the room.

'You don't have to see your mother again if it's too painful,' she says quietly.

I follow the pair inside. It feels necessary, as if I'm protecting Mum's last rights. The doctor's movements are quick and efficient. She appears relaxed when she checks my mother's airways, then closes her eyes gently with gloved hands. I notice a change when she examines Mum's arms and hands. She holds a hushed conversation with the nurse. My focus is still on losing my mother before our relationship could be mended.

The doctor turns to me at last. 'I'm afraid we'll need a post-mortem. Your mother didn't die from a stroke. I'll have to record the death as suspicious on the certificate.'

'I don't understand.'

'There's an injection mark on her arm, but the nurse never administered medication intravenously. She's the only person here qualified to do it.'

I spot the injection site on the inside of my mother's arm. It's a small red scar, surrounded by bruising, as though someone extracted blood for a sample.

'You think an intruder jabbed her with something?' Words stutter from my mouth.

'We'll need to run toxicology tests to find out. The police will be informed.'

I'm not listening when she gives me a form to sign, authorizing the post-mortem. The back of my neck prickles again, even though no one is watching me except the doctor and nurse.

Why would anyone murder a fragile old woman by fatal injection? Killing someone so vulnerable is a monstrous thing to do, no matter what she did in the past. My mother may have paid the ultimate price for the film I posted last night. I notice the doctor is assessing my behaviour, like she's trying to work out if I'm deranged enough to kill. She offers me a nod, her face solemn, instead of saying goodbye.

My first reaction is to call Rafe. I can't bring myself to explain that Mum may have been killed, saying only that she's passed, and he'll have to let Jamie know. Then I ring the police station and explain to the duty officer that my whole family needs protection. If my stalker has committed murder, their campaign has risen to a new level of violence. The female officer at the end of the line tells me to wait for officers to arrive, but I've never felt more isolated, even though the care home is thronging with strangers.

42

ME

I feel better today. Yesterday was so stressful, I'm still reacting to the excitement. My hands shake as I check my phone for details about you. I've completed one of my biggest challenges yet. It was bound to be painful for a sensitive person like me to kill someone, even a poisonous old bitch with too many secrets. I can never forgive her for what she did to me. You're both complicit, in my eyes.

Her death didn't take long to achieve. All I had to do was slip inside the care home at night, when it was so low on staff that basic safety protocols were ignored. I wore the same blue uniform as all the other carers. No one asked me to sign a register, or batted an eyelid before I hurried upstairs. They were too busy to care. I didn't even have to lie about being sent there by an agency.

The old girl barely moved when I injected tap water into her arm, a method I found on the internet. Thank God she didn't wake up. If she'd recognized me, she'd have screamed the place down. I hated that raw shrieking noise; it's lucky I'll never have to hear it again. I knew she would die a slow death, drowning from the inside, which seems a fitting punishment after years spent torturing others. I had so many reasons to kill her. She might have told you what really happened when you were a child. I want that pleasure to be mine, after waiting so many years.

I'm alone again, and fully prepared. Now you know I'm serious. You invited this, by taunting me to step out of the shadows. It's the message I've expected for months, just not how you gave it, with a mocking look on your face. The conversation between us should be private, not public. It showed a new level of disrespect. I'm waiting for you, more confident than ever, as the endgame begins.

43

YOU

The police officers at the care home look out of their depth. The station has sent two uniformed constables, a man and a woman, both too young for professional cynicism. The policeman looks anxious when he enters my mother's room, as though confronting a dead body is his worst nightmare. They listen avidly when the doctor explains that an injection appears to have been administered in the past twenty-four hours, but the only staff member qualified to use a syringe is denying responsibility. A pathologist must perform an autopsy and run toxicology tests to find the truth.

The officers question me once the doctor leaves. The young woman takes the lead, keeping her tone sympathetic. Both look sceptical about a stalker targeting my whole family, even though I've worked with offenders who've launched vicious attacks on victims' relatives just for blocking their way, with nightmarish results. This case is different. My mother played no active role in my life. My stalker may have killed her simply to demonstrate that all my blood relatives are vulnerable.

They let me leave after I finish explaining my movements for the past twenty-four hours, but tell me to remain available for interview. I'm certain they'll speak to Carla too, even though she's the one person who would never harm our mother.

Phone messages have been arriving in the past hour, including one from Jamie telling me he's still with Rafe. The next is from Lisa, checking I'm okay after leaving the private view early. She's inviting me for a drink in town later. I fire off a quick reply, giving my apologies. I want to be with Leo and Carla while the news about Mum sinks in, but I promised to attend Clive's leaving drinks. I can't let him down. I won't stay long, but must show my face at least.

I park my car then hurry towards Corpus Christi College. It's one of the most ancient buildings in Cambridge, but there's no time to admire the architecture as I cross the quadrangle to the Master's Lodge. All the colleges are built to a similar design, around central gardens, each with its own chapel, from a time when students remained in the compound all day and attended regular services. The cloistered atmosphere helped them to focus on their studies in a dedicated community with few distractions. I used to find the inward-looking buildings claustrophobic, but not anymore. I welcome the sense of enclosure tonight for the safety it provides.

The Master's Lodge lies inside the fourteenth-century courtyard, with the college crest over the entrance. I feel shabby when I step inside. Some of my colleagues are dressed for cocktails, clutching flutes of champagne. The event room is almost full, faculty members from my department mingling with university officials. Marina Westbrook gives me a chilly smile from a distance, then continues her conversation with the Master's wife. I scan the crowd looking for Clive, but I can't see him, or Noah. When I spot Hilary, I head over immediately. She's wearing an elegant dark-blue dress, her hair swept into a chignon, but her expression's panicked.

'Clive's still missing,' she whispers. 'He promised to come on the phone a few hours ago, but I haven't seen him. God knows where he spent the night.'

'He'll get here, don't worry.'

'I'm not so sure.' Her eyes are glossy with tears. 'This could be his protest about being forced to retire early.'

Clive is already late for his own celebration. Farewell parties follow a set schedule at Cambridge: the whole department assembles for an early-evening drink on a Sunday, followed by a lavish dinner. The atmosphere will turn awkward if our guest of honour doesn't appear soon.

'I should be looking for him, not drinking bloody cocktails,' Hilary whispers.

She rushes away, and my boss appears at my side. Marina remains silent for a moment, like an actor recalling her lines.

'Clive's been tricky for years, a typical saboteur. It's Hilary I pity.'

'How do you mean?'

Her voice lowers. 'You must know the rumours? He's a liability with women, always has been. I was concerned about you, at first, until I saw you could hold your own.'

'Don't attack him, please. He's a friend of mine.'

Marina ignores my comment. 'Plenty of students have complained over the years. I've saved his neck many times, always for the same reason. I still respect his work more than anyone's in Cambridge, despite his behaviour.'

The university is heaving with genius-level IQs, but her point is valid. Marina's direct speech convinces me that for once she's being sincere.

'We'll have to cancel the party.' She looks at me again. 'I've made a difficult decision about your situation. Would you like to hear it tonight, or next week, in my office?'

'Go on, Marina, don't hold back.'

'I want you to step down from your duties for now, to protect the department's reputation. You can return after the inquiry, provided the outcome is satisfactory.'

Suddenly the pain in my head feels blinding. 'You can't sack me over this.'

'It's not personal. Surely you can understand?' Her voice falls to a cold whisper.

'I'll complain to HR and appoint a lawyer. A psychologist can't be fired for acting in good faith, especially when I followed the professional code of conduct at all times.' My words are confident, but the tremor in my voice lets me down.

'It's not the only reason. Your online followers are turning against you, aren't they? And you failed to submit your report.' Her eyes glitter like a magpie's.

'The IT department will prove that was because of a technical problem.'

'Come to my office tomorrow afternoon. We can discuss this further.'

'This is bullying. I need all future conversations about my contract witnessed, in writing.'

'Your reaction disappoints me, Eloise. I'm only safeguarding the department.' She starts to turn away. 'One more thing, you asked whether a man was at your bedside, in hospital. Noah Jagiello's sports car was there, just before I left.'

Her sudden change of topic throws me off course. 'You're certain about that?'

'Positive. His car's distinctive, and the university sticker was on his front window.'

'Why didn't you say?'

'It didn't seem relevant. Ask him yourself. You two are close these days, aren't you?'

Marina walks away, stiff-backed, like a soldier on parade. It looks like our row has invigorated her, but my own strength is draining away. I had to channel Lisa's no-nonsense approach when she dropped her bombshell, but the idea of Noah performing a silent vigil at my bedside is more frightening. How did he know I was in hospital, unless he pushed me and saw me fall? It wasn't just Marina with me that night. I knew I'd seen a man as well as a woman in that hospital room.

Noah's done a great job of pretending to be innocent if it is him pursuing me. Instinct tells me that he would never walk into a care home and deliver a fatal injection to an old woman's arm, but guesswork is pointless. Everyone thinks he's laid back, which gives him the ideal cover to break down my defences, one by one. Winning my trust allowed him to observe my work and gave him access to my movements from the office next door. He was an IT expert in the States, so he could have hacked into my email and found his way inside my home to place listening devices there. Noah has charmed the whole department in the year he's spent with us, but I don't even know if his wife's death is true or just another lie. The man I slept with two nights ago could easily be my stalker.

Why risk following me to the hospital, then sit there holding my hand? I could have opened my eyes at any minute and identified him. By now he'll have seen my film, calling for a showdown. All I want is the truth. The anger brewing inside me feels even stronger than when I punched Rafe, and even more out of control. It's hard to tell if it's the pain pressing against the walls of my skull that's causing it, or the danger I'm facing. It's still there as I rush back to my car, which I leave by the entrance to Portugal Place. It's a no-parking zone, intended for buses and taxis, but I don't care about fines. I have to understand why Noah lied to me, and whether he's my stalker.

I stand outside his flat with my thumb on the buzzer, waiting for his voice through the intercom. I'm certain he can see me, staring up at his security camera, because there's a light on in his living room. He's been more cautious tonight; the curtains are fully drawn. I bet he's sitting on his sofa, replaying my latest film but unwilling to confront me.

'Open the door, you fucking coward,' I hiss into the intercom.

His trademark jazz is silent for once. It's possible that he's forgotten to turn off the lights and has gone out for the evening, but I'm not leaving. My anger is still running so hot the chill doesn't affect me. I'm prepared to doorstop him all night if that's what it takes.

44

ME

You're spoiling for a fight. I saw it in your face, but I prefer gestures to words. I'd rather show you how I feel until I'm ready to talk. Your cottage looks desolate tonight, neglected and bleak, but that's about to change. Fire and ice make a great spectacle, and this is the ideal location for a light show. The Fens provide a natural stage, pressed flat by an overload of sky. There's a drum roll of thunder while I go about my business, which fits the mood. Even the weather is applauding me.

My helper has already been here to complete the first part of my plan, but your security cameras are still blinking at me. I could have disabled them online, but why bother? They'll soon be destroyed, yet instinct makes me conceal my face as I approach the building. Then I smash your bathroom window to climb inside and enter your kitchen.

I love seeing the details of your everyday life up close. Things you handle all the time: knives, forks, spoons. It's tempting to linger, absorbing the atmosphere, even though I should hurry. I discover a photo album in a kitchen drawer, full of pictures of you as a child. I pocket one as a keepsake, then get to work. Everything you love and cherish is inside these four walls. I feel a pulse of guilt, but this is a necessary sacrifice. I have to strip away all your securities to reach you.

It's a simple task because fire is a greedy element. I use up three cans of paraffin on the ground floor and drop lit matches in each room. It gives me pleasure to stand in your garden as the flames take hold. Orange light glows in the windows as your past ignites. I want to stay and watch, but why reveal myself until you're so broken you're forced to listen? Your vulnerability will bring us together. Soon the only place where you ever felt truly safe will cease to exist.

I stop half a mile away, then watch through my binoculars, proud of myself. Your cottage is lit up like a beacon. By the time you get back it will be consumed by flames.

45

Minutes pass while I stand on Noah's doorstep with my thumb on his bell. He's not answering his phone, either. If he's the one chasing me, he's no more than a coward. I bet he's terrified of losing the safe academic life he's built, loving the thrill of terrorizing me anonymously.

My mind flits back to Jamie. He promised to call back, but never did, so I ring his number. There's no answer. When I phone Rafe, he picks up immediately. I can tell something's wrong from the flatness in his voice.

'Is Jamie there, Rafe?'

'No, I just looked in his room. He must have sneaked out, and his car's gone. Sorry, I was . . .'

'You fucking idiot. My mother was killed by an intruder at the home. My stalker could target him next.'

Killing my relatives one by one is the worst punishment imaginable, and my stalker's identity no longer matters. I'm running back to my car with my phone pressed to my ear. Jamie will be at the cottage by now, trying to be a hero, with no one protecting him. I must have been wrong all along. My stalker's campaign is about hatred, not love.

I've only driven half a mile when my phone distracts me again. I keep driving while I listen to earlier messages, hoping for clues. Noah's voice, quiet but insistent, repeats his invitation to stay with him tonight. I feel a rush of hatred for his lies, before focusing on the road.

Snow whirls in my headlights when a familiar car hurtles towards me. It's racing back into town, from the direction of my cottage. My brother is driving too fast, despite the icy conditions. I glimpse him at the wheel, his face elated. Why would he go out this late, after Simon's visit, when he already seemed exhausted? I remember him saying once that he gets in the car and drives if he can't rest. I'd love to have him at my side, but our lives are stuck on parallel lines, never quite touching.

I pass the turn-off for my old house without any desire to go back – that would be impossible now. Panic makes me grip the wheel. My long marriage feels meaningless; I don't care if it withers or survives.

The M11 is quiet when I cross it, with dirty snow heaped on the hard shoulder, thrown there by juggernauts' wheels. Conditions worsen when I drive the last mile, until something catches my eye. There's an orange glow on the horizon, like a distant bonfire. Maybe I'm imagining it after staring too hard at the road. But when I get closer, my car bumps over the rutted snow, and suddenly the picture is much too real.

My cottage is on fire and Jamie's old Ford is in the drive. Shock drops over me, numbing my senses. I think of Leo's car hurtling down the road, as though he was fleeing a crime scene, but push the idea aside. I'm still on autopilot when I call emergency services. Flames dance behind ground-floor windows while smoke billows from the chimney, dispersing on the breeze. A wall of heat hits me when I run closer, and the bubble inside me bursts at last, leaving nothing behind except terror.

I yell Jamie's name, but the front door is sealed shut, and when I look through the window, flames have taken over. The furniture is ablaze, fire leaping from floor to ceiling. I dash round the building looking for a safe entrance, but it's like peering into a furnace, flames wheeling in circles.

The bathroom's my best hope. Someone's broken the window, and I'm climbing onto the ledge when there's a noise like cannon fire. I'm thrown backwards onto the snow with a shard of glass piercing my hand, but the pain barely registers. Flames burst through the window. There could be another explosion any minute. I can't even climb a drainpipe to the first floor because they're melting from the walls.

The fire engine is arriving when I call for Jamie again. The crew spills out onto the snow, and one of them rushes towards me.

'My son could be in there,' I shout, to make myself heard above the flames.

What if he's unconscious inside, dying, because I failed to protect him? Instinct makes me run towards the building again. Another fireman grabs my arm, warning me to keep back. His voice is low and clear when he says there's nothing I can do. I must stay back until the fire's out. A team is going inside to look for Jamie.

My gaze stays pinned to the cottage. Cold air is freezing my lungs, I can hardly breathe when part of the roof collapses and flames ravage the exposed joists. My eyes shut at last, blocking it out. How did the stalker catch him? If he's inside, Jamie would have fought till the end. Whoever attacked him is a coward, tackling him unawares, still hiding their identity.

Voices hiss from the fireman's headset when he turns towards me.

'The search team can't go in yet, sorry. The structure's unsafe.'

I still can't accept that Jamie's trapped inside a place that offered me so much comfort as a child. It's a shell now; fire is consuming it, even though water from the hoses gushes through an upstairs window.

The fireman asks for my name and details again. 'Is there anyone we can contact, to support you?'

'I just need to call my son again. Maybe he's still with his friend.'

I turn away to use my phone. The fire is too loud, with pops and crackles as the building falls, its hot breath searing my face when I look back. Voices are raised as the fire crew yell instructions, and now the air is so thick with smoke I'm choking when I run back down the lane.

Jamie doesn't pick up. I only get his voicemail, telling me to leave a message in his grumpy teenage snarl. Instinct tells me to keep trying. I won't accept he's inside the cottage until there's solid proof. I have to stay rational: Jamie spends all his spare time with Billy Rawle. Maybe he left his car here and Billy drove him to his place.

The fireman who spoke to me earlier is heading in my direction, his expression sober. He explains that the police are on their way, but I don't care. They've done nothing whatsoever to protect me and my family from my stalker, but anger wastes time. I need to find out what's happened.

My hands are numb with cold as I pore over my phone, hunting for information. The CCTV cameras show a winter idyll at first, with snow falling in light flurries, pale against the dark. Then there's nothing. At 10 p.m. precisely the picture dies. Jamie's car was parked on the drive the whole time. Did my stalker want him dead, just like my mother, simply for his connection to me? Noah might be behind all this. His behaviour's gentle, but that could be part of his act. His knowledge of IT would have helped him hack into my security system and break it from the inside.

It's getting harder to convince myself that Jamie's alive. My fingers are covered in soot from the fire, mingled with blood from my wounded hand, when I rummage for my car keys. I can't just wait here, doing nothing, so I set off for Billy's house in Cottenham. It's ten minutes away, a converted vicarage beside a church, large and prosperous. I sit in my car, trying to gather myself. The village looks picturesque under its fresh coating of snow. The peaceful atmosphere reminds me that I've got nowhere to shelter Jamie now, and maybe I was kidding myself all along. I'm involved in a battle I should have fought alone.

I check my reflection in the mirror, wiping ash from my cheek. My legs feel shaky when I approach the property. Rafe liked Jennifer and Mike more than I did, his architect's eye enjoying their perfect home. They struck me as too driven by money, with little genuine warmth.

I'm not expecting a welcome when I rap on the door, after my row with Jennifer. Her face is sour when she appears, her dark hair perfectly styled. Her makeup is so perfect you can barely tell it's there, but her outrage shows. I can hear Jamie's favourite American 1970s music drifting down the stairs.

'What do you want?' she asks, frowning. 'Is something wrong?'

'Where's Jamie?'

She's blocking the doorway. 'I haven't seen him all day.'

'Let me talk to Billy, he'll know.'

Jennifer tries to shut the door in my face, but I wedge my foot into the opening. The cut on my palm is still oozing blood when I barge inside. 'I need to use your bathroom first.'

I rush down the hallway while Jennifer protests about me breaking and entering. The house is full of traditional details and muted colours. I wash my hands fast, rinsing blood from the cut. When I emerge seconds later, Jennifer is waiting with arms folded.

'Get out of my house right now,' she hisses.

'Not till I've seen Billy.'

Her eyes glitter with anger. 'Keep away from my son.'

She tries to push me back down the hall, but I'm stronger. Billy's voice drifts down from the floor above, making me rush upstairs. He's on his phone when I throw open his bedroom door. His smile vanishes fast, which isn't surprising. It's not every day that a friend's distraught mother crashes into your room. The walls are dark blue, the same shade Jamie wanted for his bedroom at the cottage, which no longer exists.

Jennifer is whining in the background, but I tune her out. The space above Billy's desk is plastered with photos, and I bet Jamie is among those smiling teenage faces. The air smells of cannabis, and Billy is slow to react, like his brain's taken a holiday. Was my son stoned too, when someone locked him inside the burning cottage?

'Jamie's missing, Billy. I need your help.'

I give him a garbled version of events and his gaze flickers from his mother's face to mine. Billy stammers in reply, words spilling out in the wrong order.

'We were in town. I followed him back to the cottage this afternoon.'

'I told you to drop him,' Jennifer snaps.

'Shut up, Mum, for fuck's sake. Didn't you hear? Jamie's in danger.'

I cut across them. 'Tell me what happened next, Billy.'

'He told me about your stalker. That's why he wanted to stay there tonight, to deal with him if he came back.'

'How, exactly?'

His gaze falls to the ground. 'He was planning to beat the shit out of him. I wanted to bring him here, but Mum said no.'

'What time was that?'

'About eight.'

'Eight-thirty,' Jennifer says. 'That's your curfew, remember?'

Billy's face darkens. 'Fix your own fucked-up life, Mum. Leave mine alone.'

His voice sounds raw, like he's just realized that Jamie might have died. But when I ask who else he could be with, Billy claims he's dropped most of his other friends recently, and hates being at college. I can see he's got nothing else to share. Jennifer grips my arm, and I don't protest as she leads me back downstairs. When I catch sight of myself in the hall mirror, soot is peppered across my clothes and there's a scorch mark on my coat. My face is blank with shock.

Jennifer looks calmer than before. Her kitchen's smart, with graphite walls, reminding me of Rafe's designs, but her movements are jerky. I remember Billy saying his parents rowed all the time. Jennifer could be going through hell too, for all I know. A confident exterior can mask the worst type of sadness.

She hands me a glass of water. 'I'm sorry about Jamie. You can spend the night here, if it helps.'

'I just need him found.'

'The police will do that for you. But Rafe should know about this, shouldn't he?'

'My phone's in the car.' The glass trembles in my grip.

'I'll call him now.'

My body feels as heavy as concrete when she hurries away. Jennifer's voice whispers through the wall from the room next door. She's keeping it low as she explains details to Rafe. Why's she calling my husband on the quiet, so I can't hear?

It dawns on me suddenly that she is his mistress. That scarf in the hallway was drenched in her scent, the bracelet expensive and tasteful, just like her jewellery tonight. It's the reason why her marriage is failing, just like mine. My eyes screw shut, trying to block out images of her and Rafe together. She's got the perfect manner for deceit, her feelings so well concealed. Does she love my husband enough to want me dead, and my son too?

When Jennifer returns, she announces that Rafe will go looking for Jamie immediately. He'll contact all his friends, like when he went missing before.

'Where's Mike tonight, Jennifer?' I ask.

'Away on a business trip.'

'Billy says you two have been rowing.'

'No more than any other couple. There's pressure at work, that's all. We're doing fine.'

'You're lying, I can see it. How long have you been sleeping with my husband?'

Her mouth flaps open. 'Excuse me?'

'I got your message, loud and clear, from those gifts you left behind.'

'You're not making sense, Eloise.'

'I destroyed your bracelet. Maybe you started the fire.'

Jennifer looks scared, like she's trapped indoors with a wild animal. I don't bother to speak again. Who cares about her screwing Rafe? It's not important now. I rise to my feet, eager to leave. This place is too pristine, as if no one ever dances here, or laughs out loud.

It's snowing again outside. Flakes spiral as they fall, muffling every sound. Billy appears as I'm about to drive away. His world-weary teenage cool has vanished. He looks like the sweet ten-year-old kid that used to sit at my kitchen table, chattering to Jamie for hours about computer games and football. I produce a smile, but my lips hurt. They're cracked and dry from standing too near the fire.

'Jamie's alive,' he mutters. 'I'd know if he was gone. He's like a brother to me.'

'Where could he be?'

'There's a place we go sometimes, to hang out.'

'Tell me, Billy. It's too late for secrets.'

'It's that old farmhouse near your cottage. I've been taking pictures inside, the atmosphere's amazing.'

He hands me his phone, showing a photo of Jamie in a room stripped bare, with winter light flooding through a broken window. The look on my son's face is pure mischief. Billy seems calmer, relieved to pass responsibility from his shoulders to mine. He offers to come with me, but Jennifer is calling him indoors, her tone shrill, so I say goodbye.

Billy offers me a broken smile. Everything else drops away when he begs me to find Jamie. Panic is still churning in my gut, but at least he's given me somewhere new to search.

46

ME

The aftermath is a let-down, of course. It's the same after any big drama. I loved seeing the flames take hold: small and delicate at first, like rose petals unfurling. That's when I walked away, certain the damage was irreversible. You'll be left with nothing. No mother, no marriage, no son, and nowhere safe to lay your head.

I half-close my eyes to watch the fire burn itself out. It was a perfect inferno, pressure building inside the cottage that once sheltered poor farm labourers, protected from the cold by a single layer of bricks. It lit up like a furnace, turning your possessions to charcoal, but now it's just a dull glow on the horizon, with occasional flames leaping towards the sky. The fire engine is still there, and its crew are crawling everywhere like ants. I can't help laughing at your predicament, even though it hurts.

My feelings don't make sense. I should be overjoyed that your refuge no longer exists, yet the idea is painful. I'm ready to face you, now that your life is stripped bare. You'll come back here soon to look for Jamie. And when you do, I'll follow you, for our last conversation.

I try to release my guilt, letting it burn away with tonight's flames, but it remains. We share the same blood, that's the trouble. I won't breathe easily until every piece of our shared history is erased.

47

The scene has changed when I drive towards the cottage. I pull up on the main road, but there's no point in going back. A police car has arrived. They'd expect me to concentrate on their questions, which is impossible. The only person I want right now is Leo. I still can't guess why he was driving away at frantic speed earlier, but he's the only person I trust to help me find the truth. I refuse to believe Jamie was inside the cottage when the fire started, and I can't stop looking for him now. His car is covered in debris, and it dawns on me that his most treasured possessions were all inside the cottage. Jamie's laptop and guitar will have been destroyed. I have to keep on believing that he escaped with his life.

When I look at the cottage again, smoke rises in grey clouds, illuminated by the fire brigade's arc lights. Its bare windows resemble sightless eyes, the gaping front door revealing the scorched walls inside. My aunt and uncle made a home that suited our needs – simple and honest. For the first time ever, I'm glad they're gone. It would have broken their hearts to see the place ruined.

My phone keeps on bleeping. I want to ignore it but check anyway, in case it's Jamie. There are texts from Rafe and Noah, and a voicemail from Lisa. When I scroll down the list there's one

from Clive Wadsworth too. It arrived half an hour ago, when I
was grilling Billy about where Jamie could be, but my old supervisor's state of mind no longer matters. I call Noah's mobile again,
desperate for answers. If he set my cottage alight after stalking me
for months, he's my greatest enemy, yet his voice is calm when he
listens to my account of losing everything.

'Let me help you, Elly. Come here, please.' I can hear the breeze
whistling behind his voice.

'Where are you, Noah?'

'Taking a walk, to straighten my head out.'

'Why did you trick me? Is that part of your fun? It was you, by
my hospital bed. Marina told me.'

There's a long pause. 'I was going to see the fireworks when
I saw you being carried to the ambulance with Marina by your
side. I drove to the hospital to help you both.'

'Why didn't you explain sooner, if that's true?'

'It felt too weird. I noticed you months ago, then suddenly
you're unconscious and I'm holding your hand. You didn't remember, so I kept quiet.'

My anger's spiralling again. 'What have you done with Jamie?'

'Nothing, Elly, you're not making sense. I've never even met
your son.'

'Tell me where he is.'

'I wish I knew. Let me help; we can find him together.'

I ring off fast. Why waste time listening to a fantasist when
there's a chance Jamie is still alive? I saw hope in Billy's eyes
when he mentioned the deserted farmhouse, like it was the cool-
est place imaginable. Maybe Jamie went there alone, smoked a
joint and fell asleep. I have to find out.

The weather is on my side at last when I follow the lane to
the old property. It's stopped snowing, but the track is in a bad
state, its surface treacherous with snow. I grab my torch from

the glove compartment, then approach the building on foot. I can see its appeal for two teenage boys. It looks spooky and atmospheric, like the only occupants are ghosts. I've feared dark spaces and confinement since childhood, but I have to search the place anyway. I find a loose piece of corrugated iron and pull it back. I call Jamie's name through the open window, but my only reply is the floorboards creaking under my feet as I climb through, and the rustling of mice scurrying away.

The farmhouse is like a museum, its details exposed by my torch. The kitchen is bare apart from a fireplace and an old-fashioned sink. When I spot something on the floor, my heart lifts. It's a grey skiing glove, like Jamie's. He was wearing them yesterday. I stuff it into my pocket, hoping it will bring me luck.

There's a thudding sound from the floor above. What if I've misjudged the situation and Noah's here too, waiting to hurt me again? I push the thought aside and go upstairs, even though tiredness and shock make me stumble, the familiar pain pressing behind my eyes. I clutch the handrail, my torchlight bouncing off damp-stained walls. A few paintings still hang there, austere portraits of a family that quit this place decades ago. It feels like they're judging me when I call Jamie's name again.

Dust rises in a cloud under my feet. The noise is coming from behind a closed door: a rhythmic thud, like a hand slapping on wood. My mouth feels like I've swallowed sand when I fling it open. Something hits my face hard, making me yell out in panic. My torch drops to the floor, the beam rolling at my feet. It was just a trapped pigeon, still flapping against the walls; it must have fallen down the chimney in the bad weather. There's nothing else here, living or dead.

I stand by the window, gazing back across the empty field. My cottage is glowing a dull red now, imploding like a dying star. Smoke is still billowing into the night sky. I have to go back, yet the idea terrifies me. I need someone to help me face whatever lies inside the cottage's broken foundations. My brother comes to mind again. Leo's condition doesn't stop him caring about me, and he's one of the few people I trust with my life. If anyone can advise me truthfully, it's him.

I pull out my phone, but another sound prevents me from making the call. It's a wrenching noise, like fabric being torn apart. My body shuts down before I can do anything except shelter my head as I collapse. Spasms grip me again, my teeth clenched together as my limbs jerk, and darkness smothers me.

48

ME

I've pushed you too far. Your body thrashes at my feet, even though I haven't laid a finger on you this time. Your eyes are stretched wide open, but I can tell you're slipping out of reach. I kneel at your side until the seizure ends. You deserve the truth about our shared past before you die, but that will be harder now. Pity is slowing me down. But before long you'll have to relive every detail of what happened to us as kids.

You're barely conscious when I drag you downstairs, which takes all of my limited strength. It's lucky you're not heavy. Maybe the cleanest way to end it would be to lock you in this place, then set it alight and walk free at last. But when I kneel beside you, my heart twists in my chest. We share the same blood, yet the biggest part of me wants you gone. You're still unconscious, too weak to fight, which is disappointing. I wanted this part of our journey to have more drama.

'We're together now, just me or you,' I whisper.

I haul you outside, with your phone in my pocket. When I look at the horizon, the cottage where you learned to feel safe is still spewing smoke into the night air. I'm your future now, your past and your present. You'll soon realize that I'm no coward.

When your phone rings, the sound is shrill and tinny. I drop it on the ground, then stamp on it with my full weight. It shatters instantly. The ringtone is soon replaced by the night's cold silence.

49

YOU

Everything hurts when my eyes open again. My legs feel numb and it's hard to breathe with my knees pressed against my chest. I'm curled like a foetus, floating in the dark. I try to move my hands, to find my phone, but it's gone. Panic floods my veins. My thoughts drift in a circle, with no rudder to anchor me.

Suddenly I'm peering through an open doorway into my past and the memories I've buried are surfacing at last. Time slides backwards, offering me no protection at all. My mother stands before me, in her late thirties, slim and glamorous, with blonde hair in perfect waves. She's in the kitchen and her back is turned. My father stands opposite, his face grave. He looks just as I remember him, in the smart suit he wore to work; clean-shaven, a man you could trust. Neither of them can see me. I want to call out and warn them that something terrible is happening, but we're separated by too many years.

'You bastard,' my mother hisses. 'I stayed in this miserable country for your sake, raising your kids.'

'I'm sorry, Ingrid.'

'Is that all you've got?' Her laughter is high and bitter. 'You'd have gone on deceiving me if that stupid bitch hadn't told me the truth.'

'I should have been honest, but it was too late.'

'You expect sympathy?'

'Don't leave me, please. I need you, and the kids. I've always loved you more.'

'It's the scandal you're worried about, Phillip. I'll tell your boss everything. You'll lose your precious job and be a laughing stock when I divorce you. Your friends at church and the golf club will all turn their backs.'

'It'll kill me if you drag my name through the dirt.' His voice breaks.

'Why should I care?'

My parents stand motionless, like pieces on a chessboard waiting for checkmate.

'You're so weak,' she hisses. 'Threatening to hurt yourself, like a spoiled child. You're terrified of dying, but it's your best option. Shame or death? The choice is yours.'

'Don't test me, Ingrid, please. We can fix this, I promise.'

'Shut up, you fool. I don't care what happens to you now.'

My mother wrenches the kitchen door open and escapes into bright sunshine. My father looks like a broken puppet with the strings cut. His body slides down the wall until he lands on the black and white floor tiles and sits there, motionless.

I reach out to him, but the present drags me back. My hands are raised to cover my eyes, even though it's too late to avoid the truth. The memories I've been hunting for years have shaken free at last. I think of Jamie and Rafe as my mind closes down again, shunting the past aside.

50

ME

I've never felt this alone until now. I make a call to my helper, confident they'll do as I say, too blind to complain, but I'm relying on them too heavily. It's time to be honest about the future. If I get caught, just two options exist: admit everything I've done and take my punishment, or make my ally shoulder the blame.

I'm sitting in your car and you're not making a sound. I could dump you by the roadside and let fate decide. You might perish in the cold or end up in hospital again. But no one gave me a chance when I broke down, so why should you have that privilege? It's too late for mercy.

It's only a matter of time before someone misses your car. They'll search for it, so I need to get back to town fast. I drive down a farm track that's rarely used. I hoped for a more elegant ending, but our final battle must be in your workplace, so the people you respect most will see you broken. No one will think to look for you there at night. The safest place is always the most obvious. When I drive back into town your car will go unnoticed. It will be just one vehicle among thousands, neatly parked among rows of ugly suburban houses.

I swing the car round, then head west. This way I can circle the city and enter through quiet streets while their residents lie sleeping. Happiness rises in my chest because the endgame you triggered has begun. You're awake again, trussed up neatly in the boot of your car. Is it your hands beating on the metal lid, or your feet? I'm glad you're ready to fight. Elvis is crooning on the radio, *Love me tender, love me true, never let me go.* I sing along, drowning your protests. I never realized how profound the lyrics are until tonight.

I will remember you tenderly, when you die, and promise not to forget you. I may even get another tattoo, with your name inked on my skin for ever.

51

YOU

I can hardly breathe. There's a rag binding my mouth, tasting of petrol. Did you wipe your hands with it after you set my house alight? Hysteria bubbles in my chest. My knowledge has failed to protect me. I've told thousands of stalking victims online to be cautious, be visible, be safe. I see now it was just empty words.

Something's wrong with my mind. There's drowsiness where terror should be; I feel like a bystander watching someone else trapped in this airless space, kicking out in frustration. I can't let the past haunt me, even though I've searched for it until now. It's too ugly to witness. I force myself to lie still, my body passive as the car judders over speed bumps. It keeps stopping at lights or roundabouts. We must be back in the city. Why take that much risk? If you want me dead, you could have done it months ago.

The past fills my mind again, overwhelming the present, even when I try to suppress it. The image is so fresh and clean, it must be true. I'm in the attic with my father. He's pacing the floor, his face rigid with tension. There's an odd smell coming off him, acrid and bitter. The window is open, but the air feels too hot, like we're trapped in an oven. My father's manner changes suddenly.

He comes to a halt in the middle of the floor and stands in silence. Then he turns to me, his voice steady.

'Listen to me, Elly. Something bad's going to happen soon. Don't look outside, just run straight downstairs and call 999. Tell the police to come straight away. It's not your fault. Let them deal with it, okay?'

I nod, but I don't understand what he means, only that he's calm again. It's the first time he's smiled for days.

'Love you always, sweetheart. You're my best girl.'

He says goodbye so casually. Then he glances up at the clouds and launches himself head first through the window, like a bird taking flight. There's a moment of silence until his scream splits the air, and instinct makes me disobey his advice. When I run to the window, my father lies on the concrete path below. His body is contorted, legs splayed in the wrong directions, like a broken statue. The terrible bawling sound coming from his mouth makes me cover my ears.

52

Monday 15 November

ME

Ambition ruled me when I arrived here. I wanted to improve my life, and the beauty of Cambridge is seductive. The streets are so freighted with history, signs of it appear on every corner. I love the gargoyles, crests and college names chipped from ancient limestone. Everyone follows the same dream, but this place was built for the young. It only comes alive in term time, when the river heaves with canoes, punts and paddleboards, competing for space. I feel overlooked here every single day, but natural justice is on my side.

I take my time driving down West Road. I don't want to trigger a speed camera or call attention to myself. My plan has worked well, so far. I'll do whatever it takes to destroy the elements of your life, leaving mine intact. The quiet helps when I finally pull up. Snow has lowered every background noise to a dull hum. By morning that will change, with the ugly dawn chorus of traffic filling these roads. Our fight must be over by then. I've never felt more powerful than now, when we're about to meet, face to face. The pretence between us will finally drop away.

I park behind the psychology building, then take your swipe card from your bag to open the security doors. It was fun hacking into the system a couple of times to cancel your details, but that was just a game. The system will record you entering the building, not me, which is ideal. The lights are out in the teaching block, leaving me hemmed in by blank walls. I fetch a trolley from the gateway. Its wheels are soundless as it trundles over snow. Porters use these trolleys to deliver supplies to the kitchen or common room. They're the perfect size to carry a human body.

I open the boot, where you're still wrapped up like a gift, tied with rope instead of ribbon. Muffled protests emerge through your gag as I haul you out, then wheel the trolley towards the building. The entrance doors part immediately. I keep my head down as we pass the security camera overhead, my face concealed by my hood.

Now I summon the lift, and we ride to the third floor. It's a struggle to lift you off the trolley when we reach your office. Suddenly you kick out, the blow to my gut winding me. It makes me so angry I want to retaliate, but it's too soon. I must clear away all the evidence before then, and you have to be ready to listen. I drag you through the doorway, then dump you on the floor, to consider your fate.

Psychological violence is something you understand better than me. Am I being unnecessarily cruel when I break your desk lamp, then unscrew the bulb in the overhead light, just in case? You told me recently that you still fear the dark, after witnessing too much suffering as a child, even though you caused it all.

I walk away, then make another decision at the end of the corridor. My father used to say, *If a job's worth doing, it's worth doing well.* I stand on a chair to open the fuse box, then throw all the switches, casting this section of the building into darkness. Now the only source of light is the powerful torch in my hand, putting me back in control.

53

YOU

I don't know where you've brought me. The oilskin has me wrapped in tight black air, stinking of smoke. It's coming from my clothes, after standing too near the blaze. My body aches from being dragged over hard ground, and my mind pulses with memories. Maybe this is how death feels? People talk about images streaming past our eyes as our strength fades, but I'm not ready to let go.

One more knock to my skull would finish me, and my breathing sounds wrong. It's slow and ragged. Am I conscious or dreaming? It feels like Jamie is nearby. Old Nashville music is playing softly, making me believe he's alive. I want to call his name, but my gag stops me. I keep trying to bite through it, but it's too thick. The taste of petrol cloys in my throat, strands of cotton sticking to my teeth.

There's nowhere to hide as my mind dodges memories that fly past like bullets. My marriage, my son and the cottage have gone, yet I can't stop fighting. I test the binding around my wrists, trying to pull them apart. The rope's so tight my fingers ache. I can move my legs, but my ankles are bound too. I'm lying on my side. My hip must be bruised, a sharp pain radiating through my back. The dark is the least of my worries, yet it still scares me, for the ugliness it hides.

I lie still for a minute, listening. There are no voices or footsteps. Even the music has fallen silent. But when I listen again, a familiar noise reaches me. The heater in my office makes that same rattling sound, all winter long.

Why bring me here, then abandon me? You've turned my office into a prison cell. What crime do you think I've committed? The words echo in my head, but the conversation feels real, at last. If it's you doing all this, Noah, why did you wait? You could have killed me in my sleep two nights ago, but kindness was just part of your act. I'm beginning to understand your mindset. It's cruelty that lights you up, not tenderness, isn't it?

54

I don't want to travel any further than necessary. It's 1 a.m. and the whole night should have been ours, but it's taking me longer than expected to set the stage. By dawn I'll be alone again, in a world where few people notice me or care how I feel.

I drive down West Road, then turn right. The block is full of university buildings, some old, some modern. The grandest is the library, its structure designed to hold millions of books. I pass laboratories and warehouses, all deserted at night, with few security guards patrolling the sites. The university owns large sections of the city, its empire too powerful to believe it could ever be brought to its knees.

There's no one in sight when I drive to a parking bay I identified days ago. It's tucked between buildings, unlit. A solitary guard strolls by, smoking a cigarette. He doesn't bother to look up, too lazy to notice that a new car has arrived. I let five minutes pass before getting out. When I check the area, there's no sign of him, only a streetlamp guttering overhead.

I leave your bag inside, then douse the car's interior with petrol and throw the can in too. All it takes now is one lit match. I hide between buildings to watch everything burn: your bag and wallet, credit cards and driving licence. Your identity is going up in flames. I never realized until tonight how glorious fire can be. It makes me long to see the whole city razed to the ground, like when London burned centuries ago, wooden buildings reduced to ashes. I love the hiss and crackle as the car windows fracture then explode. They sound like gunshots, ringing out across the city.

I retreat fast, only looking back once. There's another explosion, like a depth charge, as the petrol tank blows, making me walk faster. I'm keeping the fire brigade busy tonight. But my biggest challenge still lies ahead.

55

YOU

My physical strength has ebbed away at the worst moment. It takes effort to roll onto my back. I want to die fighting, not shuddering in fear. My head throbs as I twist from side to side. I can't feel any difference at first, but the oilskin loosens at last, and the fabric shifts, leaving my face exposed.

It's a small triumph, but it helps. The room is dark, with a trickle of light coming through a gap in the blind. I can only just make out my desk, and the chair left behind by my predecessor. Music is playing again, from the room next door. It could be Noah doing all this, yet this isn't his usual jazz. It's old American rock, from before I was born – The Eagles, 'Hotel California'. That sounds like Jamie's choice, not Noah's. The tune could be imaginary, but it helps me to keep on believing he's alive.

I scrub my face along the floor, the carpet burning my skin, to loosen my gag. I want to yell out, but the music stops abruptly. Maybe I was wrong, after all. My stalker punished my son simply for protecting me, leaving him inside the cottage to burn. I have to know the truth before I die.

All I can do is try to loosen the oilskin until my legs are free.

My ankles are still bound tight, but anger makes me kick out hard. My boots batter the wall between us, but the song starts up again, quiet and melodic: *On a dark desert highway, cool wind in my hair.* It's soft and easy, a twisted lullaby. Noah has a sick sense of humour, if it's him picking the tunes, but it could still be someone else. It must be someone smart. They've found a way to access my office, so they can probably open every door in the department.

My thoughts simplify at last. Whatever you've done to me, I'm not prepared to die here, choking on a filthy gag. I summon my strength and kick the wall again. Reg Bellamy is off duty, but someone else might hear the commotion if I make enough noise. Reg said that an intruder was reported here yesterday, which makes sense. Noah wouldn't have used his own pass card if he's my stalker, knowing it would log his time of entry. He's found a way into the building without triggering security.

The past wells up to greet me again before I can stop it. Repressed memories explode into the light. I try to blink the pictures away, but each one is more vivid than the last.

This time I face my mother, in the kitchen. Her mascara has dissolved into black trails running down her cheeks, her lipstick a gash of crimson. The rest of her face is stark white. She's inches away, hissing at me.

'You should have stopped him, you little fool. You were there. Why didn't you grab his hand?'.

She's shaking me so hard my jaw clamps shut, my teeth biting into my tongue.

'I would have forgiven him, in time. He loved me, more than anyone. There's an evil seed in you. I saw it the day you were born.' She strikes me hard across the face. 'You're the reason he jumped, not me.'

My mother's fists batter my torso, sending me reeling. Now I catch sight of Carla, cowering in the corner, frozen. It's Leo who runs to grab Mum's arm. The look on his face is desperate, like he's afraid she'll kill us all.

56

ME

I feel deflated after seeing your car burn. The hurt in my chest never goes away. I used to hate cruelty, particularly towards people I love. You fall into that category. I want to deny it, but can't. Our lives are bound together by too much history; I can no longer tell where your life ends and mine begins. We're sewn together by an invisible seam. When you die, it will be like losing my Siamese twin. What's the point of me without your sane mind keeping me whole?

I slow down by the main road as a police car approaches. It's travelling slowly, but what if you've managed to get free and summoned them? I hide behind a wall. I've been too careless since you threw down your challenge. The battle between us is already under way, and it's too late to pull back. We could have gone on with our dance, getting close and withdrawing, for months. My calmness returns when the squad car vanishes at the end of the road, leaving me free to continue. The police must be doing their usual duties, checking for people reeling home drunk, looking for trouble.

My plan only falters when I near the psychology building again, where you lie bound on the floor. The conversation between us must start soon, yet I regret our relationship ending. I respect the woman you've become – dogged and persistent, fixing so many broken minds. Pity you couldn't heal mine. I need to close the gap between us, once and for all, but I'm frozen in place.

57

YOU

My mother haunts me now the floodgates have opened. I see her in a dark blue dress, standing in the hallway. Weeks have passed since my father leapt from the window. She looks like an actor waiting to go on stage, concentrating hard, her fists bunching at her sides. Dad wore that same rapt expression the moment before he jumped. I glance around, looking for Leo and Carla, but there's no one in sight.

I'm still watching when she pushes the living room door open. The air smells of antiseptic and decay, flavouring my mouth with bitterness. I witness again how the room looked when Dad came home. He's lying on a hospital bed with handrails on each side, a plastic tube emerging from his throat. A ventilator is forcing air into his lungs, making his chest rise and fall. His eyes are the only thing he can control. My father's arms and legs lie motionless under the white sheet, like his body is made of stone.

My mother smooths his hair back from his forehead, her voice so tender, but I can't hear the words. I've forgotten how good it feels to receive her love, but my father hasn't. His eyes are sparkling. She stands motionless for a minute, then turns off his breathing machine. When I dart forward to switch it back on, she shoves me away. Now she's pressing a cushion over his face. Dad's limbs twitch as his life is taken, but he can't fight back. When I try to prise her hands away, she's much too strong.

My father's face is empty when she lifts the cushion at last. His eyes are closed, his expression relaxed for the first time since he fell. My mother lets several minutes pass before switching the machine back on, then she calls emergency services. I can hear her in the kitchen saying, *My husband's choking, help me, please send an ambulance.* Her voice is shrill with fake panic. When she returns to the living room I'm holding my father's hand, saying goodbye.

'Sorry for causing this, are you?' she hisses. 'You brought me to it, you evil child. If you breathe a word, I'll say you killed him. Do you understand?'

I stand rooted to the spot, expecting her to strike me again, but nothing happens. The hatred in her eyes hurts more than any physical blow.

58

ME

Something's wrong when I reach the back entrance to the psychology building. The entry system isn't working when I tap the pad with your card. Maybe it thinks you're still inside.

I hiss out curses while the cold, wolf-like, bites at me. Every minute increases the danger. Passing cars could see me here, under the floodlights I've triggered. I step into the shadows, beyond the camera's reach, aware that my disguise is wearing thin. Walking under that CCTV gets riskier every time.

My eyes hunt for an access point, but the lowest windows are above head height, sealed tight against the cold. I shift my weight from foot to foot, trying to keep warm. I'll have to act fast. Cleaning staff will arrive soon, paid to scour the building from top to bottom while the students are away.

I summon the same bravery that carried me inside the care home two days ago. I felt unstoppable then, injecting tap water into Ingrid's veins, knowing she would die a terrible death, choking for air. She deserved it, and so do you. My jaw keeps clenching with frustration, my teeth gritted. I should have acted long ago, straight after I won your trust.

59

I've never wanted to stay in the present more than tonight, yet my mind returns to my old bedroom in London. Mum is piling my clothes into a suitcase. She keeps her back turned, refusing to answer my questions. *Where am I going? When can I come home?*

She throws one last blouse into the case, then the lid snaps shut. Her high heels clatter downstairs and my chest feels hollow. She's already taken down the pictures I drew last term at school and removed my dressing gown from the hook on the door, wiping away my existence.

Leo is crying in his room, calling my name, but complaints are pointless. Our mother's changed since Dad died. She's crueller than before, her lips pursed tight like she's swallowed something sour. When she calls me downstairs, her voice is sharp, even though I've done nothing wrong.

The front door stands open, letting in the cold. Our next-door neighbour appears in the porch; the man is around my father's age. He gives me a tired smile as he picks up my suitcase. Mum thanks him for giving me a lift, then touches me for the last time ever. Her hand feels heavy in the centre of my back as she pushes me outside.

When I look over my shoulder, my mother has vanished. Carla is watching me leave. She's standing in the hallway with her hand on the doorknob. The look on her face startles me. All I can see is relief as the door swings shut, locking me out for good.

60

ME

I have to use a pass card that belonged to a member of staff who retired last year. My breath feels tight in my chest when I re-enter the building at last. Thank God the card worked. This university prides itself on cutting-edge research, but its security is pathetic. You only have to know the right people to cheat the system.

When I enter the psychology building, my courage fades. Someone else has got here first, their footsteps blundering through the darkness. Only one person knows I'm here. I told them to give me another hour, but it must be them. No one else knows my plan, unless I've tripped an alarm in the building without realizing. Panic is draining my strength. If the police have found their way in here, I pray they don't find the fuse box. The dark is my only protection.

I stumble through the nearest doorway, looking for a hiding place, but it's a bad choice. That's clear when I switch on my torch. I'm inside an exhibition room in the old laboratory, preserved as it was last century. Its haunted atmosphere never struck me when life felt easier, but now I realize it's a torture chamber. There's a gurney in the corner with leather straps to hold patients down. When my torch beam flickers from the walls, I see a metal box fitted with electrodes capable of charging 400 volts through a human brain. I stand by the door with eyes shut, imagining the pain and wonder of a mind electrified. I've come too far for such a cruel remedy to work. This situation is madness, yet nothing else makes sense.

I should have strapped you to that gurney for the crime you committed when we were kids. The idea should thrill me, but there's someone inside the building. I pray that it's my helper, but someone else could have found their way inside. I'll have to deal with them before finishing you.

61

YOU

Fear washes over me like a slow tide. I understand at last. Carla believed Mum's lies about me being an evil child. She kept on hearing that I drove our father to distraction, and she loved him so much, always clamouring for his attention. I've been blind because the joy of us three reuniting felt heady. I stopped being an only child and became an older sister again, linked to her and Leo like beads on a necklace. But maybe she's wanted me dead all along.

When a new sound comes, I strain to hear it again. Slow footsteps, like before. My hands are numb from the ligature, my jaw still so tightly bound my lips won't open properly. All I can do is listen. My body tenses when the noise stops outside the door, my heart thudding inside my chest. Carla must hate me with a passion if our past has hurt her for all these years. But why did she kill our mother after so much devotion? None of it makes sense. When I screw my eyes shut, panic cascades around me.

The door opens a crack. I strain to see who's there, but can only make out a figure blundering towards me. When a torch beam shines into my eyes it sears my retinas, then dies away. Someone drags their hand across my face, releasing my gag. I bite my tongue to stop myself from screaming. I won't give my stalker the satisfaction of seeing me broken.

Footsteps shift, and the door reopens, the intruder retreating. I'm alone again, and the song playing through the wall is a woman's voice, impossibly high and pure. My sister must have heard me and Jamie talking about Joni Mitchell's rare skills when she eavesdropped on us. She's singing, *I wish I had a river I could skate away on.* The song must be fifty years old, but it describes exactly how I feel.

'Carla,' I yell out. 'Come back here, please.'

Silence follows my words. She's freed me to speak, at least, but no one's listening.

62

ME

I'm stuck in this room, separated from you, just like in childhood. It was a brutal time for both of us. I know you feel the same because you've told me about the pain and isolation you suffered. And I've heard it in those crackling conversations I recorded in your home. You wouldn't believe how many times I've played them back, trying to understand you. The echo of childhood sadness remains in your voice, even when you laugh.

The truth is, my world ended when Dad died, thanks to you. It was your fault he threw himself from that window. You were in the room when it happened. I wanted to love you, so much, yet the blood we share has never been enough. You hide that evil seed at your core, but it will still be there, until you die.

Why am I faltering when the end should be easy? The connection between us makes hurting you feel wrong. I need a sister now, more than ever, but I'm about to lose you.

Tears blind me as I blunder down the corridor, heading for the stairs. I'm gasping for fresh air. It feels impossible to finish what you started. I need some breathing space, before the last step.

63

YOU

The music stops as the track ends. All I can hear now is my heart pumping too fast, blood rushing in my ears. I'm not prepared when my attacker steps back inside my office. My eyes strain in the darkness. I can only see a figure dropping to the floor, head bowed over their knees. I don't know if it's a man or a woman, but an unexpected sound reaches me. They're crying softly to themselves. My stalker is weeping, even though they must have planned this all along. I can barely move, my voice still my only defence.

My mind flits back to the facts about how stalking works. Most stalkers want total submission, giving them power and control. I should remain still and passive, becoming the perfect victim. Anything I do will be seen as a challenge, but silence consumes my energy. I want to yell for help, still hoping that someone might hear, but I know pleading won't work.

I listen hard, ears straining for every sound. My stalker is still crying. The noise is so raw it sounds like they've suffered for a lifetime and never been consoled.

64

I gasp in one ragged breath after another, trying to calm myself. I hate you for recovering from a wound I can't heal. Your child came along, cementing your perfect marriage, while I struggled to form relationships. The bitterness never left me. I decided to let you live until you reached the age our father was when you let him die. You're a success now, but with dreams and ambitions that will never be fulfilled.

I've observed you up close so many times. It's made my task harder, but my desire to hurt you remains. I still hate the girl that goaded Dad into jumping from that window. Once our father's suicide becomes common knowledge, your colleagues and friends won't think twice about finding your broken body in the quadrangle, bathed in harsh morning light. You'll be gone, and Dad's soul will finally rest in peace.

I loved him more than you ever did. You took him from me, and the same horrific death he suffered is waiting for you tonight.

65

My stalker is still crying, but the sound is fainter now. It's getting harder to remain quiet. My whole body hurts from the last attack, my hip throbbing as I move.

'Tell me what's wrong,' I whisper. 'Let me help you.'

The weeping fades. Is that the response they've craved all these months? The desire to be heard? It's so quiet I can hear a vehicle grinding along the road fifty metres away. I'd give anything to be in the passenger seat, racing away from all this, my courage too fragile to last.

'I'm sorry, Elly,' a man's voice whispers.

'Let me go, please. Whoever you are.'

'It's too late.'

I suck in a long breath, too shocked to think straight. That voice is low and sonorous. I've heard him give so many lectures over the years, I know its sound by heart. It's Clive, my oldest friend in Cambridge. I knew he was missing, but never believed he'd target me. Why would someone so loyal set fire to my house? If I can keep him talking, it'll delay him hurting me again.

'You covered your tracks well, Clive. I had no idea.'

He's quiet for a moment. 'This is about you, not me. I'm sorry. You'll die here tonight, but it's not my fault.'

I fight to stay calm. 'Tell me how it started. You owe me that much, at least.'

'She'll kill me too, for explaining. Maybe that was her intention all along. I'll tell you her secret if you really want to hear, but no interruptions, please. I'm struggling to think straight.'

I stay silent. What choice do I have, bound up like a parcel, unable to move?

'I fell for her, out of weakness.' His voice breaks down, unable to continue.

'Who do you mean, Clive?'

'She's the most powerful woman I know. Love's overwhelming, Elly. You see that every day in the stalkers you treat. It makes fools of us all.'

'You're not to blame. Just tell me the truth. She made you set my cottage on fire, didn't she?'

Music is playing again, a low pulse in the background. The melody is light and easy, like the promise of summer. It feels like Jamie's spirit is protecting me, until everything blurs. Another seizure could arrive as I wait for Clive's reply. Maybe I'm wrong about Carla. I've never introduced my sister to him, and another name enters my mind.

'Is Marina involved in this?' I ask.

'No, but she's vicious too.' He gives a jagged laugh. 'Marina pursued me, years ago. She's been trying to break me ever since I rejected her. No one would believe it, of course. She forced me to retire early, but she didn't cause this mess.'

'Who then? Why does she want me dead?'

He pauses for a moment. 'She says you ruined her life, as a child. It's the one part of your sister's personality I find ugly, that desire for vengeance.'

Shock floods through me. His words confirm what I thought before; Carla has orchestrated all of this. She found the weakest link among my friends, yet it makes no sense. Carla tries to mend people every day, yet she's killing those she claims to love.

'How did you meet her?'

'Our paths cross all the time, Elly. She made me keep it secret.'

I have to make him see sense. 'Hilary needs you at home. It ends here, okay? Untie me, right now.'

He's weeping again, too choked to reply. I can see his outline, hunched against the wall, shivering with fear in the dark. There's a new sound coming from Noah's office too. A rhythmic, thudding noise. Is someone else trapped in there, like me, trying to signal that they're alive?

Clive's still crying, with a quiet rasping sound, like he can't catch his breath.

'Untie me,' I whisper. 'I'll say you came to my rescue. You can be the knight in shining armour. Do it now, Clive, please. Time's running out.'

My words linger on the air, but he doesn't reply.

66

ME

I stand outside the door, listening to Clive sobbing. He's disobeyed me for the first time ever, proving he's even more pathetic than I realized. It was a mistake to let anyone get too close, yet company is seductive. He likes to listen, and I need to talk, but my secrets have been exposed too soon.

Trust you not to be angry, even knowing that your own sister has planned your death. Don't expect the same generosity from me. You're always so quick to accept people's frailties, but you're the reason why the man I loved most of all died in agony. My life fell apart then, like a train derailing. Nothing can change it, but your death will avenge him, at least.

I keep trying to summon my courage to face our last conversation, without any disguise. I want dawn to rise on your shattered body, for all the world to see. I've arranged everything so the person you love most will witness your fall, then we'll be even. I can escape and you'll have paid the price. Your life will end at the same age as Dad's, while you're in your prime, with so much left to achieve.

I need our last conversation more than anything, but conflict terrifies me. It always has. I screw my eyes shut and plan my first words, while my head rings with the ugly memories that drove me here.

67

'Keep talking, Clive. Get it off your chest, if it helps.'

I need to keep our conversation alive, in case he's unbalanced enough to hurt me. I still don't understand what's happened, except that Carla has mesmerized him somehow. I keep thinking about her longing for intimacy, and the way her emotions rest on a knife-edge. Mum's lies sank deep into her mind as a child, yet she killed her too. She must have broken down completely, to turn on the people she loves most. Leo was strong enough to see through Mum's deceit, but Carla was more vulnerable. My sister's smart and beautiful enough to weaponize a man who's been obsessed with her for months to do her dirty work.

My vision blurs again, until darkness swims in front of me, rippling like water. The only thing that's keeping me focused is that rhythmic thudding against the wall. Or is it just the pounding of my heartbeat?

'She wants you dead so the past can be over. It sounds reasonable when she talks, even though I've never seen you hurt anyone. She says there's evil in your character, but how could a child convince her father to take his own life?'

'You know I'd never do that, surely? Let me go, for Christ's sake.' My voice breaks.

'If she drops me, I'll have nothing. Hilary won't take me back after this.'

'You're ill, Clive. Can't you see she's playing you?' I try to keep my voice steady. 'Let me go, then your life will go back to normal.'

'I can't go home, not now.'

'You're wrong. Hilary's desperate to find you.'

'I don't deserve her, I never have.'

His voice is loud with conviction, and my hopes are dying. I've heard that tone from convicted stalkers in the past, certain that life would be perfect if only their victim loved them in return.

68

ME

I enter your office to face the darkness, at last. Clive lumbers to his feet immediately, the door clicking shut when I tell him to wait in the corridor. He's still in my grip, thank God. I know he'll help me when the time comes. All I have to do is explain why you're here, then you can die, with your mind as broken as your body.

'You and me, Elly. Are you ready to talk?'

There's no reply. I already know that silence is your favourite strategy, but now the power's mine. I've got weapons, and you've only got your faculties. I could overpower you easily, but not until the truth's exposed.

'Tell me what you've done to Jamie.'

Your tone is cold, like you think I'm worthless. Fury overtakes me suddenly. When I kick out hard, my boot connects with your ribs. There's an ugly, splintering sound, before you choke out curses. I can hear you trying not to scream. Your pain should bring me relief, yet the hurt I've carried for so long is growing all the time.

69

YOU

Clive told me my sister put me here, but her voice is different. Carla's pitch sounds lower, her words muffled and unclear. I'm struggling to draw breath. One of my ribs must be broken, the pain like a firebrand.

'Is it you, Carla?' I gasp out the words. 'You believed what Mum said, but you have to understand. She killed Dad, not me.'

Her face is concealed by the hood of her coat, and the dark, when she speaks again. 'We share the same father, but we've got nothing else in common. I adored him, you see. He was the best part of my life. Mum broke down after you let him die. You never had to witness her suffering, or mine.'

Shock hits me again. I recognize the voice now, but it doesn't make sense.

'Why did you wait so long for this, Lisa?'

'I kept giving you hints, but you were too self-absorbed to hear. Now shut up and listen.' There's no victory in her tone, just cold determination. 'Dad met my mother on a park bench in London; he didn't tell her he was married. They ate their packed lunches together every day, escapees from office jobs they hated. I was born six months after you. He was a wonderful father, affectionate and kind. I'm sure he wanted to leave your mother and marry mine. Dad's only mistake was being too weak to ask for a divorce. You and your vicious bitch of a mother poisoned his mind.'

The picture finally clicks into place. My mother learned the truth: that's why she threatened to shame Dad publicly – for having two families. It explains his suicide note.

'Mum followed him in our car when I was nine,' Lisa says. 'She finally sensed that all those business trips were a lie. She took me along to discover what he was hiding. Maybe she couldn't face the truth alone.'

'How did he keep his double life going for so long?'

'Our mothers both trusted him enough to swallow his excuses for all that absence. My life fell apart when I saw you that day, a pretty little girl about my age, living in a big house, while we struggled in our rundown flat. I realized he loved you more than me, to give you such a privileged life. A few days later we heard he'd jumped from a window. He died before I could say goodbye, thanks to you. I tracked your mother down when I was sixteen. She told me the ugly things you screamed at him that day. He would never have jumped without your cruelty; it made him suicidal.'

'That's not true. I adored him too. The decision was his, Lisa.'

'Lying won't help you now. Your mum told me you switched off the life support machine, then watched him die, with a smirk on your face. She sent you away instead of calling the police. I wanted to report you, but who'd believe a girl like me, from a poor background, about a murder I didn't witness?'

'She smothered him with a pillow. He couldn't move or speak; I think it was a mercy killing. But even if her story was true, why did you wait so long for revenge?'

Her laughter rings with bitterness. 'I tracked every stage of your life, competing with you at school and at university. I had dreams of us being close one day, but you always had to do better. I lost the race each time. I decided to let you to reach the same age as our father, then have you die with your reputation in tatters, like him. It worked, didn't it? Your followers are turning against you, calling for you to be sacked. You're broken, and I'm the reason why. Clive will help me finish it. Your life will end, just like Dad's.'

'You slept with my husband and killed my son just to get even?'

'Rafe took some convincing, but it worked in the end. The poor guy's lonely. I'll step into your shoes after you're gone. But I hate that glass house of yours, with everything on display. I'll make him build me somewhere with solid brick walls.'

I bite my tongue, determined not to give her the satisfaction of hearing me scream. 'You want my life instead of yours. Is that it?'

She ignores my question. 'Only one of us deserves to live. Once I'd tapped into your computer, it was easy to dismantle your life. I paid a guy from a village near your cottage to short circuit your electricity supply. All I had to do was ring him to put you in darkness, then drop cash into his bank account. Convincing Joe Sinclair to reoffend was harder. I found out his release date from your emails, then tracked him down in his favourite boozer for a chat. They say advice is free, don't they?'

'You told him to kill Georgia Reed?' I rasp out the words.

'Just to finish what he started. I knew you'd be discredited if the stalkers you counselled began reoffending. I thought I'd need to try several times, but it worked like a charm. It was a bonus that Georgia's dad decided to sue you for negligence.'

'You sacrificed her, Lisa. How can you live with that?'

'The blame's on *you*, not me. My past made me like this. You killed my father, then Mum broke down and I ended up in care, then a dozen foster homes. My childhood was a catalogue of abuse.'

'Listen to me. My mother planted the idea of self-harm in Dad's head. She told him suicide was his best option – that or face being shamed. Mum said it in anger, but he took her literally. And maybe you're right – Dad loved your mother more. Mine hated being second best.'

'You pretended not to remember. Was that a lie too?' Lisa hisses.

'It came back tonight. Trauma can force buried memories to the surface.'

'Shut up. I can't stand your psychobabble.'

Lisa wrenches the window open, then yells Clive's name. Cold air whispers past my face, and panic almost makes me black out again. I've flirted with the idea of death before, but the reality doesn't appeal. I didn't cause my father's agony. I can't die in the same way, landing on hard stone, my life destroyed by someone I used to trust.

70

ME

It no longer matters who's right or wrong. I've obsessed over you too long, the measuring point for all my successes and failures. I just want our battle to end, and to walk away cleansed. I call Clive's name again, but there's no answer. When I go outside, I shine my torch beam along the corridor. Light bounces back at me from empty walls.

The bastard's run away, leaving me to finish the task alone. There's an odd ringing sound in my ears. It's a hum of music that I can't identify, but nothing can distract me now. Your son will witness my final gesture. He'll see you in freefall, and the moment when you break apart, then I'll kill him too, and the past will be over.

You look pathetic, lying on the carpet at my feet. I've broken your marriage and your reputation, and taken your child. I grab your shoulders and haul you upright. You moan in pain when I shove you towards the open window to face the darkness, then heave you onto the ledge. But you're stronger than you look. You lash out with bound fists, knocking me backwards.

I come back fast, lifting your feet off the ground, until your body teeters on the brink. One more push and you'll fall. The cobbles below glisten with ice in the light spilling from the window, dawn still far away. I try again, but your fingers are buried in my hair, yanking it by the roots.

You pull me close, and suddenly I picture a different fate for us. We can both die here, together, conjoined twins. Me *and* you, not you *or* me, as I imagined. Our lives are connected, inextricable, yet there's pure hatred on your face. You wrench my hair again, pain blinding me. Suddenly the music is deafening. The door flies open, and someone's dragging me away. Panic grips me, now the link between us is broken.

71

YOU

I feel myself slipping, then a hand grips my wrist and I'm hauled back inside. When I see Jamie's face I can't tell if he's real, until his warm breath caresses my cheek. My son is white-faced with shock when he fumbles with the rope around my wrists, determined to free me at last. Once I can move my arms, I hug him close. A few seconds pass before I can speak.

'I thought you were gone, Jamie. What happened to you?'

'Don't worry about that now. Are you okay?'

'My ribs ache, and my head, but I'll live. We should call the police.'

'They're on their way. Clive brought me here, Mum. He made me wait for you next door.'

Lisa is back on her feet suddenly, trying to escape, until Jamie grabs her arm. He slams her against the wall, then blocks her way. She's broken now. It shows in her body language when she slumps to the floor with face averted, unwilling to meet my eye.

'Tell me about tonight, before the police come,' I say to Jamie.

Colour is slowly returning to his face. 'Clive came to the cottage. He told me you'd sent him to help catch your stalker.

He even said my phone was bugged, so I couldn't call you back. It made sense after everything we've seen. He promised you'd meet me here. That the police were helping you stop the stalker, at last. I let him lock me in that office to wait for you, like an idiot. He said it was to keep me safe. That bastard would have let you die.' His face crumples at last, tears leaking from his eyes.

'It's okay, sweetheart. You saved me, remember?'

'I trusted him and Hilary. Remember how they always spoiled me as a kid, with ice cream and toys?'

'Hilary's got no idea about this.'

'You almost died, while I sat there, playing music.'

'The songs helped, but I never want to hear The Eagles again.' I give a shaky laugh.

'Why did Clive help her? The vicious cow.' Jamie stares down at Lisa, but she's just a shell now, defenceless. 'I heard someone thumping the wall, then your voice. I stuck my head out the window, but couldn't see anything – until she was pushing you out.'

'So, you kicked down the door?'

'My foot's buggered, but it was worth it.'

Jamie's exhaustion shows, yet he's holding it together. I'd like to curl up on the carpet again and sleep for hours, with him at my side, but he soon rallies. He uses a wad of tissues to clean the cut on my hand, gently, like nothing else matters. It proves that I should trust him more. He's growing up fast, ready to decide his own future.

Lisa is still cowering in the corner, as though she fears the approaching daylight. I don't blame her. It will expose her secrets, and her bitterness about being my half-sister. She'll lose the job she values above all. I can't help pitying her, despite everything. Her coat is ripped open, revealing the scarlet dress underneath.

I used to believe she was confident, but now she looks like a kid after a party that no one's bothered to collect. Our friendship felt real for years, but her whole persona was fake. When I crouch at her side, her gaze is empty.

72

Jamie helps me into the ambulance. My strength's gone and pain is radiating around my body. The last face I see is Reg Bellamy's. The porter must be reporting for work early; he's standing by the gates in his black coat, sombre as an undertaker at a funeral procession. I feel like calling out to him that the threat is gone at last. There's no need to worry about me anymore. His dogged devotion to this building and everyone that walks inside no longer feels threatening.

The pain behind my eyes is getting worse. It's like a migraine, making me nauseous. Doctors pore over me at the hospital, giving me little time to think about Lisa. They take X-rays and explain that my haematoma has grown. I need an operation immediately, to drain the fluid and relieve pressure on my brain.

Rafe arrives just as I'm signing the consent form, and my anger towards him fades. He slept with the woman I saw as my closest friend, but Lisa deceived him too. We neglected each other and lost track of what mattered. Both of us spent too little time with Jamie, when we should have focused on being parents. When Rafe leans down to kiss me, his face is pale with concern. Then I'm wheeled away to the operating theatre. The anaesthetist speaks to me quietly before I drop into unconsciousness, with no dreams at all.

The pain has reduced to a dull throb when I wake up in the same hospital room as before. It feels like the past week was only a nightmare. Light floods in, leaving no space for shadows or self-doubt. Something has lifted from my mind since my childhood memories returned, triggered by the shock of being kidnapped. I'd hate to experience those sickening images again, but they served a purpose. My mother planted the idea of suicide in my father's head. Then the choice was his, and she ended up killing him for it. The guilt I've carried for decades has finally been stripped away.

Lisa fills my mind again, even though I'd rather forget her. She'll be locked away for years, leaving me to enjoy my freedom. I still can't believe that she hatched such a grand plan for revenge, killing my mother and allowing me to reach the same age as our father before attempting to destroy me. Her endless grief for him must have broken her sanity.

I look through the glass panel in the door and catch sight of Carla, and Leo in his wheelchair. He's got a newspaper open on his lap, while she fusses over him. When Leo's gaze catches mine, his smile is victorious, like we're fellow survivors of a shipwreck. I want to tell them that the past is over. We can move forward now, as a family, but sleep claims me again too soon.

Hours have passed when my eyes open again. Rafe and Jamie are sitting by my bed, waiting for me to recover. Soon I'll be strong enough to tell them the truth about my past. I can't guess what will happen to my marriage. We were pulling in different directions before the stalking began, yet I want to understand what pushed us apart, when we used to be united.

Noah deserves an apology too. He did nothing wrong. I accused him of hurting me, for no reason except a stupid hunch. It was wrong to sleep with him when I had nothing to give. I hope he finds someone soon, to help him recover from his own tragedy.

I feel a twinge of sadness about the cottage burning down, but I grew strong inside those walls. My possessions don't matter. Jamie survived the fire, and so did I. Maybe I'll book a sabbatical and take him on a trip round Europe when his exams finish, to build some good memories and release the bad.

I ask Rafe a question before sleep topples me again. I need to know if Georgia Reed is alive. He scans his phone, then tells me she's still in ICU, battling for her life with fierce determination. I say a quick prayer in my head hoping she makes it, and that my programme will protect other victims better. I hate the idea of anyone else suffering like Georgia. Soon her father will hear that Joe Sinclair was coerced into making his attack. Lisa must have cast a powerful spell over him to have manipulated him so effectively. He had no history of physical violence, only psychological intimidation, until she targeted him in that pub.

I'll fight hard to defend my reputation. No one should be sacked for following every safety protocol at work, in good faith. I let the thought go, then make a decision. I'll never post another film online. I've never liked being in the public eye, and I'd rather focus on fixing my private life.

The anaesthetic in my system is still making me drowsy, and I'm content with silence. My gaze skims Jamie's face and Rafe's, then fixes on the window. I can see the towers and spires of Cambridge in the distance, the city's architecture elegant and remote. The sky is full of snow waiting to fall, but that doesn't matter. I can sleep here in safety, at last, until it clears.

73

ME

I'm not allowed to contact you, yet I still write to you every day, keeping the letters in my notebook. They make the raw brick walls of my cell vanish, at least for a while. Six months have passed since my trial. Why didn't you meet my eye when you testified against me? We're sisters, yet you chose to ignore me.

I told the jury that we fought an epic battle, right against wrong, truth against lies. But no one listened. You have to understand that it was my duty to get justice for Dad, and that won't change. His face is tattooed across my spine, drawn from one of his old passports. I hid it from you during that spa weekend we spent together, aware that his image would expose me too soon.

Prison almost broke me at first. I hated the idea of you walking on alone, while I remain here, in darkness. A shadow can't exist with the lights turned out. I mourned for everything I'd lost: my identity, my future, even the city I loved. The view from my cell is of the prison car park and a few stunted trees. I inhabit another world now, and self-pity is pointless.

Guards peer at me every fifteen minutes through the hatch in my cell door. They're afraid I'll kill myself, like Dad, but that can't happen while our two lives are connected. The guards don't realize that I'm watching them too. Some are even more vulnerable than the prisoners, and one of them has noticed me already. It will take time to win her trust, but if I treat her like she's special, I'm certain she'll come round. She reminds me of you, trying too hard to look confident. She's weak, like Clive, and free to walk out of this place whenever she chooses.

Call me an optimist, but my dream may yet happen. It's the challenge I need to keep me occupied, even if years pass before it comes true. Time is on my side. My new friend will leave work one day with her mind reprogrammed. She'll have lost herself completely. I think of her as my emissary. My ideas will send her in your direction, so we can start over.

I wonder if you're ready for our battle to resume, Eloise. Or do you imagine it's finished? Only one of us can be right.

Either me, or you.

Author's Note

I'd like to apologize to the residents of Cambridge for changing its geography in this novel. I've used it as my location, but my imagination took over. Various real locations are included here, like the Heong Gallery, King's College and the psychology department at Cambridge University. But their appearance and history have been altered to support my story.

I do hope that lovers of Cambridge, like me, will recognize the city's atmosphere, despite these liberties. It's a heady mix of youthful excitement and ancient wisdom, with some great architecture to admire. You'll also find dozens of cafés and pubs where budding philosophers and astronomers congregate, exchanging ideas all day long.

I was given a fascinating tour of the psychology department by a senior porter, who asked me not to name him in this book. I owe him a very large thank you. He described some of the pioneering work on curing psychological illnesses at Cambridge, which gave me the idea for *The Stalker*.

Acknowledgements

I received a lot of professional and personal help while researching this book. The National Stalking Helpline staff gave me excellent advice on stalkers' motivations and behaviour. I was also advised by Paladin, the National Stalking Advocacy Service, which helped me to understand how victims can keep safe. (You can find details of both these organizations at the end of this section.)

My brilliant publisher, Simon & Schuster UK, has supported me for many years. My editor, Clare Hey, is a wonderful ally, and an expert in polishing stories to a gleam. Clare, your faith in me has really helped my confidence! Georgina Leighton is a brilliant addition to the team; thanks for your insights, which helped so much. Thanks also to lovely Jess Barratt, for putting so much energy into publicizing my books for the past decade. The digital and print sales teams have championed my books from the start. Your work goes on behind the scenes and is rarely on public display, but it's much appreciated, by me and all the other authors you support.

My agent Teresa Chris suggested years ago that I should write a standalone and predicted that I would love the process. You were right, and I was wrong. I owe you lunch and lots of Prosecco.

Thanks to the many librarians who have invited me to speak at reading groups and events in libraries across the UK. I have loved my visits and found so many folk who are passionate about reading, and I hope to visit many more libraries in years to come. Each one is a treasure trove.

Tracy Fenton, you and your Book Club are miracle workers! Thanks so much for all the hours you've spent spreading the word about my books. Thanks also to crime expert and all-round delight Ayo Onatade. You have been kind and supportive from day one of my writing career.

Writing can be a lonely business, as well as a joy. Over the years I have received thousands of supportive messages from folk online. I wish there was space to mention you all, but here are just a few of my online pals: Janet Fearnley, Polly Dymock, Louise Marley, Jennie Blackwell, Anna Tink, Joanna Blatchley, Richard Purser, Peggy Breckin, Elaine Cook, Rachel Ward, Ian Dixon, Hazel Wright, Joanna Beesley, Angela Barnes, Noemi Proietti, Caroline Cassion, Andy Aitken, Kelly Lacey, Peter Fleming, Janet Emson, Sarah Blackburn, Clare Janet Mason, Jacob Collins, Margaret@Cleobefore, Sheila Howes, Miriam Smith and Debbie Brookes.

Last but not least: Dave, my husband of three decades. Without you, and a limitless supply of tea and biscuits, this book would not exist.

National Stalking Helpline: 0808 802 0300
Paladin National Stalking Advocacy Service: 020 3866 4107